Melanie Schwapp was born in Kingston, Jamaica and majored in Mass Communication at the University of South Carolina. Melanie lives in Jamaica.

By the same author

Lally-May's Farm Suss

Dew Angels

MELANIE SCHWAPP

hoperoad : London

HopeRoad Publishing Ltd
P O Box 55544
Exhibition Road
London SW7 2DB

www.hoperoadpublishing.com
First published as an e-book by HopeRoad, 2013
This paperback edition published 2016

Supported using public funding by
**ARTS COUNCIL
ENGLAND**

ISBN 978-1-908446-47-3

eISBN 978-1-908446-20-6

To Grandma, who loved to teach, and who saw no difference in the class or colour of any soul. Mom and Dad, you are my wings, and with your support, I have never been afraid to fly.

We all suffer from the same affliction ...
adored by some, abhorred by others.
But the worst affliction of all,
is to be abhorred by ourselves.

Anonymous.

PROLOGUE

Nola's birth uncovered the secret of the great sin that Fin Thomas had committed many, many years before, but one she bellowed to the world from the very first moment she poked her kinky head into it.

The secret spoke of a lapse in judgement. Some blamed it on a hidden streak of madness which was said to rear its ugly head every now and again in some member of the outwardly perfect Thomas clan. It must have been madness that caused such a fine specimen of a 'high-brown' man to fall in love with, and marry, a girl whose skin was so black that the sun shone its reflection from her face.

The girl was Patricia Rose Leland, the only daughter of the fruit seller by the Pitts Pen train track. She was the bumptious gal who, in her unlearned, barefooted state, had had the audacity to earn the favour of the most coveted bachelor in Redding.

It happened the morning her mother was too sick to carry the fruit basket from their shack in the hills to the train tracks that ran through the village, and Patricia had taken over the chore. It was then she captivated the sweet, caramel love of Fin Thomas. That morning, as Patricia sat before her basket of fruit, Fin looked into her ackee-seed eyes and his steps faltered. He came to a complete halt as his gaze fell on those lips, thick as liver, with their soft inner flesh as startling in colour as the girl's middle name implied.

To the shock of the village, Fin married Patricia Rose Leland and, in just a shimmy of six years, bred with her four offspring. The only blessed thing about the union, people whispered, was that the children were born with skin as golden as the retreating sun.

Over the years, as those Thomas offspring bore their own golden babies, the shame of Patricia's midnight shade retreated into village history, becoming whispered warnings to anyone who showed signs of repeating Fin's sin: "Choose a girl with nice high colour. Don't bother with no 'Fin' Bride!"

The sin remained a well-guarded secret until Nola Chambers, Patricia Leland's great-granddaughter, unearthed it from her mama's loins and screamed it into her papa's shocked ears. Nola was born at dawn, but it might as well have been in the dark hours of night. When she revealed her face, as black as a moonless night in December, the muted whispers were at once amplified.

Unfortunately for Nola, there was no Fin and his unfaltering love to shield her from the disgust of the village. From the very first moments of her life everything she did, every step she took, would be directed right back towards those train tracks—tracks which led, without one bend or curve, straight out of the village of Redding.

CHAPTER 1

MAMA WAS DYING. Even before Louisa called with her swollen voice, Nola knew. That proverbial 'feeling in the gut' that put a misty haze on everything. Only the feeling remained sharp, tearing at the senses and mangling the marrow of the bones. Even when she tried to escape it with sleep, it was there, burrowing through the sheets like a maggot. It squirmed into her dreams, and lurked there for three nights.

The dream itself never showed death. But, Nola knew what it meant to see Mama standing still. Mama never stood still. She was always moving, always chopping. Always that incessant chopping! And yet, here she was standing still in the scallion field, with only the whispy, white-streaked hair blowing like dried river grass in the breeze.

The dream showed every detail of the field, every ditch, every hump, every muddy curl of worm shit. She could even smell the damp ruddiness of the soil, the spicy sting of the scallions. Mama's scallions had always bristled with the substantial girth of rain and good manure, but in the dream they were covered with fungus. Mama stood in the midst of the mottled crop, at the end of a broken trail of the stalks.

3

Her path stopped in the middle of the field, even though a gate, just a few yards away, opened wide onto another field dotted with the lush pink of rice-and-peas vines. Nola wanted to shout to Mama to go through the gate, to move away from the rot, but the words were frozen in her throat.

As Nola watched, the scallions began to collapse. One by one, they bowed to the lifeless statue of Mama. Soon there was no difference between the muddy earth and the curdled rot of the stalks. Suddenly, Mama's eyes moved. She stared out from the dream. Nola could feel the eyes piercing her. She turned fitfully in her sleep, but the eyes bored deeper to hold her still. They pierced the lifelines of her body – the blood pumping through her heart, the bubbles of air fizzing into her lungs, the tears perched on her lids. Then Mama's mouth opened, but instead of words, a blackbird flew from the dark cavity of her throat, with wings so wide that they cast a shadow over the field.

Mama's head finally moved. She tore her eyes from the mist of breath perched on Nola's nostrils and followed the bird with her gaze. Her eyes were brimming with longing as she panted with every wild caw – eyes dry, but longing for tears; mouth open in a silent circle.

Nola had not seen or spoken to Mama for eight years— eight years of no letters, no birthday greetings, no messages through Louisa's quick, sporadic phone calls, yet here she was, over 80 miles and eight years away, feeling Mama's death: drenched in sweat on a pillow musty from three nights of weeping, dreaming of the mother who had sent her away. Dreaming of her, and wondering if she still smelled of bitter onions and sweet rosewater.

"You better come, she keep callin' your name."

It was to be that simple. Nola was to jump on a bus and head to a home that had branded her soul, then dashed her

4

like a piece of trash unto the roadside. Mama was calling from the euphoria of pain medicine and the erosion of cancer, but calling just the same. Whatever Mama's body had wanted in life was not what her spirit now wanted in the face of death. After waiting eight years for Mama to call, the wail of a blackbird would do just as well.

To return was a task that Nola had never thought she would have had to face. It wasn't that she hadn't wanted to see Mama, to look into those dull eyes and share her agony. But Nola had always imagined it happening here in Kingston. Mama would come, her market basket filled with her guava cheese and banana bread, and they would sit at the table, the steam of hot cocoa rising over their faces like a hot salve. They would heal the pain without words ever having to be spoken.

Now memories would have to be faced. On that third night, the last night of the dream, Nola resigned herself to going back and the dream never returned. The ghosts came quickly, as if waiting at the door. The river came too, its gush so strong that her bed bobbed in its power. It coursed into her veins as if it had finally found its wayward tributary.

That third night, when Nola finally faced her ghosts and her river, they left her body racked dry, and her cheeks streaming with tears.

CHAPTER 2

THE STORY NOLA liked best of all Grampy's stories was the one about the Dew Angels. Grampy told her that at dawn, while the world slept, the angels came down from heaven, perched the sun on the horizon, and washed the earth beneath the pale blue light.

For many years, Nola thought that the dew-soaked soil was the remnant of an angelic cleansing ritual, the thick fog a curtain of modesty drawn to hide the naked earth beneath. Long after Grampy died, Nola believed his tale. So, when the sores started to come up on her lip, and Papa said, "You too nasty! Outside with that damn cow! That's why you have them sores all over your face!" Nola thought that the angels could make her clean and she began to wake at dawn to be washed with the earth.

Mama and Papa's bedroom was beside the kitchen, the door always held ajar by an old coal iron. Nola always stopped there to check for Papa's nasal whistle and Mama's gentle breath. Sometimes, the smell of stale whisky burned through the crack and Nola knew that, on those mornings, Papa would not wake till long after the sun had nudged the manure in the scallion beds.

After checking that Papa was in his whistling slumber, she would creep down the passage to peep into Louisa's bedroom. It had been Grampy's room where she'd spent so much time listening to his stories and massaging home-made pimento oil into his gnarled hands. For days after they'd removed his twisted torso from the house, Nola had curled up on the stained mattress and had only stopped weeping when she heard the whisp, whisp, whisp of his breath—coming from no particular direction—warm and lemony, smelling just as it used to after he'd drunk his morning mug of tea. He had feathered her forehead with kisses, assuring her that he would always be in that room. But one week after Grampy died, Papa told Louisa that she could have the old man's room.

As she stuck her head into Louisa's room to breathe in Grampy, his voice would whisper from the walls, "Mornin' Little Bird, where you off to before Massa Sun even yawn his first yawn?"

"Goin' to the angels, Grampy, to wash away the sores."

"Mind you ketch cold in the dew, Little Bird."

Louisa never stirred as they spoke. Her beautiful face always remained relaxed, golden skin glowing like one of the angels.

Not even the mongrel dog would raise his head as Nola glided past his sleeping place on the kitchen step. The fog would embrace her, and she would smell them instantly— jasmine angels, wet grass angels, cow dung angels. She would listen with glee to the light rustle of their wings through the leaves of the coolie plum tree. Ellie would be waiting, sensing her within the swirling mist, her rope winding round and round the braided trunk. Nola would sit on the old tree stump and wait.

The dew would cling to Nola's skin, the mask raising the hairs on her face. It would cap the coconut oil on her braids, till a halo of wet light surrounded her. It radiated her soul. It pulled the dirt from deep within her.

Soon the heat from her skin transformed the halo into myriad streams, trickling them over her mouth so she could taste her own skin's salt and the dew's sweet sugar.

One morning, Nola went for her wash and forgot to close the kitchen door. The mongrel dog pushed it open and went in. He'd caught one of the rats and killed it right in front of the stove, then chewed up Papa's work boots in the midst of the blood. He'd made such a ruckus that he'd stirred Papa from his sleep. Nola could hear the bellowing from out by the pen—"Stupid gal ... out with damn cow ... leave door open ... beat some sense ...!"

His voice had chased the mist away and sent Ellie tramping round the tree trunk. Even though the words had reached her ears, Nola remained frozen on the stump. She thought of running to the river and hiding within the tall grass, but she would have to come out sooner or later, and it would be worse then.

She crept back to the house and crouched beneath the kitchen window, readying herself for the blows as she stared at the leather boots that had been flung unto the grass.

Then Nola had heard Louisa's voice, hoarse with sleep, but a sweet, sweet sound to her ears. It said, "Papa, don't be vex. I didn't see Nola in her bed, so I come to check if she was outside, and I forget to lock back the door."

Papa calmed right down. Nola was able to go back into the house, walking far around him in case he spotted the truth in her wet eyes. She sent Louisa a look that said, "Thank you for savin' me."

Louisa bent to pick up Mama's scotch bonnet peppers that the mongrel had knocked out of the basket. But Papa said, "Leave them! Let her clean up the mess, and when she finish, clean my bloody boots as well!"

The day after that, the sore on Nola's lip erupted fiercer than ever before. She couldn't put anything larger than teaspoons of porridge into her mouth for three whole days and Mama painted on so much gentian violet that her face had remained stained for two weeks afterwards. When the sore eventually went down, it left a dent in the right corner of her top lip.

* * *

If anyone had asked Nola then, why Papa hated her, she would have said it was because of the baby boy. He'd only been one and a half when he drowned in a drum of rainwater.

Nola came a year after that, but she was nothing like the soft-haired baby who lay in the Redding graveyard. She was the wrong gender and was as black as that moonless night.

A black baby in Redding, where the folk were 'hard workers' when it came to 'washing out the black'. The village had earned its name because of the deep red colour of its soil, but it might as well have been so called because of the colour of its folk.

Miss Watkins, Nola's Class Three teacher, explained that Redding had been settled, many years ago, by a group of Germans who had come to seek a better life from the disease-plagued conditions of their own country. In the fertile soil of Redding, they had planted not only food crops, but tender-hued villagers as well.

Granny Pat had been lucky. Just one little girl, Lilly, had dared to be born with the ruddy hint of her mother's pigment, but she died within hours of birth. Some whispered that Marva Thomas, Pappy Fin's mama, had presided over the birth and upon seeing the tell-tale darkness tingeing the baby's ears and fingertips, had commanded the midwife

9

not to slap it and allow the life cry to fill the little lungs with oxygen, nor to wrap it for warmth during the chilly mountain night.

When Nola's papa came to Redding from Clarendon and met her mama, he saw only the golden-skinned beauty, the shy doe-eyes and sweet smile which hid the secret of Fin Thomas's sin.

CHAPTER 3

NOLA TOOK THE 54 bus from downtown Kingston. As the old bus choked over the asphalt and began its route to Redding, Nola's memory took her back eight years, right to that very schoolyard in front of which the bus would soon deposit her.

* * *

Only the end of April and already it was as hot as hell; the end of April, and still the rains had not come. Tree limbs hung feebly while flies buzzed dizzily over the empty juice boxes and patty bags scattered in the schoolyard. A slight gust teased now and then, lifting mini tornadoes up Nola's skirt as she stood under the lignum vitae tree in the middle of the schoolyard, trying to stay cool in the only shade in the yard.

"Nola, you goin' eat that?" Dahlia Daley pointed at the half-eaten bun in Nola's hand. The girl was sitting on the ground in front of her, a thick film of dust on her sweaty face. Nola shrugged and handed her the bun. Dahlia stuffed it into her mouth, with no second thought of the sore lifting the corner of Nola's lip. No other student would have eaten anything from 'Fassy-Face Nola', but, for Dahlia, as long as it was food, it didn't matter where it came from.

Dahlia Daley begged for everything. A strange thing, since her mother was none other than Merlene, owner of Merlene's Bar and Grill; quite a successful business, if you asked some men – a curse on the face of the earth, if you asked the women.

Dahlia Daley never spoke of her mother's business, and no one at school was brave enough to discuss it in front of her. At least, not since the day Portia Walker got her 'donut'. Dahlia had asked Portia Walker for the rest of her box juice. Portia suggested that, instead of begging, Dahlia could simply offer the boys some of the services that her mother offered at her bar. Slugga (Mrs. Simpson, the headmistress, so called because of the story that she had once punched a boy, much larger than herself, unconscious) witnessed the said box juice being slammed straight into poor Portia's face, leaving a scar, as round as a donut, over Portia's eye. Dahlia had been suspended for a week after that.

But, secretly, while others scoffed at Dahlia Daley, Nola found her a comfort. Dahlia Daley was ugly. Uglier even than Nola. Her dark skin did nothing to hide the pock marks of picked pimples, and her hair was always braided so haphazardly that the plaits stuck out like little blackbirds perched atop a tree. But, the ugliest thing of all was the girl's nose. A huge, bulbous thing, melding downwards and joining the girl's upper lip in one united feature.

Yet, despite the ugliness pressed unto her shoulders, Dahlia was as carefree as any of the pretty 'brownings' attending Redding Secondary. She just didn't care that the others laughed behind her back, and that most of her social interactions were limited to begging, copying homework, or pounding a juice box into someone's face.

Nola watched the girl's lips smacking noisily on a piece of cheese. There was no denying that they were drawn together, she and Dahlia; not by any formal agreement of friendship, but by the unwritten code of the two black girls being paired off.

Nola wasn't like Louisa, who was constantly being visited by Toneisha Johnson, and who sat huddled for hours in her bedroom giggling over 'boy' stories. Mama said that Toneisha was the reason Louisa had failed her exams, but Papa said that Louisa didn't need exams. She was too beautiful to worry about schoolwork. Some rich man was waiting for the opportunity to take care of her. Nola, on the other hand, had better work damn hard. So, while Louisa waited for this rich husband, she stayed at home and helped Mama with her chutneys and jams.

Nola sighed and asked Dahlia, "You do you math homework?"

"We get math homework?" Dahlia blinked back.

Nola sighed again. Slugga, who was temporarily subbing as their math teacher, had warned that anyone who hadn't done the equations would have to remain after school to help Junior plant geranium seedlings in the beds outside of the office. Dahlia would definitely be gardening that afternoon.

The bell rang and Dahlia jumped up, trotting eagerly towards the classroom. Clarice Johnson and Faith Bernard snorted scornfully as she flounced by their desks. The ever-prompt Slugga entered the classroom right behind them and silently waited as they stumbled noisily into chairs and fumbled for books.

Nola always felt a secret relief for the headmistress that her nostrils remained uncovered by the thick layer of face powder, allowing her to breathe beneath her mask of 'dusky-beige'. Truth was, Slugga was more a dusky-brown than a dusky-beige, but under several layers of the powder you couldn't really tell.

13

As the noise died down, Slugga gave them her usual greeting – a look of disdain over the rims of her green-framed glasses. Today, her blue and white striped blouse was tucked primly into the waistband of her pants, giving her the appearance of a pin-striped balloon.

"Well …," dimpled arms crossed over striped chest, "You all had the whole weekend to do those equations." Stubby nails trailed down a red-lined page in her grade book, "So quickly pass them up." Green glasses crept back up the page, down the narrow rows of desks, and rested on Dahlia Daley.

Dahlia blinked. Around her there was a flurry of activity as exercise books were passed, row by row, up to the front.

"Dahlia, where is your homework?" Eyebrows climbed above green frames.

Dahlia dug her fingers into her braids, scratching vigorously. Nola gritted her teeth in preparation for the explosion, but, miraculously, it never came—no deepening frown, no shouting about the time wasters in her school, nothing. Slugga just leaned casually over the desk and wrote something in her grade book.

"Okay, page ten in the text book. We are going to start square roots," she continued, turning to face the blackboard.

Dahlia turned merrily to Delroy Reckus and asked if she could share his book since she'd forgotten hers at home.

The rest of the lesson became a jumble of "this squared" and "that squared," and overcome by the heat, Nola drifted into a wideeyed daze. It wasn't until Slugga called her name that she jumped out of the daze and caught the end of the sentence, "… need you and Dahlia to come to my office at the end of school." Nola's heart pulsed. She couldn't fathom what she'd done to deserve a summons to Slugga's office!

The office was a mere cubicle, separated from the staff room only by a peeling dry wall. The headmistress's desk and chair dominated the space, but there was also a filing cabinet, and an additional chair had been squeezed in front of the desk. It was always a painful sight to watch Slugga manoeuvre her generous portions through the musty space to get to her chair.

At the end of school, Nola stood behind Dahlia at the office door hoping beyond hope that the headmistress had said her name by accident. But Slugga looked up from her desk and beckoned them in. Dahlia plopped into the chair in front of the desk while Nola stood hesitantly behind her. Slugga studied them above her glasses, then she opened the forever present grade book and studied the red numerals etched across the page.

"Nola ..." Eyebrows lifted again, "I think you would be a good help for Dahlia, a kind of homework police. Make sure that she does her homework every day. I notice that you always do your work, Nola. You're not into the chatty, chatty like the others. I think it would be good for you to show Dahlia how to organise herself a little better, hand in her assignments on time—hand in her assignments at all!"

Dahlia looked up at Nola and grinned. Now it was Nola's turn to blink, as she looked from Dahlia's grinning face to Slugga's set mask. She tried to speak, but all that came out of her mouth was a choked, "What?"

Slugga ignored the interruption and continued, "The two of you can do homework together in the evenings. You can meet at one of your houses, maybe take turns ... one day Nola's, next day Dahlia's, and other such delights. It doesn't matter where, just as long as you do it together. Just as long as you do it!"

Dahlia clapped her hands.

"What?"There it was again. Her throat had closed shut. She wanted to ask the headmistress if she'd gone mad. Didn't she know who Dahlia Daley was? Who her mama was? How could she go to that place in the evenings, and how could Slugga expect Mama, or worse, Papa, to allow Dahlia Daley into her house?

"What?" she muttered again, but Slugga just flashed a hand in dismissal and told them they could begin the assignment today, with the square roots on page 14.

CHAPTER 4

DAHLIA DALEY WALKED in front of Nola with a cheerful bounce. The day's activities had worked her grey cotton blouse from the waist of her skirt and two of the top buttons had become undone, so the schoolbag on her shoulder snagged it wide open. Every time she turned around to monitor Nola's progress, her purple bra beamed too.

She was 15, one year older than Nola. But, though Dahlia's body had all the physical attributes of a grown woman, she was, in every other respect, very much a child. Even now, as Nola followed apprehensively behind, Dahlia ignored the purposeful distance between them. The more Dahlia smiled at her, the more Nola checked to see who might be noticing the exchange.

Two o'clock in the afternoon always brought a rush of activity to Calabash Street. The only asphalted road in Redding, it ran from one side of the village to the other; from the turn leading to Clysdale Bend, to where it spilled onto the highway. The bus stop was on Calabash Street, to the left of the school gate. Crowds always concentrated there. Also on Calabash Street was Mad Aggie's shack, a wooden stall in the middle of the sidewalk.

Mad Aggie was Redding's very own witch. Nola stiffened as she and Dahlia approached the shack, staring ahead so as not to lock eyes with the snarling inhabitant. That afternoon Mad Aggie was leaning over her counter. The bunches of drying bush hanging from the roof seasoned the air with their pungent scent as the girls drew nearer. There was always a pile of fabric in the corner of the shack, and it was these the witch cut into strips and used to tie up her bunches of prized herbs.

Her eyes frightened Nola. They pierced through her, as if reading her very thoughts. Every time the witch looked her way, the kinks on her head unwound and stood on end. She increased her pace to hurry past the stall, but, to her surprise, Dahlia slowed down and flashed a fleshy grin at the witch. And, if Dahlia's smile was shocking, the witch's responding smile almost made Nola pass clear out!

A sudden ruckus pulled her attention away. A group of boys were kicking up a storm of dust in front of the stall, shuffling a paper-stuffed juice box between their feet in a spur-of-the-moment game of 'scrimmage'. Nola looked back at the stall, knowing for certain that the witch would not approve of the boisterous activity. Just as she thought, the woman was creeping from her shack, machete in hand! "If you ever knock over my tings, I goin' chop up every one of you and feed you to the pigs!" she shrieked.

The boys just laughed. Clinton Bailey, always up for a challenge, suddenly broke from the group and kicked the box, wadded with wet paper, with all his might. It flew like a rockstone, skimming the witch's countertop and knocking the fresh collection of bush into the street.

Mad Aggie gave a blood-curdling shriek and hauled up the hem of the faded cloth strapped around her waist. Red-crusted toes dug into the ground and she catapulted towards

Clinton, machete high above her head. "Folly is bound in the heart of a child," she bellowed, "but the rod of discipline will drive it far from him!"

Clinton chased down the street, dilly-dallying expertly among pedestrians, bicycles and goats while the rest of the boys held their bellies and fell onto the asphalt in the throes of laughter.

By the time Nola and Dahlia reached the turn off to Jackfuit Lane, the witch was already returning to her stall, quoting scriptures as she scraped up her spilled stalks of bush.

Merlene's Bar and Grill was off Jackfruit Lane, tucked safely away from the village at the end of Della Way. As they turned on to Della Way and passed Miss June's shop, Nola kept her head low lest any of the customers recognized her. She silently recited her speech of assurance, that as long as her parents thought she'd made her usual afternoon stop by the river, she would be safe from their finding out about her new duties.

It had been a difficult call, the choice between Slugga's anger and Papa's wrath, but she knew that with careful timing she could avoid Papa's. Slugga's? Well ... the only way to avoid Slugga's anger was to do what Slugga said.

The question of Dahlia Daley coming to her house was one she'd not even considered, for it would only have been a matter of time before Papa realized who she was, and chased her straight back down Macca Hill.

Nola gave an inward sigh – there were only about eight weeks left till the end of the term, hopefully not too long to keep the assignment a secret.

Anyway, she had always felt that the longer she stayed away from home the better. Papa's temperament always changed when she was around. No matter how quiet, how inconspicuous she tried to be, just the sight of her seemed to upset him. She'd tried everything – staying out of the sun so that her skin wouldn't become more blackened by its glare, eating less so that she could be as slim and neat as Louisa. But nothing ever changed that sneer. "This chile getting swartier every day," he would complain to Mama, or he would cock his head towards the kitchen door and say, "Remember what happen to Mrs. Spence? That's exactly where you headin'!"

He always referred to that steam bent rocker as if it had been Nola's fault that it had snapped apart. It had belonged to Granny Pat, the caned seat softly indented from the years of soothing many a sick or fussy child. It had been passed on to Grampy, and it was at those delicately-curled wooden feet that Nola had sat and listened to his tales.

One evening, Mrs. Spence was sitting in the chair, and while making a very strong point to Mama, she had borne down too hard on the worn seat and her rump had snapped the cane and wedged itself firmly into the rim. Her stockinged legs kicked frantically, but the action only served to lodge her tighter in the vise. Her frenzied attempts to free herself caused the chair to explode, sending steam bent missiles flying all over the kitchen while she landed with a wallop on the floor.

Dahlia's "This way," brought Nola quickly back to her current dilemma. As they drew closer to the building, Nola's heart sank further into her chest. The guffaws of boys could be heard coming from the side where the empty crates were stacked. Just her luck, to be spotted with Dahlia on the very first day of the assignment! She sped up, passing Dahlia's scraping walk. If anyone asked, she could say that she was simply cutting through the open land beyond Merlene's to pick up eggs from Tanky's chicken coops.

The voices belonged to Shane Davis, Oliver Reid, Delroy Reckus and Delroy's younger brother, Devon. They were bent over the crates, each one pushing the long veins of coconut leaves between the stacks, engrossed in the catching of lizards.

Suddenly, Devon let out a yell and yanked his vein, lifting the tightened loop victoriously into the air. A magnificently multi-hued ground lizard swished angrily from the tip, its mouth gagging open from the tight noose.

"Chop off him tail! Chop off him tail and mek it do the duppy dance!" Oliver instructed.

Obediently, Shane reached for the broom leaning beside the crates. It was an old trick, to cut off a lizard's tail and watch the severed appendage flick itself around. It always made Nola sick. She turned her head away, just in time to see Dahlia lumber past with her drawstring bag held high above her head. The same stance that Mad Aggie had had with her machete just moments before.

It struck Delroy first. Clapped him on the back of his head with a loud whack. Then the girl headed for Devon, but the boy, having had his fair warning from his brother's yelp, dropped the noose and ran. Dahlia promptly picked up a clump of soil and sailed it at his retreating back. The missile struck with another thwack, knocking him face-down into the dirt before disintegrating into a burst of red powder.

By the time Dahlia turned to face Shane and Oliver, the boys had already reached half-way to Miss June's shop. The girl swivelled to face poor Devon who was trying desperately to get to his feet. Dahlia jumped, arms pointed forward in a dive, and landed flat on him.

"How you like that, eh? How you like that round your neck? What? You can't breathe? Poor ting! You want me cut off you tail now? You ready to do the duppy dance?" Dahlia panted into his ear.

Poor Delroy seemed to be suffering from some sort of concussion, for he just stood there, blinking dizzily and rubbing his head as Dahlia strangled his brother.

Nola realized that she had to do something, for, very soon, she was sure Dahlia would find something resembling a tail to cut off of Devon. "Dahlia! The lizard!" she shouted.

It was now deathly black and its head seemed twice its original size. It looked dizzy, crawling from side to side as it dragged its coconut noose behind it.

Dahlia jumped off Devon, picked up the black body and gently worked the coconut vein loose. The lizard's eyes immediately sank back into their sockets, but the mouth remained open, gagging for breath.

"Alright little lizzie. You okay now. Them wicked boys can't hurt you no more," Dahlia cooed. The black body remained stiff in her palm and the lizard suddenly flashed its tail, and snapped on to the tip of Dahlia's thumb. Dahlia gave a startled shout and flashed her hand through the air. She pranced in a full circle, flapping her hand up and down while the lizard sailed through the air like a long, black fingernail. Finally, she gave one last swing, and the lizard's body somersaulted … one, two, three times through the air, before landing with a splat against the wall of Merlene's Bar and Grill.

The lizard had been saved from its torturous tail-amputation, but it did not survive Dahlia's launch. Nola looked to see if Delroy and Devon had witnessed the creature's attack on Dahlia, but they didn't seem to have been able to notice much. They were both hobbling down the road, Devon sobbing and holding his throat, while Delroy still rubbed his head, stumbling like a drunken patron of Merlene's into the thorny privet bushes on the side of the road.

Nola returned her incredulous stare to Dahlia. She was squeezing her bitten thumb, a tiny drop of blood oozing from the flesh. Nola couldn't fight the snort of laughter that suddenly burst from her lips. Talk about biting that hand that saved you!

"I never know that a lizard could bite and draw blood. Them have teeth?" she choked, trying to inject a note of sympathy into her voice.

Dahlia stuck her thumb into her mouth and gave Nola a broad grin, blood pooling around her dark gums. "Serve them right!" she mumbled, nodding towards the two hobbling boys. She picked up her bag and lumbered past the lizard's final resting place. "Come y'hear," she said, beckoning Nola with her unbitten hand.

CHAPTER 5

MERLENE'S BAR AND Grill! She was actually standing on the grounds of the 'den of evil'. Nola studied the side of the building on which the lizard had splattered. It didn't seem as big as she'd remembered – only about eight yards deep. Two windows each were at the front and sides, but the one at the back was much larger. They were all sealed behind their shutters in their daytime repose.

Nola hurried after Dahlia through a tall hedge of plumbago. Never had Nola seen plumbago grow to such heights. This one's purple-blue blooms almost meshed with the branches of the mango tree that hung over it. The opening led on to a beaten track, both sides lined with old paint cans of blooming gerbera, heather and speedwell plants leading right up to the daintiest pink house that Nola had ever seen.

The house reminded Nola of a newborn baby – soft and pink and pampered. Everything about it seemed to whisper tenderness and care. The verandah was just big enough to hold two plastic chairs with a little table in the centre. The windows on either side of the front door, turned up against the afternoon glare, were the same aluminium-type louvres as the ones at school, except that the school louvres were missing most of their blades, always reminding Nola of a toothless old man.

"Come nuh!" Dahlia beckoned as she skipped up the steps and opened the front door. "Mama sleeping." Dahlia's voice was a whisper as she poked her head back through the front door.

Nola stared at the girl. Was she really about to enter Merlene Daley's house? She gave one last glance at the hedge behind her and sighed with relief when she saw that nothing of Della Way was visible through the thick bramble of leaves. She mounted the little steps and followed Dahlia through the door, nearly walking straight into a formica table with its vase of cheerful yellow gerberas.

The aroma of food filled the tiny space, making Nola's belly rumble. She looked around, blinking to get her eyes used to the dim light. Everything inside was as neat and precise as the exterior. A tiny kitchenette was to the right of the formica table, with cream cupboards attached to the walls. To the left of the table was a red settee sitting in front of a coffee table and a small television set. Pink lace curtains flitted in the breeze from a standing fan in the corner of the room. Beside the television was a half-opened door through which Nola spotted items of clothing strewn over the floor—a striking contrast to the immaculate house. "Must be Dahlia's room," she thought.

"You want to change?" Dahlia pointed at Nola's uniform. Nola blinked. Why on earth would she want to change? She wasn't planning to stay forever, just long enough to get Slugga's homework done, and so as to leave before Merlene's patrons began arriving for their evening stint of sin!

"No. Let's just do the square roots quick," she snapped. Dahlia gave her a look of shock, as if she'd just suggested they cut off each other's ears. "You goin' do homework before you eat? You not hungry?!"

Nola's stomach rumbled its own answer, but she shook her head firmly. She never ate after school, afraid of Papa's disgust at her size. Dahlia shrugged her shoulders and flounced through the half-opened door. Nola, realizing she was standing alone in the middle of Merlene Daley's house, quickly followed.

Dahlia's room was an unholy mess. Even the small cot against the wall was covered in clothing. There was a large poster of birds taped on the wall above it, the masking tape peeling and tinged brown, as if it had been taken down and re-taped repeatedly. The only other furniture in the room was a chair strewn with clothing and a chest of drawers with clothing spilling from its open drawers. Dahlia's dogeared school books were thrown carelessly on top of the chest, the math book on top of the pile.

"Put this on. That uniform too hot!" Dahlia waved some sort of blue shift at Nola. "This is cooler."

Dahlia flung the shift onto the pile on the bed. Then she stripped off her own uniform revealing the purple bra in its full glory, complemented by huge green panties. She rummaged through the clothing on the chair and gave a satisfied snort as she hauled a peach-striped shift, similar to the one she'd offered Nola, over her head.

Just then, there was a creaking sound from the living room. Dahlia gave an excited giggle and dashed out of the room.

"Mama, you wake!" Her voice chirped from the living room.

"Pumkin, you reach home!"

The voice was raspy with sleep, but held a soft lilt that stopped Nola dead in her tracks. It was not the voice of a Jezebel.

"You hungry, Pumkin?" The voice thickened around a yawn.

Nola could hear the rustle of fabric, and the smell of perfume wafted into the bedroom. She pressed herself behind the door and squeezed her chest to stop her heart from pounding too loudly.

It must have been part of the charm, that voice, part of the spell that Merlene wove over her victims. Nola had heard Pastor Pepper's warnings innumerable times. "... Fall under the spell of the evil ones and stand the chance of gettin' struck by the lightnin' wrath of God!"

"Mama, guess what?" Nola heard Dahlia clap her hands.

"Nola come home with me!"

"Nola? The girl with no friends?"

Nola blinked. Dahlia Daley had described her as having no friends?

"Slugga say she must help me with homework—EVERY DAY!" Dahlia sang.

"Help you with homework every day?" Merlene repeated sleepily. "So, where she is? Where's this Nola?"

Nola felt her blood thicken as Dahlia's shoes scraped towards her hiding place. The girl ignored her pleading look and grabbed her arm, hauling her into the living room. At that very moment, Nola understood why the lizard had bitten her finger.

A vision of blue turned from the little stove – blue nylon nightgown; light blue lace rubbing against smooth, dark calves; blue bed slippers with a shock of fluff on the toes; sleep-swollen eyes cast in a face the replica of Dahlia's – same wide nose and full lips, spreading even wider in a sleepy smile. The faces were similar, but where Dahlia's clunky features overpowered her face, Merlene's own sat proportionately on hers. Proportioned and, well – quite pretty.

Nola stared in awe at the legend of Merlene Daley. The woman's skin was as smooth as a half-ripe Julie mango, framed by eyebrows plucked so thin that they resembled the precise lines of an excercise book. Nola was tempted to touch the face, to see if the softness was real or the trick of some powder, but Merlene moved before she could raise her hand. Instead, Merlene took her hand, ignoring Nola's wide-eyed assessment like it was something she got every day. She cupped Nola's hand within both of hers, one beneath the palm, the other gently rubbing the top. The film of outdoor dust grated between their flesh.

Grampy used to do that. Rub her hand, like it was a precious gem. Now, the Jezebel of Redding was rubbing her hand just like Grampy, ignoring the sore on her face, smiling at her like she was a long lost friend.

Suddenly, Nola was overcome by another type of fright. What on earth? Tears were flooding her eyes, and her lips were quivering with the effort of holding them back! No, no, no! This couldn't be happening, not in front of ugly Dahlia and her 'Jezebel' mama. It must have been the rubbing, bringing back too many memories.

Nola saw the thin brows meet before her, saw the smooth skin crinkle just for an instant, then, just as fast as it had appeared, the frown was gone.

"Nola, you is a good friend to come and help Pumkin. Thank you." The sweet lilting voice addressed her.

Nola cleared her throat, "Slugga ... I mean, Miss Simpson say I must come," she stammered.

Merlene chuckled softly and shook her head ever so slightly.

"Farmer pull cow to trough – cow don't have to drink."

Nola swallowed. She knew! Merlene knew that she hadn't wanted to come! Her sweating palm formed a slippery film between their grip. She quickly pulled her hand away and looked down at her dusty shoes.

"Mama, dinner ready?"

Thank God for Dahlia's love of her belly. The girl pranced through the thick wedge of truth that had lodged between

Nola and Merlene and yanked open the oven door. A blast of heat and the delicious smell of baked chicken filled the little room.

"Nola, you goin' to die of heat in that uniform, and you goin' get food all over it when you eat. Go put on one of Dahlia dusters," Merlene said, nodding towards Dahlia's room, then she picked up an oven mitt and took a tray of sizzling chicken and sweet potatoes from the oven.

"I not eatin' ... I not stayin' long ... I have to go home before it get dark."

Dahlia scoffed as Merlene transferred a chicken leg from the baking tray unto an oval platter.

"Foolishness!" Merlene said, not even looking up from her task. "You can finish long before night come down. You can't do homework on a empty belly!"

Dahlia picked up a piece of chicken that had fallen off the bone, blew on it aggressively, then flung it into her mouth and chewed with noisy relish. She gave a loud mmmm that made her mama laugh. Nola watched in confused silence. The way Dahlia begged at school, one would think she had come from a home with absolutely no food, yet this meal spoke of quite the opposite.

"Pumkin, give Nola a duster to put on, then wash your hands and come."

Dahlia obediently grabbed Nola's arm and hauled her to the bedroom where the blue twin to her own duster waited on the bed. She shoved the garment at Nola, gave an excited giggle, then left the room, the door slamming behind her with a decisive bang.

Nola stood there for a while, feeling more and more like the lizard in the noose. Slowly, she removed her school blouse, thankful that at least Dahlia had given her the privacy to change. What would she have told her mama about the

29

criss-crossed scars that ran across Nola's upper arms and back? What would Merlene, with her gentle rubbing hands, have thought of those?

Neither Dahlia nor Merlene showed any reaction when she floated from the room in the oversized duster.

The meal was exceptional. An exceptional meal in 'Beggin' Dahlia's' house! The chicken was soft and succulent, releasing sprays of oily juice down Nola's chin as she bit into it. But she had just one piece. Merlene insisted she have more, but she shook her head firmly. She could already hear Papa's voice— "No porridge for Nola, Sadie, just some tea this morning. She gettin' as fat as that damn cow!" So Nola just had the one chicken thigh, sucking the bone till it was grey and brittle. She watched as Dahlia slurped her way through a heaping plate, ignoring the cutlery which lay neatly at the side. She marveled that Merlene did not comment on Dahlia's loud slurps, or the amount of food she consumed. She just delicately cut through her own meal with her knife and fork, ignoring the gravy that dribbled down Dahlia's arms and formed a greasy circle on her lap.

Instead, Merlene laughed. She threw her head back and laughed a deep belly laugh when Dahlia told her how Delroy and Devon had wobbled down the road after she'd saved the lizard.

Merlene laughed till tears streamed down her face, and when Dahlia told her that the lizard had bitten her finger after she'd rescued it, Merlene had to stand up because her rocking laughter almost tipped the chair over.

Nola wanted to add the part about Dahlia flinging the lizard against the wall, but she sat in silence and watched the bubbling mirth in awe. She was used to being an outsider, wanting to be happy, but knowing she shouldn't. She held her head down and played with her bone till she heard Merlene gurgle out the words,

"Nola, you didn't laugh when the lizard bite Pumkin' finger?"

She looked up from her plate and stared at Merlene's face, at the tears on her cheeks that she hadn't even bothered to wipe off. So different from Mama, and home. She cleared her throat and dug her voice from its hiding place at the bottom of her chest.

"I laugh," she whispered. "I laugh even more when Dahlia fling the lizard against the wall and him stick like a busted breadfruit!"

Merlene laughed till she choked, and Dahlia laughed till chicken flew out of her mouth and landed on the floor beside Nola's shoe.

It felt good. It felt so good to know that she'd been responsible for that glee. So Nola laughed too, a gurgle that had tried to come out when she'd put on the shift. It now erupted with such a force that it split the sore on her lip, and her face throbbed with the pain, the sweetest pain she'd ever felt in her life. For that moment, while they laughed and slapped their thighs in mirth, Nola didn't even think about the truth. For that moment, it didn't even matter. It didn't matter that she was black; that she was ugly; that her papa thought she was fat. She reached over and took another piece of chicken, and when she bit into it, the gravy dribbled down her chin and formed a grease circle on her lap, just like Dahlia's.

After the meal they did homework at the table while Merlene washed up the plates. Dahlia listened while Nola explained over and over about the square roots. Each time she grasped something that Nola explained, Dahlia would let out a loud whoop, and Merlene would smile from the sink and say, "That's my Pumkin!"

However, when Merlene turned from the sink, wiped her hands on a towel and said, "Pumkin, I goin' to get ready for work now," Nola forgot all about the square roots, the lizard, and the laughter. Her chair scraped from the table with such a force that its plastic cushion toppled onto the floor. Work! The Jezebel! She was about to start her night of sin!

"Sorry ... sorry ... sorry ...," was all Nola could say as she scraped up her books and shoved them into her bag. She was aware that they were staring, but she didn't care. They'd tricked her with their food and laughter. She half-walked, half-ran past the bar, but broke into a full sprint when she realized that the red door was open. She could hear the faint beat of music and the swish of a broom scraping against floor, but she looked neither left nor right. She raced down the marl road, stumbling on the loose stones just like Delroy and Devon had done earlier. It was not until she neared the end of Della Way that she realized that she was still wearing Dahlia's stupid shift.

CHAPTER 6

NOLA AWOKE THE next morning with a lightness in her heart and tightness in her belly. It was the secret of the past afternoon, constricting yet thrilling her. Strange, since she'd fretted the whole way home about entering her house in Dahlia's huge shift. She'd fretted till sweat soaked the dress. She'd rehearsed the lines over and over, about her uniform being stolen at the river, about having to borrow something from Jervis Calder's clothesline, but, as it turned out, she hadn't had to speak. Mama had barely lifted her head from the stove, and Papa had been listening to the news on the radio in his room. She tiptoed past the half-open door, glimpsing the custard brown of his big toe peeping from a hole in his sock. She'd hurriedly tore off the shift and stuffed it beneath her mattress beside Grampy's worn leather belt and the faded picture of Granny Pat's shiny face. And now she'd woken up with this feeling.

At school, she even smiled apologetically at Dahlia before she could stop herself, her lips lifting as if in their own memory of the past evening. But the smile, slight as it was, didn't go unnoticed. Nola saw Clarice's eyes narrow as the girl looked from her to Dahlia. She immediately tried to assume an air of distraction, as if she hadn't been smiling at anyone in particular, but when Slugga waddled in and called for the homework, Nola grinned all over again when Dahlia passed up her ripped book with the flourish of handing over gold.

At lunchtime, the laughter came again as the image of Delroy and Devon stumbling down Della Way came to mind when she spotted Delroy playing scrimmage.

"Your glad bag bust today, Nola."

Nola jumped at the voice above her.

Clarice and Faith stood over her as she sat beneath the lignum vitae tree. Clarice's face crumpled beneath the strain of her frown and her hot-pressed ponytail shook accusingly over the peak of her chest.

Clarice was Toneisha's sister. She was no stranger to Nola, having accompanied Toneisha on many visits to their home, but as many a time as Clarice had been to her home, was as many a time as she'd greeted Nola with indifference the next day at school. Clarice was popular at school, and her loyal subjects included all of the love-struck boys and most of the girls. In fact, both the Johnson girls remained one of the prides and joys of Redding, with skin so fair it glowed luminescent in the sun. On a hot day, the pulsing network of tiny veins was actually visible on their temples. Nola would never have said it to anyone, but Clarice's skin always reminded her of that of a baby croaking lizard. Such an opinion would have been considered blasphemy by the people of Redding.

"How you laughin' so much today, Nola? You have a secret you not tellin' me?" Clarice's usually baby-fine voice was thick with accusation.

"I don't have no secret," Nola shook her head innocently.

"'Memba, Nola—chicken merry, hawk deh near!" Clarice wagged a finger over Nola's plaits, her light brown eyebrows trying to look fierce.

So engrossed was Nola in those frowns above her, she did not see when the scrimmage box flew past Clarice's legs. She only felt the breath leave her chest as something slammed into her shoulder and jerked her backward against the tree trunk.

"Delroy, why you do that?" she heard Clarice say, but the voice sounded as if the girl had slipped into another part of the world.

Nola grabbed her shoulder and watched as Delroy's sneakers joined Clarice's before her. She tried to focus on the shredded laces but found that everything had suddenly become blurred by her tears. The universe was back to normal; Nola's laughter had ceased, and the tears had returned.

The box had hit her in Papa's spot, the dent where her arm joined her shoulder. Nola knew from experience that she only needed a couple of minutes to breathe deeply till the shock dissolved and her arm became gloriously numb.

"You alright there Nola?" Delroy's voice reached her through the pain. "I kick the ball in the wrong direction. Throw it back nuh!"

Then there was the blur of Dahlia's huge shoes beside Delroy's, and the blur of her taking the juice box out of Nola's lap and flinging it right into Delroy's face – flinging it so hard that her right leg lifted off the ground. Then there was the blur of blood streaming from Delroy's nose, and the blur of him striking back at Dahlia, sinking his fist into the fleshy duo of her lip-nose.

Dahlia was already on top of him by the time Slugga made it onto the field. She had to shove through layers of students to get to the rolling bodies beneath the tree.

"Enough!" Slugga yelled, bending to grab Dahlia's collar, but in one fluid movement, Dahlia flapped her arms behind her and released the blouse into Slugga's hand without missing one stroke on Delroy's face.

Four more punches to his jaw, and Dahlia eventually jumped up, gripping half of the boy's shirt in her fist. She stood there in her heaving pink bra, trails of crimson blood decorating the worn lace.

Slugga flung Dahlia's blouse at her and pulled Delroy to his feet. Then, without a word, she grabbed Dahlia's arm and hauled the two towards her office.

Half-way across the field she turned around and shouted, "Nola Chambers, you come too!"

Slugga half-flung Dahlia into the chair in front of her desk, then pulled Delroy around to hers. Their bodies wedged for an instant between the filing cabinet and the desk, but Slugga gave Delroy a shove with her rump and sent him hurtling towards her chair. The boy's scowl deepened as he regained his balance and stood before them with his half-shirt hanging from his left shoulder.

By the time Slugga made it through, sweat drained down her face in milky brown streaks. She pointed at Dahlia. "Put on your clothes!" She spoke through her teeth, so that her words sounded like "Putch ontch yourtch clothetchs."

Dahlia looked down at her stained bra, seemingly puzzled by her state of undress. She fumbled with the blouse in her lap, trying to find the sleeves while Slugga breathed deep, rasping breaths. Eventually, with a victorious grunt, Dahlia flipped the blouse around and rammed her arms inside. However, when she attempted to button up, she could find nothing but holes where the buttons had once been. She grabbed the two sides of the blouse together and looked blankly up at Slugga.

Slugga just gave an angry snort and pointed again at Dahlia's lap. Dahlia looked from the half-a-shirt lying there to Delroy, as if unwilling to part with her trophy, but when

Slugga's breathing escalated into a threatening rasp of air, she grudgingly threw it over. Through swollen eyes, Delroy glared at the girl, but he obediently picked up the ripped garment and put it on. When he'd finished, Slugga promptly spun him around and snapped her stapler five times down his back, then beckoned Dahlia to the desk and did the same down the front of her blouse. When she turned to squeeze from behind the desk, Nola grabbed her dangling arm in fright.

But Slugga was only going to the door to ring the end of lunchtime bell.

The excited chatter of the students migrated slowly past them towards the classrooms, some of them peering into the office in the hope of witnessing the aftershock, but Slugga grunted them away. Finally, Slugga turned to address them.

"I'm not interested in who did what to who, or who start what. I just know that I'm tired! Tired of all this discord between the whole lot o' you." Her voice really did sound weary. "After much thought, I think the best thing is to force you to get along. If it's the last thing I do, I'm going to show you," a finger wagged at each of them, "How to live in harmony! H-A-R-M-O-N-Y!"

All three of them frowned back in confusion.

"Yes," Slugga nodded, satisfied with her script, "the three of you going to work together everyday—sit together in class—sit together at lunchtime, do homework together … every evenin'!" the finger wagged from Nola to Dahlia. "I am goin to make sure the three of you learn to stop this wild dog behaviour! I will not have it! Will not have it, you hear me?!"

"But … she box me in my nose and I never do nuttin' to her. She take the juice box and bust my nose!" Delroy sounded like an off-key trumpet.

"I shaid, I'm not intereshted!" Slugga patted her head, "I want the three of you off my compound right now! Tomorrow

37

morning at seven thirty sharp, report right back here and you can start the day with your new friendship."

Slugga opened her grade book, flipped to an empty page and wrote something in red ink, right in the middle of the sheet. "Alright," she said without looking up, "Get out of my office. Get out of my school. Don't ever let me see that nasty behaviour on this compound, or anywhere else, again!"

And so began the blending of three lives. Not a willful connection, but one formed by a woman whom no one dared disobey ... forged with the use of a handy stapler and a red ink pen.

CHAPTER 7

MANGO SEASON WAS a good time for Redding. Trees bowed with the weight of their bounty. The aroma from pots simmering with evening meals was replaced with the scent of mango – mango jams, mango custards, mango juice, mango chutneys, and every roadside was dotted with mango seeds sucked bald.

Mango season was a good time for Mama. The demand for her mango jam and chutney (recipes passed down from Granny Pat) was great, in Redding, in Kingston and abroad. Mrs. Spence bought such large quantities that Tuesdays and Fridays were dedicated to filling her orders alone. Some she sold in Razzle Dazzle, while the rest she packaged in thick sponge and cardboard boxes and sent to New York, where her daughter, Camille, sold them in her West Indian supermarket.

Mama hummed during mango season. This was the time that brought her closer to her goal—the extension of her kitchen. From the time Nola had been able to make sense of words, she'd heard Mama discuss her plans to take the kitchen beyond the step where the mongrel dog slept. There would be an area dedicated just to the preparation of her chutneys and jams, and space enough for a huge freezer to store fruit pulp during the off-seasons.

During mango season, Nola was in charge of peeling the mangoes and slicing the pulp off the seeds. Her hands stained yellow, and sometimes cramped stiffly into the shape of the mangoes – cup-shaped, like Grampy's. Now, with her duties doubled, she had to rush even more through her evenings at Dahlia's house.

She learned to balance her two lives—the stress of home, and the relaxation of Dahlia's. Every afternoon, she and Dahlia would walk into the little pink house to be greeted by some mouthwatering smell (Delroy refused to enter the house, waiting, instead, under the mango tree by the plumbago hedge till they came back out with their stuffed bellies). Merlene would come out of her room with her sleepy smile and colour-coded nightwear and serve them the feast while they filled her in on the day's events. Then she would wash up while Nola and Dahlia went to join Delroy's surly face, and the three of them would do Slugga's assignments beneath a canopy of Blackie mangoes.

Nola was a little surprised that Merlene had never questioned Delroy about the huge swelling he'd given Pumkin's face that day. She'd waited with bated breath on the first afternoon that he'd trudged unhappily through the hedge for Merlene's angry accusations, but Merlene had only carried plates of her delicious cooking out onto the front lawn, reassuring Delroy that she didn't bite while the sun was shining. But he refused to eat, or to laugh at her joke.

Poor Delroy, he couldn't even have tried to cop out of the punishment, for Slugga had been quite clever in her planning. At the end of each school day, she would staple ten sums into his book, a different set of ten into Dahlia's, and yet a different set into Nola's. They were each to do all 30 sums. So Delroy had no choice but to scowlingly work beside them every afternoon.

He remained silent while Nola explained the sums to Dahlia. Only once, on the second day, when Dahlia gave one of her victory whoops, he gave a scornful snort. Nola's eyes had flown to Dahlia's face in fright, sure that the girl would have upped and punched him straight in the nose, but she'd acted as if she hadn't heard, and met the snort with a blank look.

The part of the punishment served at school was nowhere as pleasant as the part at Dahlia's house. However, it passed quickly enough to be tolerable—every lunchtime they had to sit beneath the eave outside of Slugga's office where they endured crude gestures from Delroy's scrimmage crew.

All in all, it wasn't bad. All in all, it shocked Nola how often she felt laughter bubble involuntarily from her chest. Balance and timing. That was the key. Balance and timing had given her the best of both worlds, and had made her carefree. It was an intricate trick, but one in which just one shift in the elements could have sent her reeling, as it eventually did.

CHAPTER 8

ONE AFTERNOON, NOLA'S timing was very badly set off. It was the day when Biscuit, one of Merlene's waitresses, came early to work. She'd brought Bombay mangoes for Merlene, breezing through the hedge on a cloud of Matterhorn smoke, orange talons wrapped around the scandal bag of mangoes. When she flung herself into a chair on the verandah, the air seemed to crackle, every crevice of space filled with the details of her—the flaming hair; the shiny leatherette pants; the red tank top dragged low from the weight of her breasts. Even her voice, roughened by smoke, seemed to shave the air.

Nola was captivated, and Biscuit, bristling beneath the attention of a new audience, immediately embarked upon a tale. The night before, she'd witnessed the arrest of a drug don called Squid. The don had been hiding out in Nainsville (right on Biscuit's street) with one of his women. A couple weeks before, an off-duty policeman had been shot in broad daylight, within plain view of the other patrons, as he'd sat in a street-side bar. As the policeman fell to the floor, the killer had flipped his body over and removed the firearm from the waist. He then tucked the stolen gun casually into his own waistband, jumped on to the back of a motorbike across the street, on which another man had been waiting, and the two sped off as if they'd just stopped by the bar for a quick drink.

Trouble was, Biscuit expounded, the man waiting on the bike had said to himself, "Make haste nuh, Lucifer," without taking note of the drunkard lying on the side of the road. It was this drunkard who'd repeated the name 'Lucifer' to the policemen. Lucifer, well-known as a member of the Roseblood Posse which operated out of Kinte Lane.

The police entered the lane just as Lucifer had sat down to a plate of cow foot and broad beans, the policeman's gun still tucked into his waist. After much 'persuasion', Lucifer gave the name 'Squid' as the person who had ordered their colleague's murder—$10,000 for the life of the policeman who'd been trying to extort money from the don.

As soon as Squid heard about Lucifer's arrest he had gone into hiding. It turned out that the very same girlfriend with whom he sought refuge had been the one to inform the police of his whereabouts. She considered herself entitled to the money Squid had brought with him. However, she dipped a little too far into the funds for Squid's liking, and he hit her right across her face with a table fan.

Merlene shook her head. "Some woman really stupid! Them hide all the bad man them, and is always the same man that turn round and beat them near to death!"

Nola didn't know if it was her imagination, but she could have sworn that Merlene glanced at Delroy before she began her next sentence.

"You know what I wish?" she continued, "I wish our men would stop beatin' up the women. The women give them children, give them a home, make ends meet when tings get rough, and them still turn round and beat up the women!" She gave a little sigh.

Nola saw the laughter melt from Delroy's face. He began plucking at the grass.

"Not me!" Dahlia shouted, "Not me. I not takin' no beatin' from any man! I not takin' no lick from anybody! Them goin' have to fight me to the bitter end! When I go down, it goin' be in a blaze of glory!"

Merlene chuckled softly, but when she spoke her gaze seemed suddenly distant. "It's not every time you have to fight, Pumkin. Sometimes life have a way of just catchin' up to people, just like it catch up to Squid. Sometimes you just have to sit back and wait, and let the Almighty deal with them in His own time!"

I wish our men would stop beatin' up the women. Surely Merlene could not have meant your own father? Surely not, when the Bible clearly stated, "Spare the rod and spoil the child."

Nola blinked away the sting that suddenly pricked at her eyes. She looked up into the sky, trying to hide the gleam, and when she looked up, she lost her breath. The sky was orange! The afternoon had skimmed by and now the sky was ripening in the glow of evening. It was a 20-minute walk up Macca Hill! By the time she made it home, the pots with the residue of boiled mango would be piled outside the kitchen door, like an announcement of her tardiness. The pots would be waiting. The mangoes would be waiting. Papa would be waiting.

She ran one full circle around Delroy and Dahlia before she found her bearings and tore into the house past Biscuit's confused face. She tore off the duster and hauled on her skirt in such a rush that she scraped the hook against her leg. She hadn't completed buttoning her blouse before she tore back outside, grabbed up her bag, and gasped a hurried 'good-bye' to the four faces sitting in silence.

There was music coming from the bar. The deep reggae bass seemed to spur on her racing heart as she walked past the red door. A woman in a tight orange mini skirt and tubed top leaned against the jamb, blowing streams of smoke from her nose as she drew on a cigarette.

Nola ran all the way up Macca Hill, slowing down to catch her breath only when she got to the steep section before the gates of the Open Bible Church. Maybe him listening to the news, she prayed on each breath, maybe him work late at the orchard this evenin' and him don't reach home yet.

She passed Miss Terry and Miss Nan resting their heavy hips against a large boulder beside Cecil Reid's lettuce patch. Further up, Shamoney Leach waited while her four-year-old daughter peed into a pothole. In just a few minutes Nola spotted Mass Tackie's house. A single kerosene lamp burned through the living room window, even though the old man had received electricity years ago. The house sat like a crown on the top of Macca Hill. It marked the descent to the other side of the hill, where Nola's' house was.

Nola paused beside the Mass Tackie's yard to catch her breath. She could see her house lying at her feet. The kitchen light burned in the evening like a piece of sin. She could see the top of Grampy's prized thumberga vine hanging like a discarded garment over the eave of the verandah, its leaves dark and shriveled from the black fungus that had finally overtaken it. Grampy used to spray it with powdered pepper and corn oil, to keep the bugs and fungus away, but since his death, the vine had succumbed to the fungus. Nola had tried to spray it once, but Papa had gotten into such a rage over the waste of the cooking oil that she hadn't done it again.

As she stood there, she realized that Papa's car was not in its usual spot by the gate. Her heart sparked with a twinge of hope. Had her prayer worked? Had he stayed late at work that evening?

As she pushed her gate open, she thought she heard her name, spoken very softly. She froze and listened. Yes, there it was again, louder this time.

"Night then, Nola. See you tomorrow at school."

She spun around, incredulous.

Delroy! What was he doing at her gate? He lived on Bogle Lane, way on the other side of Clysdale Bend, a long way from the bottom of Macca Hill. What on earth was he doing at the top of Macca Hill? She shot him a look of confusion as she turned and ran towards the kitchen door.

The three large dutch pots were there, just as she'd predicted, stacked one on top of the other by the outside pipe. Their rims were coated in the yellow gum of boiled mango, and beside them, the charcoal and steel-wool sat accusingly on the steps. The dog lifted his head lazily as she crept past the zinc of pimento to stoop beneath the kitchen window. The house was silent except for the scraping of a knife on the wooden chopping board. The spicy smell of scotch bonnet peppers wafted through the window—seasonings for tomorrow's batch of chutneys. Then there was the sound of water at the kitchen sink, and the smell of bleach. Nola listened for Papa's voice, for the raspy whisp of his breath, but there was nothing except the water.

She had to go inside before it got any later. She pinched her leg hard. It was always a good way of preparing herself, just in case he was there. Her body would already be conditioned for pain. She stood up, then quickly stooped back down as she realized that it was drizzling. The rains had finally come. The mist fell on her braids, the coconut oil repelling the moisture and creating its glistening cap. Your halo, Grampy used to call it. How she wished it was. A halo to take her up to heaven whenever she willed it, far away from this kitchen window.

CHAPTER 9

NOLA TOOK A deep breath then opened the kitchen door, assuming a nonchalant look as she dropped her school bag on the counter, right on top of a white mound of cornstarch. The powder wafted like a disintegrating dream over her damp shoes.

"Sorry, Mama. One of Janga's goats drop in the river. It drop in the deep part, the same part where Jervis' cow did drown, so we tie rope 'round him hoof and haul him out, me and Janga 'cause I was the only one passin' by when it happen."

Nola didn't know where the story had come from. She'd been too nervous to rehearse one as she'd hurried up the hill, but here was one, pouring out of her as easy as the water from the kitchen pipe.

But immediately she saw that she'd been wrong. Her prayers had not been answered. She could tell because Mama's hands trembled as she washed the chopping board, and Louisa eyes were wide as she looked up from peeling the mangoes.

She felt the shiver begin at her feet and climb its way up her legs, through her stomach and up to her shoulders, till it chattered her teeth. She heard when Papa came from the bedroom, but when she turned, the belt was already raised.

He hit her with the buckle. He was never really fussy about where the blows landed. Nola always had to turn away to protect her face, and cross her arms across her chest to protect her breasts.

She felt the skin welt immediately. It split easily as the buckle tore into her blouse, decorating the grey fabric with streaks of red. She never cried out, for she knew that any sound, any pleading, would make him hit harder, and for a longer time. "You want someting to cry 'bout?" he would ask, and the effort of the beating would make the sweat bead on his forehead. So Nola always bit her tongue to stop the tears, till the salty blood was both in and out of her body.

She did instead, the only thing she knew how to do to escape, to pass the time till Papa's arm got slack with fatigue— she took her mind to Grampy's face. She covered her face and took her mind to the sweet wrinkled cheeks that waffled up and down in time to his chuckles. But, something very strange happened; instead of seeing Grampy's face, she saw Merlene's, thin eyebrows raised in warning, "I wish our men would stop beatin' up the women."

The voice rang through the kitchen, resounding off the walls and drowning out Papa's panting.

She heard the tinkle of metal hitting the floor, and Papa's fist found its way home. Her feet skittered, always taken by surprise by the first punch, but she braced herself on the counter, and stood fast for the ones to follow.

The voice came again, louder than before. This time it jarred her so much that her stance was shaken once again and she stumbled when Papa struck. Her hands fell from her face and she stared straight into Papa's eyes. How large his pupils were when they were dilated by anger—and something else— hatred! It flashed through his eyes and flared his nostrils. She'd never seen it so close before. She'd never seen it so real. It was because she'd always remained hidden behind her fingers. But tonight, Merlene's voice had made her hands fall away, and she'd seen it for herself.

Her eyes opened wide with the acknowledgement of the truth, and her brown gaze locked with the frigid grey of Papa's. She saw the fist rise, but it never came back down. She watched the grey eyes dart from her stare to her quivering jaw, and back to her eyes, but still the fist did not strike. Eventually, it lowered itself and reached instead for her collar. It pulled her so close to his face that the fishy hate washed over her.

"Who you think you is, saunterin' in here any time you like, while everybody else doing your work for you?" Spittle sprayed her face. "You think I send you to school to go gallivantin' by the river all night instead of comin' home to earn you keep? Eh? You think things free 'round here? We must work while you gallivant all day? How much time I must tell you to find your burro-brush head home at evenin' time and make some use of yourself?"

Then he opened the kitchen door with one hand while with the other he still held her collar firmly. He turned her around, so that the swollen coolness of the rain blasted her hot cheeks. She felt his foot in her back, the soft fabric of his sock against the curved nook of her spine—another perfect fit. Then she felt the foot draw back. As she catapulted down the kitchen steps and slammed into the zinc of pimento beans, she could taste the spicy beans on her tongue as they scattered over the wet grass.

When she finally stopped rolling, her arms were twisted beneath her torso and her left cheek was pressed against soil. The force of the raindrops splattered mud into her eyes and she had to squeeze them shut to prevent the stinging.

The rhythm of the rain became stronger on her back. Puddup, puddup, puddud, tap, tap, tap. So funny how they felt

49

like fingers, tapping at her shoulders, pulling at her shoulders, turning her over, unfolding her stiffened limbs. Hands! Hands were on her! Someone was lifting her into the cradle of arms, carrying her to the coolie plum tree where the battering drops were thwarted by the thick branches, and Nola could finally open her eyes. She gave a sob of shame. Delroy!

She wanted to wriggle free of his arms and run back into the rain, but her legs could do nothing but dangle from his arms as he pushed past Ellie's rump to put her on the empty feed bag in the corner of the pen. Nola blinked through the water droplets on her lashes and stared in awe as he lowered himself beside her. Her eyes felt raw, as if they'd been turned inside out.

"Where hurting?" Delroy's voice startled her and made her jerk her leg from the spot where it had been resting against his knee. However, the sudden movement jarred her ripped skin and bruised limbs and she moaned before she could stop herself.

"Where hurting?" He asked again, anxiously this time.

Nola wanted to scream. Why you care where hurtin' me? Instead, she shook her head slowly. The water from her braids dripped unto his legs and he leaned forward to wipe the drops from her forehead. It took all her strength not to flinch again.

"I would'a help you up sooner, but them was still at the window."

He'd seen the whole thing!

"When you leave Dahlia, you did seem so 'fraid." He was speaking again, his voice strangely unsteady. "I thought you was 'fraid to walk home alone, so I follow you, ... and then, just when I was leavin', I hear him ..." His voice trailed away.

Her head was reeling. Why would Delroy have cared that she was afraid to walk home? And why did his face seem so anxious? Hadn't he been the one who'd kicked the scrimmage box into her shoulder? She started to shiver.

Delroy pulled something from the rafters. Grampy's blue towel, the one he'd used to wipe his forehead and the sap-stained blade of his machete. When Delroy attempted to open it, it remained scrunched in a balled shape and he had to pull hard on the folds to get it around Nola's shoulders.

"You better take off those wet tings," Delroy instructed.

This time she found her voice. "With you here?"

He stared silently at her for a couple seconds before he stood up. But, as he bent and stretched his hands towards her, she flinched and covered her head with her arms. It was an automatic reaction, her body still in survival mode from her beating. Delroy crouched again beside her. He held the ends of the towel and pulled her towards him.

"I wouldn't do that. I wouldn't lick you up like that! The juice box was a accident."

Nola's chin gave a disbelieving quiver.

Delroy stared at her for a long time, his face pale in the watery light, until something in his eyes made Nola have to look away. Then he released the towel and was gone.

CHAPTER 10

NOLA STARED AT the soft light filtering through the doorway. She'd slept the whole night on the ground, and now every muscle in her body was aching. She reached for the uniform she'd hung over the rafter the night before. Still damp, but better than walking half-naked up to the house. She had to lean against the wall to pull on the skirt. As she lifted her leg, she felt a suspicious stickiness against her thighs, and her heart fell as she recognized the crimson stain on the crocus bag. It hadn't been due for another couple days, but now here it was. It must have been the fall. That, or the kick in her back.

The clank of pots from the kitchen told her that the house was awake. She walked slowly from the pen, her thighs sticking together as she tried to ignore the stiffness in her body. The dutch pots were still on the kitchen steps, the bits of mango floating within like little goldfish. She looked towards the kitchen window, straight into Mama's eyes, sunk so deep into her face that the folds of skin enveloped them like an old blanket. Her chin lifted slightly as she met Nola's eyes, then shifted quickly sideways.

Papa. He was there.

Nola scrubbed her thighs at the pipe. The water immediately turned to rust. She finally went to the kitchen door, uncertain if she should just walk in or wait for Mama to open it. She never knew what to expect after one of Papa's rages. Sometimes, it would take the slightest thing to keep him angry for days, yet at other times, just hours after he'd delivered one of his lashings, he would look blankly at her, as if her dark skin had suddenly become transparent.

She knocked. Mama wasn't sure about the state of Papa's anger either. Nola could tell by the way her eyes darted towards him when she opened the door. He didn't look up from his mug of coffee, so Mama handed her the dishcloth that had been hanging over her shoulder, her hands lingering on Nola's for a split second. Her fingers felt like fire against Nola's ice-tipped ones. Her eyes swept anxiously over Nola's face, from her disheveled braids to the ashy sky, and even though she did not speak, Nola could tell what she was thinking—"Why you can't just do what he says, Nola? Why you can't just behave? See what you cause again?"

When Mama finally released the towel, Nola pressed it to her face, breathing in the warmth and precisely clean smell of Mama as she timidly looked around the kitchen. It was exactly as it was the night before. The mango skins from Louisa's peeling were now shrivelled brown spirals all over the table. Her school bag was on the floor, still covered in its white dusting of cornstarch.

"Make sure you clean up this mess before you leave here today." Papa's voice was as nonchalant as if he were reminding her to eat breakfast, yet it made Nola jump and drop the towel.

"Yes, Sir," she nodded, making the blood gush up and down her head.

She bent to retrieve the towel and immediately used it to brush the mango skins from the table into the cupped bowl of her hand. She had to step over her school bag to stuff them into the bin, and Mama bent to move it out of her way.

"Sadie, don't I tell you not to touch nothing? That's why this pickney so damn lazy, because you do everyting for her. If you touch one more ting in here, Sadie, me and you today." Papa's voice was as quiet as before, but when he put his enamel mug back on the table, the coffee slushed over the side.

Mama dropped the school bag to the floor and turned to go back to the sink.

"Nola, my car not workin'. It in the garage again, so you goin' to have to deliver to the Spences on Saturdays. Good way for you to make up for leavin' your mother and sister to do all your work."

"Yes, Sir." Blood-gushing nod again.

She dared not argue. Mrs. Spence had told Mama that she would gladly pick up the chutneys whenever Papa's car was on the blink, but Nola did not say that. She only nodded. Yes, she would clean the kitchen. Yes, she would go to school with her raging bruises and face the shame of seeing Delroy Reckus. Yes, she would make the trek to the Spences every Saturday with the chutneys. Yes! Yes! Yes! Always her answer to a world that told her 'No!'

CHAPTER 11

L IFE SETTLED LIKE silt in the river after a storm. Nola regained her balance. She returned to Dahlia's house, getting home on time every afternoon to complete her chores. Delroy never mentioned that night in the rain, but, every now and again, she would glance up to find him staring, and she would have to look away to hide the rush of shame on her face.

But something had definitely changed in him since that night. He now added to the conversation as they sat outside Slugga's office, and then on Merlene's front lawn as they did their work. But he still refused to enter the pink house. The farthest he would go was onto the little verandah, but never through the front door.

Every now and again, Biscuit would come with her bounty of Bombay mangoes and her boisterous tales. However, no matter how interesting the stories, no matter how comfortably they all sat laughing on that lawn, Nola always watched the sky, and as soon as it began to waver in its afternoon intensity, she would grab her books and rush through the hedge. Once, she even felt Delroy nudge her with the corner of his book, and when she turned to look at him, his eyes lifted upwards to indicate the weakening sky.

It was in this comfortable existence, in this half-relaxed camaraderie, that Nola told Dahlia and Delroy about Grampy's Dew Angels. The story just slipped out one afternoon. But, she told them with laughter in her voice, in case they thought she'd been silly enough to believe the old man's tale.

Dahlia spoke first, her voice filled with wonder. "You think your grampa did see them? Ole people see things that we can't see, you know. Miss Aggie see duppy all the time!"

Delroy scoffed. "The only duppy Mad Aggie ever see is her own!"

Dahlia jumped up and jammed her hands on to her hips. "What you saying, Delroy? That you don't believe in spirits? You saying that Nola's grampa tell her lie?"

Delroy gave Nola an apologetic look. "Not a lie – just a tale, like when them tell children 'bout Santa and all those tings – no such thing as Santa."

Dahlia's face fell, her lip-nose drooping like a deflated balloon. "Delroy Reckus, you heart so tough that is a wonder that you even get it to beat! There is such a thing as Santa! People like you wouldn't know 'bout Santa cause you have to understand that Santa is not a person—it's a feelin'." Dahlia fanned her hand dismissively at Delroy.

Nola looked down at her own hands. She wouldn't have understood that 'feelin' either.

"That's why you must believe in things like the dew angels, Nola," Dahlia continued. "That's why your grampa leave you with that story, so that you can always have that feelin' in your heart! No matter how bad today is, you know that tomorrow tings can change."

Delroy scoffed again.

"You can laugh all you want, Delroy Reckus, but lemme tell you someting, if you don't believe in mystery, then you don't believe in God, and you don't believe in love!"

"So why you think God make so much bad things happen to people? Why him have to make the good things be a mystery?" Delroy almost shouted. "Why him never just make it easy for us and give us the good things right up FRONT!?"

Dahlia blinked, her lip-nose quivering slightly.

"Bad things happen because we live with bad people 'round us. But God give you the good things, the mystery, to help you deal with them better." Dahlia paused and looked towards the verandah where Merlene had come to pick up her mug from the table. Merlene waved and they all waved back. "You know we had a big house in Kingston, and a car, and Mama and Papa had a supermarket? Them used to work there all day, sometimes late in the night cause the supermarket was always full. Them used to make plenty money." She shook her head. "But my father ... my papa was a bad person." She shook her head again and corrected herself, "Papa was a good person, but him used to do bad things. Him used to take drugs."

She paused long enough for Nola to gasp and then quickly catch herself.

"Yes, my father used to take drugs! I never know, 'cause Mama used to hide it from me, just smile and make me think everyting was fine. Then him start to beat her, so bad that sometimes she used to have to go doctor."

Nola gasped again. She just couldn't imagine anyone hitting sweet Merlene. No wonder she'd been so passionate about the argument of men hitting women! No wonder Nola had felt such a bond with her, more than that of being one of Redding's outcasts.

Dahlia began to speak again. "Mama would take the licks, and when she was bleedin' on the ground, can't walk, can't even talk, Papa would say that him was sorry, that him never goin' do it again. And sometimes for a little while him would stop. Then him would go away again to where them sell the

57

drugs, stay for a while, then him would come back and start to lick Mama all over again!"

Dahlia sighed and looked up at the sky. "But the last time … the last time, I try to stop him. I beg him to stop lickin' Mama. I beg him not to kill her! But him wouldn't stop, so I take the kitchen knife and stick it right here." She pointed to her right side, her finger jabbing at the flesh over and over again as if the memory had stuck within her like a scratched record. "Even with the knife in him, and the blood everywhere, him come after me. Him lick me straight in my face." Dahlia stared down at the fist she'd made with her hand. "And him bust open my whole face, till my nose and my mouth forget where them was supposed to be. That's how hard my father lick me."

Delroy pretended to clear his throat, but Nola knew it was a muffled exclamation.

"Mama say we have to leave. She go back to the supermarket when them take Papa to hospital, and she take all the money from the office. She tie up my face with cloth, and we catch a bus that same night. Mama say we was goin' wherever God lead us. When we get to Clarendon, we come off the bus to pee-pee, and a woman who was sittin' behind us ask Mama what happen to my face. Mama tell her that I drop from a step, and she give Mama two sweet sop from her basket, and you know what she say? She tell Mama that the sweetest fruits in Jamaica come from Redding! And guess what? When we get back on the bus, the woman wasn't there! Gone, just like a duppy! Mama say that was our angel, telling us to come to Redding. So we come here, and I never see my papa since."

Delroy let out his breath in a faint whistle. "Him dead?" he asked.

Dahlia shook her head. Nola stared in awe at the girl's lip-nose. It was as if she'd suddenly discovered a secret compartment in a room that she'd thought she'd known from corner to corner. And then, right before her eyes, Dahlia's face unfolded. The thick upper lip uncurled from its tight hold on the nose, and the nose pulled up the wings that had flattened across the cheeks. Right before her eyes, Dahlia became un-ugly. Nola felt overwhelmed with shame at the years she'd made that ugliness her secret pleasure when all along it had been the result of a battle for life. Hers and her mama's. They'd had to run, to leave everything that had been familiar to them, and at the direction of a stranger, ended up in a village that despised the very air they breathed.

"But how is all that a good thing?" Delroy's voice sounded like it did that night in the rain.

Dahlia gave him a look of exasperation. "Because my father tell my mother that if she ever leave him, him goin' find her and kill her. But that angel send us here, where Papa can't ever find us. We happy, me and Mama. No matter what anybody do to us, what anybody say, them can't ever hurt us like my father hurt us. Them can't ever tear us apart." She cocked her head at Delroy.

"Yes, bad things did happen, but we can always remember the good things, me and Mama—like when my papa used to put out my presents when I go to sleep Christmas Eve, so I would believe that Santa come. Mama say him used to wake up early just to see my face when I see those presents. Now, when I think of my papa, I can know that him really did love me."

That afternoon Delroy followed Nola to the bottom of Macca Hill as he had been doing every afternoon. When he stopped at the base of Macca Hill, he said softly, "Everyting alright then, Nola?"

Nola did not look back, just nodded her head and walked up the hill, just in case she was tempted to truthfully answer his question.

CHAPTER 12

E VER SINCE DAHLIA'S story about her papa, Nola craved the chill of the waters of the Rio Diablo on her body. She wanted to feel the numbness, to feel nothing but ripples against her skin. The next afternoon, she rushed through her assignment with Dahlia and Delroy, and told them that she had to pick up something for Mama at Miss June's.

Whether angry or peaceful, the river was always beautiful. In her rage, she became a frothing mass, screaming a power that gave a glimpse of the power of the divine. In her peace, she was like glass, her ripples playing carefree games over the peeping rocks. Nola's favourite spot was the spot where children were warned not to play, where the water was too deep for washing, and the rocks too slippery for little feet. Nola had found it by accident. Years before, she'd scrambled up the bank trying to find the end of a rainbow, and she'd climbed to where tree branches had knitted themselves into a thick quilt and the rocks wore a spongy carpet of moss. The sunlight broke through the branches of two rose-apple trees, the rays playing catch across the rippling water. Where the ripples rose with the current, they shot the light upwards, so that the rays seemed to fly off the water, like tiny river angels. The air under the trees had been thick with the smell of rose-apples, making Nola heady with its sweetness. She'd jumped in, and discovered that the rocks beneath the surface of the river formed a pool, where she could stretch her legs apart and lean back to allow the current to flatten her against the rock.

She had begun to visit the spot after her papa's beatings to allow the icy water to soothe her battered body. She'd leave there with the welts flattened, and her soul soothed.

That afternoon, after she'd left Dahlia and Delroy, she stood on the high bank and stared down at her reflection. It was amazing how the river perfected what the world couldn't.

Clad only in her underwear, she jumped in and felt her limbs freeze immediately. It was a purifying cold, one that charged through her blood and electrified her spirit. But something was missing! She missed Dahlia and Delroy! She missed the silly bickering and the laughter. She was feeling guilty at having lied to them, at having left them out of something as special as this place. Just the day before, Dahlia had shared something so personal, so painful, yet here she was, hiding away in this beautiful part of the world.

Suddenly, a burst of water erupted in front of her, and she gave a startled gasp as she found herself looking straight into a glob of snot, dripping from the lip-nose of Dahlia Daley!

"Gone to get something for you mama, eh? What you was going to get, a bucket of water?" Dahlia gurgled into her face, her braids dripping streams of water into her eyes.

Nola stared incredulously from Dahlia to Delroy. The girl had stripped, and was wearing only a blue bra and bright orange panties. Delroy was on the bank, looking down at them with his best unimpressed expression.

Nola was grateful that he'd stayed up there, for the thought of him, of anyone, seeing her in her underwear was enough to sear her chilled limbs with hot shame.

"I never know you like to swim," Nola tried to explain as she followed Dahlia towards the rock, further away from where Delroy stood on the bank.

"You never know that I like to swim?" Dahlia puffed.

"Mama say that I'm like a little fish!" And to prove her point, she dove headfirst into the water. However, her torso remained uncooperative in the effort, and even with the enthusiastic propelling of her feet, her body only flipped over. When she finally righted herself and panted against the rock, there was another stream of snot draining from her nose, but she only gave a gleeful laugh and blew it away with a loud honk. Then she pressed her palms together and followed the path of her snot into the water. This time, her orange underwear filled with air, and suspended her body like a bobbing balloon.

Nola looked up at Delroy in exasperation. He laughed so hard as he pointed at Dahlia's floating underwear that his torso dipped backwards. Nola opened her mouth to warn him of the slipperiness of the bank, but it was too late. She saw the mirth on his face change to a look of shock as his shoes began a gentle glide. Unfortunately, his attempt to stop the slide by propelling his arms backwards only served to increase his speed. Nola prayed that he could swim.

The splash that his body made brought Dahlia to the surface in fright. However, Nola could not stop to explain what had happened, for Delroy was drowning! She frantically tried to remember what Grampy had told her about the time he'd saved his older brother from drowning—"Me had to knock him unconscious and then drag him out the river by his neck!" She swam quickly to the whirlpool above Delroy's thrashing body, and the minute his head broke the surface, she whacked it with her fist. She felt her fingers crack painfully, and Delroy went under again, thrashing even more wildly this time.

"Nola! What you doin' to Delroy? Is kill you tryin' to kill him?" She heard Dahlia bellow behind her.

"Him drownin'! Him drop in and him can't swim. I tryin' to save him," Nola panted back.

"Him can't swim? So how him get over there?" Dahlia's voice gurgled with stifled humour.

Nola spun to where Dahlia's finger was pointing at the bank a few yards away.

Sure enough, there was Delroy, pulling himself out of the water, dazedly rubbing the top of his head. Nola gave an inward sigh. It seemed that as long as Delroy was in hers and Dahlia's company he would be prone to head injuries.

CHAPTER 13

T HE MYSTERY AND peace of Nola's spot had not been lost on Dahlia, for the next day she begged to go back. Some days they would go straight there from school, completing their homework in the dim light of the rose-apple branches, while an old Milo tin of crayfish and lemongrass churned beside them on a makeshift stove of rocks.

Nola began to fill out. Between the food at Merlene's, and the crayfish stews by the river, her cheekbones had disappeared beneath the suppleness of her cheeks. Not only did they round out beneath their new apples, but they glowed with the ruddiness gained from the sifted light of Merlene's mango tree.

She could sense Papa's disgust. She could hear the sharp intake of breath as she walked by, and knew he'd noticed the changes, but the truth was, after that night in the kitchen, she knew there was nothing she could have done to alter his feelings. She'd seen the hatred for herself, and now she accepted that it was as permanent as the straight bridge of Papa's perfect nose. The sun would rise each day, the Rio Diablo would flow through Redding, and Papa would hate her.

It was amazing how much difference hearing Merlene's voice in the kitchen that night had made to her life. Not because she believed, with any false security, that her papa would stop hitting her but, because, for the first time, it had made her face the truth. It had made her face the futility of wishing all those years that Papa would grow to love her. The muck of hope spewed from her that night. All those years of being washed by the dew, when all she'd needed was the truth.

She soon began to feed on the hate in Papa's eyes. She began to look into his eyes at the times when she would have usually held her head low. And Papa looked away!

It was stunning at first, the faltering looks that turned away from her steady gaze. The truth—such a dangerous thing. Looking back at that time, it must have been a combination of all those things that had given her the power. The combination of the truth, the futility of the dreams, and Papa's faltering eyes. The first night, when the power surged through her, Nola waited in her room till the swish of Mama's vinegar-soaked mop had ceased, and the house rasped with the heavy breaths of sleep. She walked through the kitchen, spurred on by the ticking of the living room clock, her toes curling in the film of grease that the years had ground into the linoleum.

Their faces were slack on the pillow, Mama on the left, Papa on the right, the sheet sagging between them like a broken fence. Papa glowed like Louisa. He slept on his side, one hand tucked between his knees, like Nola. So harmless, he seemed, with his mouth slightly open, like a child, trusting the world.

Nola moved closer to the bed. Did he cry as a child? Had he been afraid of the dark? Had he wanted to be hugged when he fell and got hurt? He'd never spoken much about his childhood. His parents had lived in Hanover, he'd said that much. He had been good with numbers and had helped their neighbours with their business accounts. Any other information had been given by Mama. She told them that Papa's parents had been old, much older than the normal age for having children, so at the age of six, Papa had been sent to Nainsville to live with his Aunt Linette, his papa's younger and more 'child-able' cousin. But though younger, truth was, Aunt Linette had had a nasty temperament. She'd turned out to be as dour as any woman twice her age. A woman of God, Mama said, and one who considered the frivolities of life a direct path to hell. She'd had no children of her own, had never married, so Papa was her only companion. Mama said that Papa had sat by her bedside every evening, and read aloud her favourite passages from the Bible. He'd been right there when she'd died, yet even with that, Papa never spoke of Aunt Linette, and from the day of her funeral, he never set foot back in a church, except for the day that he married Mama.

Nola watched his temple pulse gently in slumber. Did he hate her in his sleep? Did she even exist in the perfect world of his dreams? Maybe in his dreams it was the little boy who greeted him when he came from the orchard, who sat with Mama and Louisa at the table, smiling with glee when he walked in.

She watched Papa sleep for two hours that night. The next night, she touched his face. He moved slightly when her hand brushed against his forehead, and she readied herself for the blow, but he did not wake. Her fingers continued their trail, from his forehead to his cheek. He moved again when her fingers grazed the shadow of stubble on his cheek. He raised his neck, higher on the pillow, and mumbled something that sounded like "... not in the yard," but Nola's wildly beating heart drowned out the words and she wasn't sure if he'd really said that, or "... hit her hard." She leaned close, brushing her nostrils against the curled cartilage of his ear, pulling the night smell of him deep into her chest.

The night after, when she tip-toed to Papa's doorway, the bed was empty. Mama lay sleeping, but Papa was not beside her. She spun around, frightened, thinking that he'd realized what she'd been doing and was waiting for her in the darkened kitchen, but he was nowhere in sight. Then she heard the click of a door being opened, then shut, and the minty smell of Grampy wafted into the kitchen. She wedged herself between the counter and the stove and watched as Papa walked from the passage and stopped right in front of her to take a cracker from the jar. She could still hear him crunching as he climbed into bed.

Suddenly, the living room clock was ticking so loudly that Nola had to cover her ears so it wouldn't deafen her.

Mystery, Dahlia had said, the thing that kept you going through the bitterness of life. But what if the mystery was better left undiscovered? What if the mystery of love was denied to some, and given too much to others? What then?

CHAPTER 14

REDDING PRIDED ITSELF on the power of its prayers. Every solution to life's dilemmas was given up to God in prayer. Loud, energetic prayer, that on some Sundays rattled the roof of the Redding Open Bible Church. You see, for Reddingers, prayer was also a very strong weapon. Woe to an offender who was warned, "I goin' pray for you!"

'Being prayed for' was one of the things that Nola tried very hard to avoid. It was one of the reasons that she continued smiling her way through her Saturday deliveries to the Spences. However, recently it was beginning to seem like it would need much more than weekly glimpses of her pearly whites to protect her from Mrs. Spence's prayers. As such, Pastor Peppers' Sunday sermons became an anxious experience for Nola. Whenever Pastor lisped the announcement for personal reflection and prayer, and Mrs. Spence heaved her chest towards the heavens, Nola would then fervently begin her own 'counter-prayer'. For the most part, the counter-prayers seemed to be working as she had not suffered any unusual torments.

How Nola wished she could have enjoyed the Sunday service like everyone else, singing hymns with abandon as Grampy used to do, with that deep peace on his face.

Just as important as the actual Sunday morning service was the gathering in the churchyard afterward. There was no better remedy for a spent soul than the soothing whisper of village gossip. Everyone clustered in groups, wearing expressions of concern as the news of the village passed from cluster to cluster.

One Sunday morning, as Nola stood beside her mama, Mrs. Spence ambled over. The woman's eyes did not so much as flinch in Nola's direction as she bade her mother good morning.

"Nola, say good mornin' to Mrs. Spence," Mama instructed, and as Nola mumbled a greeting, the woman grimaced as if suddenly stung by a wasp.

"Sadie, I loove the new green tomatooo chootney! Camille say that she never have hands tooo sell them! Them finish oooff the shelf before the week was oover!"

Mama smiled and nodded her thanks. "Where Mr. Spence?" she asked, looking around for the little man's head. "Him never come to church this mornin'?"

A look of concern appeared on Mrs. Spence's face. "Gas again!" she wailed. "I don't knooow what Leroy keep eatin' that give him such bad gas. Him dooon't stop belching, Sadie, even in him sleep, him belch all night looong!"

Mama shook her head sadly. "I so sorry to hear. Give him some ginger tea and sprinkle some cinnamon in it. Good for the belly."

Mrs. Spence returned Mama's sad look for a split second more, then her expression brightened again. "Sadie, yooou hear that Lydiooo get all right in her spellin' test? Every single wooord! Last week! Miss Pattersooon say that she's the brightest child she ever teach in all her years at Redding Primary!"

Lydia was Mrs. Spence's six-year-old granddaughter. The daughter of Camille, the same New York shop owner who

69

bought Mama's chutneys. The harsh life of the Big Apple being too hectic for a child, Lydia lived with her grandparents in Redding. It had always amazed Nola how Lydia, once a source of embarrassment for the Spences, had become the centre of their universe. Mr. and Mrs. Spence were two Lydia-serving inhabitants in a Lydia-ruled world.

The whispered news about Camille's out-of-wedlock pregnancy had only been bestowed on to Mama because of Camille's announcement that she was returning home right after the baby had been born. Apparently, the father of the child had decided that he was not quite ready for a commitment of that magnitude and Camille had been left with no choice but to return from New York into the folds of her disapproving home. Mrs. Spence had refused to go to New York for the birth of her grandchild, and when Camille arrived six weeks afterward, Mr. Spence made the trip to Kingston to pick up the duo at the airport by himself.

However, Camille had forgotten to mention that Lydia's delinquent father was caucasion. The light skin and soft curls that greeted Mrs. Spence was all that was required to shatter the stigma of illegitimacy. When it was time for Camille to return to New York, Mrs. Spence would hear nothing of the child returning. Didn't Camille realize how difficult it would be to raise a child in a foreign country as a single parent?

And so Lydia's brattish fate was settled.

Mama smiled as Lydia, a magnet to her grandmother's boasting, sauntered over.

"Sadie, I will cooome by for the chootneys next week, yooou don't have tooo send Noola. I need to talk to yooo and Troy because Leroooy thinking of sellin' the car, and I knooow that Troy's car been givin' all that trouble."

"Why Leroy sellin' that car and it still in such good order?" Mama asked, ignoring Lydia's stomping feet.

"Ooooh, Camille say we must get a four-wheel drive for these bad roads!" Mrs. Spence beamed. "Anyhooo, we will coome by to talk, tell yoooou all the details 'bout price and everyting."

But Mama shook her head. "No, it don't make sense, Mrs. Spence. We can't buy a car this year, with the plans for the kitchen and all. Maybe next summer, if Troy get his raise."

"Ooooh, the kitchen." Mrs. Spence frowned. "But Leroooy say that Troy tell him tooo call him when him ready to sell." She patted Mama's shoulder. "Maybe Leroooy never hear right."

Mama nodded in sad agreement as Lydia hauled her grandmother to the gate.

"But I will still coome by to pick up," Mrs. Spence shouted over her shoulder. "Dooon't send Noola. Yoooou knooow I like to pass by and catch up oon tings."

CHAPTER 15

JUNE TWELFTH. MERLENE'S birthday. Nine days before Nola's. They had a party on the front lawn. Biscuit arrived along with Birdie and Darlene (Merlene's two other waitresses), their arms brimming with food – stewed cow tripe and broad beans, rice and peas bristling with the scent of scotch bonnet peppers, pickled herring and thick water crackers, fried ripe plantains, sweet coconut grater-cakes blushed pink with food colouring, and a banana bread birthday loaf with one wax candle, all laid on one of Merlene's tablecloths around a vase of bright pink gerberas.

In between stuffing their mouths, they spent the time jerking their heads from one brightly-clad waitress to the other. The other two were as boisterously entertaining as Biscuit. The trouble was, all had a story to tell, and all told it at the same time.

Nola's expression was constantly changing from distress, to amusement, to shock. She was relieved when Dahlia shouted, "Time for the blessin's!" The women stopped speaking to cheer loudly.

Biscuit and Darlene cleared the cloth, taking the food containers into the kitchen while Merlene giggled delightedly and went to sit in the middle.

"Since Delroy and Nola never do this before, lemme explain," Dahlia said. "Every time it's somebody birthday, we all give that person a blessin'. One that will last for the whole year. That way, all the bad things other people might wish to happen to that person get cancel out, and only good things will happen! So, since today is Mama's birthday, we all get to wish her a blessin'!"

Nola swallowed. She suddenly wanted to get up and run through the hedge. No one told her that she would have to speak in front of these story-rich, vociferous strangers. How could she tell them the truth, that her only wish at that moment was for herself? That her only birthday wish for Merlene was that she was her mother and not Dahlia's?

Biscuit began. She placed her red talons on Merlene's cheeks and wished her health and happiness for the rest of her days, to be always surrounded by love, and continued success in her business so she could continue paying her employees well (Honks of laughter). Dahlia went next, wishing her mother a very, very long life, with good friends close by her side, and announced that because of her mama's smile every morning, it didn't matter what lay ahead each day, for each day became as bright as that smile. Darlene wished her beauty long into her old age. Birdie wished her romance and a companion to grow old with, upon which Dahlia expounded that her mother already had all the companionship she needed (more raucous honks).

Nola blinked in shock when Delroy stood and cleared his throat. He wished Merlene would always be in possession of a stove, so she would never stop cooking delicious meals. Everyone agreed loudly.

Then, all eyes turned to Nola. She took a deep breath and looked at Dahlia's encouraging nod and Merlene's eager eyes. She stood slowly, focusing her gaze on the little wrinkle above Merlene's raised brows.

73

"I ... I wish that you ... that you will continue to show people that life ... life is not such a bad thing. That sometimes when you feel you don't want to live anymore, you can always find something that's worth living for."

For a pulse of a second, there was silence. Then Biscuit slapped her thigh, gave a loud cackle and announced, "Life good! Life good for true!" and everyone agreed that life was definitely worth living.

Then Merlene stood up, and with her hands pressed against her heart, told everyone "thank you" for the wonderful blessings, and said that she was already blessed to have her wonderful daughter and such good friends in her life.

That evening, as Nola went to retrieve her school bag from the verandah, she turned in time to see Dahlia fling her humongous arms around Merlene's neck. She had seen them hug before. They hugged constantly—when Dahlia came in from school, when she got something correct in her homework, when she especially loved the meal that Merlene had cooked that afternoon. But there was something about this hug that stopped Nola in her tracks. It was the way they clung to each other, the way they squeezed as if they were attempting to mesh into one. There was a desperation to their grip that Nola had never seen before. She watched them silently till Dahlia gave a loud snort and they burst into laughter and broke apart.

"Thank you for that nice wish, Puddin," Merlene told her when she went to say goodbye. "It touch me right here." She pointed to the light dusting of powder on her chest, the spot on which Dahlia had just pressed her head. Then she took Nola by the shoulders and hugged her. Not a desperate hug like the one she'd given Dahlia, but a sweet one just the same.

Nola closed her eyes and breathed in the jasmine powder, and for that small moment, everything was perfect. Then

74

Delroy was behind them, telling Nola that it was time to go, and Merlene pulled him into the hug with her other arm. Delroy's forehead bucked lightly against Nola's, the sweaty slick of their foreheads sticking slightly before he abruptly pulled away. Merlene grabbed him tightly continued to press them together, as if attempting to set back the pieces of a broken figurine. Her whisper, still tinged with the spicy scent of her birthday meal, breezed over them, "Now is my turn to thank the two of you, for being such good friends to my Pumkin."

Delroy pulled away again, mumbling something about the time, and bolted through the hedge. Everyone else chuckled at his hasty retreat and Birdie shouted, "How you expec' to find a woman if you so 'fraid of one little hug?"

That evening, as Nola stood beside Mama and sliced mangoes, she couldn't help staring at her chest. There was no dusting of powder there, just the shine of sweat, and shoulder bones that jutted from her dress as if she'd forgotten to remove the hanger. Her hands expertly flipped scotch bonnet peppers beneath her knife, slicing the flesh so that just the skeleton of seeds was left behind to be discarded. Her breath was sweet. Even at the end of the day, when Mama's eyes were dazed with fatigue, her breath was always sweet, like ginger-spiced cake.

Nola reached over and gripped the briskly moving hands, causing Mama to frown slightly. She should have known to stop then, but at that moment, there was nothing else that mattered but the feel of that sweaty chest against her cheek. She wanted to hear that thud beneath, to find the proof that there was life beneath that chopping statue. But just as Nola leaned forward, Mama's startled hands flew upwards, and her fingers went straight into Nola's eyes.

Nola screamed. The acid burn crept immediately over her face. She tried to feel for the kitchen pipe, but miscalculated its direction and knocked over the bowl of mango pulp. She heard Mama gasp, and immediately, panic, ten times worse than the pain, rose into her chest.

Papa! He must have come into the kitchen to see what the commotion was about and walked straight into the mess! She whimpered as she heard Mama's footsteps hurry away. Her hands flew over her face to protect herself from the blows. She tried to back up against the sink, but crashed into the table instead, showering heavy sugar crystals over her feet. She heard Mama's footsteps hurry back into the kichen, and a knife grazed against the chopping board. Then, suddenly – the cool, slimy pulp of aloe vera against her eyes.

She heard Louisa's breathless voice, "What happen? What happen? I hear a scream. What happen to Nola, Mama?"

But Mama didn't answer, just continued to swab Nola's eyes till soon Nola could open them. Everything was blurred, but she tried to focus beyond Mama's shoulder, past Louisa's confused face. Empty! With relief she saw that the kitchen was empty except for the three of them. Her legs buckled, first with relief, then with returning anxiety as she spotted the mess of mango pulp and sugar on the floor. She pushed Mama's hands away and stooped to hurriedly scrape the sugar from the floor, but Mama stooped beside her, and it was her turn to hold Nola's hands still.

"Him have a meetin' tonight, Nola," she whispered. "Him not comin' till late."

Then she took the dishcloth from her shoulder and wiped the tears from Nola's face.

That night, Nola learned another difference between her home and Dahlia's. In Dahlia's home, hugs were safe, happy. But in the Chambers' house, hugs, like everything else, brought pain.

CHAPTER 16

THE DAY BEFORE Nola's birthday, Papa got himself a gift – Mr. Spence's red Corolla. It was in perfect condition, with the plastic still on the seats and the light grey upholstery as pristine as the first day Mr. Spence had driven it into Redding from Kingston. A huge contrast to Papa's old one, whose rear windscreen had been at the mercy of the grey electrical tape tacked around the edges.

When Nola walked through the gate and saw the car on the lawn, she thought the Spences had come to pick up an extra large order, but, as she neared the vehicle, she realized that it wasn't the Spences inside, but Papa, Louisa and Toneisha. The girls sat together in the passenger's seat, their legs dangling easily out the door, while Papa sat on the driver's side, fidgeting with the radio buttons in the linseed-polished dashboard.

"Nola, look at Papa new car. It have a radio!" Louisa beamed through the doorway, clicking her fingers to the strains of Jimmy Cliff's "The Harder They Come".

Nola stopped hesitantly, not sure if Papa would be in a good mood for having got the car, or in a bad mood for having spent the money to get it.

He was in a good mood, for even after spotting Nola he continued to rock his shoulders to the song. So Nola returned Louisa's smile and peered inside to see if Mama was in the back.

It was empty. Nola frowned. Where on earth was Mama on such a significant occasion? They'd finally gotten the reliable vehicle they'd wished for, which meant that now Mama could distribute her products to a much wider market.

Not wishing to push her luck with Papa's mood, Nola waved to the girls and went inside. Mama was there, stirring a large dutchpot of pineapple skins. Lime-Pine Jam, one of her best sellers at Miss June's. But there was something wrong. Mama's shoulders were stooped even lower than usual and her hands shook on the spoon.

With a bolt of awareness, Nola realized why Mama was not outside. It was not Papa's money, not his awaited raise that had bought the Spence's car. It was the money for Mama's kitchen.

Nola stood silently as Mama placed the cover on the dutchpot and turned to rub a kernel of nutmeg up and down a grater. Over the years, Mama's fingers had grown to resemble little hardened tools rather than flesh and bone. And for what? A new red car? She didn't even know how to drive.

The cover of the dutchpot clanked loudly as Mama added the gratered spice to the thickening syrup inside. She returned to the sink to cut up the pineapple flesh. The pulp that would give the jam its body.

It was a couple minutes well before Nola realized that she wasn't watching Mama's hands anymore, but the knife in them. It fascinated her how the blade melted through the flesh, splitting the fruit so easily. "I tek the kitchen knife and stick it right here," Dahlia had said. Had it sliced through her papa's flesh as easily as it did through the pine, or had it bucked and sputtered against bone?

The knife stopped moving. Mama was staring at her. Nola stared back at the face warped from its own harsh rub over life's grater. She'd once been beautiful. Grampy had told Nola that Mama had once been even more beautiful than Louisa, with lips that blazed like fire from her face. Nola had seen it for herself in the wedding picture tucked between the pages of the Bible on Mama's bedside table—skin that glowed from a promise, a smile that had managed to reach her eyes.

Mama's voice cracked the silent air. "Nola, I don't have that much to do this evenin', and Louisa not goin' do much anyway, with all this excitement." Her hand lifted slightly towards the door. "So you can just tend to Ellie and go to bed early tonight."

Nola didn't move.

"Go to the cow, Nola." Her voice was firmer now.

"And what 'bout you, Mama? You just goin' stay in here and chop? Chop up onion and mango and pine for the rest of your life?" The words surged like bile from Nola's gut.

The knife rattled into the sink, and Mama's eyes blazed. She'd pulled up her shoulders, her collapsed breasts heaving beneath the light gingham of her dress.

"Listen to me, chile!" The breasts shimmied beneath the strain of her voice. "That man out there work hard to look after this house, you hear me? Work hard to put food on this table and buy all the things that we need. Don't you just waltz in here and talk bad 'bout him! That man work in sun-hot at that orchard all day, so that you can go to school and make someting of your life. What he do with the money is none of your concern!"

Nola blinked. She had said nothing about Papa, or money. Yet, here was Mama addressing every thought that had crossed her mind.

A sound at the door ripped their eyes apart. Papa stood there, his shoulder resting on the jamb as he flipped through the pages of a tiny booklet with the word TOYOTA on the cover.

He barely looked up as he mumbled, "Sadie—ice water."

Hard to imagine that this beautiful man was actually her papa, half the contributor to her existence. His grater had been kinder than Mama's. Mama handed him the large cup filled with water from the jug in the fridge, the one that Nola knew was for Papa alone—and sometimes for Louisa. He took it, still without looking up, and took a long drink, his neck bulging with each gulp. Then suddenly, the cup went sailing. Over the bonnet of the red car and across the grass till it came to a stop on a pad of fresh dung by the coolie plum tree.

"Jesus, Sadie! Why everyting in the house must stink of onion?! It's like I just drink a cup of onion juice! Wash your damn hands before you go in the fridge, nuh woman!"

Mama immediately went to the sink and began scrubbing her hands. She continued to scrub them as Papa sucked his teeth and walked back to the car. Eventually she picked up the knife and began cutting the pine once again.

"Go to the cow," she said to Nola without looking up.

CHAPTER 17

THAT NIGHT, NOLA dreamt that the red car was chasing her through the pot-holed streets of Redding. She kept falling into the deep holes as the tyres screeched over her head. She woke with the screeching still in her ears, and it was not until she sat up and rubbed her eyes that she realized the sound was really there, in her room.

She peeked cautiously through the gauze curtains, blinking at the two figures swirling in the dawn haze before her. The dew angels? Outside her bedroom window? Nola rubbed her eyes. Dahlia and Delroy!——their hands bleeding with the stain of mud as they readied to throw another handful of pebbles against her window. Dahlia and Delroy, faces impatient as they stared back through the mist, dressed in jackets against the chill of the morning.

"Happy Birthday!" Dahlia shouted.

Nola rammed a finger against her mouth and frantically signaled for Dahlia to be quiet.

"We come to take you to the dew angels!" Dahlia whispered.

They were waiting by the coolie plum tree when she came out. Dahlia was rubbing Ellie's dung-caked head while Delroy leaned sleepily against the trunk. On seeing Nola, he eased up, but she found that she could not look at him. She'd been unprepared for the wave of shame that washed over her when she saw him in the spot from which he had scraped her off the ground weeks before. She kept her head low, giving nothing but a small wave as she led them through Mama's scallion and thyme patch into the tall grass beyond. Thankfully, the farther away they walked, the more the shame released its hold, and soon they were racing each other, laughing loudly as they crunched over the dew-soaked leaves. They stopped at a small clearing on the hillside. Dahlia collapsed onto a bundle of grass beneath a young guinep tree while Nola and Delroy bent with their hands on their knees and tried to catch their breaths.

It was hard to breathe deeply in the crisp mountain air. The cold mist froze the lungs and singed the nostrils. Eventually Nola flung herself beside Dahlia, playfully nudging her aside to make room. Dahlia guffawed loudly, then shoved her hand into her huge jacket and pulled out a round package foil.

"Mama say, a puddin' for Puddin'! Happy birthday!" she said, dropping the package onto Nola's lap.

It was still hot. Just out the oven!—Merlene had gotten out of bed very early to bake it. They'd planned this for her birthday! Nola blinked hastily, warding off the sudden sting behind her eyes as Dahlia leaned over and tore the foil open. The aroma of sweet potato pudding parted through the cold mist. Nola stared in awe at the thick custard, parting deliciously to allow the dark heads of raisins to poke through.

Dahlia licked her lips dramatically and poked Nola's shoulder. "Mama say, a puddin' for a puddin', but she never say it was for you alone!" She dug into her jacket again and pulled out three plastic forks, handing one each to Nola and Delroy. "Nuh true, Delroy? Not for Puddin' alone!"

Delroy shook his head. "No Sir, not for Puddin' alone!" And he dug into the foil and stuffed a huge, dripping forkful into his mouth.

Dahlia followed, slurping so noisily that a lizard on a branch above pumped its bright orange fan in complaint. Nola laughed with delight as Delroy dug out another forkful. She did the same, taking a huge, delicious bite of her very first birthday 'cake'.

It was just the three of them, damp from dew, but it was a birthday party that Nola would not have changed even one tiny detail.

Just when she thought her heart could get no lighter from joy, Dahlia jumped up and clapped her hands. "Time for the blessin's!"

Nola tried to hide the involuntary smile that lifted her lips. "Nola," Dahlia said, "I wish that you will always believe in miracles. Miracles like the dew angels, and Santa." She looked pointedly at Delroy. "But most of all, I wish that you will always believe in the miracle in here." She patted her chest so hard that the sound echoed through the mist.

Then Delroy stood up. He pulled a long stalk from one of the bundles and wound it tightly around his index finger. Eventually, when the tip of his finger had swelled into a purple nub, he cleared his throat and pointed it at Nola.

"Nola," he said, "I wish that you will always be like this grass. That no matter how the world bend you up, twist you round, try to beat you, you will always bend with it, but you won't ever break." Then he released the stalk so that it uncurled from his finger and fell at his feet.

Nola stared at the twisted blade by his sneakers. Once more, for the morning, she was struck speechless. She knew what Delroy was speaking about. He was speaking about that night, when she'd lain on the lawn, pounded first by her

83

papa's fist, then by the rain. Heat crawled into her face, even as Dahlia grabbed the curled blade and stuffed it down the front of Grampy's sweater that she had excitedly hauled over her head.

"That's the best blessin' I ever hear!" Dahlia whooped, beaming at Delroy. "You know you gettin' good at this ting? Nola, you keep that piece of grass forever, so that you can always look at it and remember your birthday blessin'. NEVER ... EVER ... BREAK!" She whooped again and jumped onto one of the bundles, splaying her arms wide as she lifted her head to the pink sky. "Wash me, dew angels! Shower me with your blessin's!"

Nola would later realize that on that morning of her fifteenth birthday, one friend had exposed the emptiness of her heart, vacated by miracles; and the other had begun the task of refilling that space.

CHAPTER 18

T HE LAST DAY of school was always a celebration. No class
work was set, everyone wore regular clothing, they were
allowed to partake of chips and sodas in the classrooms and
play board games and dominoes while teachers scrambled to
finalise reports.

It had always been a celebration for Nola too. But that was
before Slugga's punishment. That was before she had become
friends with Dahlia, and Delroy, and Merlene, and Biscuit.
Now she could not celebrate the last day of school, for it
meant the end to Slugga's punishment. No more Dahlia, and
Delroy, and Merlene, and Biscuit.

"You goin' eat that, Nola?" Dahlia asked, pointing to the
pile of cheese trix lying on a napkin on Nola's desk.

Nola smiled at the question which weeks ago would have
caused her annoyance. She now understood the ridiculousness
of Dahlia Daley's begging, Dahlia Daley whose house brimmed
with food.

One morning, as Nola, late for school, rushed onto Calabash
Street, she spotted the always tardy Dahlia Daley stopping by
Mad Aggie's shack. She'd watched as Dahlia removed a foil-
wrapped package from her bag and handed it to the wizened

85

hand reaching up from beneath the counter. For a good five minutes the girl chatted into the shack, then she'd waved 'good-bye' and lumbered off.

Nola continued to stare at Mad Aggie's grease-polished lips still smacking as she hung something from the roof of her shack. The foil from Dahlia's package, shaped diligently into a perfect cone dangled cheerily from a thin piece of cloth between the other chimes, the remnants of Dahlia's lunch glistening in the sun like a morning star.

She pushed the napkin towards Dahlia and laughed as the girl immediately pasted the paper to her face. When she pulled it away, orange crumbs speckled her lip-nose. Dahlia returned Nola's laughter with a mighty belch. Clarice and Faith, true to form, gave scoffs of disgust and fanned the air.

It must have been the recklessness of that last day, the dreariness of her heart, for without even thinking, Nola turned to them and snapped, "Why the two of you don't just get lost?"

Silence, then a gasp of shock from somewhere in the back of the classroom. Even as Dahlia guffawed and pointed at Clarice's reddening face, the realization of what she'd done made Nola want to slap her own hand over her mouth. She quickly stood up and raced out of the classroom.

It was not until she reached beneath the lignum vitae tree that she realized that Dahlia and Delroy were behind her.

"Good for you, Nola!" Dahlia shouted. "Bout time you stand up to that feisty gal!"

"Well, well, well! You three decide that the school year must finish for you before it finish for everybody else?"

All three of them jumped at the sound of Slugga's voice behind them.

"World on your shoulders, Nola?" Slugga raised an agile brow.

86

The world, and all the universe with it! Nola wanted to say, but she just shook her head.

"Good. Look at you," Slugga eventually said with a little laugh. "Look at the three of you out here."

Nola and Delroy exchanged wary glances.

Slugga sighed. "Let me ask you all a question. You think that if I never put the three of you to work together that you would ever figure out that you weren't enemies? You think the three of you would be out here, while the rest of them in there?"

Nola wanted to gasp, but swallowed the sound on a cough. This could not be Slugga standing before them with that little smile on her face!

Slugga stared at her, then wagged a finger at her bewildered face. "Ever break one stick, Nola Chambers? It breaks easy, right? Snaps right in your hand. But try breaking it while it's in a bundle, and what you think will happen?" Crisp curls shook vigorously.

"Won't," Slugga said. "Won't break so easy." She sighed.

"Sometimes you have to force those sticks together to keep them from breaking."

So there it was! The whole riddle, the whole ridiculous scenario, suddenly clicked. They had been an experiment, a bundle of stupid sticks! She and Dahlia and Delroy, forced together to prove a point.

Dahlia clapped her hands and gave a loud laugh. "Delroy!" she said, "You don't see? It's just like your blade of grass. Never break! Never break! The bungle of sticks can't break, just like your blade of grass! You don't see Delroy. You and Slugga think exactly the same!"

In her excitement, Dahlia hadn't even realized that she'd referred to the headmistress by her nick-name. But either Slugga hadn't heard, or chose to ignore it, for she only began to rifle through the envelopes she was carrying.

Dahlia grabbed Nola's shoulders and planted a wet kiss on her cheek. "Hello, Bungle," she said, then she slapped Delroy shoulder. "Hello, Bungle," she repeated, then gave a little skip.

"Never break! Never break!"

For the life of her, Nola could not share in Dahlia's humour. She was too busy watching Delroy kick aggressively at a stone. Then his eyes met hers for one second before he turned and sauntered back towards the classroom.

Slugga frowned slightly, but did not call him back. "I not going to be here next term." She eventually said.

Dahlia gasped and opened her mouth to speak, but Slugga held up a silencing hand.

"Somebody is coming to take my place, but, I really wanted the three of you to know something before I left. You see, plenty people in this world going to try and make you think that you're not worth anything. A lot of people going to try to make you feel that your lives don't mean a thing! But I know, and I want the three of you to know it too. The three of you have something special." She cocked her head to the side and studied them. "I see something in the three of you, something that I know will take you through the trials." An eyebrow brushed her sweat-beaded hairline. "You know what it is?"

Dahlia opened her mouth to answer but was once again silenced by the hand.

"The struggle!" Slugga answered her own question. "The struggle you have to deal with every day, just to come here." She waved the hand towards the classrooms.

Nola felt her face growing hot as the green frames turned on her.

"Struggle." Slugga repeated thoughtfully. "Some people think that struggle is a bad thing, but you know what? That's what makes you strong! That's what makes you better than the rest!"

Nola blinked in shock at the thick emotion in Slugga's voice. She looked at Dahlia to see if the girl had noticed it too.

Dahlia's bottom lip was quivering. "But why you not coming back next year, Miss?" she wailed.

Slugga patted the damp hair off her forehead and sighed. "I have to take care of my niece in Kingston." Her voice seemed to shake as she looked towards the noisy classrooms. "She's not ... so well." She removed a tissue from her pocket and patted her face, leaving a trail of white flecks across her forehead. "Promise me something," she continued, replacing the brown-stained tissue into her pocket.

Dahlia nodded eagerly, but Nola said nothing.

"Promise me that no matter what bad things the world tells you about yourselves, you will never believe it." She said, plucking two envelopes from the top of her pile and handing them over. "That will prove it," she said with a nod. "That will prove that you can do anything!"

With that, she gave a final nod, then turned to waddle back towards the classrooms, leaving Dahlia to whoop with delight at the 'A's and 'B's down the pages of her report.

Nola smiled and hugged Dahlia back, but, somehow, she just could not take her eyes from that classroom.

CHAPTER 19

I N ALL HER weeks of going to Merlene's, Nola had always avoided the red door of the Bar and Grill like the plague. But on that last day of school, the last day of her visits to Merlene and Dahlia's home, the recklessness of the day stayed with her. That evening, when Merlene said she had to check on something in the bar, and Dahlia, in the middle of her story about Slugga leaving the school, jumped up to accompany her, Nola went too. She followed them right through the red door.

It was dim inside. There were only five naked bulbs in the room, one in each corner, and another dangling from a cord above the bar. The entire room was just a little bigger than Mama's living room, the 'L'-shaped bar taking up most of the space on the right side. The bar itself was constructed of bamboo, the trunks bound together by rope and topped with a rough wooden counter. Everything was very basic—the bar, four round tables surrounded by four or so plastic chairs each, and shelves of glasses of differing sizes and shapes on the walls. No décor except for the plastic tablecloths on the tables and the jars of plumbago blooms in the middle of each.

The floor was raw concrete, stained throughout with spots, and a section near the bar was now swimming beneath a layer of water. The sound of grating metal echoed around the small room. When Merlene called out, a bald, sweating pate appeared above the counter.

Bertie. Nola had passed him many times, quietly sweeping puffs of dust out of the red door. Merlene had often referred to him as her 'Man Friday', speaking of him with affection when she discussed the bar with Biscuit. He now agitatedly waved a wrench over the bar and embarked upon a stammering rampage about rusted pipes and the short-term effects of duct tape. Merlene assured him that Clars would take a look at it later that night.

Nola blinked at the mention of the plumber's name. Clarence Wilks was one of Redding's prides and joys. It was said he could fix any leak with nothing more than a toothpick. He also gave one of the loudest 'alleleujahs' when Pastor prayed about the lost souls at the bottom of Della Way.

Soon, everything about the leaking pipe was forgotten. Dahlia poured them all Kola Champagnes, and they sat at a table and giggled hysterically as Dahlia described each face in the classroom when Nola had insulted Clarice. After a while, the smell of grilling chicken filled the room, and Dahlia poked her head through the back window and brought back plates of 'Janie's special, special' jerk chicken for them to sample.

As usual, the time went by before Nola could blink, and with her jaws hurting from laughing, she grudgingly got up to leave. Merlene made her promise to visit throughout the holiday, and Nola gleefully said that she would.

And so, this was the picture—Nola running out of the red door of Merlene's Bar and Grill, smiling, waving, promising to come back soon, and Merlene Daley and her daughter waving back, telling her that they were going to miss her.

It was because of all the laughing and waving that no one had seen or even heard the lime green truck, the one that

Camille had sent for her parents. Nola only spotted it when she turned from the red door to run up Della Way, but by then it was too late. By then she could only stop dead in her tracks and stare into the widening eyes of Mrs. Spence.

Nola remained immobile even as the truck ambled to the bottom of the Della Way, turned clumsily at the wide section of the road, and headed back up the road where it stopped in front of Miss June's shop.

She walked slowly up Macca Hill, waiting to hear the truck growl past her with its golden nugget of news. More than once, she thought of running into the thick twine of the hillside. She wondered how long it would be before they found her. Maybe they wouldn't, if she jumped into the river, into the section where the water frothed like icing over the sharpened rocks. Suddenly she stopped in her tracks, squinting at the figure ahead of her. The back was turned, but the stoop of the lanky shoulders, the way the hands dug deep into the khaki pockets, was so, so familiar. Her heart did its usual flip.

He turned suddenly, as if he'd felt her eyes on him. She tried to fix her lips, forcing down the sides which had shot up involuntarily. She shaded her eyes with her hand, suddenly conscious that her dark skin was probably shiny with sweat and dust from the walk. His hands dug deeper into his pockets as she made a casual gesture of wiping her forehead. Yet, through all the jittering, their gazes remained locked. Nola wondered if his hands had come out of his pockets since Slugga's revelation earlier that day. She thought she saw his shoulders give a little shrug, as if answering the question that had traveled on their stares.

Eventually, she dragged her legs across the space between them.

"Merlene was askin' for you." She started to speak before she got to him, trying to break the strange tension that had arisen between them. "She wanted to know how you did in your exams. Me and Dahlia did good. Merlene say that she goin' cook a special dinner for all of us one day next week, that is, if you want to come. She say it would be our own end of school party. I know we had one at school, but this would be ours, you know, since we study together and all ..." She knew she was rambling, but she also knew that if she stopped speaking she would have to hear what she didn't want to hear —Delroy Reckus' goodbye.

He shrugged in response to the speech, then kicked a stone into the fern fronds beside them.

Nola took a deep breath. "You should'a come to say goodbye to Merlene, Delroy. She really like you, you know."

This time, he picked up a stone and threw it down the hillside. Branches cracked their protests and two ground doves cawed and fluttered angrily away. But Nola could pay attention to nothing but the scent that had wafted from Delroy's throwing arm—musky sweat mixed the residue of sweet deodorant.

"Redding not that big, I'll see them round town," he shrugged.

See them round town! First of all, Merlene didn't go 'round town', and second of all, what was he planning to do—walk up to her at the bus stop and say, "Hi Merlene Daley. How are you on this fine day in Redding?"

"So, how was your report?" She decided it was better to switch the topic.

Delroy gave a bitter laugh. "You never hear what Slugga say? Sticks in a bungle." He shrugged again. "Of course I did good! It was a successful experiment. A successful bungle of sticks!"

"It getting late," Nola said quietly as Miss Terry nodded a suspicious greeting. "I have to get home ..." her voice trailed

93

off. The word 'home' had suddenly brought back the memory of that green truck.

Delroy nodded. "I comin' up with you."

"No!" The sharpness in her tone frightened even herself, but the thought of him once again witnessing Papa's rage towards her was just too much to bear. She shook her head and pointedly softened her voice. "Him ... Papa goin' be washin' the car today. If him see you with me ..."

He hesitated, then nodded again, studying her face through slightly squinted eyes. She looked away, once again painfully aware of her sweaty ugliness.

"Nola, I ... I have to tell you someting." He touched her shoulder.

She flinched from the heat of his fingers, even though it was just a light brush on her blouse. Dear God! She was melting, right there in the middle of the road! She looked up at his face and drank in every detail of him for the last time—his lips, slightly pursed now, and lighter on the inside where it glistened with his saliva ...

"I want you to know that I never mean for that box to lick you. The scrimmage box ... I never wanted it to lick you that day."

His eyes! Light brown, with dark inner rings panning out like the river ... .

"I saw Clarice there, and I was just tryin' to get her away from you ... ."

His eyebrows were slightly askew, one a little higher than the other...

"... but it hit you instead."

So beautiful, he was. So beautiful that he could lie to her all he wanted. She would listen.

"When Slugga say that she wanted to prove that we weren't enemies, I know what she was thinkin'. She was talkin' 'bout

that day with the juice box. But you wasn't my enemy, Nola."
His hands dug deep again. "That day when Dahlia never do her
math homework, and Slugga call the two of you to the office,
I went too. I thought you was in some kind of trouble, so I
went in case I had to tell Slugga that you never do anyting. I
was there, outside the window, listenin' to everyting she said.
That evenin', I follow the two of you. Shane and Devon and
Oliver did come too, because when them see where I was
goin', them say them wanted to come and catch lizards ...."
His mouth suddenly snapped shut as he focused his gaze on
something behind her shoulder.

Shamoney Leach, jostling up the hill.

"I just wanted to make sure that you was okay, you
know," he continued, whispering now. "I never know that
Merlene was so nice, and I thought she would ... ." He gave
an apologetic shrug. "You know what everybody say 'bout
Merlene."

Nola's head was spinning. Make sure she was okay? Then
suddenly, it clicked. The thought that rushed to her mind sent
a bolt of awareness through her chest.

It was a trick! She was being set up, by Delroy, and
Clarice, and the rest of the class, in retaliation for what she'd
said earlier. They were probably all hidden in the bushes, in
between the ferns and cocoa leaves, holding their mouths
against the snorts of laughter!

Nola looked suspiciously at the feathery fronds of fern and
the thorny spines of privet as she shouted. "You neva even like
me! You forget what the whole lot of you call me—Fassy Face
Nola?!"

He shook his head and reached out as if to hold her hand,
but changed his mind and dropped his arms by his sides.

"Not me! I never called you that! The others did, but not
me. You don't know ... ."

But Nola never got a chance to hear what it was she didn't know, for at that moment, the blaring horn of the Spence's truck rang from the bottom of the hill. Her anxious glance in its direction did not go unnoticed by Delroy, and he backed away, for even without knowing about the incident on Della Way, the danger of Mrs. Spence's tongue was legendary. Nola shook her head to indicate that it didn't matter anymore, the damage had already been done and the Spence's truck already carried her fate in its bright cab.

"It's okay," she assured him, "You can talk. It don't matter if them see us now."

But he'd already started down the hill. "Next week, when Merlene cook for us, we talk then, okay? I follow you home afterwards, and we talk."

He walked backwards, not taking his eyes off her face, then he did something which knocked the breath right out of her. He picked a blade of grass from the roadside, then rolled it around his finger, touched it to his lips and placed it inside his shirt pocket beside his heart. And, whoosh, her breath left her chest just like that.

Then he was gone, turning to skitter around the bend just as another blare from the truck rang over the hill.

CHAPTER 20

THIRTY-EIGHT MINUTES. THAT was how long it took for the Spences to finish their business on Della Way and arrive at the Chambers's gate. Thirty-eight minutes to deliver its news. The vehicle had not come to a complete halt before the driver's door was flung open and the white loafers descended from the cab. They almost tripped over the mongrel as they hurried through the gate, followed by Lydia's pretty yellow flip-flops skipping excitedly over the animal.

Nola had just made it through the gate when the truck belched its arrival. She did not go inside. Instead, she stooped by the zinc sheet of drying pimento, beside Papa's new car, and began scraping the sun-crisped balls into the folds of her skirt. The smell of the spice forced itself within the cracks of the still air and was somewhat comforting to her raw nerves. She did not look up as Mrs. Spence lumbered by, but she heard the woman sniff angrily, and the sweet headiness of her perfume brushed the pimento scent aside.

Mrs. Spence's voice shook with anticipation at the kitchen door. "Sadieee! Sadieee!"

There was answering confusion in Mama's. "Mrs. Spence? I forget to give you something? I thought I filled the whole order on Tuesday. Camille need more already?"

"Nooo, Sadie, I don't need nooo more chutneys. I had tooo coome here because sooomething come tooo my attention that I think yooo need tooo deal with right now! Right now, Sadie! This is a matter that can't wait. I knooow if it was Lydioo, yoooou would dooo the same thing for me!"

Mrs. Spence was ushered concernedly into the kitchen.

"Sadie, yoooou know I love yoooou like my own daughter, and I would never want anything bad tooo happen tooo your family, but sooomething very bad, sooomething very evil is going ooon, Sadie. Sooomething yooo have to deal with before the devil get his evil claws any deeper in yoooour family!"

Mama was confused. The devil's claws? In her family? Surely Mrs. Spence was mistaken.

"Ooooh, Sadie, nooo, nooo, nooo! Not the rest of yoooou! Not the whole family. Just that chile. Frooom the moment I saw her as a baby, Sadie, frooom the moment I saw her look sooo different from the rest of yoooou, I knew the devil had something to dooo with that chile." Mrs. Spence's voice fell to a harsh whisper. "She born with the evil in her, Sadie."

Nola heard Papa's voice asking what the commotion was all about. She stood and allowed the pimento balls to clatter back onto the zinc, then walked slowly towards Ellie's pen. She emptied a bag of grain into the dirty trough. Ellie spread her lips greedily over the grain and immediately began to chew, her frayed rope dragging in the dung like a sawed-off noose.

Papa's voice bellowed from the kitchen, "NOLA! NOLA!"

Nola sat on the rotting stump and stared into Mama's scallion plot. The stalks were that deep green that promised a spicy shock of flavour, a result of Mama's home-made fertilizer – Ellie's dried dung mixed with the discarded rotted peel of her vegetables and fruits. Her gaze traveled to the field of wild guinea grass beside it, the same field where she and Dahlia and Delroy had gone for her birthday. That morning when they'd raced through it, the angelic dew had made the grass lush and straight, but now the blades hung low, their tips bowed as if pining for the cool relief of the absent breeze.

"Where's that damn pickney?! She think she can hide from me? Sadie, you always beggin' for that child. You see what I tell you, though? No damn good! She come to no good just like I tell you!"

Mrs. Spence stepped from the kitchen, her eyes going straight to the zinc where the pimento seeds lay scattered. Her shoulders shook in an annoyed huff and she said something over her shoulder, then ushered Lydia towards the gate.

Mama didn't see them out. Nola could see her head by the kitchen window, bent over the sink. But this time her hands weren't moving.

"I want her out this house! If she can't behave like a decent person, then she can go live somewhere else! Spending time with whores?! Not in my house! Not in my house, Sadie! What you think she was doing there? You think she never took part in all the nastiness goin' on in that place?" Papa was almost screaming.

Mama's head jerked sharply as his finger rammed into her temple. She remained rooted in the spot, though, and when Papa stopped poking her head, she bowed it again.

"It's your damn fault, Sadie! You raise a sinner, and then mek me have to deal with the shame!"

Louisa came to the door and looked out, straight at the spot where Nola sat. Funny how well Louisa knew her. Funny how well she knew her even though they'd barely had much to say to each other for the last couple years. Truth be told, they hadn't had the opportunity to speak much, ever since Louisa had been moved out of their room, yet her sister always seemed to know exactly where she was. Nola recognized the quick flick of the hand, giving her the signal to run, telling her to go quickly as she closed the kitchen door.

Nola sighed. Run to where, Louisa? Tell me, and I'll go.

But Papa flung the door open again. His eyes flashed across the lawn. Grey flames licked up her spine and sent her body into a shivering fit.

Nola heard her sister's voice, in that calm of calm, the calm that had always worked like magic on Papa's rage, tell him that she thought she saw Nola heading out the gate, maybe to the river.

But Papa's rage was too much for Louisa's voice to temper that evening, and even as he stormed from the kitchen towards Ellie's pen, he was already hauling the belt from his waist. It chafed the loops of his pants, twisting the zipper across his hip. He seemed to glide, graceful despite his twisted pants. Mama had told her that he used to play cricket, and when he ran for the pitch, he'd looked as if he were dancing. That's where Mama had first seen Papa, and had instantly fallen in love.

He reached Nola in one second, arm raised for the pitch. The belt glided with the same liquid grace as its carrier, the silver buckle glimmering in the evening light.

Nola didn't move. Papa's lips drew back from his teeth in the hiss that announced the commencement of her beating, but she did not put her arms over her face. She needed to look into those eyes once again. Those eyes that held the mystery of the man who'd fathered her, yet hated her.

The ripples of his pupils finally pulled her to her feet. She stood right beneath the harsh breeze of his nostrils. He stared back, and once again, his hand faltered. Slowly, he lowered the belt and pointed a finger in her face. "You turn whore, now?" His voice was like a thin thread through the blanket of dulling light.

She could smell lemonade on his breath, bittersweet on stale saliva. She could see Louisa, now behind him, eyes flashing wildly from Nola's face, to the back of Papa's neck. Her eyes begged Nola not to say anything, just to take the licks so that it would be over soon.

So Nola explained nothing of Slugga's experiment. It was the least she could do for her sister for the times that she'd saved her. Instead, she lifted her hand and touched Papa's face.

He flinched. The breath wedged in Louisa's throat. But Nola cared about nothing but the feel of that skin beneath her fingers. So different while he was awake. The jaw bone which had been slack in sleep was now tight beneath ropy muscle.

Suddenly, a loud phwapp ripped through the air.

Nola pulled again at his cheek, smiling at the sound it made as the lips plucked sharply from the teeth. The sound ripped the air again and Louisa gasped louder this time. Nola could not stop. She had to see the expression in Papa's eyes when she touched him the way her sister had done. She'd watched them play this game so many times, the one where Louisa pulled at his lips till they lay pink and taut against his teeth, and commanded him to say words from the distorted mouth. Say 'hit', she would say, and Papa would say, 'Shit', and they would both crack up. Nola would laugh too, but the truth was, watching them play that game had always left her with a gaping hole in her chest.

Papa's head suddenly jerked, and she had to bring her other hand up to hold it still.

That was when Louisa screamed.

This time, the sound cracked the air right open. Nola looked curiously at Louisa's frantic face, at the mouth, wide open, at the tears streaming beneath her chin like the ribbons of a church hat.

Mama was running from the kitchen now, her arms flailing above her head. She was shouting, words that sounded like Hop, hop, hop! Dab it, Louisa! Dab, dab, dab!

But as Mama got closer, her words became clear. She was not telling Nola to 'hop', but to 'stop', and she was not telling Louisa to 'dab it', but to 'grab it'. So Nola looked at her hand, the one she'd raised to hold Papa's face, the one that had been resting by her side. In that hand was Grampy's machete.

She looked confusedly at the rusty blade against Papa's cheek. How it get from the rafters of Ellie's pen and into my hand? She'd used it yesterday, to cut a fresh bundle of grass for Ellie, but she'd put it back, standing on Grampy's milking stool to cotch the blade on the rafter where it was kept.

Louisa screamed again. She and Mama stood with extended arms, pleading with her to drop the machete. But she couldn't do that. That would mean letting go of Papa's face, and she couldn't do that now. Not when she'd finally gotten a taste of something she'd wanted all her life. Not with him looking like that at her, waiting for her next move.

She shook her head, knowing that Mama would understand. Mama knew they were the same, the blade and Papa's eyes— the same cold steel.

For years to come, in Nola's memories of the events that followed, everything seemed to have happened in slow motion. She would remember Louisa's screams as the long, drawn-out sound of time being stretched like a stiffened piece of old gum. She would remember Papa's hand sailing in its graceful dance through the air, sailing for an eternity before it struck.

The fist was closed. She knew that because of how it struck, with a concentrated force below her jawbone. It sent her chin cracking up so far that her head felt as if it had separated from her neck. Her first thought as she sailed through the air was that she would look up from where her head had landed and be able to see her body still standing there beside Papa, with the belt at its feet. Her second thought was of Dahlia's lip-nose, the features joined forever by her own papa's fist, and she knew that from now on, she and Dahlia would forever be kindred spirits in their deformities.

She flew a good distance, rolling until she stopped on her side, right beside Ellie's stomping hooves. Her face slapped so hard into a pile of wet dung that it packed the cavity of her ear. It was hot, like steaming cocoa tea. She was able to register that. It seemed to be flowing from her head down to her shoulders. The warmth covered her like a blanket. If it weren't for the dull screams that continued around her, she would have pulled her legs up to her belly and gone to sleep in the warm cocoon.

But the screaming wouldn't stop, so she opened her eyes. The dung was around her like a river of syrup, but it was doing something strange to her hearing. It was reversing sound. Louisa's hysterical screams were coming from far away, from way down the bottom of Macca Hill, while Mama's barely audible 'Dear Heavenly Father' rang through Nola's head as if the words had been bellowed straight into her ear.

She tried to sit up, but her head dropped heavily back into the manure. It splattered into her mouth. It was the taste that eventually told her that she was not lying in manure. She was lying in a lake of blood!

Dear Jesus! The machete! Papa! She tried to rock herself up unto her hands and knees, her movements slushing in the pool. She wobbled to her feet, using the tree trunk as support. She wanted to scream for Papa, to bellow his name, but she was frozen, all except the wild searching of her eyes.

She found him by the door of the pen, his head bowed and resting on one arm on the door jamb. There wasn't any blood on his body. The relief of seeing him there almost sent her fainting back to the ground, if it weren't for Louisa's screaming.

It hit her then. The blood had to have been coming from somewhere, from someone! Mama and Louisa were okay, huddled together on the lawn, Louisa screaming into Mama's neck. Mama was crying too, staring with wild eyes at a spot behind Nola.

Nola turned then, to the spot where she'd landed after Papa's blow, the spot beside Ellie's hooves. There she was. Ellie. Dear Ellie, lying on her side with her hoof twitching as if desperately trying to get someone's attention.

Nola didn't see the machete till she was standing over Ellie. It was as precisely placed into the cow's neck as if it had been a deliberate chop by a butcher. Even now, it pulsed a fountain of black syrup. The eyes were open, looking up at her for help, and her mouth ... her mouth gasped, the grain from the trough still on her tongue.

Nola sank to her knees, flinging her arms over Ellie's sopping chest. "No God! ... Please Jesus, don't make her die".

The cow's last breath left her in a mixture of a gurgle and a sigh. Nola only knew that the sound vibrated through her own chest. She stared into the shimmering pool around them and gave a relieved sigh of her own. Grampy was there! Right there in the blood. She could see him taking Ellie's rope and leading her away, his half-smile waffling in the ripples.

"Take me too, Grampy, don't leave me again."

Someone tugged at her shoulder. "I want to go with him!" Her voice was louder now. "I goin' with them! I goin' with Grampy and Ellie. Them can't leave me here!"

The hands were determined. She began to fight, was about to kick them away, until the arms grabbed her, and the smell rendered her immobile. Grampy! He'd come! He'd really come! She could smell him—old clothes, old skin, old sweat, old breath, old love.

"Grampy, why you took so long? You know how long I been waitin' for you! I ready to go with you," she sobbed, resting her head in the brittle cavity of the chest, eroded now by both life and death. Another perfect fit.

Then he spoke, and Nola wondered at how much death had changed his voice. So much deeper now. "Come child," he said, "Get yourself outta this mess. Come make we wash. Ellie gone, child. Nuttin' you or me can do 'bout that now."

"Grampy, . . . I ready to go," she whispered impatiently into the furry ear.

It was not Grampy who whispered back. "Not Grampy, child. Tackie. Just ole Tackie."

Nola looked up at the creased face then. Mas Tackie tried to smile, but his lips quivered, then gave up as he looked back at her bloody face.

Mama and Louisa took her from him at the pipe. Silent Mama, her lips blue, like she'd just walked out of the icy river, and Louisa, stifling her sobs with hiccups. They stripped off her clothes and scrubbed her with ash. They rubbed the soot into her skin with the laundry brush, softening the crust of blood and dung and tears. The bristles tore her skin, but she didn't complain, for the friction was bringing life back into her numb limbs.

Over by the coolie plum tree a crowd had grown. They'd heard the screams. That was the thing with the hill. It was generous with its noise. They mulled over Ellie's body, passing the story around till it was clearer to them than it was to the people who'd witnessed it.

For the second time in her life, Nola stood by the outside pipe and turned the clear water into rust. Nola Chambers had

105

turned clear water into blood when she tried to kill her papa. What would the dew angels have made of that? Nola giggled.

Mama and Louisa looked up, startled. They wouldn't have understood the joke, about the tale of the angels, about how Dahlia had told her to believe in miracles, and how she'd believed, so much so that she'd thought that Grampy had come to take her away. She laughed again, this time so loudly that it was a shock to her own throbbing head. There was a stunned silence from the crowd by the pen, and Louisa gave Mama a frightened glance. It all made Nola laugh more.

The laughter bubbled out till she had to bend over and hold her belly. It brought tears streaming down her cheeks, and when Mama tried to cover her head with a towel, she flung it off. She stood there before them all, in her soaking bra and panties, the scars on her back and upper arms shining like purple snakes in the dim light.

CHAPTER 21

NOLA WAS BOUND tightly in red cloth, fetched from the back room of the Open Bible Church for occasions such as this. It had been sent for with such urgency that poor Sister Norma had broken the key in the lock in her hurry to get it. The cloth had been rushed up to the Chambers's home in the cab of the Spence's truck, dutifully delivering the antidote to the news it had earlier deposited. The cloth was sprinkled with white rum. Both the colour and strong smell were the perfect combination to keep the evil at bay.

Most of the residents of the hill had left their half-eaten dinners to witness the results of the evil rampage for themselves. God-fearing people that they were, they'd immediately set about the task of saving Nola Chambers' soul. The prayers had been unceasing.

If the prayers and white rum weren't successful, then Pastor's palm certainly would be. The palm had slapped so hard against Nola's forehead that her teeth had rocked in her gums, and where her jaw had grown a swelling from Papa's fist, there grew a matching one on her forehead. By the time Sister Norma and Mrs. Spence had bound her in the cloth, her body was so swollen and bruised that no spirit, good or evil, would have had much use for it.

She lay still in the bed for hours after the wailing and prayers had died down. No one had spoken a word to her since her fit of laughter, addressing only the brazen spirit within her.

The events had proven too much for Papa to bear, and he'd disappeared while she'd laughed by the pipe. But Mama had stayed, and while the villagers prayed, she had stood silently by the pipe. When the elders took Nola into her bedroom, Mama followed them into the house, but sat at the kitchen table, eyes staring straight ahead, not even looking up at the red bundle of cloth that was her daughter. Nola craned her neck over the screeching heads to try to catch Mama's stare. She'd wanted to let her know that she was sorry, for the blood on her front lawn, for the bombardment of villagers in her small kitchen, for Papa being gone, but when she finally caught Mama's eyes, all she could see was dullness—dullness beyond even that of the death in Ellie's eyes.

It was the memory of those eyes that had made Nola lie still as they cleared her room of all her tainted belongings. After they left, she closed her eyes and searched the whirlwind in her mind for any hint at the darkness there. Maybe the blackness of her skin really had been an indication of the darkness of her soul. She slumped deep into the cloth. She wanted at once to feel nothing. Remember nothing. Know nothing.

Then came the dream of the river. She, lying at the bottom with the red water above her, them standing on the banks, laughing at her embedded in the silt—Papa, Mrs. Spence, Pastor, Sister Norma, Mama. Merlene was crying. Tears rolled down her cheeks as she stared at the spot beside Nola. It was Dahlia, lying beside Nola, her lip-nose sticking from the silt like a river slug. Her skin was the grey shade that water made of everything, like she'd been there for a long time. Nola desperately tried to free the girl, but her own arms were buried deep, and the more she tried to break free was the farther and farther away that Dahlia moved. Then suddenly, miraculously, Nola was free from the loamy layers so she could swim to Dahlia and pull her out of the river bed. She heard the girl calling her name, but again, the more she tried to swim to her, the farther she drifted.

"Nola!" The voice was louder now. "Nola!"

Her eyes flew open and focused through her wild tears on the face above her. Louisa! Bending over her with anxious eyes. Nola sat up and stared wildly around her. She was naked, the cloth lying around her in strips.

"Dahlia! Dahlia!" Her words were garbled, as if the water was still in her throat. "Louisa, Dahlia need me! I have to save . . ."

Louisa's hand clapped roughly over Nola's mouth, "Ssshh, Nola, don't make them hear you! Them still out there. Them don't know that I'm in here."

The tears flooded from Nola with such a force that her shoulders shook and Louisa had to press her face into her chest to mask the sounds. She cried for a long time, shedding tears that had been waiting for many, many years. When she finally stopped, Louisa tried to wipe her face with the red cloth, but Nola shuddered away. Louisa immediately gathered the strips and shoved them through the bedroom window. Then she put her finger to her lips and disappeared through the doorway. She reappeared with clothes, all her own, and gently guided Nola's shaking limbs into them. They were a tight fit.

Nola studied her sister's face as she helped her pull her arms through the t-shirt. The eyes were bloodshot and swollen, the tip of her nose still red.

"You want some sour sop tea?" Louisa asked when she'd finished dressing Nola. She sat back on her heels. "Them did make some for Mama. Some still on the stove. It will calm your nerves, Nola, give you some strength."

Strength? Strength for what? I just goin' to do whatever them say. Whatever I suppose to do from now on. No more trouble — whatever them tell me to do. Don't need no strength for that.

Nola shook her head. "Where Papa?" she croaked.

"Him don't come back yet." Louisa eventually whispered.

"I so sorry," Nola looked down at her hands. "I never mean to hurt Ellie, or Papa. I don't know how … " Louisa once again put her hand over Nola's mouth, gentler this time.

"Ssshh! I know," she said. "I know you! I know you wouldn't do that."

Nola nodded, biting her lip to stop the tears. She just didn't have the energy to start crying again. "And Mama? What 'bout Mama? She … she okay?"

Louisa nodded thoughtfully. "Them give her the tea and she sleepin' now. She wanted to see you before she go to bed, but them tell her in the mornin'. I not suppose to be in here either, but Miss Terry drop asleep. Is her watch now."

"Mama wanted to see me?" Nola asked.

Louisa nodded again, and Nola's heart lifted. Mama had wanted to see her! Even after what she'd done, Mama had wanted to see her. This was her chance to start over, to prove that she could be good. She would be perfect from now on. Not even to the river she would go.

The river! The dream suddenly rushed back. She had to explain to them! She had to explain everything to Dahlia and Merlene before they heard it through the village. After all they'd done for her, she owed them that. She owed them a proper goodbye.

She tried to stand, but teetered forward and would have fallen onto her face if Louisa hadn't jumped up and grabbed her waist.

"Nola, what you doin'? Sit down before them hear us!"

"I have to go to them, Louisa! I have to talk to Dahlia and Merlene just one last time. They will understand when I tell them what happen. Them don't mean no harm, Louisa. Them is good people—good people ..." Her voice broke as she pleaded with Louisa.

She had expected her sister to shake her head and push her back down on the bed, but Louisa didn't. She didn't even look surprised. Instead, she bent to the ground, took the rubber slippers off her feet, and placed them in front of Nola's.

Louisa looked up, into Nola's face, "I knew 'bout you goin' there in the evenin's. I knew for a long time. Clarice tell Toneisha, and then Toneisha tell me. But I tell them that if them say anything to anybody, I was goin' tell everybody 'bout Clarice and Tulia meetin' Shane and Oliver behind Razzle Dazzle in the evenin's."

Nola jerked her head and looked into her sister's weary eyes. "Louisa, I only went 'cause Slugga told me to! I wasn't doin' any nastiness."

"I know. I know that. At first ... at first I was goin' to warn you to stop goin'. Then when I saw the look on your face when you come home in the evenin's—you had that smile. You was just so happy, Nola. I couldn't stop you."

Louisa stared down at Nola's hands inside of hers. A black pearl within a bronze oyster. She eventually said. "I used to think that you never had the same Papa that I had. I couldn't understand why he was always so vex with you. I used to wish that your real Papa would come and take you back to your house. Not because I wanted you to leave me, but because I just wanted you to know what it was like to love your papa."

Nola swallowed hard and finally managed to squeak, "I love him, Louisa. I love my papa. It's just that, him don't love me."

Louisa hugged her, fierce and hard. "I sorry I couldn't do more to stop it."

111

CHAPTER 22

NOLA STOOD OUTSIDE the kitchen door and breathed in deeply, gulping the fresh air she never thought she'd feel again. The act only wrenched another sob from her chest as she inhaled the raw tinge of acid-metal—blood! Ellie's death still hung in the air.

Nola negotiated the potholes of Macca Hill by memory. Eventually, the lights of Calabash Street filtered through the trees. Running at a trot, by the time she got to the bottom of the hill, she was gasping for breath. Flowing into her nostrils was the unmistakable smell of smoke.

The shadow billowing into the sky was over Della Way, strongest over the spot where the pink house stood. Suddenly, she understood where Papa had gone that night.

She ran, right down Jackfruit Lane, on to Della Way, into the bustle of villagers running in and out of a wall of smoke. She could not make out the faces through the thick curtain, but she could see that Miss June's shop still stood. She squinted at a group huddled in the middle of the road with dripping cloths over their noses—Miss June and Tulia, Skengy and Jervis, shaking their heads agitatedly as they pointed down the road.

She ran towards where the blaze rose high into the sky.

The crates were gone. So was the red door. Nola stood frozen in the heat and watched the shutters and walls of Merlene's Bar and Grill crumple like paper. She raced through the crowd, searching wildly for a familiar feature—an elaborate hairdo, pencil-thin eyebrows, the girth of a co-joined lip-nose. She recognized Clars and Tanky, their chests shirtless and gleaming as they chopped at the prickly privet on the other side of the street.

She ran behind the bar, Louisa's rubber slippers softening on the searing ground and sticking to the soles of her feet. She found Bertie there. He stood a few yards back from the crumbling building, his neck craned backward as he watched the flames lick the sky. He held a bucket of water in one hand. In the other, his broom.

Nola grabbed his arm and her fingers slid downward in the mulch of sweat. He jumped, startled from his daze, but even as he stared into Nola's face, his expression remained blank. It took a good few seconds for the bewildered mask to lift, and for his eyes to register her face.

"Bertie! Where everybody? Where Dahlia ... and ... Miss Merlene?" Nola rasped.

"Don't know where them gone. Miss Merlene and all of we was in there ..." Bertie shook his head and pointed his broomstick at the flames. "Then Miss Merlene tell everybody to go home 'cause nuttin' we can do."

Nola gave him a reassuring pat and rushed towards the hedge. The blue flora was now just a speckle of shriveled buds, the once intertwined branches now baring open in sections to reveal the rotted stakes of wood beneath. She raced to the front door. It was locked, and the lights were off. Nola banged on the door, the louvres rattling beside her.

"Dahlia! Merlene! Is me! Nola! Open the door! It's Nola! Open up, quick!"

But no one came. No sound from within. Could they have already left? Would they have left their beloved home unprotected from the fire?

Suddenly, something brushed against her leg and she gave a startled shriek. Streaky! The pig that lived behind the bar was shaking, his body spinning in circles at her feet. Nola gave a happy laugh and grabbed up his heat-marinated stench.

"Streaky, where they gone? Where Dahlia? She wouldn't leave you." Nola banged on the door again and bellowed. "Dahlia! Streaky is 'fraid. He out here lookin' for you!"

It took just a couple of seconds, but the distinct click of a door being opened reached Nola's ears. Soon, the front door cracked open, and Dahlia's lip-nose appeared in the flickering light. It was when the girl's eyes widened at the sight of her face that Nola remembered her bruises.

"Dahlia! Thank God! I been callin' and callin' you! What you and Merlene still doin' in there? We have to get water and stop the fire before it reach the house. Bertie out there waitin' to help us!"

Dahlia spoke so calmly that Nola blinked in shock. "Nola, the house goin' be okay. The fire goin' burn out before it reach the house. We okay. You need to leave now. Take Streaky with you." She paused and her lip-nose quivered slightly as she studied Nola's face.

"Go away before them hurt you some more."

Nola shoved her shoulder into the door with a strength that surprised even herself.

"You mad, Dahlia? You can't leave Streaky with me. She love you! She need you!" Nola set the pig on the floor, and it promptly ran up to Dahlia and rubbed itself on her leg. "See?"

"Nola, Puddin', you have to leave. Take Streaky and go now!" Merlene's voice came from the bedroom door.

114

She looked like an angel. Her purple nightgown shimmered in the silver haze of smoke that had followed Nola through the front door. Her brows became drawn into a deep frown as they registered Nola's swollen face.

When she spoke again, her voice was gentler. "This have nothing to do with you, Puddin', just me and Pumkin. This is someting we have to deal with – nothing to do with you."

"Yes, Merlene, it is about me! It's all about me! I think … I think …" Nola swallowed. "I think that is my papa who set the fire. Him find out that I was coming here in the evenin's."

But Merlene's expression did not change. She just kept looking at Nola with that knowing look, then shook her head. "Puddin'," she said. "If it wasn't your papa, then it would'a been someone else. It was just a matter of time." She flinched slightly as the sound of crashing wood reverberated through the room.

"Go now, Nola. Please take Streaky and go before them catch you here!"

"No!" Nola stepped towards Dahlia. "I not leavin' if you not leavin'." It was becoming harder to speak. Thick smoke was creeping into the room from beneath the front door, slivering in between the cracks of the louvre windows.

Dahlia grabbed Nola's shoulder and gave it a slight shake and Nola's heart froze as she looked into the girl's face. Her skin was grey and ashy within the smoke. Just as it had been in the dream.

"Nola," Dahlia said, "Mama and I not runnin' no more. We can't let people keep drivin' us out of our home."

"You don't have to run, Dahlia," Nola cried. "Let's just go outside. We can build back the house if anyting happen! Me and Delroy and Bertie and Biscuit and Darlene—everybody! We can build back the Bar and Grill and whatever else the fire burn down."

Merlene coughed and fanned the air. "Nola," she eventually rasped, "Biscuit and the others couldn't wait for me to build again. Nobody could. Them pay is what them live on. Them couldn't live without a job for so long, not for the time it would take to build the bar back."

Nola's throat was closing, but she made one last pleading effort. "Then Merlene ... we can build ... a different kind ... of business this time. A restaurant ... where everybody would want to come ... or a supermarket, like you had in Kingston. Please, please let's just go outside!"

She gripped the back of a dining chair. She was going to faint. She knew it. They had to leave now!

Dahlia coughed too, a bellow of a spit that cooled Nola's face. She felt her arm being grabbed and then she was being hauled towards Merlene's room. The smoke was less behind the closed door of the bedroom. A whispy mist swirled persistently behind them as they piled in, and Merlene had to hurry into the bathroom to get a dripping towel to place along the bottom of the doorway.

Another ruckus rang out from outside. Shouts. Frantic instructions. Then banging on the front door.

"Fire pon the house! Fire pon the house!"

It sounded like Tanky, but Nola couldn't be sure. The louvres shook, and a sudden intolerable heat seemed to swell everything. Nola's head pounded with the heavy pressure. Merlene and Dahlia ran into the bathroom and brought more wet towels that they wrapped around theirs and Nola's wracking shoulders. Dahlia held Streaky tight beneath hers while Nola used the dripping tips of hers to squeeze a soothing stream onto her face.

Another shout from outside. "Them must be gone! Nobody in them right mind would still be in there! Wet round the back before it spread to Tanky farm!"

116

Nola saw them look at each other, and she saw the message pass between them. One look was all it took, and the decision had been made.

Merlene nodded at Nola. "Alright, Puddin', we goin' to have to run. We have to run through the front door, so keep the towel tight round your head, and try not to breathe till you get outside. Don't make the smoke get in your chest or it will seize up and you won't be able to run!"

Nola nodded back with eager relief. They positioned her at the bedroom door to go first. They claimed she was the dizziest and the weakest. Just before they opened it, Dahlia shoved Streaky underneath Nola's arm and said, "I need to help Mama". Their faces weren't visible anymore, but she felt them put another soaking towel around her shoulders. She could hear them coughing and gasping as someone opened the bedroom door.

The heat was unbearable. It slammed into Nola's face like a physical blow, sending her reeling backwards until a hand shoved her through the doorway once again. The flames on Merlene's lopsided sofa were so blinding that it felt as if her eyeballs had gelled into liquid. Her lashes disintegrated, leaving her eyes vulnerable to the ribbons of soot that floated through the living room. Someone pushed her towards the dining table where the plastic cushions melted into sizzling drops onto the floor. Never break! The words rang through the room. They were depending on her! They were depending on her to lead them out of there.

Never break! Suddenly, survival took over from fear. Nola tucked her head into the towel, squeezed the squirming pig firmly against her hip, and raced towards the front door. The moisture in the towel became steam. Her instinctive reaction was to fling it off, but remembering Merlene's words about the smoke, she gripped it over her face and felt for the bolt on the door. Her fingertips melted onto the metal. Never break! Never break! The words screamed through her head as she felt herself about to pass out from the pain. She grabbed the tip of the towel and wrapped it around her blistered fingers, then tugged the bolt again. The latch gave, and a hot gush of air burst into the house.

The fire cackled with new energy, rising to a crescendo which was deafening. Nola jumped.

The lawn was simmering. She lost her grip of Streaky as she rolled, but heard him squealing beside her and knew he was okay. Instinct got her to her feet once again and took her through the glowing twigs of the hedge, past the crackling skeleton of the Bar and Grill, and flung her in a choking heap on the road.

The bile rose as if on cue. She vomited till all that was left was the dry retching that protested against the smoke still in her chest. It took a while for her to realize that the road was empty. The villagers had gone. The shouts and clink of machetes were now coming from up the road, by Miss June's shop.

A movement at her feet, told her that Merlene and Dahlia were also coming out of their daze. She lifted herself feebly onto her hands to check on them, but all she could see was Streaky, spinning dizzily by her feet. She sat up sharply, her eyes searching through the haze over the road. They were nowhere in sight.

They were not by the burning bar. They were not visible through the barren hedge. Empty. Everywhere was empty. Dahlia and Merlene were nowhere to be seen.

"NO! DAHLIA! NO! Somebody help! Them still inside! Them still in the house!"

She tried to inch closer to the house, but the heat was a wall. The roof collapsed and the flames almost touched the

moon with their roaring belch. Something exploded. The
sound made her jump backwards. She looked up just in time
to catch the spark as it lifted from the house, rising so high
into the sky that she had to crane her neck to follow it. It
arched delicately over the moon, and then headed back down
to earth.

Cold. It registered to Nola how strange that the fire that
had just singed her skin could have felt so cold. It froze her
cheek. Numbed her entire body so that she fell to the ground.
She just lay there in front of the burning house, willing the
cold, refreshing fire to swallow her up too.

Then she saw it. A vision of white. It moved swiftly through
the smoke, gliding on wings spread wide. It swooped down on
her, and covered her in the coolness of its wings. A dew angel!
It had come, even before dawn, to rescue them. Wet with its
dew, it poured its soothing moisture over Nola's twitching
body, breathing its own breath into her mouth before lifting
her out of the smoke.

CHAPTER 23

NOLA DRIFTED IN and out of the blackness to cool salves being slathered over her body and bitter liquid being dripped down her singed throat. Many times she wandered from the abyss thinking of Merlene and Dahlia, wanting to ask where the dew angel had taken them, but her throat had locked against speech. Sometimes she saw the river, tranquil as the golden light played across its surface. Sometimes Ellie would nod at her over its gleaming ripples, and sometimes it was Delroy's face that smiled from the banks.

On the day that her eyes finally opened, it was silver light she saw. Her eyes were hazy, but she could tell that the light came from above her head. She blinked to clear her vision, and her sticky lashes sealed shut once again. She tried to lift her fingers to wipe the paste away, but her hand could not budge.

There was a shuffle. Someone was moving! Someone was beside her! Something cool was being dabbed onto her eyes, wiping the paste away. This time, when she opened them, she could see. Blurred, but the image before her was clear enough to make her chest heave with shock.

Mad Aggie! She was in Mad Aggie's stall!

The wizened face was creased into an anxious frown, but when Nola gave a frightened sob, the sparse brows lifted in warning.

"Shush! No talk! Them come take you wey!" she rasped.

The woman was on her haunches, knees wide apart, like an animal about to pounce on its prey. Nola stared wide-eyed as the witch cocked her eyes and held a finger in the air. Nola listened, hoping to hear another voice to which to scream for help. That's when she realized that noise screamed all around them – the moan of traffic, the hum of chatter. Life in the village was back to normal.

Nola tried to speak, but produced only a racking cough. Mad Aggie immediately scurried to the corner of the stall and retrieved an enamel cup, then hurried back to gently place the rim at Nola's lips. Nola gulped, grateful for the wetness on her parched throat, but coughed violently again when the severe bitterness of the liquid registered. However, when the coughing stopped her voice was able to scrape from her throat.

"Dah ... lia?" she asked. "Merl ... Merl ...?"

Something flashed within Mad Aggie's eyes. But just as quickly as the look had appeared was as quickly as it disappeared. A shutter was pulled, and all trace of emotion vanished from her face.

She flung her arms into the air and stared up at the cobwebbed roof. "The Great Book say, there is earthly bodies, there is heavenly bodies. What sow in dishonour, raise in glory ... what sow in weakness, raise in power ... ." The arms lowered slowly and the blank gaze focused, once again, on Nola's frightened eyes. She leaned closer, her bitter breath fanning Nola's face. "They raise!" she whispered, "They raise in glory and power, right beside the Mighty Father. No more pain, no more tears. No more shunnin' by them earthly devils!"

Nola closed her eyes and allowed the witch's riddles to unravel within the haze of her mind. Tears sprung from her lashes, even though her body was as dry as chip.

Right beside the Mighty Father! The dew angel had come too late!

They'd made the choice. They'd chosen to stay together, while she'd chosen to run like the traitorous coward that she was! A blaze of glory! Just like Dahlia had said. Nola envied their crisp, charred bodies.

Her eyes flew open at the loud scoff beside her. She'd forgotten where she was for an instant. She stared frantically at the face above her, but to her surprise it was not anger she saw. The gaze was actually soft as the turbaned head bent closer, wafting the nutty, bitter smell of breath over Nola like a musty blanket.

"The Great Book say, the last enemy we have to destroy is death. No more enemy after that!" She whispered, as if imparting another sacred secret within the midst of a crowd.

They had conquered death, all of them—Granny Pat's newborn Lilly, Grampy, Ellie, Merlene and Dahlia, now all heavenly bodies along with the dew angels. What the witch didn't know was that it wasn't the conquering of death that had made Nola weep, it was the conquering of life.

Suddenly, another scuffle above Nola's head made her give a startled jump. She craned her stiffened neck to see who else had been in the shack with them.

This time, a sob did manage to escape her throat. It was Streaky! The sight brought such a jolt of painful memory that laughter burst from Nola alongside the tears.

Mad Aggie scoffed again, but her face remained blank. It was a sound that sounded something like 'ffsshh', which, in the days to follow, Nola would come to decipher as 'foolishness'.

The woman dug into the wrapping of fabric around her chest and removed a piece of red-checked cotton, dabbing it across Nola's wet cheeks. She ffsshed again when Nola flinched sharply.

Nola's face felt as if someone had suddenly rammed a million needles deep into the skin. Then she remembered— the spark, sailing from the pink house like a farewell. She remembered standing there, mesmerized by the beauty, remembered watching with awe as it had turned in the sky, then headed, of all places in the wide expanse of land, for her face.

She panted with agony, both from the memory and the wakening throb on her face. Her deep breaths sent the witch scurrying again, across the shack to grab a plastic vial. With deft hands, the woman lifted Nola's head and poured the entire contents of the vial down her throat. Nola tried to wring her head away from the grasp, but the wiry hands held it so firmly that she had no choice but to sputter, till every drop was either down her throat or streaming along with the tears down her cheeks.

Mad Aggie chuckled. "Good, good! Make you good again. See? You strong! Try fight Aggie! When you come, can't even move your little finger! But God say, 'Daughter Aggie, I not ready for that chile up here yet, lot more for her to do down there. You take that chile and fix her so she can finish down there!'"

The potion fanned out in Nola's belly. Long, burning fingers, tearing through her insides.

It was evening when she opened her eyes again. Panic ripped through her as she focused on the strip of dull orange sky. She'd fallen asleep at Dahlia and missed washing the pots! She tried to get up, but her legs were heavy. Someone had tied them to the ground!

123

Then she remembered, and the memory jolted her like a punch to her gut. All that blood ... Dear Ellie ... And Dahlia and Merlene within those flames!

The shack was empty. Not even Streaky was there. Just the pile of old cloth, and in the far corner the gauze that covered the enamel mugs and vials. A large pile of wild bush and dusty yams lay beside it, a few flies taking turns to pitch onto the exposed flesh of the yams. She really was in Mad Aggie's shack. The world had turned upside down, and dropped her at the bottom of Macca Hill.

A slight movement above her leg suddenly caught her eye. Sweet Jesus ... a rat, easily the size of a mongoose! It was climbing down the post with its eyes focused on the spot where Nola's toes had slipped from beneath the covering. Nola squealed and wiggled her toes, but the rat remained undaunted. It pounced, and as numb as her legs were, the heavy weight of the rodent registered. She screamed again as it scrambled towards her feet, and just when she felt she would pass out from fright, it suddenly stopped moving.

A stick, its sharpened point piercing through the creature's neck and out again through the underbelly, had been rammed with unerring accuracy from above the counter.

"Hah! See that? Make good soup, good for lungs! Make you breathe clear and strong. Aggie skin rattie later. Make good soup to clear smoke-black out your lungs!"

If Nola had had the energy, she would have vomited right there and then. The witch, obviously tickled by the expression on Nola's face, cackled loudly. She continued chuckling and mumbling to herself as she took a pile of bush from beneath her arm and added it to the pile on the floor. She turned and gave Nola a curious stare.

"Your sistah come," she eventually said. "She say she come back later when you wake."

Nola couldn't describe the sound that came from her own throat. A gurgle? A sob? A snort?

The witch ffsshhed and turned back to the bush. "She come plenty, all those days you was sleepin'." She kept her back to Nola as she spoke. "Cry plenty! Aggie have to get bringle with her and tell her, No more cryin' in this place! No more bawlin' to stop that chile from healin'!"

"Lou ... Louisa ... come here?... To see me? In this ... place?" The witch turned to give her another long stare, but did not answer. Eventually she gathered her skirt between her legs and turned back to the bush. She selected two stalks from the pile and pulled the leaves off, dropping them into the bowl with the rat. Then she picked up a plastic bottle and studied the amber contents above her head for a while. She eventually pulled off the cap she held it to her nose and took a long sniff before pouring the contents onto the rat.

Nola watched with no reaction, with not one sickening jerk of her belly. Nothing else mattered but that Louisa had come for her. If Louisa knew that she was there, then Mama and Papa knew too, and if Louisa had come for her, that meant that she was forgiven.

Her heart soared. Maybe Papa would tell her how sorry he was. Maybe he would explain that he only meant to frighten them, and now he was beside himself with grief.

"Mama ... Papa ... them come too?" She whispered at the witch's back.

Mad Aggie did not pause in her labour. She was now tying some of the bush into bundles with strips of cloth, while other bunches she threw into a black scandal bag. Nola was about to repeat the question when the witch swirled around and held up a warning finger. Nola's mouth snapped shut.

"Blessed are you!" she hissed, "Blessed are you when they persecute you and say all kind o' evil against you because

125

o' me. Rejoice and be glad, because great is your reward in heaven!" Her eyes blazed for an instant, then she blinked and turned to look out the doorway. "When your sistah come, you talk with her! You talk to your sistah and ask her if madda and fadda come."

CHAPTER 24

L OUISA NEVER CAME the next day, nor the day after that, nor even the day after that.

As the days passed, the hope inside Nola fizzled away. But even as the hope inside her died, the strength of her body returned. Each day, Mad Aggie forced her to do something more, and by the fifth day of waking from the dark sleep, Nola was sitting up for several hours without her lungs flapping like a deflated balloon. Each morning, the witch cotched her against the wall beneath the counter and brought fresh river water for her to wash her face, and chewstick to freshen her mouth. She was wrapped in fresh cloth, the ends tied in a huge knot behind her back, her breasts bound as flat as bulla cakes. At first, Nola had resisted, thinking the fabric held within it the rotting carcasses of rats and lizards, but to her surprise, the cloth the woman had pulled from a box under the counter smelled of blue soap and sweet river water.

So Nola was wiped every day from head to toe, the burns on her hands, feet and face slathered with thick paste. She eventually got used to the witch chanting loudly about 'the enemy' over the raised scars on her shoulders and back.

Truth be told, it wasn't so bad, her existence in the shack. The witch's constant ramblings about God and the prowling 'enemy' were a distraction from the sadness that sat like a boulder on her chest. It was just as Grampy used to say—the mind had the power to change any situation from bad to good. "Suppose you was in a wide open field," he would say, "and somebody stuff you under a box and sit down on top of it so that you can't get out? You best believe you goin' kick and scream with all your might, and beg them to let you out! But, Little Bird, suppose you in that same field, and the person tell you that a wild dog lookin' to bite you, and the only place you goin' be safe was under that same box? You best believe you goin' stay happy crouch up under there for as long as it take for that dog to leave! Same field, same box—but the MIND, Little Bird, the mind is what different— feelin' trapped in one instance, safe in the other."

So that was what Nola told herself as she lay on the sidewalk within the pungent shack.

Soon she found that she began to look forward to the witch's boisterous company. She took pleasure in watching the woman's nimble fingers sort through her bush, and in being able to recognize some of the branches that she picked out—dogblood, serese, sour sop, even the miserable cow itch vine that most villagers avoided like the plague. The ruddy scent of bush always filled the shack like a third inhabitant, but by the end of the week Nola had become so used to it that it lost its offensive grate against her nostrils.

Nola learned to accommodate herself to the strictures of the shack, to speak in whispers and to limit her movements in the day. Mad Aggie had warned her that the villagers thought she was a 'bad, bad gal', and if they found her, they would send her to the home where all bad gals were sent.

The most uncomfortable aspect of the shack was the use of the 'bathroom'—the old paint can that Mad Aggie brought to her each time she shyly indicated her need. The witch would hold her by her shoulders above the can, ffsshhing encouragingly, then she would disappear with the waste.

She began to help Mad Aggie with her bush sorting and tying, listening in silence as the witch rambled about doctors being disciples of the enemy, taking people's money and making them addicted to man-made drugs that weakened the body. More people sick, more money in doctor pocket!

And it truly seemed that most of the village believed this too. In secret, Mad Aggie was the provider of antidotes for complaints ranging from failing eyesight, to women's 'bleeding' problems, to swollen veins. At nights, Mad Aggie went from 'witch', to 'Madda', disappearing through the doorway with her pail of 'medicines' as if she were just one more wedge of the thick darkness beyond.

On the night that Louisa finally came to the shack, she found Nola sitting up beneath the counter, picking caterpillars from sour sop leaves and listening intently as Aggie listed out the names of the bushes before them—Neem, Chigganit, Man to Man, Rat Ears. Even with the stench of the wild bush sitting thickly within the shack, Nola smelled her sister before she saw her.

Louisa was pale and gaunt. Nola's heart lurched when she noted the deep stoop of her shoulders. Oh God, she look just like Mama! Nola could not speak. A lump had risen from her chest and wedged itself into her throat. Seeing Louisa was making every scab on her body sting with awakening, as if the fire had resurrected itself inside her.

Louisa stared back, as if she, too, were seeing a ghost. Then slowly she stooped to touch Nola's cheek, running her fingers over the raw skin that Mad Aggie had left unbandaged that day. Nola saw the tremble of her sister's bottom lip, then the deep, sad frown. She turned away from Louisa's hand, suddenly aware of the hideous sight she must have made.

Aggie had been watching them silently from the corner, but she suddenly gave a ffsshh, grabbed a jar of the black liquid she'd brewed that morning and disappeared through the doorway.

Louisa hesitantly took Nola's hand, staring at the cracking scabs.

"Nola … I so sorry. I never know all this would happen." She shook her head slowly, her eyes swimming beneath a fresh pool of tears. "I thought you would just go and tell them goodbye and it would be all over."

Nola stared at Louisa's trembling lips and a sudden, horrible thought freed her voice from beneath the lump.

"Louisa, them never …? Pastor never hit you for freein' me?" Louisa gave a soft, bitter laugh. "No! No! No matter how I tell them that is me who let you out, them never believe me. Them think I was just tryin' to protect you. Pastor say that is the spirits put Miss Terry in a deep sleep and take you outta the house. Him say your spirits was stronger than any him ever see in him life."

Nola sighed with relief. Better she stay in their bad books than Louisa enter them. She could never live with herself knowing that she'd put a stoop in Mama's shoulders, and Louisa's as well.

"What 'bout Mama and Papa? Them think that is the spirits that free me too?"

Louisa did not answer immediately. She touched the raw tips of Nola's fingers, the ones that had grasped the hot latch on Merlene's door. She drew a sharp breath when she saw that the fingernails had lifted completely off the skin.

"Nola!" She eventually said, "Why you never just go there and leave like you said you would?"

Nola pulled her hand away. Louisa wouldn't have understood. She hadn't known them.

"What 'bout Mama, Louisa?" she asked again.

"Mama believe me," Louisa eventually whispered. "But Papa ... Papa made us lock up your room. Him say that nobody must go back in there till Pastor say all the evil gone out of it."

"Is that when them goin' come for me? When they think all the evil gone? Louisa?"

"Nola," Louisa finally spoke in a low whisper. "The witch come and tell me that she have you two days after the fire, when everybody already think that you burn up with the others. When she tell me, I run and tell Mama, but Mama tell me not to say nothing to Papa, or nobody! She tell me that we have to wait till everyting settle down before we tell them, that if they know you're alive, them goin' come for you. And this time, it going' be worse, because you went back there."

Nola stared at her sister, the reality of her words slamming hard into her head.

"Nola, them say we had to hold your funeral quick, quick," Louisa continued, "so that the spirits couldn't get a chance to come back. And by then ... Mama say we couldn't tell them again."

"Funeral, Louisa?"

Louisa nodded, "Them never have no body, so them bury your clothes and all your tings. They say they weren't leaving' nothing for the spirits to linger 'round in."

Louisa's head flew up at Nola's gasp. She grabbed her shoulders tightly as if she thought Nola was going to faint. "The fire was bad, Nola!" Her voice begged for understanding. "There was barely anything left of your friends. Just a few bones ... and their teeth."

Teeth! Dear Grampy's Sweet Jesus! That's all that had been left of them! Nola grabbed the pail that Mad Aggie always left beside her and retched till she felt as if her very soul had been expelled.

Those beautiful smiles, that lip-nose that had warmed her heart, now just remnants within a scorched pile! She wanted to ask for the details—which section of the house had they been found in? Had they returned to the bedroom after they'd pushed her out? But while one part of her wanted to know, another part could not deal with the facts.

"Everybody think that the witch took up what was left of you. When them went there the next mornin', they found her walkin' through the house with all kind of tings in her hand. She was screamin' at them, tellin' them that God goin' come for all of them. They thought she took you away."

"What they did with what they found, of ... of ... Dahlia and Merlene?"

"The waitress that live in Nainsville come and take everyting back to Nainsville. She say she would dead first before she see them buried in Redding dirt."

Biscuit! Dear Biscuit. She knew they wouldn't have wanted to be left in the hands of those who'd despised them. Nola felt a deep nudge of peace within her. She remembered the hug that afternoon on Merlene's lawn, the one in which Dahlia and Merlene squeezed each other with such desperation. Somehow, they had known that the end was near. They'd wanted to squeeze the last bit of goodness, the last ounce of love, out of life.

Nola pulled a palm across her wet face and sighed. "How long I been here?" She nodded at the shack walls.

"Three weeks," Louisa said. "We keep you funeral last week Thursday."

"Three weeks?!" The words slipped out so loudly that Louisa 'sshhed' her anxiously and jumped up to peep over the counter.

She soon sat back down with relief and whispered, "Nola, if you ever knew what you look like when the witch bring me to see you that day. She say that when she took you out of the fire, you was breathing out smoke, like the fire was inside of you."

So it had been Mad Aggie who'd scraped her from the burning lawn. No dew angel after all. Nola felt the last essence of Grampy's tale waft away. Sorry, Dahlia, I tried to keep it alive, but it gone now—gone just like you.

Louisa continued speaking, oblivious to the revelation she'd just given Nola. "Mama send me to see you, and when I look on you, Nola, I thought you was dead! You wasn't even breathin' good." It was Louisa's turn to sob. "I really thought you was going to die. I never know the day would come when you would be able to sit up again, and talk! And Mama, she never know what to do with herself. She wanted to come and see you, but them wouldn't leave her alone. Every day, every minute, somebody was with her, and she never want nobody to know that you was here. She never want you to have to go through all those tings again. But Mad Aggie ... Mad Aggie save you! She tell me, Tell your mama I fix this chile like new. No worries. You just keep prayin' and Mighty One will do the rest. I can't believe is really you sittin' here with me." She grabbed Nola's shoulders and hugged her tight.

"What 'bout Papa, Louisa? What Papa say when him hear that I was ... dead?"

Louisa gently cupped Nola's cheek and gave a deep sigh. "Him say that you get what you deserve, that you bruck out the house to go back down to the devil's place, so you get what you deserve— brimstone and fire."

Nola nodded into Louisa's palm. Nothing had changed.

"And Delroy? You see Delroy Reckus?"

Louisa nodded slowly, "Nola, him never leave the burn-down house for one week! Him go there every day and sit down on the road side, in the middle of all the ash. Hours, just looking. "

Nola grabbed Louisa's arm. "Louisa, You have to tell Delroy that I didn't burn up."

"Nola! You crazy? Mama don't want nobody to know! You want them to come for you and beat you again?"

"So, I must just stay in this shack forever? Live with the witch forever?"

Louisa shook her head. "Mama just want everyting to settle down. Right now, everybody talkin' 'bout you and the fire, and how God finally strike down the sinners."

"God strike us down? Louisa, you know dat is Papa set the fire!"

"Don't say that! The fire never start on the house. The fire start on the bar, and it spread! Them could'a come out, Nola, and they didn't. Papa never kill anybody!"

"I know that him never mean to burn them up. I just want Delroy to know that not all of us died. Him know everyting, Louisa … 'bout Papa and me. Just please, please tell him, Louisa! Please!"

Louisa hesitated, then nodded. Nola flung her arms gratefully around her neck just as Aggie crept back into the stall, "Dark! Dark! Late dark!" she hissed. "Mind you make your fada come look for you!"

"When you goin' come for me?" Nola whispered against Louisa's ear.

"Soon," Louisa whispered back. Then she stood and pulled the blue towel back around her shoulders.

"Louisa, you know that was Grampy's towel?" Nola smiled fondly at the stained cloth.

Louisa removed the towel from her shoulders and placed it gently around Nola's.

CHAPTER 25

A FTER LOUISA'S VISIT, Nola's anxiety at being discovered in Aggie's shack grew. She was becoming more and more impatient about the time of her departure. Every day she prayed, "Mama, come for me! Mama, please come soon!"

The message was given to Aggie by Louisa, who in turn gave it to Nola—she could not return to her home. Papa was still too enraged to be told about her rescue. So Nola was to leave the village to be spared Papa's rage. She was to leave with Slugga when the headmistress left town the next evening. It was exactly four weeks after Nola had left her house to tell Dahlia and Merlene 'goodbye'.

Nola absorbed the instructions from Aggie, asking no questions. Not if Mama and Louisa would come to say 'goodbye'; not how she would face a strange world with her ugly, burned face. None.

The morning of the day she was to leave found Aggie quiet and watchful. Nola woke to find the woman squatted over her, staring with glazed eyes. From then on, the eyes never left her, not while she peed in the paint can, not while she washed up with the river water, not while she sipped her mug of hot cocoa.

She lookin' for someting, Nola realized. She think I'm sad to be leavin'.

Little did Aggie know that there was no more sadness left in her. It had all been spent. Fifteen years spent. She was as numb as when the cold spark had crashed into her.

Later, as they sipped peppery calalloo-cocoa soup, Nola finally asked the question she'd wanted to ask for weeks.

"Why, Aggie? Why you live on the sidewalk and make people think that you're mad. Why you want people to be 'fraid of you?"

Nola watched as the lips pulled back into that half-snarl, half-smile. "People think Aggie mad? What 'bout Nola? Nola think Aggie mad too?"

Nola studied the weathered face—the dark, piercing eyes, the yellowed teeth and dark gums, the sparse brows which furrowed with concern when she'd moaned in pain.

Nola shook her head. "No. No Aggie, I don't think you're mad at all."

Aggie gave a soft chuckle. "Well, you wrong! Aggie mad! Mad like the dark in the night! Mad like the ripple in the river! Mad like the Son who nail pon the cross! Mad just like the Almighty One say Aggie must mad!" She threw back her head and downed the rest of her soup with a noisy gulp. "All of the Lord's people mad! World not our home, you know, so we have to mad to live here 'mongst the sinners! True home in heaven with Mighty One. World 'fraid of us mad people 'cause we know the answers. Mighty One talk to us. When shit a come, pee-pee have to wait!" She flung her head back and cackled up at the foil chimes. "It's the ones who not mad have the problem!"

She cackled again, and this time Nola joined in. They laughed till they had to hold their bellies, bits of green calalloo speckling their teeth.

It was not until she felt the rough shake of her shoulders that Nola realized she'd fallen asleep.

"Near middle night, now. Come. Time! Time!" Aggie whispered.

Nola looked around in confusion and shook her head to clear the foggy daze. The last thing she remembered was Aggie telling her to drink all the soup for strength, then—nothing. Aggie had put something in her soup, sneaky woman that she was! Whatever it was, it was still in her system, for her head felt as if it were floating above her shoulders, like a balloon on a string.

"Put this on," Aggie hissed. "Can't go on bus ride in that wrap-up cloth."

Nola blinked at the pair of faded orange sweat pants and brown leather slippers that the woman held up. Aggie shook the pants at her impatiently. "Make haste! Don't want you to miss taxi!" She pulled Nola forward and roughly tugged at the knot at her back. She sniffed. "'Memba something, them think Aggie head mix up, but Aggie no mix up! Aggie live on street 'cause people can't watch Aggie. People 'fraid of Aggie! So Aggie watch them! Nobody trouble Aggie in this house on road, 'cause nobody want this house on road. Nobody want old cloth on Aggie body. Only Aggie want it. Nobody come with no jealous, jealous over Aggie, nobody envy Aggie … and Aggie no envy nobody! Aggie have eye on village from this spot on road, right in middle of them, and them don't even know that Aggie watchin' them!"

Her fingers moved deftly, unwinding the cloth from Nola's body, then lifting her legs to haul the fabric from beneath her. "'Memba the Son when Him walk on this earth, carry nuttin' but robe on Him back, slippers on Him foot. And to this day, that Man is King, with nuttin' but slippers on Him foot!"

She wagged a finger at Nola's face. "You! You think you sad 'cause you think life bad for you. Cry plenty, cause you think

137

nobody love you, nobody want you. But the Mighty One plan it like that! Mighty One have big plan for you! Him nuh want you here with these sinners, chile." She directed her wagging finger at the doorway. "Them hold you back, make you no hear what Lord voice say, 'cause you only worry 'bout what them think, what them goin' say, what them goin' do! No, no! Lord nuh care what them think! When you go from here, you make sure you listen! Listen good for that voice tell you what to do!"

She gripped Nola's shoulders. "You think Aggie nuh see you? You think Aggie nuh see you walk past? Aggie see you—'fraid of world, 'fraid of village, lookin' to see who watchin' you, hurryin' home before fadda beat you!"

Nola stared in shock at the wizened face. Another face she'd shunned. Another face that had made her see beneath the rat-race that she'd called life, and showed her something worth living beneath it.

"Aggie," she whispered, "I . . . I glad that is you save me from the fire. Nobody else would'a take care of me like you did, Aggie. You . . . you save my life!"

Aggie hmmphed and turned away to fuss with the waist of the sweat pants. "Aggie do it for Lord. Do it for Dahlia!" she mumbled. "Dahlia say, Nola good fren', Aggie, talk to me when everybody else laugh!"

With that she hauled Nola up unto her legs and pulled the sweat pants over them.

The last time Nola had smelled the outdoor air, it had reeked of smoke and death. Now it was sweet. Headily sweet to her nostrils after lying so long beneath the pungent blanket of herbs. Aggie supported her with a wiry arm as they walked down the empty main street.

She could hear the rush of the river, amplified by the heavy silence of the night. Nola looked neither left nor right; not toward the hole-pocked road that marked the way to her home, nor at the purple scarred tree-tops that marked the site where the pink house had once stood. She looked straight ahead as Aggie led her past the familiar track that led to the river, past the Spence's Razzle Dazzle store, past the Redding Secondary gate, past the decapitated bus stop. Her legs buckled, and Aggie ffsshhed as she helped her to sit on a night-chilled rock on the roadside. She spread Grampy's towel like a blanket over Nola's trembling legs. The moon seemed to wink down at them from between the branches of the water-pump trees. Nola stared up at the mellow light, realizing that as exhausted as she felt, it was good to be outside again.

Aggie stood beside her, also staring silently at the sky. Nola was stunned by the sudden sadness that overcame her as she thought of saying 'goodbye' to the woman. They had formed a bond. Aggie had shielded her all this time from a world that would have preferred to see her disintegrate into soot, and then happily bury her teeth. Nola reached out and touched Aggie's arm, running her fingers up the taut coil of tendons till she gripped the elbow. She wanted to ask her to allow her to stay, to allow her to remain hidden in the shack during the day, then walk the streets with her at nights, but she knew it would have been impossible.

Nola heard the crunch of car tyres edging towards them. The bright glare of its lights pierced her lids, her nostrils flared from the combined scents of old gasoline and sweet air freshener. She heard Aggie commanding the driver to switch off the engine before he woke the village, she heard the slam of a door, followed by crunching footsteps approaching the rock. Nola's nostrils flared again as it detected the thick, powdery scent.

"Come, time to leave!" Aggie commanded, giving Nola's shoulder a rough shake.

Nola slowly opened her eyes and stared at Aggie squatting before her. Then her gaze lifted towards the wide shadow standing in front of a battered grey car. The dusky-beige mask was not there. In its place, just dusk. Dusk, with darker freckled spots across the nose and cheeks. Neither were the green-framed glasses on the face, clutched instead in a tight fist by the wide hips. Without them, the eyes seemed so tiny, lost within the roundness of the cheeks.

The person who looked like Slugga waddled up to her and hesitantly touched the top of her head.

"Nola, my child, I'm so sorry ... I didn't realize ..."

Aggie ffsshhed loudly and brushed Slugga's hand away. "Nuh sorry!" she said. "Nuh sorry when Mighty One make plan!" She slapped Nola's knee. "Sometimes when fire bun, everyting turn to ash. Everyting get black and ugly! Ah! You think it no good! But listen, when that ash stay and mix up with the dirt, it make that dirt rich! Good farmer know to wait! Wait for that soil to get rich, and then when he plant, he yield plenty. Plenty yield from that burn up ash!"

Aggie removed something from the cloth wrapped around her waist, releasing the hem that had been caught up to expose her knee. She held up a small roll of pink sateen and pressed it into Nola's hand.

"You take Lord's medicine with you, for life or dead! Just memba, one in the meal will heal, two in the head will dead!"

The car horn blasted and Nola almost dropped the package in fright.

Slugga swirled to face the taxi. "Youngsht mansht," she hissed, "We're picking upsht a very sick person here, and it's going to take some timesht to getsht her in the vehicle. If you wish to earn the goodsht money that I'm paying you, then sit yourself in that car and wait! If notsht, please feel free to go back to Nainsville, and I will find other meansht of getting us where we needsht to go!"

The driver blinked, opened his mouth to speak, then snapped it shut and sank dejectedly back into his seat.

Nola tried to stand, and Aggie immediately began to help her to her feet.

"No, no ..." Nola wheezed, pushing at Aggie's bony chest. "I want ... do this ... by myself. I want walk out of here on my own."

Aggie cackled proudly and slapped her leg with glee. "You see?" She pointed at Slugga. "You see how the Lord workin' a'ready? The girl ready to go! Of course she ready!"

By the time Nola made it to the car, she was breathing like an old truck.

Aggie placed Grampy's towel on her lap, then she put a hand on Nola's cheek. "You ask why Aggie live on street," she whispered. "One time Aggie did love till her heart beat boom, boom when she see that face! Aggie did love, till Aggie never know where Aggie start and where him end! Aggie only joy in life was to make him happy. Aggie do everyting him say. Him say, Aggie, that nose of yours spread out too far when you smile, so Aggie stop smile. Him say, Aggie, that skin of yours get too black in that sun hot, so Aggie stop go outside. Then ... Aggie gone! Him suck up all of Aggie! But the Mighty One have too much tings for Aggie do on this earth for her to disappear! Mighty One take Aggie back! Mighty One lead that man to someone else, someone that have nose that stay straight as a stick when she smile! Mighty One free Aggie before too late!"

"You have to be brave, girlie. Brave to take road alone. I will lead the blind by ways they have not known, along unfamiliar paths I will guide them, I will turn darkness into light before them, and make the rough places smooth!"

Nola grabbed the sap-stained hands on the car door and choked "Thank you, thank you." So, on her last night in Redding, instead of thinking of the mother and sister who'd stayed away, and the father who preferred her dead than alive, Nola thought only of that yellow smile and the pride in those eyes as they waved her away from her home.

CHAPTER 26

WHEN NOLA AND Slugga dismounted from the bus in Half Way Tree, everything seemed to be behind a watery haze, as if a curtain of vapour had been hung over the city. And the crowd! As Nola hustled behind Slugga's rump in between the blaring buses and shouting pedestrians, she felt as if she'd entered the birthplace of all crowds.

Slugga hailed a taxi and ushered Nola into the back as she shouted an address to the driver, and nodded pleasantly as Nola shuffled over so that she could fit beside her. The freckles glimmered on her sweaty face. It was so strange to see this new Slugga—no makeup, no mask, just the freckled brown skin of a regular person. She had shot Nola so many concerned looks on the bus drive from Nainsville that Nola wondered if it really was the headmistress who'd picked her up last night, or some dusky-faced imposter. A few times she had even patted Nola's head, an action which Nola realized was the woman's way of showing concern.

She had remained standing behind Nola as she handed her the mirror to look at her face for the first time since the fire, and she'd held Nola's shoulders firmly when she flinched at the face staring back—the eyes with their patchy eyebrows, the skin, dull and grey, tight across the cheekbones. But, those were not the things that had made Nola lurch away from the reflection. Not even the large mass of cracking scab on the side of her face had shocked her as much as the grin that greeted her. She was smiling. With no effort, with not even the slightest movement of her facial muscles, she was smiling back at herself. The spark that had sailed from the pink house and landed on her face had seared on it, a smile. A smirk.

At first, Nola had shrunk away, then when Slugga had held her in place, she began to shake with laughter. That Dahlia! She tried to explain the humour to Slugga, but she couldn't get the words out for the laughter, that Dahlia had gone and left her with something she'd always claimed that Nola hadn't done enough of. "You know what your problem is Nola Chambers, you don't know how to have fun and enjoy life! Always worryin' 'bout this or that! You need to just laugh! When you feel bad 'bout tings, just make yourself laugh, and watch how you feel better!"

Dahlia had left her with a smile, with just the right amount of sadness and just the right amount of glee.

The taxi finally stopped in front of a two-storey building with an outdoor staircase leading from the garage up to the roof. Nola craned her neck through the taxi window to see where it led.

There were concrete railings around the perimeter of the roof, like some kind of roof verandah.

Nola followed Slugga slowly through the metal gate, holding Grampy's towel close to her chest. Ahead of them was a garage, empty except for a clothesline stretching from one concrete column to the other. Hanging from it were a few white napkins, some tee shirts, and two white merinos. Beneath the clothing Nola could see that there was a closed

144

door marking the entrance into the house, but Slugga ignored it and walked instead along a narrow dirt path at the side.

It was dim in the backyard. Two huge ackee trees blocked out most of the sun. The air was cool and Nola stopped beneath the branches, appreciating the break from the ferocious city heat. She noticed that someone, or some others, had also used the trees as refuge from the heat, for a wooden stool and two plastic chairs had been arranged around a Red Stripe beer bottle bearing a half-burnt coil of mosquito destroyer.

Nola gave an involuntary jump as her eyes focused on the mound beside one of the chairs. It was not a pile of dirt as she'd first thought, but a dog! Its coat was the same dark brown colour as damp soil, and it had fooled her eyes in the dim light. She was about to turn and gallop back to the front of the house when she spotted the chain leading from the animal's neck to one of the tree trunks.

Nola stopped nervously behind Slugga's wide frame as the woman sang from the doorway. "Hallooo! Tiny! Hallooo! Tiny! It's me. Aunt May! I'm here!" Slugga waddled further into the house, still calling for 'Tiny' in that strange, melodious tone.

Nola lingered by the doorway, noting that they were in the kitchen. The smell was overpowering—overripe bananas and spoilt milk. Gingy flies swarmed to meet Nola at the doorway. She fanned them away with Grampy's towel, but Slugga walked unperturbed through the flies, continuing through the kitchen and turning left through another doorway.

"Tiny!" Slugga sang again, her voice echoing cheerily against the walls of the house. "Tiny! Aunty May's here!"

Then suddenly, she stopped. They were in a passageway that curved beneath an indoor staircase and led to another closed door. Beside the door was a young girl, fast asleep in a rocking chair. She couldn't have been more than 17. Her face was plumped with youth, her dark hair so thick on her scalp

145

that it seemed as if she were wearing a cap. Her mouth pouted in a juvenile expression of displeasure, as if she were having not-so-sweet dreams. Slugga watched the girl with a strange half-smile on her face.

Nola stared at Slugga in amazement. She looked as if she were about to explode with love. Her face actually glowed, the freckles beaming like stars on the dusky skin.

This was the sick niece that Slugga had told them about.

Slugga bent over the girl and whispered, "Tiny. Tiny, my darling, wake up! It's Aunty."

At first the girl's lashes fluttered in confusion, then as they focused on Slugga's face they widened with joy. She gave a broken sob as she jumped out of the chair and flung her arms around Slugga's neck.

"Aunty!" was all she said, her voice muffled in Slugga's chest.

"Yes, my dear, Aunty come. No worries, Aunty's here now."

She must have been very sick, for Slugga's voice shook with emotion. It was not until Nola shuffled her weight from one shaky leg to the other that Slugga seemed to remember that she was standing there. She gave Nola a stunned look before lifting the girl's head from her shoulder.

"Nola!" she exclaimed. "Tiny, this is Nola, the young lady I told you about. Nola, this is my niece, Tiny."

The young lady I told you about. Nola wondered what words had pre-empted her arrival. Had she told Tiny of the fire that her papa had started and of the two people who had burned to death? Or had she told her that she'd lived on the sidewalk for the past month, and that she, Slugga, had been forced to take her out of Redding?

Tiny looked up from Slugga's chest and Nola was washed with new shame when she saw the look of shock that marred the girl's face.

"Wha' happen to ..." Tiny whispered.

"Remember, Tiny?" Slugga's voice was soft and coaxing.

"Remember I told you that Nola was in a fire. Tried to save two very good friends of ours."

Nola's head shot up. Two very good friends of ours? Two? She hadn't known that Slugga even knew Merlene Daley, much less to have considered her a friend.

But Slugga just smiled at her shocked look and nodded. "Brave girl, very brave girl," Then she turned again to Tiny. "Nola's going to be staying with us for a while, till she's better to go back home."

The girl tried to smile, but even though her lips moved, her eyes remained stiff with shock.

She was very pretty. Not like Louisa, with her delicate prettiness. This girl's beauty was more brazen—thick, dark eyebrows to match her cap of hair, slightly slanted eyes that hinted at a tinge of Asian heritage, and full, pouty lips which glistened as she licked them to conceal her surprise.

"Aunty," she protested, "Stop tellin' people that my name is Tiny. It's Petra! My name is Petra, you hear!" She gave Nola a firm nod. "Only Aunty call me Tiny," she gave Slugga a playful pinch, her slender fingers sinking into the dough of flesh.

"Tiny!" Slugga cradled her arms and rocked them back and forth as if holding an imaginary baby. "The tiniest thing she was! They brought this squealing little thing out of the hospital room and told me that she was my niece! You sure? I asked them. You sure it's not a rat you picked up off the floor by mistake?"

Petra laughed delightedly and pinched Slugga's arm again.

"Five pounds, two ounces!" Slugga continued, "but the loudest cry you ever heard in all your life! Not even a ten pound baby could have made that much noise!"

"And you, Aunty, look at you! You're not anything near tiny! I thought you tell me that you was goin' to lose some

147

weight. Goin' to stop eatin' all that oxtail and dumplings, and start walkin' for exercise in the evenin's after school."

"Chu man, you don't worry about me! One day when all the rest of you starving, Aunty going to be just fine. Plenty sustenance on my bones to keep me going when everybody else hungry!"

The two of them cackled at Slugga's joke, and Nola smiled hesitantly, wondering again if she'd jumped into the taxi with the wrong person.

Suddenly, the smile faded off Petra's face and her expression became sullen as she looked down at her waist. "I lose everyting except this." She lifted her tee shirt and jiggled a fold of skin that flapped over the waist of her pants.

Nola blinked at the wedge of flesh that the girl jiggled. It looked so out of place on her tiny frame, like she'd strapped a bicycle tire tube up around her waist.

Slugga placed a hand on to the protruding flesh and gave it a little pat. "It will go Tiny, just give it time," she said. "Just give everything time." She gave a heavy sigh and patted Petra's head.

"I'm so sorry I couldn't come sooner, but you know how things happen."

They all stood in silence, staring down at Petra's belly. Beginning to feel a little shaky from a combination of the long trip, her strange surroundings and standing for so long, Nola shifted again from one leg to the other. She was just contemplating whether she should brush past them and collapse in the rocking chair, when Slugga said, "I want to see her. Nola, sit there till I come back, and then I'll show you where you're going to sleep." She pointed at the rocking chair with one hand while she took Petra's elbow with the other.

They went quietly through the door beside the chair, leaving Nola to stumble to the rocker. She looked into the room as they opened the door, but nothing was visible within the darkness. She sank into the chair, folding Grampy's towel on to her lap and trying to keep her mind alert by imagining what the rest of the house must look like.

She leaned forward and peered out the sash window at the end of the passageway. She could see only one of the ackee trees from there, the one on the right that had been closer to the house. She hadn't noticed the grill leaning against its trunk before. There was a bed of calalloo plants behind it, the leaves large and succulent in the coolness of the shade. Someone had obviously spent a lot of time tending the plants. Petra? No, the girl somehow didn't seem that way inclined. Digging in the dirt didn't seem the style of such an exotic looking thing. There were even tracks of a rake in the bared soil beneath the tree, smoothing the area into neat, symmetrical lines.

Suddenly a shuffle at the top of the staircase sent Nola jerking backwards into the rocking chair. Someone was up there!

She stared wildly at the closed door that Slugga had just entered. Should she run in there? Her heart raced at the thought of meeting another Kingstonian without Slugga there to explain the condition of her face.

As the footsteps began descending the staircase, Nola pushed with suddenly strong legs, knocking the rocking chair against the wall behind her. The owner of the footsteps did not seem to notice, continuing down, slow and unhurried. They stopped at the bottom, shuffling around as if searching for something, then they continued again, but much to Nola's relief, they faded away, through the kitchen and out the back door. Nola peered through the sash window, anxious to see who'd come down the stairs. Before she spotted anyone, another sound pulled her attention from the window.

It was the soft mewing of a cat, and it seemed to be coming from the room into which Slugga and Petra had disappeared.

Nola cocked her head closer to the door and listened carefully. The sound escalated, changing from a mew to a downright wail. Nola blinked. That was no cat! That was a baby! A very upset baby!

However, just as fast as the sound had escalated, was as fast as it was muffled, as if something had been quickly put into its mouth. Nola heard Slugga's voice, a gentle murmur behind the door, then Petra's voice, a rushed whisper, then silence once again. Suddenly, the image of the clothesline in the garage rushed back to Nola. Those were no large napkins on the line. They were diapers! Diapers for that baby in the room! Slugga's niece hadn't been sick, after all, she'd simply had a baby! The reason for the bicycle tube around her belly and the bags under her eyes. A baby! Slugga had left Redding to take care of her grand-niece, not her niece!

When the door finally opened, Slugga emerged alone. She waved to Nola to follow her back into the kitchen and took her through the mesh of flies to a door which Nola had not noticed before.

It was beside the fridge, hidden by the cumbersome appliance. Slugga had to turn sideways to get her body through the obstructed doorway.

"This is where you will sleep, Nola." Slugga was still whispering, as if her mind had remained inside the darkened room. "We rent out all the other rooms in the house. Tiny and I will share that room by the stairs. You will use this one." Her eyes stared straight ahead and took a deep breath. "When my brother passed on, it seemed such a shame to waste all this space, so we advertised the rooms, and they filled up before we could even shut the newspaper."

The room was as dark as the one under the stairs, the curtains drawn tight over a single window. When Slugga flung the curtains open, dust particles spiraled agitatedly through the new light, and a sash window similar to the one in the passage revealed her new home. It was a tiny space, with just a single cot against the wall and a warped formica night table.

"Tiny has clothes that you can use till we get you some of your own." Slugga said, fanning the dust from her face. She clicked the latch on the window and gave a hefty pull, lifting the bottom half upward with a resounding crack. A draft of cool, soil-scented air entered the room, sending the dust into another vigorous whorl up to the ceiling. The mixture of ackee, damp earth and plant growth reminded Nola of the hillsides of Macca Hill, when the soil had been plowed and seasoned with seeds and young saplings for a new crop.

"Nola," Slugga continued to stare out of the window, "You've been through a lot, I know … And I know that I've been the cause of most of it. But … I'm not going to go into all of that, now. What's done is done. This is your home for as long as you want to stay." She waved a hand at the little bed, then she turned to face Nola again. "Remember what I told you about that bundle of sticks?"

Nola nodded.

"Well, this is my bundle." Slugga pointed towards the reeking kitchen. "And now you're a part of it."

Nola blinked hard and tried to swallow the wedge of emotion that blocked her throat. It was so hard to adjust to this new Slugga speaking to her in this whispering, gentle tone.

"You need to stop doing that," Slugga said. "When you want to cry, just cry. When the time comes to smile, for the tears to dry up, they will. But you have to get it out Nola. All that pain has to come out, so you can move on." She nodded gently, as if coaxing Nola's tears to come, but Nola just looked down at her feet, blinking vigorously.

They stood there for a while, then Slugga sighed, gave Nola a final pat on her head, and backed precariously out of the door.

The springs creaked in protest as Nola sank wearily onto the bed. She clutched Grampy's towel to her chest and peered out of the window. She could see the dog happily wagging its tail. She leaned forward, curious to see what had miraculously roused it from its slumber, and gasped. A dew angel! Its hair as white as the clouds, its skin as pink as a pomegranate. It was rubbing the dog's head and murmuring softly. As Nola watched in awe, the angel removed something from its pocket and gave it to the dog. Then it unhooked the chain from the tree and Nola heard the click of its tongue as the dog followed it around the side of the house.

Nola sank back against the bed. Was Aggie right, that she would come to Kingston and hear the Mighty One's voice, and be visited by his angels?

She got up and pushed open the door beside the bed. A bathroom. A cubicle with a white plastic curtain around it that Nola supposed was a shower, a toilet and a mirrored medicine chest sitting over a sink the size of a small mixing bowl. Nola stared at her smiling reflection. The scab was almost all gone, the skin beneath shiny and warped, like the wrinkled skin of a dog's underbelly. She traced the shape of the scar with her bald finger. Yes, she was supposed to be here, that was why she'd been given this smile.

Slowly, she covered the mirror with Grampy's towel and went back into the room. She pulled the pillow from beneath the bedspread, dropped it to the ground and lay on it, breathing in the smell of the linoleum floor. Musty and cool. It reminded her of the pungent blanket of Mad Aggie's stall, of the yellow-toothed cackle and soothing chants. Immediately her body began to relax into the hard floor.

CHAPTER 27

ONE CHRISTMAS, A beggar had come to Redding. He had come bearing a tattered, lady's handbag and a dirty sheet of cardboard. He had spread the cardboard on the sidewalk beside the bus stop and made himself a bed on which he slept most mornings. At noon he would parade up and down Calabash Street, palms turned upwards and saying to anyone who turned their eyes in his direction, "Mi hand empty, mi belly empty, a little someting in mi hand will put a little someting in mi belly."

In the evenings, he would pull sheets of white paper and stubby sticks of charcoal from his handbag and would proceed to draw, as if in a daze, till the sun went down. Every time he completed a sketch, he would cock his head to the side to appraise his work before fastening it with thin strips of wire to the fence behind him. Each 'sketch' was just a mass of lines and smudges; some sheets a jumble of shades of black, some intertwining spirals of wispy streaks.

One evening, Nola stood on the other side of the bus stop. She giggled to herself at the way the man leaned back to study his scribbles before adding yet another streak to the smudged chaos. That was when she saw it – a woman, standing with arms outstretched, breasts heaving from her chest like great boulders towards the sky. Nola blinked in surprise, shook her head, and looked again at the sketch, but the man had moved to the fence with the paper, and as he hung it, the image was lost within the smudges.

The beggar disappeared after just two weeks of his sidewalk stay. When he left, the only sign that he had been there were the blackened smudges of his charcoal shavings on the sidewalk.

Nola's memories of Redding were like those smudges. People and experiences in her life that should have been crisp and clear in her memory were hazy and blurred. When the lines became too crisp, when the faces cleared and their voices rang through her memory, her heart began breaking all over again.

Petra did not like Nola, but it did not matter. The curl of the girl's lip, or the narrowing of her eyes when Slugga insisted that Nola call her 'Aunt May', did not matter. Nothing could faze Nola now, for she'd been through worse, and she'd survived, with her sketches, and a grin to show for it.

Aunt May tried to clear the haze; to get it all to matter. She tried to speak to Nola, tried to squeeze her hand and pat her head, but all the woman received for her efforts were stiff hands and blank looks. Nola swore she would never again fall for that trick. Never again would she become attached, to begin to feel that within all the pain, that life did hold some happiness. Never again would she let her guard down.

She sought to fill her time with busy things that allowed no spare room for memories. She was assigned the housecleaning duties, once Petra's job. With the baby, it had become difficult for the girl, so Nola was given the task of cleaning the kitchen and the other common areas like the living room and garage. Aunt May said it was just until the new school term began. Nola had wanted to ask, school? What's the use of school in a life filled with smudges? But she did not say this to Aunt May. Instead, she agreed to help.

She became so busy that soon she forgot the smudged sketches in her mind. Each day she swept the floors, then mopped them till the house reeked of pine. She wiped down the kitchen counters with bleach so that the flies could not find any scraps to pitch on. She wiped the mildew from the cupboards above the counter and packed the washed dishes in them. She hauled the bags of garbage from the drum, tied them shut with the twist-ties, and dragged them out to the gate for the garbage truck to take away. She swept the rug in the living room till its mustard-coloured fibres rose in soft balls and clung to the straw of the broom, and she lifted the cushions from the settee and dusted the lizard mess and cockroach eggs from beneath them. She even learned the bus route to the market, every Thursday grinning her way through the crowds and the meat and vegetable stalls to purchase the items Aunt May needed for the week. At night she collapsed onto the musty comfort of the floor in her room, grateful for the fatigue that sank her limbs into the linoleum, leaving no energy even for dreaming.

Aunt May worked in the house, too, seeing to the bills and preparing meals for which the tenants paid extra in their rent. Nola marveled as the headmistress stood before the stove in her stained apron and her head crowded with curlers, tasting stewed peas from the bubbling pot and clapping her lips with a pondering expression. She would always then add a pinch of salt or a sprig of thyme, her curlers rattling as she nodded with satisfaction at her decision.

Without the dusky-beige mask, Slugga was not really Slugga. In her place was Aunt May, with her freckled skin and her concerned looks, and her fierce protection of Tiny and whatever mewing thing was behind that closed door. Without the mask, Nola was able to see the little quirks that broke free the new persona of 'Aunt May'—Aunt May laughed heartily at jokes, holding her head far back and chuckling till her eyes streamed with mirth, and at the end of the laughter, she would wipe her eyes and announce, "Oh, how I laugh!" Aunt May would rattle out a list of things that had to be done, and at the end of the list she would say, "... and other such delights." Nola, the cesspool truck is coming to suck out the pit today. When they come, tell them to make sure that they drain out everything, and throw in the acid ... and other such delights. Slugga, without her mask, without Redding Secondary, became like a mother hen—to Petra, to the tenants of the house, and to the baby in the room.

The baby! If Nola had not heard the cries and witnessed the piles of soiled diapers that came from the room each day, she would not have believed that a baby existed. The baby was never taken out of the room.

Just once, early one morning, Aunt May and Petra emerged with a bundle of yellow blankets, but they did not stop for Nola to see what was inside as she stirred cornmeal porridge on the stove. They rushed through the front door and into a waiting taxi at the gate, Aunt May mumbling something about the clinic. They returned early afternoon, while Nola had been sweeping dried leaves from the garage, but again they walked quickly past, the blanket cooing happily as it jostled against Aunt May's chest.

It was a 'she'. That much Nola grasped from the dropped words about her formula, or her bottles, or her diapers to be soaked. No name, just her. Even the tenants commented on the mystery of the child.

Only one other person, besides Aunt May and Petra, was allowed into the room. Mrs. Lyndsay, the cotton balled dew angel whose dog was attached to the ackee tree. Mrs. Lyndsay had been the dew angel, the pink and white enigma who'd stunned Nola that first day with her whiteness. Almost completely blind, she was from Connecticut. She had moved to the island with her Jamaican husband 36 years ago. When her husband had died after just seven years of marriage, Mrs. Lyndsay did not have the heart to leave the place where her beloved had been laid to rest, and was now a Jamaican in every way except for her cotton ball colouring.

She had cataracts, thick jelly that covered her eyeballs and made her blue eyes seem as if they were staring up from beneath a thick layer of ice. Her neck stuck forward permanently with the habit of trying to focus, but all that penetrated the film were blended shadows. Thus the dog. Not a useless watch dog as Nola had assumed, but a guide dog.

Anyway, Mrs. Lyndsay was the only other person allowed to go into the room and 'see' Petra's baby. She'd been a nurse in Connecticut, and had even worked as a receptionist in a 'foot doctor's' office in Jamaica for many years before her eyes grew their film. It was through Mrs. Lyndsay's reports that Nola learned that the baby's name was Kendra, and that she was now gripping things and taking them to her mouth. "Love her belly, that little one," Mrs. Lyndsay would laugh, "suck the bottle so hard that she nearly take off the whole nipple!"

"Not healthy, not healthy!" Nathan would exclaim, shaking his rattling old head emphatically. "Baby need fresh air! Can't spend all him days lock up in a room!"

One day Nathan cornered Aunt May as she came down the kitchen steps with a pailful of diapers. "Maysie! I was just tellin' Lynsie here that what you and Petra doin' to that baby is not right! Not right at all! Babies need outside air. You should be takin' him for some early mornin' breeze and some evenin' breeze, make him lungs strong!"

157

Aunt May sighed. "Yes, Nathan, the baby gets the early morning air and other such delights—just that all of you are still sleeping or gone to work, so you wouldn't know!"

Nathan gave a satisfied hhmmphh and gave Mrs. Lyndsay an 'I told you so' look which was wasted on the woman's icy gaze. Then he picked up his rake and set about raking the smoothed dirt around them.

Mrs. Lyndsay coughed. "Nathan! It wasn't you just talkin' 'bout catching asthma from dust?! What you trying to do, kill us all with your damn raking?!"

Nathan was the tender of the garden. He was a gardener by profession, working in homes in the upper St. Andrew area of Jack's Hill, mowing lawns and plowing beds of gardens that he claimed were so big that some required his services twice a week. During the evenings he pottered around Aunt May's backyard, tending lovingly to his personal crops—the rambling pumpkin vines at the side of the house, scotch bonnet pepper plants and gungu pea shrubs. The luscious calalloo plants behind the ackee tree were Nathan's eighteenth batch that had flourished in the man's special mixture of rat-bat and donkey dung. If one wished to see Nathan's leathery forehead become shiny with excitement, they need just ask a question pertaining to the ratio of dung to soil.

Olive, Aunt May's third tenant, was in her early twenties, a curvaceous package of rambunctiousness who was very rarely actually spotted in the house. During the days, the woman was either working or sleeping, the latter being the more probable, and at nights, she toured the town. Olive claimed she was a maid, employed to a 'stocious' hotel in New Kingston, but Nola was never certain how many days of the week the woman went to work. Most evenings did not see her return till the sun winked through the thinning darkness, and most afternoons when her shift was to begin, the woman

158

complained bitterly about a bout of flu that she could not shake, and refused to leave her room.

The only reason Nola was familiar with the hours in which Olive stumbled into the house was because when the woman came home, she could never seem to find her way out of the kitchen. Of course, Nola, being in the room right beside it, was awakened by the holy racket she made in her frantic search for personal belongings. The first time Nola heard the pandemonium, she leapt up from the floor of her room and peered frantically round the fridge to see the strange woman rocking precariously over the cutlery drawer. All its contents were on the ground, and when Olive spotted Nola's alarmed face by the fridge, she loudly accused her of taking her toothbrush out of the drawer and replacing it with knives and forks.

The next time, when the clatter brought Nola racing again to the fridge, she found the woman throwing the broom and mop out of their narrow cupboard and trying to ram her body into the tiny space. This time, when she spotted Nola peeping from the fridge, she accused her of stealing the toilet.

So, from then on, when Nola heard the racket begin, she would race to the kitchen and lead the woman up to her room before she could accuse her of stealing something else. As they stumbled up the staircase together, Nola would have to shush the woman as she sobbed about how much she loved Nola since she was the only person in the house who ever smiled at her.

It was Olive who asked Petra one afternoon where the baby's father was. It was one of those days when Olive had shaken the 'flu' long enough to appear in the kitchen dressed in her pink and white checked uniform.

"You nuh see that the baby drainin' the life outta you, Petra?" she said as she slurped a cup of ginger tea. "Where

Ricky? From that baby born, I don't see him come back here. After is not you make the baby alone! Why him think that is you alone must raise it?"

Petra froze in the middle of loading the sterilizer with bottles. With Petra's back turned to her, Olive had not seen the girl's reaction, and continued the conversation, oblivious to the tension rising thickly in the kitchen.

"Me say, them man round here worthless you see! Every one of them! Them just love breed up the young girls, then them leave them with the pickney to raise while them gone to find another girl to breed! Look how you was a nice, nice girl, Petra – goin' school and everyting, and now you just draw down and mash up like any street dog."

Petra still said nothing, but her lips were tightly pursed and she was ramming the bottles in so roughly that some of them tumbled back out and she had to thrust her hips against the cupboard to catch them.

"Nice, nice girl you was, goin' to school and everyting, draw down now to nothin' because of them nasty man!"

Nola dropped the pot into the sink. "Olive," she said, turning to face the woman, "I thought you say that you had to be at work at two o'clock? Is twenty to two."

Olive sucked her teeth, "What them pay me can't even buy me a pack of Craven A for the week!" But she dumped her cup of tea into the sink and sauntered off, giving a dismissive wave at the doorway.

Nola gave a silent sigh of relief as the clip-clop of the girl's shoes disappeared up the stairs. She sneaked a look at Petra. She was shoving the cover onto the sterilizer, but when Olive's bedroom door slammed upstairs, she stopped and gripped the counter, her knuckles yellow beneath the strain on the taut skin. Then suddenly, she spun to face Nola.

160

Nola blinked with shock at the expression on the girl's face. It was not with shared relief that Petra stared back at her, but blazing anger.

With just two steps, Petra's face was so close to hers that Nola could smell the bitter rage on her breath. "Let me just tell you someting, you smoke-stink country gal!" She practically spat out the words, "I can fight my own battles. I don't need you, or anybody else tryin' to fight them for me, you hear me?!"

Nola was speechless, shocked even more at the tears than of the anger that pooled in Petra's eyes.

"The next time anybody ask me 'bout my private business, you make me answer! Don't feel sorry for me, country gal! I don't need nobody feelin' sorry for me!" Her nostrils flared as she cocked her head to the side, the heat of her breath still rising like a fire into Nola's own nostrils. "You think you better than me just cause I make a mistake? You think you better than me just cause Aunty dig you out of your little country hole and bring you here? Well, lemme tell you something, gal, Aunty know that my mistake not goin' stop me from makin' someting of my life, so you can just get off your high-donkey thinkin' that my aunty love you any more than she love me!" She gave a bitter laugh. "The only reason you is here is 'cause Aunty think that she owe you someting; owe you someting for mekkin' your parents kick you out of your own yard!"

She opened her mouth to say more, but as the tears spilled from her eyes and dripped down her cheeks, she snapped her mouth shut, turned on her heels and marched out of the kitchen, leaving Nola to blink in shock at the empty space in front of her.

CHAPTER 28

NOLA STOOD THERE for a long time, unable to move, unable to register the outburst. By Petra's reaction, anyone would have sworn it was Nola who had spoken out of turn and not Olive. But even more than the girl's inexplicable rage, something else snagged on Nola's mind. It was the way Petra had kept referring to her baby as a 'mistake', and how when she'd said it, her lips had curled with something very close to disgust.

Very soon, Nola understood why.

She was mopping the floor beneath the staircase beside Petra's and Aunt May's shared room when she heard the familiar whimper. At first, she ignored the sound, assuming that Petra was in the room with the baby, but when the cry escalated into its irritated wail, it became clear that the baby had been left unattended. Aunt May was outside with the Jamaica Public Service man checking the electric meter.

Nola dropped the mop and raced to the front door to signal to her.

"Aunt May!" she shouted, "the baby cryin'!"

Aunt May turned to look at her, a frown plastered on her forehead. "What's that, Child?" she asked.

"The baby, she cryin', and I don't see Petra!"

Aunt May nodded. "Run in for her," she said, and turned back to the JPS man.

"Wha'?" Nola asked, taken aback by the flippant instruction.

Aunt May's arm jiggled irritatedly. "Run in for her!" she shouted again, and waved Nola off.

So Nola ran back towards the room where the cries had become such emphatic screaming that they were now punctuated with harsh hiccups. She winced as the sound pierced her ears. The crib was in the corner of the room by the window, on the other side of a double bed laden with unfolded diaper shirts and rompers. Through the rails of the crib, Nola could see a vigorously moving blanket. She rushed to the crib and lifted one end of the squirming cloth. A little foot, stiffened by temper, kicked its reddened toes up at her. Nola hurriedly lifted the other end of the blanket, and gave a startled step backwards.

The face beneath was red with anger and swollen with tears, but so much more distorted than from mere hysteria—the eyes sloped upwards and the tongue hung heavily out of the the full lips, swollen from crying and laying squat and slimy on its chin. The look of fear in the baby's eyes shook Nola loose from the shock that had frozen her, and she hurriedly picked up the stiffened body and cooed gently, holding it tightly against her chest. The baby caught its breath and gave another piercing wail, flailing its tight wrists against Nola's cheeks as she bounced up and down.

She murmured in the calmest voice she could muster, "Don't cry, little baby. It's alright. Don't cry."

The baby hiccupped and whimpered again, but thankfully the screaming stopped, and very soon Nola felt the little head turn and rest its cheek against her shoulder, the tiny fists gripping her blouse as if they would never let go. The little body was

163

still shaking, so Nola pressed her palm behind the fat folds of the neck, trying to assure her that she was safe. The soft down of curls brushed Nola's fingers, and the sweet, baby smell of her wafted around her like a soft cloud. Nola could not explain it, but suddenly her heart felt as if someone had just poured steaming water over it. It melted right there in her chest.

Nola heard hurried steps coming towards the room, followed by Aunt May's panting breaths. "What's the matter with this little one, now?" her cooing voice called from outside the door.

But when she got to the doorway, she froze. "Nola! What are you doing?"

The little head turned towards Aunt May's voice.

"She was cryin'. You told me to run in .... " Nola began to explain, but Aunt May's shaking head stopped her.

The woman looked anxiously back down the passage. "No child, I said that I was coming for her." She walked hastily up to Nola and took the baby out of her arms. "Go! Go back to the mopping."

Coming for her ... Run in for her! Nola had heard wrong. She turned to leave the room quickly, picking up on Aunt May's anxiety, but just as she got to the door, she was met by another set of clicking heels.

Petra said nothing, looking in disbelief from Nola to Aunt May before she pushed roughly past Nola and walked over to Aunt May.

She was dressed up, Nola noticed, her high heels clicking smartly on the tile, her turquoise linen dress belted neatly at the waist and thick hair braided into six tight cornrows. Her lips gleamed beneath pink gloss.

"You let her in here?" Her voice was a hoarse whisper.

Aunt May shifted the baby from one shoulder to the other and patted Petra reassuringly on her head. "It was an accident,

164

Dear. Nola heard the baby screaming and tried to call me. She thought I said to get her."

"Thought you said to get her?" Petra turned a stiff chin to Nola. "You ever see anybody else in this house touch my pickney except Aunty? You ever see me ask anybody in this house for help with my pickney except Aunty? You neva thought Aunty say to get her, you just damn fast! You just wanted to come in here and laugh, don't it? Eh? Who tell you to come? That whore, Olive? Well you can go tell her! You can go tell the whole lot of them 'bout the freak that come out of me. Go on, nuh!" She pointed at the doorway. "Go tell them 'bout the freak!"

"No, no," was all Nola could say, shaking her head vigorously, her eyes racing helplessly from Petra to Aunt May.

"TINY!" All of a sudden, it was 'Slugga' from Redding Secondary School who stood before them. "Tiny!" Slugga rasped again, "don't you ever refer to this child as a freak again! I told you it was an accident! Kendra was crying and Nola only came to help!"

As if on cue, the baby began to cry again. It must have been the crackling tension in the room, the anger in its mother's voice, for it lifted its head from Aunt May's shoulder and wailed as if it were once again trapped beneath the blanket. Aunt May began to bounce just as Nola had done.

"Nola," Aunt May nodded reassuringly at the door, "You can go to your mopping. I soon come."

"NO!"

Nola blinked in shock as Petra grabbed the wailing baby out of Aunt May's arms.

"No!" Petra repeated, "She came to see the freak, so let her see it! How 'bout we show everybody, eh? Might as well, cause she goin' tell them anyway! She goin' tell everybody, and all of them goin' to laugh at me, Aunty!"

"Tiny! You're frightening Kendra! Give her back to me till we all calm down."

But Petra shook her head.

"You know what them say at the home, Aunty? That them don't have no space for a retarded chile, that the home can only take children that have a chance for adoption cause them can't afford to keep them indefinitely! You know what the lady tell me to do? She say I must leave her at the police station!— at night, when no one can see. Leave her right there outside the station so them will have no choice but to find a home for her."

Nola gasped, and Aunt May flashed her hand irritatedly at the door again, indicating that she should leave. But she couldn't move. She stood rooted to the spot.

"No, Tiny, no! Stop that nonsense about a children's home. I told you we can look after Kendra! You and me, we can manage. She's not retarded. She's not a freak. She doesn't need any home but this one!"

"Aunty, you don't see? All her life people like this ... " she jabbed a finger in Nola's direction, ignoring the Kendra's escalating wails as her elbow jarred the baby's back, "goin' sneak to look at her, to laugh, and tease her ... all her life! All her life!"

Suddenly, the baby turned her head and Nola looked straight into her eyes. They were brimming with tears and wide with fright. Something in that look, something familiar in the helplessness of it, jarred Nola so deeply that the words were out of her mouth before she even realized it.

"So what you think, Petra? That givin' her up goin' stop people from laughin'? Or is just that you don't want to be around to deal with it?"

Once again, Petra's blazing eyes were on her, but it was not Petra's eyes that Nola saw. The hatred in them was so strong,

166

so fierce and familiar. Cold, grey flames of hate. Nola did not quiver. The baby's pleading eyes had given rise to an anger of her very own.

"Stop pretendin' that it's 'bout the baby, Petra! You know that it's just yourself you're thinkin' 'bout, and the shame you feel! Look at her," Nola pointed at the baby's head, pecking anxiously at her mother's breast. "All that matter to her is that you love her. It don't matter to her what nobody else think!"

"You want her? You want her? You think that you could deal with a retarded chile better than me?" Petra pushed the screaming baby into Nola's arms, and immediately Nola began to bounce, reassuring the fearful eyes that stared up at her.

Aunt May grabbed the girl by the shoulders. "Tiny, you gone off of your head or what? That's your child! Nola is right, you have to deal with it, and you know that I'm here to help you. I tell you, these things happen all the time, and the children grow up to be strong and independent. They grow up just fine, Tiny, going to school and everything! Kendra is going to be fine!"

Petra was sobbing now. "No, Aunty. " She buried her face in her hands and shook her head dejectedly, "Look at her! Look how she ugly."

Nola's heart cracked. Right down the middle, it cracked. Is that how Mama and Papa had felt about her. We're the same, little Kendra, you and me. Don't worry, I'll be here for you, too.

"Take her!" Petra was shouting at her again. "Take her for everybody to see! Take her in the street and make them laugh, so that she can grow used to it from now!"

"Nobody goin' laugh unless you make them feel there's someting to laugh at, Petra," Nola said quietly.

Aunt May gave Petra's shoulder another little shake "Tiny, you can't lock her up forever. Six months of hiding is enough! Look at Nola, she's not laughing! Everybody will know that it's just one of those things, Tiny, and everybody will love Kendra, just like us!

"Okay, Aunty. Okay then! Time to show my mistake to the world, eh? Time for everybody to see what I been hidin'!"

And with that, Petra grabbed the baby from Nola's arms and clicked out of the bedroom. Aunt May gave Nola a bewildered look before waddling after her.

"Come everybody!" Nola could hear Petra shouting from the kitchen. "Come and see what Petra been hidin'!"

Then she heard Aunt May's voice, "Not like this, Tiny! Tiny, stop this behaviour right now!"

Nola ran after them, just in time to see Petra rush out the kitchen with the baby held out from her chest like a bag of waste. Petra rushed around the side of the house and out the gate, right into the middle of the street. She stopped there, and hoisted the baby high in the air. The baby smiled, liking this new game.

"Come, everybody! Come and see Petra's freak! Come and see the thing that Petra made, the thing that not even its own daddy can bear to look at!"

Nola had overtaken Aunt May's puffing body by the side of the house, and now she stood before Petra in the middle of the road, not knowing what to do next. People were watching – two women by the gate of the house next door, three up at the top of the road by the Rasta's cook shop, and one pair of eyes that peeped through the window of the house opposite them. All had turned to see what the commotion was about, and when the two women by the gate spotted Petra spinning the baby high above her head, they nudged each other and pointed at the unfolding spectacle. The girl jiggled the gurgling baby towards the eyes at the window and shouted, "Miss Myrtle! Miss Myrtle, come see nuh? You keep askin' for the baby. Now you can see it! Come and see Petra's retard!"

168

The two women by the gate, overcome with curiosity, walked over to Aunt May, fanning their faces with excitement.

"What goin' on, Miss May? Petra alright there?" one asked.

Aunt May walked over to Petra and jerked her arms up for the baby. "Tiny! Shamesh on yoush, making a mockery of your own childsh!" she hissed.

A car was coming. Nola heard the rev of the engine, from up at the corner by the Rasta's cook shop, shrieking an obnoxious warning as the vehicle tore at full speed towards them.

"Lawd Jeeesus!" One of the inquisitive women grabbed her head, and hobbled back to the sidewalk. "Unnu don't see that car comin'? Get out the road, May!"

But neither Aunt May nor Petra moved. The driver slammed on his brakes, skidding across the road towards Nola. The gravel sprayed Nola's face as the other inquisitive woman grabbed her and screamed for the mighty Lord to save them all.

The car did not stop, straightening itself with a irritated screech in front of Aunt May's gate, then continuing on its way. The driver stuck his head out of the window and shouted, "Unnu get unnu backside out the road! You ever see car inna hospital yet?"

"Miss May, you and Petra gone mad or what? What you doin' in the middle of the road with that baby?" Miss Myrtle came down to the gate, eyes wide, and her head laden with colourful rollers under a black hairnet.

Aunt May dropped her hands to her sides in defeat. "It's okay, Miss Myrtle. Petra just playing with the baby. We're going inside just now."

"Petra," Aunt May's voice still sounded shaky, but there was a warning edge to it that Nola knew well. "I think you need to get that baby inside the house right now. If not, I'm going to have to call the doctor."

Slowly, Petra lowered the baby; and still cheerful from the treat of being outdoors, the baby gurgled playfully and tried to grab her mother's ear.

"Wha' happen, Maysie? Wha' happenin' to Petra there? Everybody up by Ab say that car nearly lick the two of you down, and Petra down here screamin' like a mad dog with ticks!" It was Nathan, returning from work. He walked up to Aunt May and Petra, squinting as he focused on the baby in the glare of the afternoon light. Nola saw the unmistakable widening of his eyes as he stared at the thick smile on Kendra's face, and she heard the loud whistle of breath as it was expelled from his nostrils.

The man's reaction did not go unnoticed. Petra immediately rested her forehead on Kendra's head and began to sob quietly.

"Come then." Nathan was the one to finally speak. He took the baby from Petra's shaking arms. "Make we get this little one inside before she catch cold in her mole. Night dew soon come down on us out here."

Petra looked up at him with red-rimmed eyes. "You see her, Nathan, you see her?" she whispered.

"Yes, Pet, me see her. Come now. Come off of this street before car lick we down." He walked off with Kendra staring curiously up at his shiny face, her tongue flapping heavily with the walk.

CHAPTER 29

IT TURNED OUT that Aunt May did call the doctor for Petra. While Nola, Mrs. Lyndsay and Nathan waited in the kitchen, the doctor's and Aunt May's murmuring voices could be heard trying to soothe Petra in the bedroom.

Mrs. Lyndsay fed Kendra. The baby sucked contentedly, rivulets of milk drained down her chin, forming a white ring around her neck. They all sat in silence, the baby's sucking noises oddly soothing to their frayed nerves, until Aunt May came heavy-lidded out of the room to see the doctor out and to take Kendra in for bed.

Nola didn't realize how exhausted she was till she collapsed on the floor of her room later that night. Her body felt heavy with the effects of the evening, the baby's distorted face snagging on her brain like a loose thread on a macca bush. She put her head on the pillow and took a deep breath of the comforting musk.

She sighed, remembering the helplessness in Kendra's eyes when her mother had wailed over her head. All she'd wanted to do was to grab her and run away. Run and never stop till they were far from every human being who would ever make that child feel ashamed of who she was; of how she looked.

A quiet knock on the door sent her scrambling up onto the bed. Aunt May's sweat-limped curls poked in, followed by her side-turned body. She nodded at Nola, then went to stand in front of the sash window, peering intently into the darkness.

When she finally spoke, her voice sounded thin. "Down's Syndrome. You know what that is? Mongoloid. Kendra was born like that, and Petra wanted to leave her at the hospital, to just get up one night and leave, so that they couldn't find her to force her to take the baby home. But," Aunt May sighed, "I told her that everything was going to be fine, that I would come and help with the baby and everything was going to be fine. Every morning, every day I have to be coaxing Tiny not to give up on her baby. You know where she went today? To a home, a children's home! She went there to beg them to take Kendra, even though I told her not to, even though I told her that we could manage."

She leaned wearily on the side of the window jamb. "Tiny suffers from depression. Been on medication from she was 13. Of course, you not supposed to get pregnant while on such things, but it took her by surprise when it happened. It took us all by surprise. Anyway, as soon as she found out, she came off. The depression wasn't so bad while she was pregnant, hormones, and other such delights, the doctor said. Some people get better, some get worse, and Tiny was one of the lucky ones. But then, the baby came, and you can see how that would set her off. The doctor said it could have been from the medication, maybe not, maybe it's just one of those things that happen."

Her voice cracked and she cleared her throat, "Anyway, Tiny went back on her medication, and now, she has her good days and her bad days. It's just that when it comes to Kendra she's not so rational. She thinks that everybody's out to get her—to mock her. The doctor told me just to give her time to adjust and she would learn how to deal with it, but … time has to run out some time. If it wasn't you, Nola, then it would have been something else. Tiny's been waiting to explode for some time now."

Nola didn't know what to say. Depression? A beautiful girl like Petra, so loved and adored by everyone, suffering from depression? It just didn't make sense.

"When I saw you holding Kendra in the room today, it felt so good to see that baby getting a little loving. She deserves all the love she can get, if it's not going to come from her own mother, then maybe it's better if it comes from someone else." Aunt May smiled gently. "You musn't feel guilty about today, Nola. Thanks to you, Kendra's free from that room now."

"Remember the bundle of sticks? Well, Kendra is part of it, and she needs all of us to band around her. Alright, bed now. We have a long day tomorrow. Remember, we have that appointment to look at your new school."

New school? Oh God, she'd forgotten that! Aunt May had said she'd registered her to start in September, but who was going to take care of Kendra?

"But …," Nola began to protest, but when Aunt May turned back with those eyebrows pulled high by their strings, she looked away again.

"That's that, then." Aunt May nodded, satisfied, and turned to squeeze herself out of the doorway.

CHAPTER 30

NOLA WATCHED THE woman pull on the cigarette till the tip gleamed red, then ash white as she expelled a puff of smoke. She coughed again, that dry, racking cough that pulled her shoulder blades so far forward that they almost met in the centre of her chest. Eventually she looked at her watch and flicked the cigarette stub into the car park.

She was in charge of the supermarket—the manager. Nola had figured it out because of the way she cussed the workers, especially the young boy who packed the items on the shelves, and the way she smiled widely when any of the richer looking patrons entered the store. Her favourite customer, the one with whom she smiled the most, was a young man who drove a sleek black Honda and always parked right in front of the entrance, right over the 'NO PARKING' words painted on the asphalt. She grinned from ear to ear when he came into the supermarket and never accepted payment for the Wriggley's gum he took from her cage.

The woman sat in the tiny grilled area on the left of the doorway and it was from there she barked her instructions to the employees. The first time Nola walked into the supermarket the woman had scowled at her from the cage, guessing that since Nola was in a school uniform, she wouldn't have had much money to spend.

Save Rite Supermarket the sign read, just as Dahlia had said the name of her parents' supermarket was. But there was no sign of a man with Dahlia's features inside. Nola had even lingered by the door leading into the back storeroom, searching through the cooler bin and pretending to have difficulty with the choice between the processed cheese and cheddar cheese. However, the only people she saw going in and out of the room were the packing boy and an older man with a limp. No handsome, handsome, man as Dahlia had described her papa.

Nola had found the place from memory of Dahlia's proud descriptions—the plaza by the taxi stand in Cross Roads—and there it was, right under the billboard advertising the variety of goods in the little square of shops. It was as if the world went silent when Nola spotted the sign. There it was, the place that Dahlia had spoken of so reverently, where she'd lived happy times with a sober papa and dear Merlene. Nola stood in front of the doors for a long time, imagining carefree Dahlia and smiling Merlene going in and out of them, walking over those same cracked tiles, thinking life so wonderful.

At first, she hadn't even intended to go inside, just to pass by to see if the place had really existed and wasn't one of the 'miracles' that had existed in that dream-happy land of Dahlia's. But when Nola had seen it was all true, she felt a deep need to see the man responsible for chasing those two souls into her life. But he was not there. She went back a week after, and the week after that, and the week after that. He never showed up.

One afternoon, Nola sauntered through the produce section where the shelves held their boxes of yams, plantains, onions and other vegetables.

"What you want?"

She spun around and blinked in shock at the smoking woman standing in front of her.

"What?" Nola stammered.

"You must need someting, cause every minute me see you watchin' me like you give me someting to hold for you!" The woman crossed her arms and studied Nola's shocked face. "You're the schooler who come in here every day and just walk round, nuh? What you want in here?"

"I just waitin' for my mother. She work in the music shop, and she soon finish work, so I just waitin' for her to go home."

The woman placed her hands on her hips, raising her eyebrows slightly.

"She work in the music shop, eh? Which one of them is you mother, Donny or Rupert?"

Nola opened her mouth, then closed it again. Damn!

"Merlene." Nola felt the name slip out of her mouth. It must have been because it was the name always at the forefront of her mind when she came into the supermarket. "My ... my ...mother name is Merlene. She new, just start to work there ...round the back. She mop up at evenin' time."

Nola saw the woman's squint as her arms fell heavily to her sides.

"Is Merlene send you in here?" She hissed into Nola's ear, looking anxiously around.

Nola shook her head quickly, shock gripping her chest at the woman's hysteria.

The woman hissed again, "Why you come then? You mad or someting? You don't know him will kill her. Is fool you fool, or what?"

"No ... she ... I just come to ... "

"What she want? Eh? She get everyting already! Tell her to be happy with what she have and keep her ass quiet!"

176

"No, she don't want nothing. She ... she gone." Nola fanned her hands wildly to emphasize the 'nothing'.

"Good! Tell her to stay where she is! What you comin' in here for, callin' her name like is nothin'? You crazy?" She grabbed Nola's arm and pulled her towards the front of the store. "Tell her don't send you back in here again!"

And with that, she pushed Nola towards the front door and turned to go back into her cage.

Nola left, her body shaking. She was so disoriented that she did not see the person coming in from the other side of the doorway, and only felt the pain of her wrist cracking against a hard, sinewy arm. She grabbed her wrist and looked up to apologize. It was the black Honda man.

"Oy gal, why you don't watch where you goin', man? Look how you dirty up me shoes!"

"Sorry," she stammered, cradling her wrist.

He didn't even look at her, just pulled a hanky from his pocket and sucked his teeth as he bent to rub the tip of his shiny right shoe. Nola stared at the top of his head, at the hair clipped short but curling softly, glistening in the sunlight as if it had been coated in oil. His smell was strong—minty and musky at the same time.

CHAPTER 31

THAT AFTERNOON NOLA'S mind was buzzing too much to face the confusion of the house. Kendra would be demanding a bottle with her hunger-pitched whine; Mrs. Lyndsay would be commenting on how the baby was getting so strong and boisterous; Nathan would be expounding on the miraculous healing powers of the Rockfort Mineral Bath and insisting that Petra take the baby there; Petra would be cussing that he was chatting nonsense, and poor Aunt May would be trying to quell the brewing argument with instructions to everyone to hush so as not to agitate Kendra. No, there was definitely no space in Nola's racing mind for the chaos of Aunt May's kitchen.

She hesitated at the top of the road, pondering a way to sneak past the noisy kitchen and climb in through her bedroom window, when a voice called out.

"Wha'ppen, African Princess, you lookin' lost pon this nice evening here."

It was the Rastafarian who ran the shop at the corner. His locks were such an unusual colour, like bleached cloth. They were wound on top of his head like a roll of rope, tilting precariously to the right with their weight. Once, Nola

178

had heard Papa tell Louisa that to get their locks matted, Rastafarians used cow dung to bind the shafts. When the rasta beckoned for her to come closer, she remained where she was.

Like his locks, his face was also unusual—very wide, with cheekbones that jutted out like handles on a clay jar, parenthesis to the fine, pointed features within them. He reminded Nola of a round plasticine patty, with a finger-pinched nose and pencil drawn lips.

"Wha' mek a beautiful princess like you look like you carryin' the world pon you back, eh?"

Beautiful? Princess? Nola tried not to raise the other side of her mouth into a full blown smile.

"Yeh, you! You look like somebody chasin' behind you with a knife. You don't know sey nobody can trouble you once you live pon this street? You safe, man! Safer than a Bible inna Jah briefcase with Abediah watchin' over you! Abediah know every soul who cross them yah streets. I and I will always watch out for a beautiful princess like you!"

The other side of her lip lifted disobediently to match its frozen half and Nola had to drop her head to hide it.

"Dat's right! Smile, man! The world not dat bad! But don't hide it! Why a princess like you must always a hold her head down? Nah, man! A pretty sistren like you must hold you head up high and let the world bask in your beauty."

Nola's hand flew to her mouth to stifle the giggle.

"Come here, nuh. Come here since you lost, mek Abediah show you someting."

Nola felt her feet moving even as her mind screamed – Thief! Cow dung head! She walked towards the grinning face, the same face she'd turned away from so many times when it had nodded in greeting as she went to and from the bus stop. But this afternoon, her feet took her straight up to the shop window.

He chuckled. "Dat's right, you safe, man. Miss May know Abediah, you know? From before the I and I could walk! Me and Petra grow together, man. Petra is me bonified sistren."

The shop was a tiny square of a building, with a window on one side and a door on the other. All details purely functional. The Rasta and his mother lived in the corner house behind, with gates on both sides of the street so that one entrance was on Palm View Road, and the other on Preston Road. Nola had glimpsed them walking back and forth from the house with the pots of the vegetarian food they cooked and sold in the shop. The mother, also Rastafarian, kept her locks bound in woolen scarves that formed tall, colourful towers on her head.

The shop was a lunch, and sometimes dinner, stop for many residents of the area. Even Petra and Nathan sometimes brought home the sweating cardboard boxes filled with steaming calalloo and whole wheat dumplings, or steamed fish and soft dasheen. Today, Nola could smell fish. She peered in through the window and saw a plate of crisply fried sprat beneath a meshed food cover on which flies pitched hysterically, teased into a frenzy by the scent. Most of the interior of the shop was occupied by a rusted chest freezer with the words, IRISH MOSS, BUILD UP YOUR STRUCTER written crookedly across it. On the wall opposite was a wooden shelf bearing a two-burner hot plate with two large, dented aluminium pots.

"You know what is the right ting for a young princess like you? —The good, good, fish! Yeh, man. Keep your skin pretty. Nuh block up you system like meat! I can see you eat healthy, though. Your structure lookin' good and healthy, man, just like Jah intend." Nola laughed again, feeling suddenly careless. "No meat?" she asked, "But I love stew pork!"

"Sey wha? You eat trenton? Nah man! You jokin'! You musn't put dem tings in your system, man! Trenton is an abomination

180

to Jah! Come, mek Abediah give you someting dat mek you nuh want even look pon dat nastiness again."

He reached above his head and took a paper plate from a shelf and put three of the tiny, fried sprats onto the plate. Then he lifted the cover off a yellow pail and spooned two tablespoons of pickled onions and scotch bonnet peppers on to the fish. The spicy smell made Nola's tastebuds brace beneath a rush of saliva. She took the plate gratefully from Abediah as he gave her a knowing nod.

"Righteous ting for a princess like you!" he grinned.

Nola stared at the mound of onions and fish and swallowed the saliva that streamed into her mouth. "I don't have no money," she whispered.

"Nah, man. Abediah fix dis up for you! Rasta nuh tek back what him give!"

Nola continued staring at the plate. "You have any fork?"

He laughed, his teeth gleaming with fish juice. "Fork? Come, man, a nice African princess like you don't need no fork! Look!" He used three wide fingers to scoop a chunk of flesh and fine bones from his own plate, then dropped it into his mouth with exaggerated flourish.

Nola laughed and immediately imitated the action. The sprat was fried so crisply that the tiny bones were like chips, and Nola was able to chew every delicious morsel and swallow it all in one big gulp. Delicious!

The Rasta gave a pleased chuckle in return. "Yeh, man, good ital food!"

Suddenly, a voice called from behind him. "Ab, Patrick comin' for six bag of coal. Put dem round the front for me, nuh?" The voice was gravelly and coarse.

It was the mother. Nola saw the top of her black and green tam as she peered through the shop door. She blinked in surprise when she spotted Nola.

"Is May chile dat?" she thrust her chin at the window.

"Mams, look pon dis nice young princess who tell me dat she eat pork!"

The woman's turban shook sadly. "Dat's why dis country can't fix, Ab. Everybody doin' tings them own way and not Jah way."

"We goin' fix her though, Mams. See how she love the little sprat there? Nyamming it like is the first meal she eat in days! We goin' fix her up, Mams. Put her pon the right track."

Suddenly the area was overwhelmed with a strong odour – perspiration and engine oil? Nola turned to see two men approaching the shop, their faces and clothing marred with the black stains of grease sealed in with an overlay of sweat. One of them leaned right onto her as he poked his head through the shop window.

"Ab, beg you two spliff quick, Bredda," he called through the window. "Me boss gone to airport to pick up him wife and me takin' a little break before him come back. That boss man love to watch us work, while him just sit in him air condition office all day and give us orders, you see me?"

"But don't you tell me dat him pay you extra for every car you wash, Barry?" Mams asked the man as the Rasta put two rolls of paper into his outstretched hand.

The man called Barry handed one of the rolls to his silent companion. Thankfully, he straightened off of Nola to light a match and suck noisily on his own roll. He leaned back against the shop wall and exhaled a thin stream of pungent smoke, looking Nola up and down with narrowed eyes. He took another draw, then, as he exhaled another stream, he offered her the roll. Nola shook her head and walked quickly to the corner, bowing her head low over her plate.

"Yeh, Mams, so the boss sey. But man have to take a little break every now and again, Bredda, build back him strength, you see me?"

The Rasta laughed. "Build up you strength for what, Star? All you do all day is lay under dat tree!"

Suddenly, Barry's companion began to dance. No music, no singing. Each time he took a long draw of the spliff he would slowly release the smoke from his nose, then do a dip, first with one shoulder, then the other.

"Barry, warn Rat not to bother with dat bad behaviour him put down last week, you nuh! Him bruck up nine beer bottles dat I could'a exchange for good, good money!" Mams wagged a finger through the window.

Barry smiled as his friend sidestepped across the road and back. "Rat cool, Mams. Him just chillin' to the vibe in him head, you see me. Ab should'a know not to leave no bottle on the sidewalk when Rat under him cushungpeng!"

"So what you sey, Princess? You not eatin' no more trenton after dis?" The Rasta asked, nodding at Nola's empty plate.

Barry sucked his teeth. "Ab, stop tell the young jubie rubbish, Bredda! Pork is the sweetest ting to eat! You don't see how her skin smooth and pretty? Is pork do that, you see me?"

"Move from mi shop before Jah strike you with lightning and miss you! Why you think all of the world dyin' from cancer and all kind of disease? Every year a new disease arise and everybody cry out to Jah and askin' Why? Why? You don't see dat is only Rasta live long and healthy? Cause Jah way is the only way, and Jah sey you NOT TO EAT PORK!"

Barry sucked his teeth again and waved away Ab's outburst. "Chu, stop chat nonsense, Bredda, and gimme a Irish mash. Pay you next week, you see me."

"How you goin' pay me next week and you don't do any work? You boss goin' fire you backside when him come back and see dat you don't fix no car since him gone!" But Ab took a plastic bottle of grey liquid from a small fridge beneath the counter and handed it to the man.

183

"My boss can go wey! Him have big house in Beverly Hills while me have to rent one little room in one mash-down house. Every night me sleep on rotten mattress like me is some street dog, you see me."

The Rasta looked over at Nola and shook his head despairingly, his locks rocking emphatically from side to side. "Whose fault it is dat him don't have big house? Nuh him not workin' hard enough to get it?"

Nola didn't answer, but walked instead to throw her plate into the garbage drum.

"Come, y'hear Rat. Make us go back to the slave work before the boss come back and tie us to the tree and whip us for runnin' away!" Barry's voice mimicked Ab. "You see dis informer here, sey him is Rasta, but him is just like everybody else, just want see the Black man work till him drop down and dead, you see me?"

Barry nodded a farewell to Nola and flung his hand dismissively at Ab before he sauntered down Preston Road, while Rat jigged silently beside him.

Abediah sucked his teeth and wagged a finger at Nola. "You see dat bwoy, don't believe none of the rubbish dat him chat! Him just wastin' him life.

Abediah's Ital Food became Nola's regular stop on her way home from school. There Nola met the residents of Palm View Road and those from the neighbouring Preston Road. They all stopped by the shop, some just for a chat to break the distance in their journeys home from work.

Abediah sat within the shop window like the king of the streets, passing out 'spliffs', cold ales, or steaming plates of food. Sometimes he would haul large crocus bags filled with coal from behind the house, packing them into the trunks of waiting vehicles as Mams collected the money and stuffed the bills into the huge front pocket of her apron. The two always shared in the cooking of the meals for the shop, although sometimes they were helped by one of the many 'Empresses' that streamed in and out of Abediah's life. They always came with helpful hands, dark skin glowing and teeth grinning with adoration, and they left with their skin darker with rage and teeth bared in angry snarls.

It was there at Ab's shop that Nola realized that to some, black skin was a glory. To some, it was a sign of beauty. She watched the women as they paraded in and out of Ab's house, some with hips as wide as Aunt May's, some with noses that stretched from cheek to cheek, some with hair so kinky that it curled too tight to grow any longer than a few wary inches from their scalps, and all with skin so dark that it shone like polished steel.

Nola watched in awe as Ab grabbed their waists and pulled them onto his lap, and she pretended not to look when the women flitted their sensuous fingers across the rocky boulders of his shoulders. Nola swore that each new woman would be the one to stay, but none ever did. Not for long, anyway. And no one ever seemed surprised when it was once again just Ab and Mams who carted the pots from the house.

CHAPTER 32

NOLA WAS FAILING everything in school except English. The report showed it—all Ds and Fs, with a C in mathematics. She dropped the report on the kitchen counter, leaving it for Aunt May to sign so that she could return it to the form teacher on Monday morning. She was not there when Aunt May opened it, but she found it lying on her bed when she returned that evening, with a note in Aunt May's precise letters—"You can only achieve if you believe in yourself. Don't leave until I get back home. I need to have a word with you". Nola folded the report and put it in her school bag, then crushed the note and dropped it in the bin beside the toilet. Then she climbed out the bedroom window and made her way back to Abediah's.

It was Friday night, so the corner was more crowded than usual. Everyone welcomed Nola with surprised pleasure that she was back so soon, and Barry asked if she'd finally come to her senses and taken up his offer to be his woman. Nola sucked her teeth but gave a secret smile of pleasure. Barry was lazy and unambitious, but Grampy's saying was true— after your mouth get lace with pepper, you would'a take sugar from a mongrel dog!

Nola took a carrot juice from Mams and told her she'd pay her on Monday when she got her lunch money from Aunt May, who didn't give her the weekly allowance until Monday mornings after all the weekend chores had been completed.

Barry sidled his sweat-stained body beside her on the curb and puckered his lips. Nola stared in disgust at the white foam that had hardened in the corners of his mouth.

"Cho man, Nola," he crooned with a lecherous grin, "mi boss don't pay me this week, you know. Trust me a stout on your bill nuh, and week after next me buy you back someting nice, you see me?"

Nola turned her head to escape the stench of his mouth. "Barry," she said, "me goin' to school, and you is the one with a job, and me must buy you a drink?"

Barry scratched his grease-matted head and frowned. "Cho, what wrong with everybody, man? All them can talk 'bout is work, work, work, you see me! You don't see that is the weekend, man? Time for relaxation and good sensation."

Nola sipped her juice and looked around. "Where Rat tonight?"

Barry sucked his teeth and jiggled his crotch. "Cho, Rat is a joker, man! Say him gone to work for one big car company uptown that sell pure expensive car. Say that him need better pay to look after him five pickney. But hear what, is white people own the company! Imagine that? Rat is a traitor, man, put himself right back in the path of slavery, you see me?"

"Nola, Petra start feed that baby with a spoon yet?" Mams shouted through the shop window. "Is not good for dat chile just'a get milk, milk, milk all the time, you know? Bet you when them start give her some good fish tea you see her start look normal, face straighten out like any paw-paw tree trunk."

"Mi cousin in St. Mary did have a chile like dat, you know, tongue hang down pass him chin! But all mi cousin do is give

187

the baby little ganja tea every mornin' and every evenin'. And she boil up the doctor fish with the eye and guts and everyting in it. By the time dat chile reach one year, him a run up and down normal like every other pickney in the yard, tongue pull back up in him mouth and face pretty like anyting!"

"Mams, not a thing was wrong with Hya baby," Ab laughed. "The baby just born ugly like sin, dat's all, and thanks to Jah merciful grace, him face just get better lookin' the older him get!"

Barry sucked his teeth. "That's why me tell my baby mother them, 'nuh look pon NO ugly face while you breedin' my youth!' Me nuh want no ugly pickney come out and call me Papa, you see me?"

Barry removed a pencil-thin spliff from behind his ear and sucked noisily on it as he held up a match. Then he closed his eyes and took a long draw. Nola watched curiously as the angry set of his jaw slackened with each puff of smoke, till soon a crooked smile crept over his lips again, and his shoulders moved rhythmically to the beat of the reggae. When he eventually opened his eyes, Nola recognized the familiar pink glaze.

Maybe it was the mellowness of the moment. Maybe it was the fact that she needed an escape from her bad report and Aunt May's note. Maybe it was the glaze that had crept over Barry's eyes, the same glaze she'd envied of Aggie, the glaze that had separated the woman from the rest of the world. Maybe it was the longing for that separation. Maybe it was all those things that made Nola take the spliff from Barry's greasy fingers. She took it, put the wet tip to her lips, and took a long draw.

She did not even cough. It was as if the smoke had been the long lost filling for the searing cavity in her chest. At first, it crept into her like a single thread of cobweb, twisting delicately like a sliver of light through her. Then suddenly, the thread swelled, expanding within her head till it crushed everything against the sides of her body, stretching her like a taut balloon. She felt so light, so free, as if just one touch, one tiny prick, could make her explode into smithereens of silver-white sparks.

Nola looked to see if Barry had noticed the swelling of her body, and giggled delightedly when she saw that his head had swollen too. It was floating over hers with that wide grin as he reached to take the spliff from her fingers.

"See how the ting good? Make everyting copasetic, my girl!" He looked thoughtfully at the smoking tip and gave it a proud shake. "Gift from God, this ting. Gift from God, you see me?" Then he handed it to her again.

This time her head did explode, but not into silver-white sparks. It exploded into a whirlwind of colours. They were so beautiful, so stark and clear against the night sky. Nola reached out to catch them, but they flitted away from her fingers. She heard when Abediah asked Barry what was wrong with her, and Barry answered that Nola was irie. Just chillin' to the vibe in her head.

She floated for the rest of the evening—over to the shop window to get a fish tea from Mams, back to the curb for another draw from Barry, back to the window for a stout, back to Barry for a draw, and somewhere within her floating, it hit her—how funny her life had been! Somehow, from within that glaze, she was able to see the humour of it all. And when she told Barry the story, about the witch that lived on the sidewalk, about Papa and his beatings, about the burning of the pink house, he thought it was funny too, and they chortled till they fell off the sidewalk into the stinking gutter.

Later, when she floated home, she didn't climb through her bedroom window. She floated right through the kitchen door where Slugga was waiting over her cup of Milo, and she told her as bold as anything that she wasn't going back to that damn school with its 'risto' girls looking at her funny. She told her to stay out of her life, that she'd done enough damage the first time she'd tried to fix it, and that if it wasn't for her stupid bungle of sticks, Merlene and Dahlia would still be alive. And, furthermore, from then on, she would be calling her 'Slugga', because she wasn't any damn aunty of hers! And when Nola saw the pained look overtake the woman's face, saw the wobbling jaws snap tight, she was in awe of the power that she had discovered. She preened like a child who'd just discovered a secret button on a toy that could make it fly. It was a rush as powerful as the one she'd experienced from the weed, a magnificent surge that shot her ten feet tall, towering her over Slugga's wilting face. It was so pitiful to see the face crumble before her. Fight, nuh! She wanted to shout at Slugga. Fight for yourself, you worthless cow!

Finally! Finally she was free.

CHAPTER 33

THE DAYS MESHED into weeks as Nola stayed away from them all, doing whatever she wanted. She hardly saw Kendra or the other residents of the house, sometimes for so long that when she eventually glimpsed them, they seemed to be just part of the daze of faces that mulled on and around Palm View Road.

She spent most of her time on the curb in front of Abediah's shop, or beneath the tamarind tree in the yard of the garage where Barry worked. Beneath that tree was where Barry took his numerous 'breaks'. Every time his boss, Monty (the mongrel) Spaulding, drove through the gate in his sparkling blue Benz, Barry would scramble up from the cardboard and dive beneath a car, and Nola would, on cue, grab a tool and pass it to his outstretched hand.

It wasn't that often that Barry had to leave his cardboard, for 'the mongrel' hardly left the cool walls of his air conditioned office to face the dusty heat outside, unless it was to go out for one of the lunches that kept him out for most of the afternoons.

Even from within her glaze, it entered Nola's mind that it was quite a miracle that the garage stayed in business. Cars

191

remained parked for weeks in the dusty yard while customers gesticulated angrily at the engines and steering wheels that sat idly in the shade beside Barry.

Truth was, under regular circumstances, Barry would not have been Nola's first choice of companionship. But, that was the beauty of the glaze. Under the glaze, Barry's stench miraculously disappeared, and when her pockets flapped emptily, Nola just followed the man's lead and cheerfully made promises to Ab and Mams to settle her bills 'soon, soon'. Barry became her glazed confidant, whose depth of feeling for her went no further than the depth of her pockets. It suited Nola just fine. She was tired. Tired of paddling around, barely able to keep her head above the choppy water. She didn't have to with Barry—Barry and his hatred of the 'White oppressors'. Barry and his love of ganja.

Even Abediah and Mams smoked. Nola saw them rolling the browned leaves in the squares of paper, then taking long draws, their eyes fading into that tell-tale mellowness as the smoke ribboned through their locks. Abediah explained to Nola that 'collieweed' was good for the brain. He told her that it unblocked vessels, cleansed the bloodstream. But he always frowned when he spoke of those who used smoking as an excuse to behave violently or to be lazy. Nola knew he referred to Barry. She knew Ab was disapproving of the man's ways, but ever since his warning on that day when Nola had first met them both, he never interfered in their 'friendship'. Never interfered except for the comments to no one in particular as she walked past the shop towards the garage—"The fast lane can come to a sudden end round the bend."

As to Slugga, she withdrew her speech. She didn't even look up when Nola crossed her path beneath the ackee trees in the evenings. It was strange, to see this once commanding figure now silenced just by her presence. Truth was, if Nola hadn't been so enthralled by her new-found 'glaze', it may even have seemed a bit sad. But all feelings of regret were quelled by the glaze. Instead, Nola assumed the stance of defiance, eyeing everyone with dismissive glances as she passed them in the backyard. Sometimes the baby, curious despite the disinterested cast of her features, would call "guh, guh" as Nola sauntered past, but Nola refused to focus on the child. Only stubborn Nathan would call out, "Just cut some nice fresh callaloo from the patch today, Girlie. Maysie cook up a nice pot on the stove there. Best callaloo I ever eat in all the years I walk this earth. Have some in there, Girlie. Best callaloo you ever eat!"

Mrs. Lyndsay would then murmur, "That Nola there? But I thought she and that chile Olive move out of the house?"

Petra just wore a smug look of satisfaction, one which deepened every time she saw Slugga turn away from Nola.

The only member of the household that Nola still remained in contact with was Olive. Olive continued coming in late, announcing her arrival with the customary racket. Nola was always wide awake, sometimes smoking a leftover stub of spliff as she stared into the darkness beyond the sash window. At the sounds from the kitchens she would jump up eagerly, desperate to share in the glaze on Olive's face. Most times, Nola would help Olive up the stairs to her room, but sometimes, if the woman's limbs were too saturated with beer to take her any farther than the kitchen, Nola would lead her into her own room and drop her onto the bed, where Olive would fall into a deep, pungent sleep. Nola would lie in her spot on the floor, finally falling asleep too, as Olive's raspy snores coaxed her mind out of the glaze just far enough to remember that shack with its own snoring inhabitant. Sometimes, when Olive moved on the bed and rustled Nola awake, in her half-slumber Nola would think that it was Louisa up there. It was at those times that she would find the floor beneath her face wet.

Along with her attendance at school, Nola's chores ceased. So, therefore, ended her allowance. As such, she was forced to find other means of earning money to pay for her new-found pastime of smoking weed and buying Guiness stouts from Ab. She began running errands for the people in the area. On Tuesday and Saturday evenings she watched Milly, Ruthie's four-year-old daughter, while the woman carried food and laundered clothes to her grandmother in a nursing home. On Fridays, if the garbage truck missed its pick-ups, she would haul bags of pastry scraps and discarded dough from Mattie's bakery to the dumpster at the end of the lane. Some mornings, if Mams was in the mood for company, Nola would sit on her kitchen step and help cut up the carrots, cho-cho and pumpkin for the stews. As payment, Mams would squeeze a couple dollars into her hand, or offer her a plate of food from her aromatic pots.

Life was good. How could it not be when nothing mattered? After a couple of months, Nola even returned to the Save Rite Supermarket. Who was the smoking lady to tell her where she could go and couldn't go?

Nola went when the taxi stand was at its busiest—after lunchtime when the traffic was thick and the crowd of pedestrians swelled like the laden Rio Diablo. The same heat and crowd of Kingston that had at first stunned her now became her blanket. She was able to shove and push her way on the crowded buses like everyone else, haggling with the taxi drivers over fares to go from here to there. She was able to blend into the crowd and watch the supermarket, undauntedly, to search for Dahlia's features coming in and out of its doorway. The smoking woman's words still rang through her head—You don't know him will kill her? The evil creature was still alive! Now it was just a matter of Nola being at the right place, at the right time, to find him.

One day she saw a man walk up to the door, pause for a second, then continue down the walkway and into the fabric store at the corner of the plaza. Nola's heart raced. He was tall and dark, and something in his gait seemed familiar—the carefree way his feet had scraped the sidewalk, each foot turned out slightly as it stomped forward. She'd followed behind such a walk so many times. Nola chased after him, nearly running straight into a taxi as it was moving off. She held up a hand of apology at the curse words which spilled from the window, but continued to run till she was inside the plaza's parking lot. She thought better of passing the supermarket entrance, so she entered through the exit gate. She got as far as the music shop.

The smell of the cologne immediately overpowered her. Shit! Black Honda man! What the hell was he doing on the other side of the plaza! Nola repeated the words the taxi man had just used to her, casting the man an angry look. He stared calmly back at her, a toothpick hanging from the side of his perfectly formed lips.

"Oy, girl, what you doin' runnin' in the plaza? You know you nearly knock me down?" Then he frowned. "Nuh you same one nearly run me over couple weeks ago in the supermarket?

Girl, why you don't look where you goin'? You want me to ban you from this place?"

"Ban who? You don't own the road!" Nola hissed. She tried to pull her arm away, but her rude response had tightened his grip and her arm just pumped helplessly in his hand.

He made a sound that may have been a laugh, but when Nola looked up at him, his eyes reflected no humour. The toothpick bobbed, denting his lip as his eyes narrowed. "Don't own the road, eh?" he said, removing the toothpick and using it to point at something behind Nola's head. "Look good round

195

you, gal! Every ting you see, every piece of concrete in this plaza, every hinge on every door, Me! Me own it!"

Nola blinked up at him as he gently placed the toothpick back into his mouth and flung her arm roughly back at her. "So watch where you walk, or, like I say—mind I have to ban you from my plaza." And with that, he sauntered off, looking neither left nor right as he crossed the parking lot and entered the supermarket doors.

Nola watched him disappear, then slowly turned and walked towards the fabric store.

The man was gone. She looked in every store except the supermarket, peeping in every doorway in case he'd wandered into somewhere else while she'd been so rudely stopped, but there was no sign of him. Her shoulders sagged as she headed back towards the taxi stand. She stopped by the entrance to the plaza, pondering if within her extreme disappointment she felt like battling the crowd on the bus, or whether she should just splurge on a taxi. She didn't see when the black Honda crept up beside her, exiting through the gateway where the sign read, ENTRANCE ONLY. She did not see the car, just felt the blast of cold air as the window was wound down and a voice said, "Oy, Clumsy, get in and I take you where you need to go before you run into my car this time!"

Nola gave a stunned look into the dark interior. The cool air wafted temptingly over her face, soothing the drops of sweat that had burst free in her search for the tall man. What the hell, she thought. What worse could he do after threatenin' to ban her from the plaza?

She repeated her inward shrug, this time so he could see, and bent to open the door. It was locked, and the man made no effort to open it, so Nola had to stick her hand through the open window and pull up the lock herself. She climbed in, the smell of cologne engulfing her again.

It was amazing how the crowd parted like the Red Sea when the vehicle turned out of the plaza, as if its driver commanded control of the bustling throng even outside of the plaza. As Nola sat in the cool breeze of the air conditioning and watched the sweaty, tired faces outside, she remembered the Spences, driving their brand new lime-green truck through the streets of Redding.

"So, where you live?" the man asked, his tone conversational for the first time since he'd addressed her.

Nola mumbled the address of Aunt May's house, sure that his next question would be how to get there, but he did not ask. The car just turned left by the sunglass higglers, right by the Chinese betting shop, and began the drive through the streets that led to Palm View Road. He did not speak again, just chewed on his toothpick and nodded in time to the music. She noticed that his shirt glimmered as his arm moved on the steering wheel, as if it had been spun with silver thread. His hands were slender on the wheel, the fingernails filed perfectly straight across. They were almost like a woman's, except for the fine dusting of dark hair on the backs of the fingers. He wore a ring with a large yellow stone on the middle finger of his right hand, the stone pulsating mesmerizingly as it reflected the red lights from the stereo.

Suddenly, he turned and looked straight into her eyes. The man flicked the toothpick to the other side of his mouth and cocked his chin at her.

"So ... you goin' tell me what you big interest in my little plaza is?"

Nola looked quickly down at her feet, at the toes so wide, the skin so rough with its tell-tale stain from the Redding dirt.

"You don't hear me talkin' to you, girl? I ask you a question. What interest you have with my plaza, why you comin' there to run up and down and knock people over?"

"I ... I just lookin' round, that's all."

The man sniffed as he pulled the toothpick from of his mouth. He wound down his window and flicked it into the street.

"Lookin' round, eh?" He feigned deep thought. "Lookin' round at the chewing gum that stick on to the walls, or the juice boxes and patty paper lyin' in the walkway?" His voice raised a notch with the last word.

Suddenly Nola realized how stupid she'd been to have gotten into the car. She knew nothing about him except that he drove this black car and claimed he owned the plaza. He could be a rapist, or a murderer!

The man gave a dry laugh. "Just chill, man. I not doin' nothin' to you—yet!" He laughed again as Nola shot him a frantic look. "You look like you just see a duppy," he said, then shook his head. "Nah man, Eric cool. Eric cool. Eric nah hurt you. I just want make sure that whoever send you down there know that I on to them, right?"

"Nobody send me. I just lost a friend there, that's all."

"How you can lost a friend? The only way you can lose a friend is if them don't want to be friends with you no more, and that mean them don't want you to find them!"

Nola studied his face as he turned his attention back to the road. It was cool, skin smooth, with a slightly darker haze around the cheeks and chin where he shaved. Smooth like a dark river. Smooth and cold.

"So, Clumsy," he said, "here's what you goin' do for Eric. I want you to do this for me. You see, I have to watch my interests carefully. Believe it or not, plenty people out there might not love Eric." He tapped his chest with his slim fingers. "You know how it is, you can't be nice to everybody, so not everybody goin' love you all the time."

Nola looked out the window.

"That's how business have to run. If you don't know what goin' on round you, then you might as well give up your business! So, anybody who come into my place, I make it my business to know what them come there for, whether to buy tings ... ." He flicked his head mockingly towards her, "... or whether them come to look for lost friends. So here's what you goin' do for me, Clumsy. You goin' check in with Val, my manager, you goin' check in with her every time you set foot in my plaza, and you goin' let her know what time you come, and what time you leave – understand? That way, both of us win. You can look for you friend, and I can know that my interests are safe."

"Check in? What I checkin' in for? I tell you a'ready, nobody send me there. I just lookin'... "

He stepped on the brakes so suddenly that Nola flew straight into the lights on the dashboard.

"Clumsy ... ." His voice was frighteningly quiet. The hairs on Nola's neck prickled with warning. "Clumsy, you not understandin' someting. Eric watch tings. Maybe two, three times, then when Eric see that someting not addin' up, Eric know someting not right! So, like I say, if you want to put your foot back in my place of business, even if is just to stand by the gate and count the pick-pockets, you go in to Val first, and you let her know that you is there, and then after that you can return to the gate. Understand me, Clumsy?"

Nola stared straight ahead. They were at the bottom of Preston Road, four doors from the garage. How far could she get if she opened the door and ran?

Not far. His car looked pretty fast, and he looked like the type who would simply run her over and drive off. Besides, she'd stupidly given him Aunt May's address, so he would know where to find her anyway. She shrugged, "My name is not Clumsy, it's Nola."

He smirked as he pushed the car into gear and began to drive again. "I like 'Clumsy'. Pity your mother neva know what I know 'bout you, so she could'a give you the right name when you were born."

But she did, Nola thought, her cheeks suddenly burning. 'Nola', as in NO-love, NO-beauty, NO-damn luck to end up runnin' into, of all people, the owner of the stupid plaza!

The car turned the corner unto Palm View and drove past Abediah's shop. Nola could see the Rasta hauling two bags of coal from the house. He looked up as the black Honda drove by, and Nola sank low in the seat to prevent having to answer numerous questions later, but thankfully, Ab did not pay attention to the car and quickly turned his concentration back to the bags.

They pulled up in front of Aunt May's gate and Eric nodded at the numbers painted on the post.

"Eighteen Palm View Road," he said, looking straight into her eyes.

She shivered again and quickly turned to open the door, but froze when she spotted Petra walking up the road towards them. Damn! Damn! Damn! NO-damn luck!

She sank back into the seat again, and turned to face Eric. "Thanks for the ride."

He gave that cold, half-smile and shook his head in mock sadness. "Clumsy, Clumsy, Clumsy! Playin' round in big man game and can't manage it." Then he leaned over her and flicked the car door open. "Get out, and remember this—don't play with tings you can't handle!"

Nola turned to leave, almost falling out of the car, right at Petra's feet.

The girl stopped and watched curiously, her eyes going from Nola to the black car with its frosty breath blasting into the street. She said not a word, just crossed her arms and gave Nola a look that said, "So this is what you been doin'? Gallivanting round with men!"

Nola said nothing either, cutting her eyes dismissively at Petra when she stood up. But even in her annoyance, she shut the man's car door with care.

"What a pretty little ting like you doin' walkin' round in this sun hot?"

Nola's mouth fell open before she could catch herself. Eric was out of the car and walking towards them, his eyes unabashedly giving Petra a head to toe assessment. He liked what he saw, for the hand with the yellow stone winked flirtatiously as he offered it.

"Eric McKenzie," he said, and gave a little bow.

A bow? Nola wanted to scoff, but she just scratched her forehead so that her arm could cover her bemused expression.

Petra stared up at him, the smug expression she'd rained on Nola now faltering as she took in the sheer perfection of the man.

And Petra crumbled. Just like that, it was over.

"Petra." She gave a delighted giggle as she put her hand in his.

Eric gave it a little shake, not letting go even after the pumping had stopped.

"Petra," he crooned in a voice as mellow as his radio. "Petra for 'perfectly pretty'. You live near here?" Eric asked.

Petra nodded and pointed at their gatepost. "Right here, with her."

Eric passed a dismissive glance over Nola.

"You want to come inside? I can make some mint tea …"

Nola watched with amused interest as Petra blushed.

Eric flashed his wrist, a gold watch gleaming from beneath the sleeve. "Next time," he said. He smiled again before turning to go back into his car. "Definitely, next time!"

The car skidded off dramatically. Petra and Nola stared as it raced to the bottom of the road. The horn blared obnoxiously as it turned the corner without even slowing down, almost colliding with a car coming from the opposite side of the intersection.

When Petra eventually tore her eyes from the road, she threw Nola a sly glance before she sashayed through the gate.

Nola could not stop thinking of the man's smile. It was the realization that, even with all the sweet words pouring from it, that smile had never once removed the cold glint from his eyes.

CHAPTER 34

THE BLACK HONDA became a regular fixture at the gates of 18 Palm View Road.

Eric McKenzie's sweet words, as perfectly timed as a stunning sunset, swept all off their feet. He reminded Nola of the magician at the church fun day, wielding his wand so that every face turned to stare with unabashed admiration and awed expectation.

But, by far, Nola thought his greatest trick was the one he performed on Slugga. With just one sugary compliment, Eric's magic wand transformed Slugga into a skittish schoolgirl. He brought the woman's hands fanning at her face, and made her cheeks flush as red as otaheiti apples – her cooking was the best; her eyes were so dark and deep that if she'd been 20 years younger he would have drowned in them; her hands were as soft as feathers when their fingers touched as she handed him a frosted glass of ginger beer. Nola was shocked but, admittedly, a little awed by the man's prowess. May 'Slugga' Simpson, crumbling as easy as Petra had? The woman chuckled at the man's easy jokes, tapping his shoulder playfully as if she'd known him for years, flushing coquettishly when she said, "I laugh. Oh, how I laugh!"

There was no denying that for some reason, Eric McKenzie had developed an interest in 18 Palm View Road, an interest which had tucked the serrated weapon within its smooth sheath.

Eric McKenzie knew everything about everyone. Poor Nathan melted the evening that Eric brought him a dome-shaped object to put in his callaloo bed. It supposedly gave off a vibration, undetected by humans, which kept slugs and snails at bay. "Poison-free, trouble-free," Eric announced as he handed the dome to Nathan.

As to Mrs. Lyndsay, she was a goner from the moment Eric sadly mentioned that his mother had passed on five years ago, but had been a nurse all her life. When asked the mother's name, since Mrs. Lyndsay was certain she might have known her, Eric explained that his mother had worked in Montego Bay at the Cornwall Regional Hospital, and no, Mrs. Lyndsay could most definitely not have known her. But no matter, Mrs. Lyndsay was satisfied that Eric had come from good stock, and beamed proudly in the general direction of his voice and scent whenever he was around.

It was as if Eric had researched every single resident in the house. He knew all their interests. No one was exempt from the spell of Eric McKenzie's velvet tongue. No one, that is, except three stubborn souls—Nola, Kendra and Nero.

Nola had already glimpsed the barbed spikes. She'd already seen the bristle hidden beneath that velvet sheath, and she knew that that was all it was—a magician and his tricks.

And, no compliment, no joke, could do anything to endear dog or child to the man.

Whenever Nero spotted Eric's smiling face, the animal would begin a barking that sounded like a persistent dry cough, interrupting the conversation so much that Mrs. Lyndsay would have to take him to the front of the house and tie him to the column.

And Kendra. Poor Kendra. At first Petra hid the child from Eric, keeping her tucked away in the bedroom when he visited. But on that fateful day, when Kendra was finally brought to meet Eric, the child never stopped wailing. From that day on, every time Kendra laid eyes on Eric McKenzie, her head would fall back to release a wail that Nola was certain must have done just as good a job at chasing away the slugs as the vibrating dome. "She just tired," Aunt May would murmur, whisking the baby out of the kitchen lest she chase the man away with her dour demeanor.

It was Mrs. Lyndsay who'd insisted that the baby be brought out. After about Eric's sixth visit, during which the woman repeatedly asked where the little 'boogsie' was and caused Eric to raise curious brows, Petra had had no choice but to reveal her offspring.

Nola was there. "Clumsy," he'd greeted softly, squinting for no one else to see but her. Then he'd been bombarded with questions about the nickname for Nola, and he'd laughingly explained how they'd met when Nola had bumped into him at his supermarket and had subsequently looked so lost that he'd offered to drive her home. His story had been followed by a chorus of "Him so kind!" and "What a genkleman!" and a deep frown from Petra. Nola had wanted to shout at the girl, Open your eyes! You don't see?! You don't see that squint? You busy watchin' me when you should be watchin' him!

"Such a good heart ..." Mrs. Lyndsay had crooned, "... must love children!" And then, "Petra, where's that little boogsie? Bring her out to meet Eric, nuh?"

Petra mumbled something about the baby falling asleep.

"Foolishness!" Nathan had exclaimed. "This time of day Kensey love to come outside and get little afternoon breeze."

So Petra had hesitantly explained to Eric that her daughter was not normal. She'd tried to prepare him for the sight, tried to tell him about the 'Down's Syndrome', but Eric had lifted his hand in protest and told her that any daughter of hers must be perfect. So Petra had retrieved Kendra from her hiding place, and Eric had smiled gently when she returned with the baby, and crooned in his sweet voice that the baby was even prettier than her mother. Tears came to Petra's eyes, and Aunt May nodded her head firmly, as if an important decision had just been made.

Then Kendra started to wail.

After the next couple times of the baby screaming into Eric's face, and Nero howling in unison from the garage, it became clear that there was nothing they could do to stop the hysteria, and her exile was resumed. It was never outrightly stated, that Kendra was being kept away, just that things were immediately found to do with the baby whenever the black car drove up—a bath, or a bottle, or a walk down the road. Eric pretended not to notice the baby's coincidental disappearances upon his arrivals, and persistently asked for her each time. Sometimes he even brought with him a stuffed toy or new dress from the plaza, handing the gifts to the teary-eyed mother.

But he was smug. While everyone else had been enthralled at his crooning smile that afternoon when Kendra had first been brought out, Nola had been the only one who'd watched his eyes. It had been a very subtle movement, and probably would have even been undetected if not for that drive home in his car that day.

When Eric was not pleased, he squinted. Almost an involuntary reaction, a very slight narrowing of the lids, but a movement that was definitely there. And, sure enough, that afternoon when Petra had walked hesitantly towards him with Kendra, Eric had squinted ever so slightly.

One afternoon, while Nola sat on the curb outside Ab's shop with Mattie, sharing a bottle of Dragon Stout, she blinked in confusion at the familiar figures of Eric and Petra walking towards the shop. She handed Mattie the bottle and stood up, thinking they were coming to summon her for something, but they just casually walked up to the window and ordered two stouts from Ab.

Why here?—The place she came to get away from the whole lot of them? Stupid Petra, coming to show off her prize.

She sat back down quickly and grabbed the stout from Mattie. He wouldn't stay anyway, she shrugged to herself. His crisp shirt and shiny shoes didn't go with Ab's décor of cracked sidewalk and piss-stained walls.

But, she was wrong. By the time Barry and Bunty, and Keshawn and Panhead came by, they all fell into position— into the awed circle around Eric McKenzie.

Nola sat on the curb and steamed while Petra beamed beside her prize, nodding sensibly as he told Abediah that he would do better business if he put some tables and chairs on the sidewalk. Ab explained that he had tried over and over, but had been denied the permit that allowed for a restaurant on that street. Eric said he would help him, that he had 'contacts', and Ab handed him two more stouts, 'on the house'.

The next week, four round plastic tables and 16 chairs arrived at Ab's. Mams hurried downtown and bought four yellow plastic tablecloths and four plastic bouquets.

Later that evening, when Eric's car screeched up to the shop, before they could even thank him for the tables and chairs, he unloaded a boom box from the trunk.

"Now you can add some real spice to you place," he told Abediah as he handed the man some cassettes. "Music always make food go down better. People stay longer, buy more drinks." When asked by Ab if repayment could be made in installments, Eric simply brushed him off and said, "We'll work someting out, man."

So 'Abediah's Ital Stop' adopted a different tone. On Fridays music now blared so loudly that the base vibrated Slugga's kitchen. But no one complained. In the beginning, Miss Myrtle's frowning face was brought to the window, but after Eric commissioned a truck to churn globs of black asphalt into the craggy gaps on Palm View and Preston Roads, the head only appeared to beam at the sparkling new road outside her window.

Very soon, strange faces began to appear at Ab's shop—friends of Eric who came to visit him at his new 'hang-out'. Ab and Mams happily increased their supply of drinks and food. Even the garage that Barry worked at began to see a rise in business. Cars of Ab's new patrons were left there for quick washes and tunings while the owners relaxed at Ab. And, with popular requests for 'something sweet' after their meals, Ab asked Mattie to supply him with plantain tarts, sugar buns and rock cakes from the bakery.

It was a good time for everyone. Palm View and Preston Roads were booming, and everyone beamed at Eric as if he was some kind of angel sent from above. And to think, all because of Nola's clumsy collision with such a 'nice, nice' man.

Of all the friends who visited Eric at the Ital Stop, he seemed closest to a younger man named Pedro. From afar, the two even looked like brothers—same smooth, sifted cocoa colouring, same slim build that allowed for clothing to hang gracefully from their shoulders. But, where Eric's features were finely sculpted, Pedro's were thicker. His brow jutted out above his eyes like a shelf, so that the eyes retreated into the shadow of his forehead. Where Eric's eyes made Nola shiver inwardly, Pedro's shaded eyes made her quake in her shoes.

Eric always beckoned for the man to sit beside him, instructing whoever was in that spot, even Petra, to get up.

Nola noticed that as the men sat and sipped their drinks, neither of them ever sat with their backs to the road, always favouring the table closest to the shop window, facing the street and shifting their eyes to the road whenever a vehicle drove by. But, while Eric ate happily of the meals that Ab and Mams prepared, Pedro refused all offerings of food. Instead, he sucked on bottles of hot Dragon Stout, all of which he insisted on opening himself. Pedro also never smoked the ganja from Ab's shop, or from anyone else for that matter. He always pulled his own delicate rolls from his shirt pocket.

CHAPTER 35

THE TWO MEN were afraid of something. Nola could tell that much from their shifting eyes.

She decided to try as best she could to remain part of the laughing, swooning crowd, for she knew that was the only way she could watch them. Let them believe her guard was down, so they would eventually lower their own.

Then the thing she'd been fearing finally happened.

Four or so months after Eric entered their lives, Petra's smile froze on her face. The adoring looks she had once given Eric were replaced with quavering, unsure looks, and instead of nodding proudly when he spoke, Petra looked down at her feet.

It happened so quickly, the switch from adoration to fear, that the others didn't even notice. It must have been Nola's familiarity with the signs that allowed her to see so clearly. Then one afternoon, she saw it in living colour.

She'd been sitting in her room, quietly watching Eric and Petra as they sat beneath the trees. She'd watched as Petra got up and went into the kitchen, and she noticed with weed-glazed amusement how the girl almost ran to complete whatever chore it was she'd been sent to do. Nola had actually giggled, and had to cover her mouth to prevent the laughter from blaring out loudly when she remembered her own anxious run when Papa had instructed her to do something.

Petra had rushed back with a glass of ginger beer, and even beneath the glaze, Nola's laughter quickly died when she saw Eric grab Petra's wrist, twisting her arm till it wound like a piece of rubber behind her back. He hissed against her face, his teeth grazing at her temple, "Don't I tell you to bring the bottle and make me see you open it? You think I want to drink your spit?"

Nola had heard the sob swallowed in Petra's throat as she'd said, "Eric. You know I wouldn't do that."

But Eric had just sucked his teeth and dropped the glass of ginger beer at her feet. "No," he'd said, "I don't know that. All of you bitches is the same!" And then he'd left.

Nola saw Petra look anxiously into the kitchen to check if anyone had seen the exchange, then cover her face with her hands. No, Petra. I can tell you that you're not dreamin'. When you tek down your hands, everyting goin' still be the same!

Then Petra picked up the glass and walked slowly into the kitchen.

After that, Nola spent more and more time stooped by her bedroom window, listening to the exchanges outside. Eric was always different when Slugga or Mrs. Lyndsay were around—easygoing and pleasant, but the monster always emerged when he was alone with Petra.

Soon, it began to affect Petra's everyday chores. Once, she emptied salt on Kendra's diapers instead of detergent. Another time she forgot Kendra's porridge on the stove, and by the time Slugga walked in, it had become a black, smoking mass caked to the pot.

Slugga frowned at the girl's distraction, but thinking this was another of Petra's depressive episodes, upped her medication.

Nola pondered telling Slugga what she'd seen, but she knew she would think it was just one of her weed-induced rants. Besides, Petra had made it clear she wanted Nola to stay out of her business, and who would believe Nola's glazed tale over Eric's velvet-sheathed one anyway?

It turned out that she didn't have to. One afternoon, the barbs on Eric McKenzie's tongue wore through their velvet sheath. It was the day that Petra walked into the kitchen and announced that Kendra was to be placed in a children's home.

"Tiny, what you talking about?" Slugga croaked. "We're managing so well with Kendra. I thought we decided not to bring up that home thing again since she was coming on so nicely?"

Petra shook her head, her smile firmly in place. "Auntie, it's already decided. Eric know someone who work in Liguanea at a nice children's home. Them say them have space for one more, and Eric say them tek good care of the children there, really love them and everyting. Even the ones like ... Kendra."

"Stop chat nonsense, Pet!" Nathan exclaimed, dropping his bowl of gungu pods on the counter with a loud 'clank'. "When them say it take a village to raise a chile, them mean your own village, not a stranger's own!"

"Look, I know everybody love Kendra, but I am her mother, and I know the best ting for her. Eric say that children like Kendra do better with people who know 'bout those kinds of tings. None of us know anyting 'bout it, Auntie. Memba the doctor say that she goin' to need plenty help to live a normal life."

"Love, Tiny! Plenty love, that's what the doctor said! And we give her that every day! She's a happy little girl." Slugga's voice broke.

Petra shook her head firmly, but Nola could see that the smile faltered. "She still a baby now, Auntie. What 'bout when she have to start school? What happen when all the children start laugh at her?"

"Don't start that again, Tiny! No one is going to laugh at Kendra any more than they laugh at the rest of us. No one can escape that, Tiny. Look at me. You think no one has ever laughed at me? All the time! Right, Mrs. Lyndsay? What about you? Don't people laugh at you?"

Mrs. Lyndsay nodded emphatically.

Nathan gave a honk of laughter. "Yes bwoy, and me? You memba the time when I work all day bendin' over the garden bed them, and when me done work me jump on the bus to come home and me notice people lookin' at me strange the whole way? Is not till me reach the front gate of the yard that Miss Myrtle call out and tell me that my pants tear right out, and you could'a see all an' sundry underneath! 'Memba that day, Pet?"

Nola cleared her throat. She had so many stories about being laughed at that she didn't know where to start, but when they all turned to look at her, she found that the words could not leave her lips. Slugga's eyes were so shiny with pain that they made her heart quake. They begged for help, even from her.

Nola cleared her throat again, "Petra," she finally whispered, "I know the two of us neva really see eye to eye, but trust me when I tell you that somebody laughin' at Kendra is not the worst thing in the world that can happen to her. Her own family. Her own mother not wantin' her is worse than that."

At first Nola thought she'd reached the girl. At first she just stood there, blinking erratically as if absorbing Nola's words.

But suddenly, she took a step forward, and her voice shook with rage. "Don't talk to me 'bout nothin' to do with my pickney, you lazy, good-for-nuttin' weed-head!" she ranted. "You think Eric don't tell me 'bout you? You think Eric don't tell me how you is a good for nothin' thief! How him had to take you home that day in the plaza cause you was lookin' for something to steal!"

213

There was a collective gasp. Through the corner of her eye, Nola saw Slugga's head fall. It was something in that movement, something in that defeated action, that triggered something deep in Nola. It was as if her heart shifted from one side of her chest to the other, causing a wrenching pain. Even in Kingston, she'd given someone Mama's look.

Nola took a deep breath and moved towards Petra. "Since Eric know so much, why you don't ask him why it's so important to him for Kendra to go into a home? Him not around her, him don't spend no time with her to know what kind of treatment she need? Why is it so important to Eric that Kendra go into a home, Petra?"

Petra blinked again, and for a split second, her aggressive frown slackened with confusion, but it was only for an instant. She also took a step forward, her face drawing close to Nola's, her lips baring back to reveal clenched teeth. "Why you don't mind you own business, stinkin' country gal?"

Nola forced herself to take one more step, and this time their noses brushed. "No, Petra, why you don't mind your business? Is you bring Kendra into this world, and you have people to help you with her, and you still want to send her away. For what? A man?" She cocked her head to match Petra's stance, "... I suppose that is what you did mean when you sey you wasn't goin' to make your mistake stop you from makin' someting of your life!"

She felt, rather than saw, when Petra raised a fist, but she did not step away. She continued staring into the girl's eyes, just as she'd done in another kitchen with another attacking dog. Petra's fist dropped heavily back to her side and she whirled to face Slugga.

"You see what happen when you bring dutty dog into your house? It fill it up with shit!"

214

Slugga nodded slowly. Her cheeks were wet. "And that shit is the truth, Tiny."

Petra let out a defeated sob and covered her face with her hands. "All of you turnin' on me and it's not for me to decide! Eric ask me if I was sure, and I say 'yes', and him say once him commit to the space we have to take it or them goin' charge him money for holdin' it."

"Rubbish, Pet! Rubbish, Rubbish!" Nathan threw his hands into the air again. "Is your pickney! Nobody can charge you money if you decide you want keep your own pickney!"

Mrs. Lyndsay shuffled forward and reached towards Petra's voice, "We'll talk to Eric, Chile. Don't worry 'bout a thing. You just go hug up you little boogsie."

Petra went to the baby.

Nathan and Aunt May stood silently. Nola could not look at them, only at the safe blankness of Mrs. Lyndsay's widened eyes.

She was so ashamed. She knew that her own behaviour had caused those same looks. She'd hurt them too, and worst of all, she'd been the one to bring Eric McKenzie into their lives. How could she have stepped aside and allowed Eric to cast his spell over them when she'd known the truth all along? They must have been thinking, What a nerve! Who this gal to talk to Petra 'bout not minding her business, when her own business gone to shit?

Nola knew they were thinking it, because she felt them not looking at her. She felt them bristling from her past hostility and her rare presence in the kitchen.

Nathan was the first to move, storming out the door and towards his callaloo bed. He emerged with the slug-chaser and, with all his might, he flung the dome across the yard.

CHAPTER 36

I T WAS THAT very evening, when he came to pick up Petra, that 'we'll talk to Eric' happened. This time, when he squinted, everyone saw.

He squinted down at Aunt May, his toothpick bobbing as she told him that Petra had changed her mind about the children's home, and she would gladly refund him any money he would lose because of her niece's confusion. He smiled his beautiful, perfect smile, picked up a banana from the basket, peeled it, and after he had bitten it, he drawled, "Since is never you born the baby, Lady, I don't think you have any right to decide what to do with her. The baby mother tell me she want her chile in a home, and that's exactly where she goin'!"

Aunt May blinked in shock, Nathan blinked in shock, even Mrs. Lyndsay blinked in shock.

Aunt May cleared her throat and tried again. "Eric, I don't think you understand. What I'm telling you is that Petra did say that she would put Kendra in the home, but she's changed her mind, and the baby will be staying with us."

"Us? Who is us?" Eric looked around the kitchen curiously, chewing nonchalantly on the banana. "Us? Tell me, Lady, is that what you goin' to tell the judge? That us goin' look after a special needs chile? Us being a mad-ass gardener who talk to leaves, and a blind woman who can't tell if she feedin' a cat or a rat, and a fat ole woman who soon dead from heart attack? What you think the judge goin' say to that, Fatta? That you is a the perfect role model for the baby when you have a teenage girl in your charge who drop out of school and smoke weed all day?"

Oh God! Nola felt the room drop from under her feet. Oh God! They were going to lose Kendra, and all because of her! Oh God! She grabbed on to the counter as Eric smiled and gave her a wink.

"Nah! Nah! It can't go so! Who the hell you think you is to come in here and tell us wha' to do with our Kensey?!" It was Nathan, rushing from the kitchen door with his hands waving emphatically through the air.

"No, Nathan! No need for that!" Aunt May held up a hand. She stepped towards Eric and looked up at him with unflinching eyes. "Yes, Eric, call us anything you wish, but the fact remains that before you allow Kendra to leave this house, you're going to have to go through that same mad-ass gardener, that same blind woman, and this fat ole woman! Kendra is ours, and judge or no judge, she's staying here."

Eric chuckled and dropped the banana peel on to the floor. "Fatta, you swimmin' in water that too deep for you, man. What you don't seem to understand is that Petra and I linking up as in man and wife! As in mama and papa! That's right. Kendra goin' finally have a daddy, and this daddy happen to know exactly what's best for his little girl. My wife-to-be and I discuss this already, and we decide that a children's home is the best place for our little 'boogsie'." He laughed softly.

"Getsh outsht! Getsh outsht of my houshht!"

But Eric just sneered. "Your house? No, no Fatta! Not your house. This is Petra father's house, that him leave to Petra." Eric laughed again as Aunt May's mouth snapped shut in shock.

"Which remind me, thank you very much for remindin' me." He bowed graciously at Aunt May, "I think all of you better start lookin' for a place to live, since Petra and I have other plans for this house. From what I been sussin' out, I can see that this area in need of a proper nightclub, not that Rastafari shit up the road, but a nice club that decent people can go to. Who can tell," he pointed at Nola with his car key, "maybe we will even have some use for you, Clumsy. Put you in a little sexy skirt, make you show off them nice titties."

Nola's hands flew up to cover her chest and Nathan screamed. Nathan uttered a high pitched wail and flung his whole body at Eric.

But Eric had been waiting, and when his elbow cracked up into Nathan's face, the horrendous sound of ripping skin and bursting cartilage resounded through the house. The sound brought Petra running from the room where Aunt May had told her to stay while they spoke to Eric. She stood at the doorway with wide eyes, holding Kendra tightly against her chest. When she saw Nathan lying on the floor, with the blood pouring from his face, she buried her head in the baby's neck and released a stifled sob.

Aunt May shouted for someone to get ice out of the freezer as she dropped to the ground and cradled Nathan's head.

Mrs. Lyndsay froze, "What him do, May? What him do to Nathan?"

And within all the cries and moaning, Eric simply jingled his keys at Petra and said, "Get your things. I don't want you stayn' here till we sort out the business of this house. Get your clothes, and make sure you don't bring that thing with you."

That thing! Even with the shock of the night still numbing her body, Nola felt the rage rise into her chest. She wanted to race after him and knock him senseless with the dutchie pot! She could take a lick from him, she'd taken them from her own papa, and she knew she could take one from Eric McKenzie, even for the satisfaction of seeing the blood spew from his glossy curls! She looked around the kitchen for something, anything—the dutchie pot or a rolling pin, and that was when she saw it—the machete! She saw it! Right there on the rafter in Ellie's pen. She saw it up above her head, she saw herself pulling the stool beneath the rafter to reach it, felt the hate bubbling in her chest as she'd imagined the stained blade ending Papa—ending her misery forever.

She grabbed her mouth, willing the sudden surge of bile to stay down. Aunt May looked up from sopping Nathan's nose, the woman's eyes brimmed with tears, but even through the moisture, Nola could see the clear message—Don't do it! Let him leave!

She knew! Aunt May knew! She knew that she'd tried to kill her papa. They'd all known! No wonder they'd tied her up. No wonder they hadn't wanted her in their village. No wonder Mama hadn't come to say goodbye. Only Aunt May had taken her. Aunt May and Aggie. Dear God, how could she not have remembered?

Petra came back into the kitchen with a bag clutched to her chest, her eyes refusing to look down at the squirming Nathan. She looked neither at Nola nor Aunt May, but turned instead to face Mrs. Lyndsay's milky gaze, and said, "Miss Lyndsay, I leave Kendra in the crib. She ready to sleep, just check her and see if she ... ." She took a shaky breath, "Check on her in a while and see if she okay for me?" And with that, she was gone.

They quietly dressed Nathan's nose. Nola boiled some pimento and placed a poultice on the grotesquely twisted face, but the bruise was uncontrollable, creeping its purple stain from beneath the eyes right down to the chin.

* * *

Everyone was shocked. Eric? Their knight in shining armour! Surely there had been some misunderstanding! Nola was certain that if they had not seen Nathan's distorted face for themselves, they would not have believed the story. It was not until after taking a tub of chickpea soup for Nathan that Mams believed, and after confirming the man's injuries to Ab, the tables and chairs from the sidewalk were promptly packed up and stacked beside the light post.

It had only been Nola, Mattie and Barry on the sidewalk when Ab had angrily thrown the chairs one on top of the other, and while the women had clapped and cheered, Barry had not. Just short of the time that Barry had sauntered back down to the garage, the black Honda screeched to a stop in front of the cook shop. It was midafternoon, not a time Eric usually stopped by.

Eric exited the vehicle slowly, despite his hurried arrival, and sauntered towards the shop, not even so much as glancing in the direction of the lopsided stack of chairs. He had Necka with him, the skinny boy who always plaited his three-inch beard into a thin, ridiculous looking rat tail of a braid. He was not one of Eric's regular companions.

Eric pulled himself up onto the freezer beside Ab's stool, resting his elbow casually on his raised knee.

Necka leaned his lanky frame beside the window.

"Not so happy today, Ab?" Nola heard Eric ask.

"I and I don't like what you do to my brethren the other night, man. We don't live like dat pon dis road, Star. We look after each other. We live in peace pon dis road, my youth."

Eric chuckled, a quiet, humorous sound. "But who say we can't live good? We can live good, but if the man rush me, what you want me to do? You don't expec' me to defend myself, man?"

220

"Where Petra?!" Ab shouted. "Why you take her from her pickney? "

Eric plucked the toothpick from his mouth and leaned forward. "Tell you what. You see how you and you mother live, and you mek your plans each day, 'bout what you goin' to cook, and when you goin' to eat, and when you goin' to sleep? You see how you do all that and nobody say to you, No Ab, me don't think that you should eat right now, or me don't think that you should sleep right now? Well, the same way that nobody not interfering with your business is the same way nobody not to interfere with mine!" He plopped the toothpick back into his mouth and cocked his head towards the window. "Speakin' of business, I notice that my chairs pack up outside."

Ab nodded his head slowly. "Just like you sey, boss, dis is my business, and right now, I and I not interested in havin' no more tables and chairs in my business."

Eric laughed again, but this time, there was no humour in it. He looked over at Necka who grinned cheerily back through the window.

"Necka, tell me what you think 'bout this Rasta here. You think him understand anyting 'bout business?"

Necka chuckled. "Nah, man, him don't know a ting 'bout business!"

Eric leaned closer to Ab and nodded again at the window. "Let me tell you 'bout business, Rasta. You see that permit, and those tables that you say you don't want no more? Them cost money! Money that you don't start pay back yet. Every penny that you make when everybody did sit off in them chairs— every penny that you make was because of me!" He laughed that mirthless laugh again. "Now, what we goin' to do now is get our business sorted out. You owe me a lot of money, and as of now, you goin' start payin' me back each week till I tell you when you finish pay!"

But Ab was not giving up. "It don't work so, Star!" His locks rocked emphatically. "Tek your chairs and sell them back, man. Me will pay you for your permit!"

Eric shook his head with mock display of sadness and jumped off the freezer. He gave Necka a calm flick of his hand, and the boy immediately gave Mattie an apologetic nod and walked around to the shop door.

It wasn't until Nola saw the glint of sunlight relecting off the boy's hand that she realized what was about to enfold, right there … right in front of herself and Mattie. She tried to scream a warning to Ab, but as she opened her mouth, she heard Mattie's wail of "Murder! Murder!" and saw the woman racing towards the house, her breasts shimmying as she waved her arms.

Nola could not move. She remained staring at the shop window even as the glint sliced through the air. Suddenly, her head spun towards the sidewalk even as one part of her brain screamed for her to stay alert.

CHAPTER 37

S HE TRIED TO move from beneath the stifling overlay, but her
head was too heavy. The thing was holding her down. A
gasp wheezed from her chest and she managed to tear her
eyes open, her heart pounding with relief when she saw that it
was just a fan beside her, blowing hot waves into her nostrils.
Slowly, she pushed herself up unto her arms and cautiously
looked around.

She was in Ab's and Mams' house, lying on the settee in
the living room. She reached up and felt her head. Throbbing!
The weight she'd felt was a thick bandage, fastened carefully
over a spot on the side of her forehead. She remembered now.
She'd fainted and fallen on to the sidewalk when Necka had
… Necka … knife! … Ab! She scrambled off the settee and
raced through the front door.

Everyone was out there. They all surrounded Mams, and
they spoke in hushed tones as the woman rocked back and
forth on a chair. Her tam was gone and her locks tumbled
freely around her shoulders. Even Aunt May was there,
perched precariously on the tree stump on which Mams
chopped the wood for coal, patting Mam's shoulder and
shaking her own head in disbelief. Nola's heart pulsed at

the look on their faces. Those grimaces that she recognized immediately—Pain. Terror. Defeat.

"Where is he?" Nola managed to squawk from the doorway. "What them do with Ab?"

Mams looked up from her chair. Her locks were dark, not bronzed like her son's, but peppered with white. Their marbled lengths tumbled way past her waist, pooling in her lap as she sat. When she spotted Nola, she beat her chest with both hands, and wailed "Me lion! Me young lion!"

Aunt May waddled over to Nola and took her hand. Nola looked down at the dimpled fingers. "What them do with him?" she whispered.

"He's in the shop, Nola, but... don't ... ."

Too late. She was already running. They shouted for her to stop, but the hysteria in their voices made her run even faster. She had to see him.

He was still in there, his torso hunched over the freezer, his head on his arm as if he was merely resting.

Nola grabbed her chest. She didn't know if it was the relief of seeing Ab's chest moving with the passage of air, or the shock of seeing his head shorn of its locks that sent her head spinning into a faint once again. She grabbed the door jamb to stop herself from falling, and the movement made Ab look up.

There was still the rust of dried blood around his nostrils, and a red slit above his right eye, but he looked nothing as bad as Nathan. What struck Nola more than anything else was how youthful his face looked without the heavy locks around it. Youthful, and so ... vulnerable. The chopped hair left on his scalp was almost two shades darker than the sun-bleached locks that had once covered it, making the man before her seem like a stranger. His eyes were the only familiar thing staring back at her, those soulful eyes that had warmed her that day when he'd offered her his fried sprat. They rested

224

now on Nola's own bandaged forehead, and she saw them pulse with something unrecognizable before he lowered his head once again.

"I tell them nobody must come in here right now!" his muffled voice said.

Nola leaned against the door jamb, her legs made even weaker with the relief of hearing his voice.

"I wanted to see if you was alright," she said.

His shoulders shook slightly. "Alright? I and I not alright, man. Them tek away my glory. Better them did just kill me, Rasta."

Nola straightened from the door jamb. There it was again—that word—Glory! The word that culminated the suffering, the pain of life. She felt a pulse of anger as she stared at Ab's bent head. Even this calm, easy-going Rasta, who'd seemed so—untouchable, 'the watchman and protector of the street', had fallen under the pain of trashed glory. How she hated that word!

"Better?" she asked, wondering at the anger that cast the relief aside. "Better them kill you? And what 'bout Mams?! What she would' a do if them did kill you?"

"What she goin' do now that them neva kill me? Pay them back for the rest of her life—for some plastic chair and table?!" He sucked his teeth. "You know say Rasta don't tek nothin' from nobody? Rasta suppose to know better than dat. Rasta work hard for everyting him have. But I and I fall for the tricks, man! I and I fall for the tricks and now them actin' like them own the Rasta!"

"All of us fall for the tricks, Ab. Everybody." She sighed, shaking her head in disbelief. "So what we goin' do now?"

Finally Ab stood, and Nola flinched when she saw that Necka had left two of the long locks to hang comically down his right shoulder. He looked like a mangled spider.

"What we goin' do now?" he repeated her question on the expelled breath of a sigh. "I and I have nowhere to go,

225

Princess. This here is what Jah gimme." He looked around the little shop and sighed again. "What we goin' do now is pay for the permit, and the tables, and the chairs, till the betrayer sey dat we done pay. Live we life best as we can in the meantime."

"No, Ab! We have to call the police! We have to make them lock up Eric and keep him away! What him doin' isn't right!"

"Princess, you nah talk sense, man. Man like Eric McKenzie have the police in them back pocket. Police nah help Rasta over sweet boy like dat."

"So what if him never say that you finish pay, Ab? What we do then? Pay him back for the rest of your life, like you say?"

Ab took a deep breath, then bent to pick up his tam from the ground. He studied it for a while before he pulled it over his hacked locks. "Tell Mams to start the cookin'" he said over his shoulder, "Enough time waste already, and the evenin' crowd soon come down pon us."

Nola stared disbelievingly as he poured a puddle of bleach on to the freezer and began wiping it down. Eventually she turned to leave, but then she heard his voice, ever so quietly, "Princess ... 'memba what I sey—Rasta don't defend violence. Rasta leave justice up to Jah. Trust me, Princess, Jah will look after the whole of us, watch and see. Leave people like Eric and Necka and Barry up to Jah. All you can do for me, Princess, is keep your heart clean. When time come to face Jah, I and I don't want know sey your heart nuh righteous 'cause of me."

Nola nodded, and turned to leave, but something caught her eye and stopped her in her tracks. Ab's prized locks. His bronzed glory, tied into a rough bundle and nailed above the door jamb like a bouquet of drying herbs. Nola stifled a sob and turned to face him again.

He didn't look up, just continued to wipe the freezer and said, "Leave it to Jah."

CHAPTER 38

LIKE SCOLDED CHILDREN, they replaced the tables and chairs. As promised by Eric, Necka was there at the end of the week to collect the first installment of his 'repayment'. As it turned out, Necka collected payment that week not just from Ab, but from every other business that Eric had been 'helping'—from the bakery, as repayment for a small generator that Eric had 'contributed' to them to combat the pesky power outages; from the garage, where Barry had moved into an air conditioned office under his new, Eric-imposed title of 'manager/watchman'. Eric had persuaded the Mongrel that the garage was in need of 'protection' from undesirables who were waiting for the chance to rob it. It was for this 'protection' that Eric collected his weekly dues; and from Aunt May, as a percentage of the rentals for Petra's house.

The whole community developed the shell-shocked expressions of those who'd just been through a war and were not quite sure if another phase of bombings would ensue. For days after Nathan's and Ab's incidents, everyone spoke in whispers, as if they'd expected Eric McKenzie to suddenly appear out of the woodwork and pummel them for their treason.

At 18 Palm View Road, on top of the financial strain of Eric's 'rental' collection, everyone waited anxiously for word on Petra. The girl had not visited or called, not even to enquire about Kendra. Nola guessed that it was Eric who had probably laid down the rule of no contact, and she told Aunt May as much, but it did nothing to ease the clamp of the woman's jaw.

Every greeting in the mornings or evenings was pre-empted by the question, "You hear anyting?" But all eager inquiries were met with the same sad shake of the head.

To top it all, Petra had not taken her medication with her that night, and the little brown vial of tablets sat beside the sterilizer as a reminder of the dark confusion that threatened the girl while she was away. Many times Nola would walk into the kitchen to find Aunt May staring at the vial in her hand.

But, the most surprising thing of all was that Kendra began to thrive. Kendra began to thrive despite the thick tension that surrounded her. And it was mostly because of Nola.

It was the guilt that caused it. The guilt from those words—a teenage girl who drop out of school and smoke weed all day. Those words, and the vision of herself removing the machete from the rafter, were too torturous to live with. She wanted to give up; to throw her arms up at the world and say, 'Ok, you win! I can't do it no more. You're stronger than me.' She wanted to just curl up until it was all over, but she couldn't—because she'd been the one to cause it all.

The first thing she had to do was to fight the need for the glaze. It was hard. Sometimes the pain and rage rose so strongly into her chest that she craved the dullness that it granted. She saw them all watching her, giving her the same wary looks that they'd worn as she'd sauntered past in her ganja high. Ab was right—she had to clean up her heart.

Nola buried her shame in the one person who knew no better of her. Kendra. Nola became Kendra's caregiver. She bathed the child in the mornings, fed her, took her for walks to visit Ab and Mams, and rocked her to sleep when she began her tired whine. She even learned to differentiate the child's cries.

Since Kendra's uncooperative tongue made it difficult for clear speech, instead of trying to talk, Kendra would just wail in frustration when she wanted something. Nola learned to interpret the cries—the on and off moans of hunger, the whines of exhaustion, the wails of pain or fright, and the frustrated hiccups of boredom.

It was Nola who discovered that after most of Kendra's meals, the child was still hungry. Mealtimes always left Kendra cranky and restless. After tackling the bowl and spoon for almost 20 minutes, the baby would just stop eating and moan till a bottle was placed in her mouth.

Nola realized why. The child's heavy tongue made it difficult for her to accept the spoon, pull the food off, and swallow in sequence. It was just too much coordination for her clumsy tongue, and, as a result, at the end of the meal most of the food lay on the bib instead of down the child's throat.

Nola decided to try something new. She began to give Kendra her meals before she became too hungry, a half hour or so before her scheduled meal times. Nola tied a bright orange ribbon with a wooden spoon attached to it above the kitchen door, and placed Kendra's high chair in the middle of the doorway. Throughout the meal, Nola constantly hit the spoon so that the child looked up and gurgled happily at the swinging spoon while she was being fed.

The results were amazing. Kendra, not being ravenous, accepted the challenge of the bowl and spoon in better spirits, and, holding up her head to gaze at the swinging spoon, elongated her squat neck to be able to swallow.

In time, not only did the child's disposition improve, but her neck and tongue muscles became so much stronger that she actually began to speak.

Nola was overcome. She could not believe that she had actually made such a difference to someone's life. She could not believe that the smile that shone from Kendra's face every time she walked into a room, was for her. It was euphoric. The baby came to mean so much to her that there was actually a pain in her heart whenever her mind rested on any business to do with her. Was it love? Was that a type of love, this feeling that caused a combination of a physical pain and a soaring joy? Was that the love a mama felt for her child, or was it just that Nola saw so much of herself in Kendra? Was she taking care of the baby, or was she taking care of the ugly, attention-deprived child she had been? She did not know, but she knew one thing. She would die for Kendra.

The child's striking steps in her development were such a cause for celebration that it temporarily lifted everyone's minds off the sadness of Petra's absence and Eric's cruel impositions. It wasn't so much that they forgot about Petra as much as it was that they all came to realize that the girl's actions had not been selfish after all. They all chose to believe better, and came to the conclusion that Petra had made herself the sacrificial lamb. She was keeping herself away from Kendra in the hope that for Eric, the child would become 'out of sight, out of mind'.

Aunt May aged. Where her face had been plump and creased by the weight of fat, it now lay in the crumpled folds of a soul sucked hollow by worry. She reminded Nola of a swollen version of Mama.

The strange thing was, the more Nola looked at Aunt May, was the more anger she felt at Mama. Many times she tried to tell herself that it was not Mama at which she felt that surge of rage, but Eric. But, when she slept at night, it was Mama's face that wafted through her dreams and woke her up with her fists clenched.

Then she realized why. It was because Petra had gone away. It was because Merlene had run away. It was because they'd run away to save their children, and Mama had not.

The anger formed a ball in Nola's gut. What was it that had kept Mama there? Why had she preferred to stay and work her fingers to the bone, to allow her face to sag to her chin, while her child was beaten? What was it that made one mama try save her baby, while another stayed and stirred pots?

Fear! Fear! It had controlled Nola too. Fear of pain. Fear of rejection. Fear of failing Mama and Papa. Fear of being different. Fear of being the same. Fear that had done nothing to change anything!

Fear had made Mama weak, made not even love for her daughter worth the bargain.

And then it hit her, like the proverbial ton of bricks—It had been in Papa's eyes too! Just as it had been in the shift of Eric's and Pedro's eyes. Fear existed even in the creatures who demanded it of others. It was just a matter of finding what caused it. It was just a matter of finding the right thing to bargain for, and the strength to do the bargaining.

CHAPTER 39

THE IDEA CAME to her one night, during one of her kitchen trysts with Olive. The girl was crying, having just learnt that the man with whom she'd been spending most of her time, and who had promised her a big Christmas wedding, was, in fact, already married and about to host his own daughter's wedding—at Christmas.

That night, as Nola helped her up the stairs, Olive clung to her and slobbered into her neck about men and their trickery. They were all wolves in sheep's clothing, she wailed.

Wolves in sheep's clothing! Nola had almost dropped Olive on the stairs. A disguise! That was it! That was what she needed to get closer to the supermarket and to Eric McKenzie. Maybe then she could hear something of Petra. Maybe she could even discover what Eric's bargaining tool was.

The next morning, she paid Mams a visit. Luckily, the woman did not share her son's opinion about leaving Eric to Jah, and while Ab was loading the freezer with bottles of freshly made Irish Moss, she called Nola into her room and removed a paper bag from the drawer of her wardrobe.

"Them chop off the lion's mane, and them think them win!" the woman snarled as she pressed the bag into Nola's hands.

232

"Them think them tek him power, but sometimes the beast have to rise back from where them don't expec' it—out of the quiet forest!" She tapped Nola's forehead. "Out of the quiet forest the beast will pounce!"

Nola nodded as the weight of the bag was released into her hands.

"But this ..." Mams grabbed the bag again and shook it hard. "This dead already. This can't dead again! You have to tek care of yourself, girl! I pray to Jah, dat as him give little David the power over the great giant, him will give you the power to strike dat Lucifer down!"

Nola rushed straight to her bathroom and locked the door. For the first time since her first night in Kingston, she removed Grampy's towel from the mirror.

The eyes that stared back at her seemed like those of a stranger. How they'd changed. Before, they had been lost in their sockets. They'd been weak, like watery tea. She realized then that she'd never ever looked at herself through her own eyes. She'd always looked with their eyes. Redding eyes. She'd only seen what they'd seen. The blackness. That was all.

Nola leaned forward, her breath misting the mirror. Her eyes pulsed. They shone. Her eyes had broken free of the glaze, and pulsed with the gleam of the release.

She opened Mams's bag and peered inside. The musty bundle didn't even look like hair. The bronze colour was gone, as if the very energy had fizzled away after being severed from its lifeforce. Nola removed a lock and stared at the chopped ends, her heart raging as she remembered Ab's bent, defeated head. She would have to tie them together to keep them on her own scalp.

She used her memory of Aggie and her wrappings to complete the disguise. First she rubbed her unused bed sheets in dirt, then ripped them into three pieces, one for her top,

233

one for her skirt and one for her turban. The turban she used to hold the locks into place, ensuring that a few of them hung over her face to hide her distinguishing smirk. Then she added a splatter of kitchen grease across her cheeks and blackened her front teeth with shoe polish.

There! A ragged street beggar stood before her in the mirror. Nola bared her teeth at her reflection, laughing out loud at the illusion of the gaping hole in the front.

She had to sneak from the house through the front door, knowing that she was more at risk of meeting up with someone in the kitchen or beneath the ackee trees. She walked down the street instead of up past Ab's shop, hunching her back and dragging her left leg the way she'd watched Grampy do so many times.

The beggar was in his spot, leaning against the stop sign. He always grinned at Nola when she passed, exposing a gap matching the one she had just simulated, hissing like a deflating tyre and crooning, "Sexy Jubie, come and give a man a little someting, nuh?"

Now, as she dragged her leg past him, he looked up and scowled. He thought she was another beggar, trying to trespass on his domain. The disguise had passed its first test!

She stopped by the bus stop and bought a bucket of brightly coloured heliconia blooms from a street vendor. If she was to sit by the taxi stand for hours, then she needed an excuse to be there. She'd just have to remember to call out every couple minutes, "Pretty flowas! Pretty flowas! Three dollar a stem!"

She arrived at the taxi stand a little before ten-thirty in the morning, a time which she knew would not yet see Eric at the supermarket. No one seemed to notice her as she pushed through the crowd and plopped her bucket of flowers on the ground. She chose a spot on the wall beside the 'exit' gateway of the plaza, the spot she thought would be the safest to watch from since it was the gate Eric never used. From there she could see the supermarket doors clearly. They were just being opened by the old man from the back room, his back bent as he shuffled to fasten the grills to the outer wall. No sign of the smoking lady.

"What you doin' in my spot, Mammy? You don't know say nobody but Imo sell in this spot?!"

Nola squinted up at the wide shadow. It flung a huge duffle angrily at her feet, and waved a roll of blue tarpaulin in front of her stunned face. Nola jumped up quickly, afraid that any sort of confrontation would draw attention from the supermarket.

"Sorry, Sorry . . . ." She caught herself. "Sarry, sarry, missus." She switched to the flat, drawn out patois of the street. "Me just lookin' for somewhere to sell mi flowas." Her mind raced, remembering Nathan's passionate argument about Kendra's health. "My son! My son need some medicine for him asthma, and me need to get little money to buy it."

"You can sit over deh so," the woman said, "But just for today! Mr. Mac say that nobody must sell on him sidewalk without payin' rent."

Mr. Mac? Eric! He charged rent for the sidewalk? Nola disguised her involuntary gasp of anger with a cough. She nodded quickly in surrender to the woman's instructions and hoisted her bucket to the garbage drum. There was a sign on the light post beside it, NO PISSING HERE, but the smell of urine was stifling. There was no way she would get any customers in this spot, but she had to admit that it was a little more inconspicuous than the first. The bougainvillea gave some shade, but was so prickly that it scratched her back and neck as she tried to sit on the wall, so she just sat on the sidewalk.

To see the supermarket doors she would now have to lift her head and peer over the low wall, but who was she to complain since she wasn't paying rent?

The woman pointed at the other higglers along the sidewalk who were also setting out their wares. "You think tings come easy in this place?" She bellowed. "You can't just come and take up prime space like that! Nah, man, you have to earn your spot! Imo start sellin' here from before this plaza even have all them other shop!" She waved her fingers at the plaza. "When just the so-so supermarket and cloth store was there—that's why Mr. Mac treat Imo special!" She beamed. "Give me special price, cause me was here long before all of these other 'prentice!"

Just then, Nola glimpsed the smoking woman. She was walking towards the entrance gate from within the crowd on the sidewalk. Nola shrunk beneath the bougainvillea. Shut up, shut up, she wanted to hiss at the higgler. She quickly looked down and pretended to sort through her flowers, trying to release the higgler's interest towards her.

The smoking woman stopped by the pushcart at the gate and bought a newspaper. Even as the vendor gave her a toothless grin as he handed over her change, the woman did not release her scowl. Nola gave an inward shrug. What would anyone who worked for Eric McKenzie have to smile about anyway?

Eric's car entered the plaza at about one o'clock that afternoon, just when Nola's stomach had begun to rumble so loudly that even the flies appeared startled and buzzed more erratically beside her. She'd been about to pull out the raisin bun she'd tucked into the waistband of her rags when she heard the tyres screech into the parking lot. It stopped in its usual spot in the 'no parking' area in front of the supermarket doors, but Eric did not alight immediately. As Nola watched from behind the wall, the car sat purring like a contented cat.

After what seemed like an eternity, Nola eventually spotted Eric's gleaming crown alight from the car, followed by the angry slam of his car door. He strode purposefully into the supermarket.

The next head that emerged caused Nola's breath to catch in her chest. Petra! The girl exited the car slowly, her head bent so low that Nola wondered how she could possibly see where she was going. She turned to carefully shut the car door and Nola's hand flew to her mouth to stifle a gasp. Petra was as slim as a stick, with the long, shriveled face to match. How could she have changed so much in so little time? The beauty on her face was barely recognizable, spread thin like a sparse film of butter on cold, warped toast.

Petra lifted each leg slowly, hesitantly, towards the supermarket door, as if what she really wanted to do was to turn and run. Nola felt as if she was watching Mama with her jaded, robot-like movements as she swished her mop over the kitchen floor, as she chopped her onions and stared at nothing.

Nola clutched at her chest.

"Missus, is what happen to you? You just see a duppy?"

Miss Imo bent over her and fanned energetically with a soiled sheet of cardboard. "Breathe deep, m'dear. Don't make your chest seize up!" She coaxed Nola.

"You want me call a taxi, Mammy? You think you need to go hospital?"

"No, no ..." Nola choked. "No hospital! I just choke, that's all. I'm alright now... just little water."

A thermos appeared and cool water was hastily poured down her throat. Nola pushed gently at the meaty chest in front of her, nodding vigorously to let the pourer know that she'd had enough.

Nola, left to once again peep over the wall, was relieved to see that Eric's car was still there. But now a police car was parked beside it. She frowned. It was not the first time that she'd seen that police car in the lot beside Eric's car. Ab's words rushed back to her, "Man like Eric have the police in dem back pocket." He'd been right after all.

237

It was about 30 minutes before Eric appeared again. Alone. Nola watched as he sauntered over to the police car and tapped on the window with his keys. She couldn't see what he pushed through the window, but he definitely took something from his left pocket and handed it over. He did not speak to the person inside, just handed the item over and sauntered to his own car. The police car immediately left the plaza, passing Nola as she bent low over her bucket of heliconias. Eric drove out soon afterward, through the entrance gateway. Alone.

So he'd put Petra to work. Nola wanted desperately to go inside. She wanted to get closer to Petra, to see if the sham she'd just seen was really as bad as it appeared from the roadside. But it was just too risky, even with her disguise.

Nola stayed by the garbage drum all day, watching the patrons of the plaza come and go, and listening to the animated conversations of the higglers. She even sold five more stalks of heliconia blooms.

Eric never returned, and Petra never came back outside. By late evening when the higglers began folding up their tarpaulins and packing their duffles with the goods that had not been sold, Nola began to think that it had been her imagination that had produced the meek figure entering the supermarket earlier. She was just thinking that, and about to take up her bucket and leave when she spotted the downcast head. It came outside followed by the smoking woman who carried a black scandal bag. Nola watched as they stopped by the same cart at the entrance where the smoking woman bought a *Star* while Petra stared down at her feet. They eventually crossed through the traffic and squeezed into a mini-bus bursting with arms, legs and sweaty faces.

Nola sighed. From shiny black Honda to packed mini-bus. Fate had such a cruel sense of humour.

CHAPTER 40

BARRY STOPPED COMING by the cook shop. As a matter of fact, Barry stopped walking on Palm View Road altogether. He now approached the garage from Preston Road, not willing to brave the curses, spits and calls of 'Traitor' and 'Dread Hater' that greeted him on Palm View Road.

Only one person still embraced Barry wholeheartedly—Eric McKenzie, who tucked the man beneath his wing. He had embarked Barry on a new business venture, which saw him actually up and about the garage. 'Working' was probably not the word that a regular person would have used to refer to the pastime into which Eric had launched Barry, but it did see great profit for the garage, and, therefore, earned the hearty favour of the Mongrel.

They began stealing cars. Yes, the garage took on a brand new portfolio—instead of repairing cars, they stole them. From the gleaming new, to the rickety old, they were all brought to the garage and separated into prized parts—fenders, bumpers, engines, steering wheels. All were harvested like butchered cows, and sold to a market which seemed to have been miraculously waiting in the wings.

Mattie was the one who filled them all in. She was able to tell them that Necka had shown Barry how to use a flattened rubber tube, sealed at one end, to slide through the top of the car windows and pump it with air so that the tube swelled and released the top of the window from its frame. A wire hanger was then snaked through to lift the lock, then the vehicle was pushed out of earshot of the owner's home before the car was 'hot wired' and driven away.

At first, Nola did not believe that lazy, cowardly Barry would have engaged in such a foolhardy and dangerous pastime. Then she remembered the man's weed-induced rantings beneath the tamarind tree. Barry believed that all rich folk owed him something. They were the reason that he was poor. In Barry's eyes, he was not stealing—he was taking back what was his.

In due time, even more strange faces began to appear on Palm View Road and Preston Lane. The new faces parked their cars in the middle of the road, forcing traffic to manoeuvre around their vehicles. The new faces crossed the streets in front of moving vehicles, without so much as a glance in the direction of the car, continuing on their way even as the tyres screeched to panicked stops within inches of their bodies. Soon, the cars that had once used Palm View as a throughway found other routes to travel, and the traffic became considerably less, except for the new faces.

The residents adjusted quietly, no one wanting to incite any confrontations, especially after what had happened to poor Nathan, and, not to mention, what could happen to Petra and little Kendra.

Barry, in the meantime, settled nicely into his new occupation, generating so much money for the garage that the Mongrel became even fatter, his car even bigger, and his lunch breaks even longer. Eric, in turn, having set up the contacts for the successful organisation, stayed away from the garage,

240

sending Necka to monitor the operation and to collect his 'fees' each week.

One day, Barry came back to Abediah's Ital Stop. At first Nola thought she'd made a mistake, that it was not Barry who strutted towards the shop, but someone who looked like him. The person didn't even walk like Barry.

But, it was Barry strutting towards them, except that Barry now walked like Eric McKenzie.

He approached the window as if he had not been absent from it for months. He walked right up and hailed Ab with a casual flick of his hand, then nodded at everyone else and ordered a Red Stripe Beer. Red Stripe Beer? This from a man who had once emphatically claimed that nothing held the essence of a true man like a hot stout.

Everyone became silent, looking from Barry to Ab, then to each other, as if a duppy had just wandered into their midst. He certainly didn't look like the Barry they'd once known. The tight, scruffy rolls of uncombed hair had been replaced by tight, neat cornrows which met at the nape of the neck in a tiny puff of hair. The smelly, grease-stained shirt had been replaced by a silky gray one, the buttons undone to just above a diamante studded belt, exposing Barry's fur-spattered chest. But the most spectacular change was the shoes. White! White, patent shoes, toes pointed to kingdom come, the fine tip ending in a spectacular finish of shiny stainless steel.

Ab was the first to speak, handing Barry a hot stout with a nod and a 'Wha'ppenin' Rasta?' Mams sucked her teeth and held her chest. Ab nodded for her to go into the house and she went, muttering bitterly about the lion's mane.

Ab pointed to the empty chairs and tables which everyone else had pointedly ignored. "Barry," he said, "Tek your seat, Star."

Barry nodded and raised his stout in an exaggerated salute before sitting in a chair beside the window—Eric's old seat.

241

In a while, the conversation resumed, none of it directed at Barry.

"So Ab, how business, Star? Tings lookin' good?" Barry called above the chatter, rocking casually on the chair.

Ab continued to wipe the counter, not looking up as he said, "Well, Brethren, I and I can't complain. Jah look after him own, you nuh."

Barry nodded and sucked on the stout bottle noisily. So not everything had changed.

"So I say, too, Star. So I say!" Barry chortled as he released the bottle spout and wiped his mouth with the back of his hand.

"And wha' 'bout you, Rasta? How business down the road?" Ab asked.

"Well you know how tings go … some days better than some, you see me?"

Ab nodded. "So it go, sometimes."

Suddenly, Barry looked over at Nola.

She was caught off-guard, especially since she'd been staring so intently at him. When he turned, his eyes locked with hers. She blinked in surprise, but found that she could not look away. There it was again—that surge of familiar emotion. Guilt.

She'd encouraged this! All this—the clothes, the shoes, the stealing … she'd encouraged it all! All those hours she'd lain beside Barry in that haze of smoke, she'd listened to his gibberish and nodded in agreement to his stupid reasoning. Then she'd dismissed him like everyone else! It was as if it was happening all over again— reaching for the machete for Papa, and killing Ellie instead.

Barry's tree had been the pen. He had accepted her just like Ellie had, and what had she done? Left him to the mercies of that serrated tongue.

242

She should have warned him. She should have gone to him and tried to speak some sense into him. She should have told him of Eric's deception, warned him of what lay beneath that sheath.

She gave him a weak smile, to let him know that she was willing to talk, but he turned his head away and looked back at Ab.

"You know, Ab, someting I been meanin' to say … to everybody … been just waitin' for the right time to say it." Barry crooned.

Ab stopped wiping and looked up. Everyone else's gaze joined his to stare at the lone, occupied chair. Barry, seeing that he had finally gotten everyone's attention, grinned broadly, righted his chair and removed his hand from his pocket. He stood slowly, with the exaggerated movements of someone acting in a play, and placed his stuffed fist on the counter in front of Ab. Then he leaned forward as if to whisper, but spoke loud enough for everyone to hear.

"Sometimes, Star, when you make your enemy think you is their friend, you can get more from them than when you fight, you see me?"

He released his fist, and a wad of money, as if falling in line with the man's dramatics, flipped open magnificently. Some of the bills fell off the counter and floated to the sidewalk.

Ab stared at the notes for an instant before looking back at the shocked faces outside. Then he turned away as calm as ever and began to pour a bottle of fresh vinegar into the bucket of pickled peppers.

After a few seconds of silence, he spoke over his shoulder.

"Tek your money off me food counter, Rasta. I just finish wipe it."

Barry's face fell. He looked around at them, embarrassed like, but the look lasted only a few seconds before he was grinning again.

"Is yours, Brethren! Yours, man! To pay back for… everyting, you see me!"

Ab slammed the cover onto the bucket.

"I and I don't need your money, Rasta. Everyting cool, Star."

"Not my money, Bredda, Eric money! Listen to me, when him tell me to collect up everyting for Necka to bring to him at weekend time, me just hold back little-little each time. After all, who doin' all the work? Nuh me! Who you think risk them life every night, risk gettin' caught by the police every night to get this cash? Nuh me! And that fat dog, Mongrel and the one named Eric think them must get more than me? Nah man! This is mine! And me givin' it to you!" Barry flicked his wrist at the money.

"WHOSE MONEY YOU SEY?"

Ab's bellow made Nola jump. She watched as he leaned forward to shove the money off the counter, sending it floating like discarded leaves onto the sidewalk. Mattie stared at a hundred dollar bill that settled beside her, but she did not touch it. No one moved.

"Don't bring nothin' dat come from any iniquity round here again, you hear me, Rasta?!" Ab shouted, pointing a finger at Barry's shocked face.

Barry stared at Ab in disbelief, and this time when he spoke, his pompous tone was gone.

"Ab," he said, "'Memba how you and me use to talk, man?— 'bout one day when you goin' to open your big restaurant with live, fresh fish in a pond, and how me goin' to open a store that sell all them fancy TV and video? 'Memba that, Star? Well, see the start we need here, Bredda! Now we get the chance to do it! Now we can live the dream, you see me!"

"Nah, not dis way. Hard work, Star. Me tired to tell you dat. Hard work! Is only hard work bring tings dat stay for good. Anyting else will fade away before you blink!" The anger seemed to have left Ab's voice as quickly as it had entered it, and he nodded gently at the sidewalk where the money lay scattered. "Dat is not good money, my Brethren. Dat money goin' only bring more trouble, more problems, man. When time come for Jah to bring the dream, Him goin' bring it the right way, Star—not like this."

Barry gave a bitter laugh and whirled around to look at the other faces, "All of you is hypocrite! Big hypocrite! All of you a cry everyday say unnu hungry, say unnu pickney can't go school, say the rich man a keep you poor. Well, now you get your chance, you see me, and you turnin' it down! Where you think this money come from? It come from the rich man who drive round in him pretty car all day, gettin' richer and richer while unnu down here starvin'! You think them rich people care 'bout you? You think them big time insurance don't just buy them back another car? This money can feed unnu pickney!"

He scooped a handful of bills from the sidewalk and walked over to Mattie, dropping the money over the woman's head. It floated over her like giant confetti, but still Mattie did not move. Even when Barry frustratedly slapped a bill against her chest, she continued staring straight ahead.

"See it there! See it there!" Barry ranted. "Now you can buy food! What the hell you think Eric can do to you if him don't know? You think I stupid, to make Eric know? You think anybody would notice if a few blade of grass missin' from a big field? Oy, Mattie, nuh the same ting Eric do to everybody else—take what don't belong to him? Thief from a thief and him can't call you a thief, you see me?"

"Take up your money, boy. None of us want any part of it!" Nola spun around. Aunt May! She must have heard all the shouting. Now she stood in the centre of the road, arms on her hips and a glare on her face that Nola remembered so well.

"When you bring back my niece, then you can talk to us about a chance! Then you can talk to us about a start!"

"And when you can put mi lion's mane back on him head, put him pride back on him shoulders, then you can talk to me 'bout hypocrite!"

Mams had come back from the house. But when Nola saw what she gripped in her right hand she gave a panicked gasp. Mams was holding the cleaver she used to chop the heads off the fish.

Barry backed up at the sight, but his feet misjudged the closeness of the curb and he flew backwards into the road, his arms flailing wildly.

"Easy Mams," Abs said quietly.

He'd moved so quickly. He was already beside Mams, removing the cleaver from her hand. "We nuh defend dat kind of ting, Mams, you know dat."

"NAH!" Mattie finally jumped up from the curb. "Don't tell Mams to take it EASY, Ab! Him deserve for someone to teach him a lesson once and for all! I tell you long time 'bout this bwoy—this no-good, dutty bwoy! Him come here with him nastiness and bad ways, and look what him do? Bring nastiness and badness to people just tryin' to live a honest life!"

Barry took another step backwards and opened his mouth, but he quickly snapped it shut as if he thought better of speaking. Suddenly he turned helpless eyes to where Nola sat in stunned silence.

She pleaded back with her own eyes. We have it all here, Barry! We don't need no Eric and him thiefin' ways! We have each other. Nobody to beat us and kick us down stairs, nobody to tell us we can't eat cause we too fat, or ugly, or black.

But the shutters closed over Barry's eyes. They shut, like Ellie's had shut, and he turned to walk away.

"Hold it, Star!" Ab called.

Barry stopped and turned slowly. Ab pointed at the money scattered over the sidewalk.

"Don't leave your litter on mi sidewalk, Rasta."

Barry's shoulders fell as if someone had leaned on him from behind. He looked at Nola briefly again, and she stared back steadily, willing him to break his resistance and apologize for his betrayal, but he just headed slowly back towards the sidewalk and picked up the scattered bills. The only sound on the street the click, click of his smart white shoes.

When he'd finished, and stood with the notes crushed in his fists, he turned to face them once again, the look on his face saying, "This is your last chance", but Ab just nodded, and said, "Thanks, Star. We have to keep our streets clean, you know?"

Barry turned and walked away, just like the old Barry.

CHAPTER 41

IT WAS ONE of his babymothers who raised the alarm. She'd gone to his rented room to pick up the thousand dollars that he'd told her to come and collect, found the door broken and the mattress smeared with blood. She'd raced to the garage to see if Barry had been somehow injured the day before, but no one knew of any injury.

Some days later, a cane worker in St Catherine found his body. At first the worker thought the suspicious mass of ants in the cane field where john crows had begun to circle was the carcass of another dog or goat. They often got hit by the speeding cars on the highway, and ran into the cane fields where they eventually died.

It took a while to distinguish which parts of the body had been devoured by the ants and wild dogs, and which parts had been removed before it had been dumped into the cane field. The wailing babymother identified the long scar across the back as the one that Barry had gotten when he'd tried to crawl under a barbed wire fence to escape her demands for money. It was agreed that the body belonged to one Barrington Dickson, and it was also agreed that the fingers, eyes and tongue had been hacked off before the victim had died.

As soon as Nola had heard, despite her grief, she felt as if a piece of her soul that had become loosened, a piece that had been clanking noisily around within her, had clicked back into place. She'd known. She'd felt Barry's death, and that night, her spirit had bade him farewell.

She told no one of this 'feeling', of 'knowing', for she was sure none would have believed her. None except for a cackling old woman, miles away.

Two police cars visited the garage the day after Barry's body had been identified. They questioned the man's co-workers and wrote report after report, including one from his devastated boss, the Mongrel, who tearfully slobbered that Barrington Dickson had been one of his most hard-working mechanics.

It was shocking for the residents to see the garage so radically transformed. One evening, the garage had been the grimy yard with parts stacked everywhere, and by the next morning, the day after Barry had been reported missing, the garage had become a spanking facility, with five cars and a motor bike parked neatly at the side, awaiting their turn to be cranked up on the brand new lift.

The police left Monty's Garage with no leads as to Barry's brutal demise. Then one of the man's co-workers suggested that they visit Barry's favourite watering hole. Maybe someone there would have an idea of any enemies the man might have had. By that afternoon, the police cars had migrated from the garage to the sidewalk of Abediah's Ital Stop.

They were all sitting on the curb, sick and numb over the news of Barry's torturous death when the police cars pulled up. And yet, even in the midst of their grief, the silent warning passed between their eyes, like a shared bottle of stout. Petra! Kendra! Don't say nothin' ... bout Eric or Necka or the money Barry had brought to them! Nothin' bout the car ring!

That was when Nola realized how smart Eric McKenzie really was. In Petra, he'd created his own little insurance policy. Wasn't that something? He'd got Petra through the threat to Kendra, and had got them through the threat to Petra. They were his—his little men on his little board game of life. The barbed tongue was finally, truly out of its sheath.

So they all masked their knowing with their grief and obligingly answered the detectives' questions. No, no one they could think of who would want to hurt Barry. No, no, no arguments. No, no money borrowed that they knew of. No, Barry had no questionable associations. No, he didn't do drugs. The only women they only knew of in his life were his three babymothers—Judine, Rosie and Irene, the one who'd raised the alarm 'about him missing'.

They questioned Nola last, maybe because she was the youngest. The detective offered her the chance to get a drink of water before he sat beside her on the curb. She declined the offer and stared down at his shoes. Shiny, like Eric's. He smelled good too. She looked up at his face, and her breath stopped within her chest. His eyes! They were hard eyes, and even though he made his voice soft with coaxing as he asked her how well she'd known Barrington Dickson, his eyes remained as hard as a rock stone. They made Nola shiver. The detective misunderstood her action and told her not to be afraid, that he just wanted to know if Barry had ever mentioned having a problem with anyone.

But Nola could not answer 'yes' or 'no'. The eyes stifled her voice. She looked away again, and another detective came up and asked if she was hiding something why she looked so 'fraid'. The nice smelling detective waved him away, asking if he wouldn't be 'fraid too if his friend had been found minus his eyes. Then they both chuckled, and the nice-smelling detective handed Nola a piece of paper and stood up. There was a phone number on it, and the name 'Winston' written above.

"Call me if you think of anyting. Your friend never deserve that, did he?" he said.

Did he? Nola's eyes flashed upwards to meet those eyes. Did he? It was the way he'd said it. Not like a rhetorical question, but like he was really asking her if Barry deserved it.

But he just winked at her and went to join his colleagues at Ab's window.

The cars eventually screeched off, complimentary stouts balanced along with their guns through the windows. They left on the sidewalk, eyes wide with fear, and silenced voices wanting to scream for help.

* * *

The night after Barry's funeral, they all sat beneath the ackee trees and allowed Kendra's noisy chatter to soothe their frayed nerves—Nola, Aunt May, Nathan and Mrs. Lyndsay. When they spoke, it was in halting whispers because the air seemed too heavy for speech. The fear had forced itself between the cracks in the air, granting them immobile within the sludge. No one could shed the painful memory of Irene, stripping off her clothes in grief and flinging her naked body onto Barry's pine casket. It had taken Nathan, Ab and Panhead to scrape her off the box so it could be lowered into the earth. Five children, all bearing features that had once characterized Barry's face, had stood silently around the gaping hole. Even Mattie had wailed, tearing at the long weaves in her hair and screaming, "Barry neva deserve this! No Lawd, not even Barry deserve this!"

Eric had not come. Neither had Petra, Pedro or Necka. Nola was half grateful, half regretful. She'd hoped to see Petra

251

for Aunt May's sake, just to know that she was okay. As Nola had watched Barry's casket disappearing beneath the dirt, she couldn't help herself imagining Eric's face down there—his cocky mouth with its toothpick being covered beneath the layers of soil.

Afterwards they could do nothing but sit beneath the trees. Nathan held his face with hands pale and ashy from drained blood. Ever since he'd heard about Barry's death, his hands periodically flew to his face, as if the thought of the Barry's demise made him grateful that he'd gotten away with just his purple mask.

Then the phone rang. It vibrated the thick air and scraped against their raw nerves. They all jumped, looking at each other with stunned expressions. Finally Aunt May bleated, "Tiny!" and waddled up the kitchen steps. She was back at the door in less than a minute.

"Nola, come child," she called quietly.

What now? Nola thought. No more, Lord! Not Petra! But when she looked at Aunt May's face, she noticed with relief that it was no more panicked than before. Not Petra, Aunt May's eyes said.

The voice at the other end of the phone was so low that Nola wondered if the caller had hung up. She shrugged questioningly at Aunt May, and was about to put the receiver back in its cradle when she heard "Nola".

Nola gulped. "Louisa?" she whispered into the mouthpiece and to Aunt May at the same time.

Aunt May waddled away as the voice whispered back, "Hello, Nola … I can't stay long. I … I just wanted to see how you was doin'."

"Louisa! Where are you? Where you callin' from?"

There was a slight pause. "Razzle Dazzle … I workin' here for a little till Mama start to make chutneys again. It's my turn to lock up this evenin', so I get to call you before Mrs. Spence come to pick up the keys."

Despite the shock at hearing Louisa's voice, the words snagged on Nola's brain. Mama wasn't making chutneys? Impossible! That's all she did—chop, stir, bottle. Even when sick, she'd bound her head in bayrum-soaked rags and made her chutneys.

"What happen to Mama, Louisa? Why she not makin' chutneys?"

Another pause. "She tired, Nola. Takin' a little break, you know?"

Nola closed her eyes. "Louisa, is she alright? Mama alright?"

This time Louisa was quick to answer, her voice gaining a sudden spurt of brightness. "Fine! She fine! Mama good … and Papa too."

The mention of Papa's name gave Nola's heart a sharp pulse.

"And you?" she quickly asked Louisa. "How you doin', Louisa? Workin' at Razzle Dazzle, eh? That's nice."

"You can believe it, Nola? Me! Have to dress up nice every day in skirt and blouse, and high heels! You should see me, Nola. Papa say I look just like a secretary in a fancy office!"

Her heart pulsed again, but Nola forced a laugh.

"What 'bout Aggie, Louisa? You see her round town?"

A little expulsion of breath. "She gone, Nola. From 'bout a week or so after you leave. Tanky was passin' the stall one mornin' and him notice that everyting was gone—the cloth, the bush. Everyting! Nobody don't see her since, so them tear down the stall."

Nola gasped. Aggie—gone? The shack—gone? It was like hearing that the Rio Diablo was no longer flowing through the village. The sadness that poured into her heart was overwhelming, and Nola had to bite her lip to stop from bursting into tears. Louisa would think she was crazy to be crying over the witch and her rancid stall, but that spot on the sidewalk meant as much to Nola as the room that had held Grampy's whispers. That spot had saved her life.

"... sey that them saw a pig just like the witch's own up by the river somewhere." Louisa was still speaking, and the word 'river' halted Nola's thoughts. She remembered that Aggie had often spoken of moving up on the riverbank. Could she have gone there?

"Louisa ..." Nola stammered, "You see Delroy round the place?" "Mmmm. Him come by the shop sometimes. You know, to buy things." Nola could sense the shrug in Louisa's voice. She didn't know if it was because of her own reaction to the news of Aggie's disappearance, but Louisa's voice now sounded a little thin, a little strained.

"You did tell him for me, Louisa, that I neva die in the fire?" "Mmm hmm." Still strained.

Nola felt ashamed for asking. She shouldn't have made Louisa uncomfortable, especially when she was taking such a risk to call her.

"What 'bout you, Nola? Slugga treat you good?"

Nola sighed. "Very good. Everybody here treat me good." She swallowed and took a deep breath. "But someting bad just happen to one of our ... ."

"Nola, I have to go! I hear Mrs. Spence calling. I have to go, okay Nola? Take care of yourself till we talk again, okay? And Nola ... We couldn't come to see you leave because ... we couldn't let Papa know, you understand?"

"Yes, Louisa." She whispered to the loud echo of dial tone. "I always understand."

CHAPTER 42

THE POLICE CAR was in the plaza again, but this time the officer sat casually on the trunk, speaking to Eric.

Nola had had to swallow the bile that rose up in her chest when Eric had emerged from his own car earlier. Every cocky jerk of his neck made her wish that she could put her hands around it and squeeze. She gritted her teeth till her head pulsed, watching as he spoke to the plain-clothed policeman. He seemed agitated, pulling the toothpick in and out of his mouth and pointing it every now and again at the man. Nola squinted to see if she could distinguish some of the words, but he was standing sideways, making it difficult to read his lips. What on earth could have upset Eric again? She had to hear what he was saying!

Surprisingly, the thought of approaching the men brought no fear. She searched her heart for the quiver that always shook it when her thoughts settled on Eric McKenzie. No quiver—just a desperate need to do something—and to do it right away! It must have been the thought of eye-less, tongue-less, finger-less Barry, and the memory of Irene's naked body flung over the casket—it must have been those memories that made her realize that she would rather be dead than to face someone else's demise at the hands of the creature.

Her chest heaved as she watched Eric cross his arms and rock back on his shiny heels. She would go. Right up there and listen to what he was saying! And if it wasn't about Petra, then at least she would find out what you had to say to get a policeman into your back pocket!

That morning, Petra had arrived on the bus. Nola had blinked in surprise when she recognized the rail-thin frame walking behind the smoking woman. When Petra lagged behind in the crowded street, the smoking woman grabbed her arm and pulled her forward. Nola had watched from beneath the bougainvillea, each haul of Petra's rail thin shoulders making her own fingers tighten on the tray of sweets that had replaced the bucket of heliconias. By the time Petra's feet had skittered into the supermarket, Nola's knuckles had become the pale grey of dead flesh.

As she watched Eric making another point to the police officer, his beautiful fingers pointing at the street at nothing in particular, the urgency to save Petra deepened. She picked up her tray of Wrigley's gum and Icy Mints and limped over to the noisy higglers on the other side of the gate. They didn't notice her approach.

Nola coughed loudly as they chortled and slapped each other's shoulders in mirth. "Imo ..." she tapped Imogene's meaty shoulder. "Sorry, Imo. Beg you watch me tings for me while I go to get a cool drinks up in the plaza."

Imogene and Maxine stopped mid-chuckle and looked up at Nola.

"But dis woman gone mad or what?" Maxine wheezed. "What you think, Imo? Is nuff she nuff, or fool she fool? Woman, you don't know dat Mr. Mac don't want the likes of you in him plaza?" Her eyes flew up to the parking lot where Eric was leaning forward to hand something to the policeman.

Nola quickly racked her brain for a different ploy. She grabbed her belly. "Me have to pee-pee, and me can't pee-pee on the sidewalk, right?" Nola cringed at the crudeness of her words, but grabbed her crotch in the most brazen stance she could muster.

The women broke into raucous laughter and slapped each other again.

"Is what do dis woman though, Lord? See dat sign cross the street?" Imo wagged a finger at the crowded bus stop. "The one dat say, PUBLIC LAVATORY? Well, dat is where you go to pee-pee, not in Mr. Mac nice, nice plaza! Dat bathroom is for patrons only!" Nola gave a deep sigh before dropping the tray onto Imo's lap. "Me can't hold the pee-pee long enough to reach all the way cross there. Me just have to take my chances with Mr. Mac!"

She decided to approach from the rear. She dragged her leg dramatically as she walked up from the exit gate. Thankfully, he was in such deep conversation that he did not notice her approach, and by the time she'd gotten to the column from which the large plaza light was mounted, she could hear his voice.

"... know the date ... nuh suspect ... keep him far till ... ." His words drifted like a sporadic mountain wind, teasing her first with its intensity, then becoming a distant drone. She moved closer, not dragging her leg as much this time lest he hear the sound of her slipper scraping the asphalt. She stopped when the familiar spice of his cologne reached her nostrils.

"What 'bout the ones round him?" The policeman was speaking now, his voice as steady as a block of ice. "You sure them will keep cool, or we have to deal with them too?"

Eric chuckled, and Nola didn't have to see his face to know that his eyes had remained steely in their squint.

257

"What you a chat 'bout? You think them could work for me and give any trouble? Them is all my people. Them know where them bread butter... just like you." Another chuckle.

The policeman grunted. "Yeh, but is cause of me you can even think 'bout gettin' the butter, don't forget that!"

They laughed together.

"What you say him name? Patrick?"

"Peter! Peter Ellis! See, me write it on the paper! Don't forget. June 23rd, 17 Pine Crest Avenue."

Eric's gaze casually lifted from the policeman and snagged on Nola's hunched form. His eyes narrowed and his upper lip lifted into a disgusted sneer, jerking the toothpick sharply upward.

He shouted at Nola, "Get your stinking, old ass out of my plaza before you chase away all my good, good customers."

She opened her mouth to speak. She wanted to tell him what an evil, no-good ceature he was; that she couldn't believe that God had breathed air into such a murdering, lying son-of-a-bitch like himself, but she caught herself just in time. She snapped her jaws shut and quickly turned to limp back through the gate.

Nola limped towards the cackles of Imogene and Maxine, and as she sat down on that piss-stained sidewalk beneath the prickly bougainvillea bush she felt her own laughter gurgling up within her chest. Before she knew it, she had joined in their boisterous cackling.

However, as Imo and Maxine guffawed, "What happen to the pee-pee? It run back up in your mad head?" Nola laughed for a different reason. Nola laughed because Eric McKenzie, with all of his cunning and wit, had looked straight at her, and had not recognized her!

CHAPTER 43

TWO MORNINGS LATER, when Nola returned to the sidewalk, she saw both the smoking woman and Eric go into the supermarket, but not Petra. When she returned three mornings after that, Petra was absent again. Nola tried to tell herself that Eric had merely changed his mind about Petra working at the supermarket, but no matter how she tried to convince herself, her heart told her otherwise. A nagging voice within her head kept saying, "Who would know? Who would know if Petra was missin' like Barry?"

That evening, as soon as Nola spotted the smoking woman buying her newspaper at the pushcart, she headed to the bus stop. She waited in the crowd, and when she saw the woman heading towards the bus, Nola rushed on to it.

It must have been her aged appearance and her limp, but Nola noticed with relief that as she tried to push her way towards the back of the bus, some of the passengers tilted aside so that she could pass, with murmurings of, "Easy Mammy." By the time the smoking woman had boarded, Nola was deep into the crowd. The bus did not leave for another 15 minutes. Nola used the time to study the woman.

Her face was very thin, making her jaw seem long and never ending. She was not ugly, but the sharp set of her face made her seem stoic and unreal.

Nola noticed that the woman remained close to the doorway, moving aside at each stop to allow passengers on and off, but venturing no deeper into the crowd. After about 35 minutes, Nola saw that she had positioned herself in front of the conductor's legs. She was about to come off. Nola discreetly moved forward, and by the time the bus stopped and the woman jumped off, she was close behind.

They had come off in front of a building with a sign reading, STEELE'S HARDWARE. Thankfully, there was a crowd milling by the doors of the hardware, so Nola was able to quickly conceal herself within their midst. She watched as the woman tucked the thermos beneath her armpit and lit a cigarette, taking a long draw before expelling the smoke in what seemed to Nola like a deep sigh. Then she began walking up the road. She eventually turned on to a little slip road where she stopped to speak to someone whom Nola could not see, waving her thermos as if to make a point, then she turned on to another side road on the right, and disappeared.

Nola searched for the name of the road. No name, just a rusty pole with a jagged tip, as if the sign had been sawn off. There was only one building to the left of the van, an abandoned factory or warehouse of some sort. Most of the windows were boarded up, and those that were not boasted the shredded gaps from flung missiles. To the right was fenced off open land, the grass tall and untended like the thick Redding hillside.

Nola resumed her limp and followed the woman's path down the slip road. There was an awful stench and she would soon see why. A dead goat kid lay in the grass near the roadside, its legs stuck out grotesquely from a torso swollen with the energy of death. Nola hauled up her hem to pass the animal quickly but a voice stopped her dead in her tracks.

"You lost you way, Mammy?"

Nola jumped. She'd been so distracted by the dead goat that she hadn't seen the man on the right of the road. She pulled the locks over her mouth and turned to face the figure leaning against the wall of the boarded-up building.

His cap was pulled low over his forehead, so his features were hidden in the shadow of the brim, but the narrowness of his shoulders and the spindly beginning of sinew in his arms told her that he was quite young. Her mind raced for an answer to quell the younster's suspicious glare.

Just as she was about to stage another 'asthma' attack, the boy jerked off the wall and pointed a thin finger.

"Hold on . . . You . . . you is Hitler auntie?"

Nola swallowed the 'cough' that had been perched on her chest and nodded, a little too eagerly, making the locks teeter dangerously.

The boy dissolved into childish guffaws. "Him tell us, you know! Him tell us you was goin' come! Him say you just know when him get little money! What? You smell it? Bumbo! You good, Mammy, you good! The money not even in him pocket good and you reach to beg for it already!" He grinned, gold-decorated teeth shimmering from the shadow of his huge cap.

"Alright, Mammy, gwaan through. You deserve to get every penny!"

Nola stared in shock. That easy?

He flicked his wrist towards the bend. "Gwaan nuh, Mammy! You want the money finish before you reach?"

Nola turned and quickly limped towards the turn that the smoking lady had gone down.

"Hold on!"

261

She froze. Had the locks given her away? Had they rocked to the side and exposed her own dark braids beneath? She didn't turn to face the boy, holding her skirt in readiness to tear down the road if he tried to stop her. She was sure she could outrun him, especially with his skinny legs stuck in those ridiculous boots.

But the boy just screeched, "Make sure that if you squeeze anyting outta Hitler pocket, you squeeze some for me too!"

Nola hurried away, leaving him to laugh hysterically at his own joke.

Her heart fell when she saw that the road veered to the left, forming a sharp bend which obscured the smoking woman's path from her view. She picked up her pace, hoping she hadn't lost her all over again, but, as she turned to the bend, her feet skidded to a halt.

What the hell?! A ditch! Two feet deep and right smack across the middle of the road! Enough to crack an ankle or rip the underneath off of any car. It was deeper than any pothole she'd ever seen! A mucky collection of sweetie wrappers, juice boxes and cigarette butts floated in the brown water at the bottom.

Nola peered anxiously down the street. There she was! She nearly shouted with glee when she spotted the woman, again standing in the middle of the road, again talking to someone out of Nola's vision. "This must be Lucky Nola Day," she thought, watching as the woman gave an irritated kick at three dogs who'd run up to sniff her legs.

Realizing that she was standing in plain view of the woman and the dogs, Nola scurried to the side of the road. Thankfully a guinep tree grew half inside, half outside of the wall that separated the street from the open land. She hid beside the trunk and continued to study the street ahead. Nice houses, some painted in bright colours, lined up closely on either side like a rainbow. Quite a surprise, to see such nice houses on that street!

The woman waved at the person to whom she'd been speaking and continued down the road, the dogs scampering playfully behind her. She walked about three gates down, then stopped before a grey one on the left side of the road. She stood there for a while, lighting a cigarette and taking a few puffs before flicking it at the dogs. They sniffed the cigarette excitedly as the woman opened the gate and went inside.

Nola followed, using the little beaten path on the side to pass the ditch. The houses seemed taller than regular homes, some three stories high, and they seemed to be built extremely close.

"Hey Madda, where you think you ah go?"

Nola jumped. Not again!

She turned slowly to face the green house on her right, the one into which the smoking woman had been speaking. To her surprise, the speaker was not in the house as Nola had thought, but leaning against the gate outside, and there was not one person there, but three. This street was proving to be a little more dangerous than she'd anticipated.

She studied their faces from behind the safety of her locks. They were definitely older than the first boy. One of them had a green rag tied around the top of his head, his afro shooting out at the sides like a coconut broom. The other two had cornrows, but were no less intimidating to look at. It was their eyes—expressionless, even though waiting for Nola's answer. As lifeless as the goat kid that lay stiff on the corner.

Nola quickly looked down at her dusty toes, her words snagging in her throat. She shivered inwardly as the coconut broom raised himself off the gate and sauntered towards her. She felt the urge to take a step backward, and she had to dig her heels into the ground to stay put. As he got closer, she saw that

263

he was even more unkempt than he seemed from afar. He was unshaven, but the beard did not grow in a uniform manner but splattered unevenly across the cheeks. A thin roll of spliff was tucked behind his left ear which boasted a diamond so huge that most of the lobe seemed to have disappeared beneath its white gleam.

"Madda? You deaf? WHERE ... YOU ... T'INK ... YOU ... AH ... GO?"

Nola swallowed and tried to keep her voice steady, but only two words squeezed out of her throat. "Hitler ... m ... money."

The eyes frowned slightly, then to her surprise, they became alight with recognition. The man whooped loudly, the stiff lips bursting into a gleam of gold that put the first boy's gleam to shame. Every one of his teeth, both the top and bottom rows, were magnificently capped in gold. Between that and the earring, he was almost blinding to look at. Like a Christmas tree, this one.

"Yow!" he called to the pair of cornrows. "Frog! Sasquatch! Hitler auntie ... She come for true, my yout!"

The pair broke into guffaws, grabbing their crotches in the apparently extreme hilarity of the situation.

"Down deh!" The Christmas tree pointed after he'd grabbed his own crotch a few times. "The house with the pineapple on the gate ... HITLER HOUSE!" He bent to shout into her ear, and she had to steal herself not to flinch. "HITLER HOUSE!" he shouted again as her gaze followed his finger jabbing at somewhere down the road.

Nola hobbled off, but as she went further down the road, her heart fell when she saw that the pineapple gate was past the smoking woman's grey one.

Damn! Damn! Damn! They were probably watching her, waiting to see her enter Hitler's gate. She would have to just head for the pineapple house and hope that the luck of the afternoon was still with her.

She shuffled to the bright yellow house. The two giant pineapples sat on the gateposts like braggadocios landmarks. As she stood staring at the yellow front door with the pineapples carved into the panels, something tugged at her hem and she jumped in panic.

The dogs! They were pulling at her cloth, threatening to unravel it right there on the street.

"Shoo!" she hissed, kicking at them as she'd seen the smoking woman do. "Go away!"

They gave her a wounded look but ran off, stopping to sniff each other's rear ends by the grey gate. Nola glanced over her shoulders to check if the men had as yet re-directed their attention, but no such luck. They were still watching, hands poised, ready to grab.

She sighed and searched the ground resignedly for a stone. There was a chunk of concrete on the sidewalk, so she picked it up and made as if to knock on the gate. Sure enough, the men engaged in another round of guffawing, and when Nola looked back and saw them exchanging high-fives, she ducked behind the huge yellow post.

She remained there, crouched in that familiar position till her back screamed and her legs tingled with pins and needles. She stayed there till the sky glowed and the pineapples on the posts lit up. She prayed that the dogs wouldn't come back and sniff her out to the watchmen. She alternated her frantic looks between the windows of the house and the gate on which the men still leaned. One of the times, she saw that the Christmas tree had gone, leaving the other two behind. You see?... she encouraged her stiff legs, just two to go! However, when she heard the hum of a car engine coming from the top of the road, panic shattered her once again. Suppose the car was coming this way … to this gate? Suppose it was that damn Hitler?

She held her breath and peeped out. Sure enough, a car was at the top of the road, idling in front of the ditch. As she watched, the cornrows sauntered up to the bend, where one of them jumped over the wall and retrieved a long metal grate. He passed one end to his companion, and together they carried it to the ditch and placed it across the hole. The car drove over, the driver tapping the horn and gave a friendly wave through the window.

Nola gasped. That was no pothole, it was a security system! A moat, no less! Wonder of wonders! If only Palm View had had one of those, they could have kept out the likes of Eric McKenzie! Her thoughts were suddenly interrupted as she realized that the car was now speeding towards her hiding place. She pressed back against the post, holding her breath on a prayer, then expelling it with relief as the car sped past, stinging her with a barrage of gravel.

Suddenly, a realization hit her. The grate! It had to be replaced, which meant the cornrows would have to still be up at the wall! She peeped out once again, and sure enough, there they were lowering the grill behind the guinep trunk.

Nola ran. Hauled up her rags and ran straight across the street to the grey gate. The dogs, ecstatic at the apparent offer of a game, joined in the gallop and raced ahead of her, straight up the street to where the cornrows stood.

Nola's heart did a painful flip when she saw that a thick padlock hung from the gate, but as she rammed her hand through and grabbed it, she realized that it hung open. Lucky Nola Day! She nearly laughed with relief as the latch slid aside, but the feeling was short lived as the metal grated loudly across the bar. She did not stop to check if the sound had been noted by the cornrows, just hurriedly pushed the gate open and slipped inside, searching wildly for another hiding place. She spotted a June Rose bush in the corner of the yard and rushed behind it, anxiously holding her breath as she waited for the cornrows and dogs to come galloping through the gate.

Praise God, they hadn't heard! Again, Nola almost laughed again, the relief obviously making her giddy. She released her breath in a loud whoosh, but was suddenly aware of another sensation. Burning. Her skin was burning all over, as if someone had lit a fire beneath her rags. She squinted at the bark of the June Rose bush and saw that the outer layer was moving! A fine, golden army of Pickle-Dickle ants marched hysterically along the branches, some having already launched the attack.

Before she could stop herself, she jumped from the bush and began stomping her legs, trying to knock the creatures out of her rags. However, as she jumped around, her eyes snagged on something, and she froze.

Eric's black Honda sat in the garage right in front of her! As Nola stared at the vehicle with her jaw lolling open, everything suddenly began to make sense—the missing street sign, the watchmen hidden within the woodwork at every corner, the moat—everything reeked of Eric McKenzie! This ugly grey house that looked like the fly pitching on the rainbow, belonged to Eric McKenzie!

Nola stared, the burning on her skin miraculously disappearing beneath the shock of her discovery. Surprisingly, the house was not one of the extravagant three-storey ones. It had just two levels, but two levels peppered with so many windows that it reminded Nola of a castle. A prince's castle to go with the moat.

There was music coming from within the house, the faint bass of reggae reverberating from somewhere on the second floor. The acknowledgement of activity shook Nola from her shocked trance and sent her scampering over to the car. She ducked between the shiny vehicle and the wall of the garage, trying to figure out what the hell to do next as she rubbed at her welted neck. If this was Eric's house, and the smoking woman was here, then Petra had to be close by!

She gathered her rags and scurried to the front of the car, but just as she reached the bumper, she became aware of another sound—a low, grating hum. She peeped out cautiously and spotted a white front door. But the sound was from somewhere to the left. She stuck her neck out a little further and gasped, quickly withdrawing behind the car once again. There was a man asleep in a chair! It was his loud snores that she was hearing.

She'd gotten this far, there was no way she could stop now. As another grating snore rang through the garage, she hauled up her rags and ran to the closed door, grabbing the handle. Open! In three seconds flat, Nola was inside Eric McKenzie's house!

CHAPTER 44

T HE SMELL OF hot oil and onions flamed Nola's nostrils as she tried to adjust her eyes to the dim light. She pressed herself back against the wall, her feet stumbling over something on the ground as she blinked to force her eyes into focus. She panicked for a few seconds, not knowing which part of the house she'd entered. Was she being watched as she stood there, blinking like a peenywallie? She braced herself for a blow, listening carefully for the sounds of someone's approach, but she could only hear the clank of pots.

In a few seconds, her eyes focused on the narrow passage, and she jumped when she saw a silent figure standing beside her. Just as she was about to tear through the house screaming Petra's name, she realized that it was just a wooden hat rack, its four-pronged arms covered with caps and one brightly-coloured umbrella.

She tried to move quietly up the passage, but stumbled again. Eric's shoes were lined up against the wall, shining even in the dim light. Nola sneered in disgust at the sparkling leather. They were probably left there so that they wouldn't soil the floors of his precious house.

She hurriedly tiptoed towards the light at the end of the passage. The left side led to the clanking pots, the right towards another dim room. Nola squinted into the room and made out an ironing board, a chest freezer, and several white cupboards mounted on the wall. But it was the freezer that caught her eye. Huge, taking up most of the wall on the right side of the room. The type Mama would have died for.

The room to the left was obviously the kitchen, for the smell of the food and the sound of the pots were stronger now. Nola peered cautiously round the wall. Pristine and white. Everything white—the cupboards, the toaster sitting on the counter, the plates stacked in the drainboard, the stove with its steaming pots, even the plastic garbage bin beside the sink. The only thing not white was the woman standing in front of the sink.

She wore a faded orange dress with white bleach marks splattered down the back. She was a big woman, wider even than Aunt May and Mrs. Spence. Her socked feet were shoved into bedroom slippers with the stitching bursting open at the sides. From behind, her shoulders sloped dramatically, as if someone had removed the bony blades causing the heavy flesh to sag like old lumpy cushions. As she energetically scrubbed something in the sink, the loose flesh under her arm slapped nosily against her sides.

As if sensing that she was being watched, the woman turned, and once again, Nola gasped.

Ugly! As much as Nola had said she would never use that word to describe another human being, she could find no other word for this woman. Her face looked like it was slipping off the skull. The skin drooped even more than her shoulders, the jowls of her cheeks almost reaching her chin and waffling erratically with the momentum of her sudden turn. One eye was sealed shut, a solid blanket of skin pulled taut over the section where the split should have been. The other one was barely visible beneath its own sagging lid. Her skin was the colour of weak tea. But her lips! They were the most shocking feature of all—the deepest pink Nola had ever seen on a human face. They rounded into an 'O' of surprise as her eye registered Nola peeping from the doorway.

Again, Nola's panicked mind told her to run and scream for Petra, especially now with the woman frozen with shock, but something in that half-open eye kept her rooted to the spot. Surely she'd made a mistake. This could not be Eric McKenzie's house with this hideous woman in it!

"Ratta!" The woman spoke, pointing at Nola's head.

Nola's mind raced along the familiar channels which had given rise to the many stories to buffer Papa's belt.

"Water," she eventually croaked, grabbing her neck and making her voice crack as if with thirst. "Please for a drink of ice water."

The woman smiled, sending the cheeks waffling once again. She slapped her soapy hands against her skirt and beckoned for Nola to come in.

Nola looked behind her shoulder to make one last check that no one had followed her into the house as the woman took a glass from one of the cupboards and filled it at the pipe. Then, with both hands wrapped carefully around it, the woman handed Nola the glass with the reverence of handing over a gift.

Nola accepted it with a grateful nod and drained it. She handed it back to the woman who took it with another pink smile. She beckoned again, this time with a little jump on her pulping feet.

"Baba!" she said, in a voice childlike with excitement. Childlike, despite the grey tinges along her hairline.

Grampy would have called her 'feeble minded', like Lincoln, Miss Terry's first son. Lincoln used to pee his pants

271

every day, even after he'd grown a beard. He would walk behind his mother, twisting his fingers and looking down at his feet, and suddenly there would appear a big wet spot at the front of his pants. Grampy used to say that there was nothing wrong with the boy, that he was just a little feeble in the mind like some people were feeble in the limbs and couldn't lift heavy things.

"Baba!" the woman said again, pointing at the counter beside a white fridge.

A doll was cotched up against a telephone directory beneath a white wall phone. It was as hideous as the woman pointing to it. Just a few tufts of black matted hair remained on its stained head, the rest of the scalp dotted with the large holes which once held the absent tufts. Both eyes were missing. It was dressed in a tattered yellow blouse, the bottom half of the body left bare, exposing the joints where the legs were wedged into the rigid torso. The woman picked it up gently, rocking it in her arms before offering it to Nola.

"Baba . . ." she whispered, her face softening with tenderness.

With another look behind her shoulder, Nola stepped forward and took the doll. The woman handed it over as gingerly as if she were handing over a live infant, one hand beneath the bottom. Nola followed suit and held the doll gently, imitating the woman's rocking motion. The woman giggled and touched Nola's head.

"Ratta," she said in awe, fingering Ab's dreadlocks. Then she put a stubby finger against Nola's lips and whispered "Ssshh."

She smelled good despite her tattered appearance. Baby lotion. Nola knew the smell well from having rubbed Kendra's skin with it every morning and evening.

"Baba sleep," the woman said, then touched her own lips, 'Sshhh'.

272

Nola nodded. "Baba sleep ... no noise ... no talkin'," she whispered eagerly.

The woman giggled again and pulled Nola by the elbow to a white chair in the corner. It sat in front of another door, which Nola hoped beyond hope was not a room from which Eric or the smoking woman would suddenly emerge.

The woman pushed gently on her shoulder, indicating that she should sit in the chair, but Nola shook her head, looking nervously at the doorway. She could still hear the music coming from the upper floor.

She grabbed the woman's hand. "Eric? Eric live here?" she asked anxiously.

The woman's cheeks seemed to fall even more, shaking violently as her eye widened. She bit hard on her bottom lip, the pink disappearing into white gashes beneath the pressure of her teeth. It was her turn to look anxiously behind her shoulder as she took a step back from Nola.

"No! No! Opi behave. Opi cook! Opi wash! No tell Eric!" she pleaded, waving her hands hysterically.

"No, no!" Nola dropped the doll into the chair and grabbed the woman's hands. "I not tellin' Eric!" Nola pointed at herself. "I not tellin' Eric. I just want to know where him is!"

But the woman had spotted the doll lying on its face in the chair. Her breath escaped in a noisy rasp from her nose. "Baba!" she shrieked.

"No! Sshh! Sshh!" Nola quickly grabbed the doll and put it on her shoulder, bouncing like she did when Kendra fussed. "Baba sleep! Sshh! See? Nola put Baba to sleep."

Nola plopped into the chair and hummed, noting with relief that the woman's lip popped back out from beneath the teeth, the pink rushing back even stronger than before. She returned to the sink, happily eyeing the doll on Nola's shoulder as she removed four ears of corn, still in their pale green husks, and

273

began shucking them. She stopped to caress the silken threads that lay around the buttery kernels.

"Ratta!" she grinned as she plopped some of the golden threads on top of her head. She pointed at Nola's own fake locks. "Opi ratta too!"

Rasta! That's what she'd been saying all along! Ratta! Rasta! There was something about the woman that warmed her heart. The simplicity of her. The purity within the heavy folds of her face. The pink, eager smile. That smile, so similar to another that had also transformed heavy features. She watched as the woman plopped the naked ears of corn into one of the pots on the stove and held her face over the cloud of steam. Her skin soon gleamed with fine droplets of precipitation— just like the dew angels wash!

Nola shook her head hard. What was going on with her, getting so weepy about Dahlia and the dew angels while she sat in Eric McKenzie's kitchen, of all places!

Suddenly a door slammed, and the sound sent Nola flying out of the chair. Eric! The doll fell to the floor, but this time she grabbed it up before the woman could react. She stuffed it into the woman's hands and gripped the spongy shoulders.

"Hide!" Nola pointed at herself. "Ratta hide! Eric don't like Ratta!"

Nola watched with relief as the eye cleared with understanding, then blinked with thought. The woman pointed at the door behind the chair and hauled Nola over to it, opening it and then shoving Nola inside before shutting it again.

It was dark inside, but just before the door had been shut, Nola had glimpsed shelves of canned goods and other food items. It was a pantry. She leaned against the door and listened carefully as the woman's heavy feet shuffled towards the stove. Soon, another set of footsteps clipped into the kitchen and Nola heard the smoking woman's voice.

"Hopey," she rasped, "Why the hell you have to mess up the stove every time you cook? See the pot boilin' over! You better clean it up before Eric come down!"

Hopey. Opi? ... Hopey!

The sound of hurried, shuffling feet, then running water, then shuffling feet again.

"Good ting him not eatin' here tonight. Him goin' out, so just take up dinner for the girl."

The girl! Was it Petra she was speaking about? Nola nearly jumped out of the cupboard with excitement.

"Nuh eat!" Hopey moaned. "She nuh eat!"

"Well, keep tryin'! I sure she not goin' starve herself! She will eat when hungry bite her good and proper!" The woman's voice was closer now. Right beside the cupboard. The soft creak of wood indicated that she'd sat in the chair. "Me don't have no time to run after her like she's some pickney! Just take the food up and leave it there till she ready to eat! And the kitchen stinks. Hopey, mind you make Eric get vex again, you know! You know him don't like the food smell in the kitchen!"

Eric didn't like the food smell in the kitchen! Where else would the food smell be? Nola bit her lip. A monster even in his own home.

Something was sprayed, then sweet air freshener crept beneath the pantry door. Someone coughed.

"Stop that, Hopey! You spray the damn ting straight in my face!" The smoking woman sucked her teeth and Nola heard her feet clip hurriedly towards the passageway. "I gone! I come back tomorrow and try to dress her again. See another spot of grease there by the oven handle! Wipe it off before Eric come!"

Then the feet clicked down the passage and towards the garage door. Nola stayed inside the pantry, waiting for a signal from Hopey that it was safe to come out. But none came. Had the woman forgotten about her already?

275

Suddenly, another smell crept beneath the doorway, and Nola realized why the door had not been opened. Eric's cologne! He had entered the kitchen without so much as a scrape of heels, as silent as the serpent that he was. Nola sucked in her breath, suddenly fearful that her breathing could be heard through the door.

The sound of the fridge door being opened, the hiss of a bottle cap being popped off.

Nola leaned closer to the door—there was no heavy shuffle of feet. Hopey was standing still.

And then he spoke. "If you cook any more of that nasty food and stink up the kitchen like this again, you goin' be sorry." His voice was quiet. Quiet and calm as if he were wishing Hopey a good night's sleep. "Throw that nastiness in the garbage and put it outside so it stop stinkin' up the place!"

"Opi nuh eat, Peta nuh eat yet."

Then, that very, very familiar sound. Nola would know it if she heard it through an iron wall—skin striking skin. The woman grunted in pain, and Nola's hand flew to her mouth to stifle her own gasp.

"You don't hear what I say? Throw it away, now!"

Shuffling feet, hurrying across the kitchen, metal grating against the stove, rustle of food splashing against plastic, a hhmph from Eric, then silence. Nola pressed her ear hard against the door for the thudding of her heart was suddenly drowning out all other sounds.

Eric's voice came muffled from the passage. "And how the hell all my hats get on the ground?"

Then Nola heard another shout. This time it came from the garage. Then another thwack of splitting flesh and plastic scraping against concrete. Eric had found his sleeping watchman.

Nola remained in the pantry even after the distant hum of the car engine told her that Eric had gone and the shuffle

276

outside told her that Hopey had resumed her tasks. She stayed as still as one of the cans on the shelf, wondering if someone else had silently entered the kitchen, preventing Hopey from opening the door.

After a while, when her skin began to sweat from the stifling heat in the cupboard, she slowly cracked the door and peeped out. Hopey was bent over the garbage bin, ladling stew into a white bowl.

"No, Hopey, dirty! Make you sick!" Nola whispered.

The woman turned to face her. The right side of her mouth was even more crimson than before, a bruise beginning to lift the upper lip. A smudge of blood smeared down to her chin, but she smiled when she spotted Nola and beckoned eagerly.

"No. No dirty! Look! Opi put clean bag ... no dirt. Opi take out dinner – clean, clean!"

Nola stared down at the crisp garbage bag in the bin and laughed out loud. The woman had obviously been prepared for Eric's command. Not so feeble-minded after all.

"Hopey... the girl upstairs? Petra? Petra is upstairs?"

Hopey stopped ladling and cocked her eye at Nola. Then she heaved her heavy frame up from the bin and placed the bowl on the counter.

"Ratta take Peta home?"

Nola nodded, "Yes, Ratta take Petra home. Show me! Show me Petra!"

Hopey took two bowls from the cupboard and ladled first rice, then stew into them. Then she plopped an ear of corn on the side of each bowl and placed them on a tray along with two glasses of water. She picked the doll up from the counter and placed it between the bowls, then picked up the tray and nodded at Nola.

"Come," she said, and left the kitchen.

Nola hesitated. There were probably more watchmen hidden within the walls of the house.

"Come!" The woman was back at the doorway, arms waffling with the weight of the tray. "Come! Ratta make Peta eat!"

Nola followed her. They walked through a dining room with a huge glass table surrounded by eight white leather and aluminum chairs. A crystal chandelier hung low over the centre of the table, its icy drops reflecting the light and casting silvery spots over the walls. They approached a flight of stairs which led up from a living room just as white and pristine as the kitchen and dining room. Two white sofas faced each other across from another glass table, a large painting of a white horse running through white, frothy sea surf hanging on the wall. Nola sighed as she stared at the collection of crystal ashtrays arranged in a circle on the coffee table. No wonder poor Petra had chosen this place over the plastic chairs and mosquito-riddled ackee trees of Palm View.

Nola stopped and listened—the music had stopped. The house was silent.

The landing upstairs boasted the biggest television set Nola had ever seen. A small sofa and reclining chair sat in front of it. A wooden table between them was littered with cash register receipts. Nola's gaze locked onto the black scandal bag in the midst of the receipts— wads of money fastened with elastic bands were sticking casually out of it. Poor Barry. The temptation must have been irresistible.

CHAPTER 45

THERE WERE THREE closed doors on the landing, all between the many windows Nola had seen from the gate. Hopey walked to the farthest one in the corner and placed the tray on the ground. She opened the door slowly, peeking in as if expecting a wild animal to jump out at her, then she picked up the tray and entered the room.

Nola followed. The room was small, painted in soft blue with a blue bedspread on the bed and blue curtains drawn over windows. Nola stared upwards in awe. There were white clouds painted on the ceiling, as wispy and light as if in the midst of a bright June sky.

A lamp burned on the bedside table beside the twin bed, illuminating the little figure covered from head to toe by the blue bedspread.

"Peta?" Hopey shuffled over to the bed and placed the tray on the night table.

The figure moved slightly, a little jump of fright, but then it was still again. When Hopey pulled gently at the bedspread, it made a small grunt of objection, but there was no other movement.

"Food come, Peta. You eat up food for Opi?" The woman's voice was as gentle as her movements.

But the head in the bed turned away. Nola could see that the hair was uncombed, sticking above the bedspread like river weed. Hopey turned and gave Nola a hopeless look with her weepy eye, beckoning for her to approach the bed.

Nola walked slowly, suddenly unsure about Petra's reaction when she saw her there in Eric's house. She bent over the bushy head, and the strong odour of sweat and stale breath wafted thickly over her face.

"Petra?" she whispered.

The figure jumped again, but did not turn to face her. Nola pulled the locks from her head. "Petra ... it's Nola!" She said, a little louder.

She could hear Hopey gasp and mutter something about the locks hanging from Nola's hand, but she could pay no attention to the woman at that moment, because, very slowly, Petra's head was turning.

And then it was Nola's turn to gasp.

Her hands flew to her mouth and she gagged in disbelief at the face below her. This battered, swollen, distorted face could not belong to Petra! This face, with both eyes swollen almost shut, covered with mucous that had hardened, one layer on the other, into yellow scales over the purple flesh, was someone else! Those could not be the eyes that had flashed so angrily over Kendra's head. The bottom lip now protruded way past the top lip, a yellowish split positioned right in the middle as if meticulously placed there. It had started to fester, the puss seeping through the split like a busted serese pod.

Hopey touched Nola's shoulder and whispered. "Opi and Val try dress Peta face, but Peta nuh want we touch."

"Nola?" Petra was whispering. "Where … am … I? Ho …
Home?" Her voice cracked on the word 'home'. "Where …
Auntie … and … Ken … Kendra?"

"I come for you, Petra. I goin' take you home, okay?" It was
all Nola could say and not burst into tears.

The battered head nodded.

"But first, we have to put something on your face. We have
to dress your face and you have to eat. You have to eat to get
strong to make it home."

Hopey gave another glance at the locks in Nola's hand, but
at the word 'eat' she nodded and murmured, "Ah! Peta eat.
Nola make Peta eat. Fix Peta back pretty, pretty."

Petra tried to make a facial movement, but only her bottom
lip quivered.

Hopey picked up the tray. "Come Nola! You give Peta food!"
But Petra said. "Hurt … can't … eat."

Once again, rage rose within Nola like a new appendage
within her chest. How dare he saunter into Petra's life with
his sugar words, take her away from her baby, from her aunty,
just to beat her and leave her lyin' under this pretend sky? She
touched Petra's blackening cheek, causing the girl to wince.

"Drink then, Petra. Drink something for me." She whispered
against Petra's ear.

Petra did not answer, and Nola took her silence for a 'yes'.
She dropped the locks onto the floor and took one of the
glasses from the tray, signaling for Hopey to go ahead and eat
her own dinner.

The woman did not move, just stood blinking that one eye
at Nola's bared braids.

"Hopey, I goin' to get Petra to eat. She just need to wet her
throat first, okay?"

With that, the woman hesitantly picked up one of the bowls
of stew and lowered herself onto the floor by the foot of the

bed, placing the doll beside her. Nola watched as she dipped a spoon into the stew, then offered it to the doll before plopping it into her own mouth.

When Nola was satisfied that she was totally engrossed in her meal, she removed something from the rags around her waist. Aggie's package. The one she'd placed into Nola's hand before the taxi had driven off that night. Nola didn't know why she'd had the inclination to push the thing into her waist, but ever since donning her disguise, she'd always left the house with the package and the policeman's slip of paper tucked into the folds of her rags. Maybe it was because as she'd wrapped herself, the memory of Aggie had been so strong that she needed something else, some real part of Aggie with her.

As soon as she untied the pink sateen, the familiar pungency of Aggie's stall filled the room. She took a deep breath and felt a strange twinge deep within her chest. Power. Yes, power. It was as if the power in that sachet of herbs was actually diffusing through her like a physical force.

Nola checked to see if Hopey had noticed the smell, but the woman was busy alternating the spoon between the doll's stoic face and her own slurping mouth.

Nola pinched up some of the herbs, careful to measure to the first line of her finger as she'd watched Aggie do so many times. One finger in the meal and it will heal, two in the head and you will dead! Praying that she had the correct measurement, Nola ground the flakes between her fingers and sprinkled the powder into the water, then stirred vigorously with the spoon from the tray. She put a spoonful against Petra's lips.

Despite their swollen, infected state, they tightened firmly and turned away.

"Sshh, Petra, drink it. It will make you better. Trust me, make you better." Nola pleaded.

And Petra drank. She opened her lips slowly and allowed Nola to pour the liquid onto her tongue. She coughed at first as the bitterness grated against her parched throat, but when Nola lifted her head off the pillow and murmured encouragingly, she swallowed. The girl painstakingly swallowed nearly a quarter of the glass, but soon she shook her head and turned away from the spoon.

"Okay, enough," Nola laughed softly, and placed the glass back on the tray.

Hopey's spoon clattered into her empty bowl and she released a belch so loud that both Petra and Nola jumped. The woman chuckled and rubbed her great belly.

"Food nice!" she said. "Opi cook nice for Baba. Peta eat?"

Nola shook her head. "Hopey, Petra not goin' be able to eat your nice cookin' till her mouth get better. We have to dress it so it will get better, then she can eat."

"Opi and Val try. We put untmint on Peta, but Peta nuh want we touch! Peta cry, Want go home! Want me auntie!"

Petra groaned, her tongue flicking for an instant over the split on her lip. Nola watched the girl's face grimace, then relax back into sleep.

"Bring the ointment for me, Hopey. She can't fight us now."

Opi nodded and took the tray out of the room, the doll nestled between her empty bowl and Petra's untouched one.

"Nola ... "

Nola jumped. Petra's breathing was so deep that she'd thought the girl had already succumbed to the effects of Aggie's potion.

"Nola ... " Petra said again, "How ... is ... my ... ?" She grimaced slightly. "Lie ... beside ... me."

Nola stood still, unsure if Petra was aware of her words beneath the daze of the herbs.

"Nola ... beside me, please. Hold ... me ... "

Nola hesitated for an instant before she knocked off her slippers and, for the first time in over one year, climbed into a bed. She lay beside Petra's frail body, and as the girl shuffled closer, Nola put her arm around her waist. This was how she'd hugged Grampy, and he'd felt just like this, like broken, discarded sticks lying on the riverbank after a heavy rainfall.

"Nola, I ... sorry to ... do all ... this. Aunty ... I too bad ... for this ... world. Don't belong ... here." Then Petra sighed, and Nola felt the body relax. Finally, she succumbed to that glorious, healing darkness that Nola knew so well.

"No, Petra," Nola whispered into the girl's stale, unaware breaths, "You too good for this world, that's the problem. Too good for this bad place."

It was not until Hopey lumbered back into the room that Nola realized the pillow beneath her face was wet.

"Nola sleep?" Hopey bent over the bed and blinked her weepy eye.

Nola extricated her limbs from Petra's body. The girl did not budge.

"Thanks," Nola nodded at Hopey as she took the jar from her thick fingers.

She turned her back to the woman and added a pinch of Aggie's herbs to the dark purple ointment, then she smeared the cream over Petra's lips and face. When she'd finished, she pointed at Hopey's bloody lip.

"Come, Hopey," she said, "Your turn."

But Hopey shook her head anxiously and her hands flew over her mouth. "Eric no like untment! Eric sey, Opi look like duppy. Opi get outta house!"

So that's how it was, Nola thought. He injured them, then refused them the things they needed to get better.

"Hopey, is Eric who do that to Petra?"

The woman blinked her eye again, then began plucking at the doll's hair. Nola reached over and held her hands still.

"I know is him, Hopey, you don't have to answer." She swallowed the lump that blocked her throat. "Hopey, I have to take Petra home. She have to get home." She thought for an instant. "She have a little baby. A baba!" She pointed at the doll in Hopey's arms. "I have to take her back to her baba."

Hopey clutched the doll against her chest. "Baba sad without Mama!"

Nola nodded, happy that she'd hit the right nerve. "Yes, Hopey, baba very sad, so I have to take Petra back, but ... but I can't let Eric see me."

The thundercloud passed over Hopey's face again, but this time she did not shriek. Instead, she picked at another tuft of hair on the doll's head. Suddenly Nola realized what had happened to the missing hair from those dark holes.

"Baba want come. Opi and baba come with Peta!"

Nola sighed. It didn't make sense to argue at this crucial point. "Okay, Hopey, but not now. Petra too weak, now. She need to sleep and get better. I goin' to come back in a couple days for her, but make sure you don't say nothin' to nobody, okay? Don't say nothin' to Val, or Eric, or nobody!"

Hopey's cheeks waffled eagerly.

"You have to take care of Petra, for me, okay? When she wake up, she goin' want to eat, so you make some soup, some callaloo soup. You can get some callaloo, Hopey?"

Hopey nodded again. "Opi go market, buy plenty callaloo for Peta."

Nola stared into Hopey's eye, a pulse of excitement jerking her heart. "You go to market? When you go to market, Hopey?"

Hopey thought for a while. "When Gwenny come to iron clothes, Necka take Opi and baba to market. Opi buy yam, corn, potato, tomato ... and callaloo for Peta!"

285

Necka! Nola gagged at the mention of the man's name. "Yes, callaloo for Petra. Hopey. Which market you go to?"

"Coralation! Opi go Coralation Market when Gwenny come to iron clothes! Buy yam, corn, potato, tomato, and callaloo! Opi buy plenty callaloo for Peta!"

Coronation Market, downtown Kingston. Nola thought for a while, twisting her fingers anxiously in her lap. If only they could find a way to get Petra to the market with Hopey, then Nola could meet them there and take Petra back to Palm View. It sounded so easy, but would Eric let Petra leave the house with Hopey? And, even if Hopey took her secretly when Eric had left for the day, what of Necka? He would definitely rat to Eric, with his stinking fish breath! And, most importantly, how was Nola going to find out what the hell day Gwenny came to iron the clothes?!

Nola sighed. She would just have to come back. She would once again have to sneak past the 'guards' on the street, into the house, and steal Petra. Unless... her hand flew to the slip of paper tucked beneath her bra strap. Unless she could get help from someone not intimidated by the likes of Eric McKenzie! She dug the paper out of her rags and opened it up to reveal the numbers scrawled across it.

Winston, he'd written his name beneath the numbers. Winston, the detective. Nola stared at the paper. Was it a sign? She'd taken the paper and Aggie's herbs from her drawer and she hadn't known why, and it had turned out that she'd needed the herbs for Petra's injuries, so was she also to call the policeman? Was he the one who would get Petra home and Eric out of their lives forever? Was it her spirit again? That loose rattle instructing her to do something that her brain hadn't yet registered, just as it had niggled her about Barry's death?

Nola tried to recall the policeman's face as he'd sat beside her on the curb. There had been something about his eyes—

yet he'd offered her a drink, and that had made her feel there was some kindness to him. He'd wanted to help. He'd wanted to help to find Barry's murderer, and he'd known they were all holding back, that's why his eyes had seemed so strange. Nola gripped the paper tightly.

"Hopey, where's the phone?"

She blinked at Nola's question. "No phone," she eventually mumbled.

It was Nola's turn to blink. "No phone?!" Eric McKenzie didn't have a phone in his house? Impossible! "There must be a phone somewhere, Hopey!"

Hopey rested the doll on her shoulder and began to pat its back, making its limbs rattle.

"Phone in Eric room. Nobody use Eric phone, 'cept Eric and Val!"

Nola nearly laughed at Hopey's imitation of Eric's authoritative tone.

"And Eric's room door is locked, of course?" Nola threw her arms in the air.

"But why him have him money just put down easy as cheese on the table and then lock up him room,?" Nola spoke half to herself, half to the woman. Then she remembered Eric and Pedro's shifting eyes as they'd sat on the sidewalk outside of Ab's shop. Cowards, with their shifty-eyed fears, sending Necka to do their dirty work. No wonder there were watchmen on every corner! Oh well, she'd just have to call Winston when she got back to Palm View.

"Okay, Hopey, I goin' leave now before Eric come back. Remember, you have to dress Petra face. You have to take care of her till I come back for her, okay?"

Hopey nodded and her eye flicked toward the bedroom door.

"Promise me that you not goin' make Eric hurt Peta again."

But, as Nola looked into that sad, blinking eye and the wobbling jowls, she realized how futile her request was. She left the room with her heart heavy, but she kept telling herself that she would be back for Petra in no time. The detective would help her. She knew he would. She prayed he would.

It wasn't until the smoking woman's voice rasped, "What the hell you think you doin' here?" that Nola's heart collapsed.

CHAPTER 46

Hopey had called the smoking woman. When she'd gone to get the 'untment' for Petra's face, she'd called from the phone in the kitchen.

How stupid Nola had been, not to have remembered that when Hopey had first beckoned her into the kitchen, the doll had been leaning against a phone book on the counter, right beneath a white telephone. It must have been the shock of finding Petra in that state that had chased all details out of her mind. Never once in Hopey's speech about the only phone being in Eric's room, did Nola have the slightest memory of the one in the kitchen.

Not that Nola could blame Hopey. The woman was terrified of Eric. Terrified that he would have discovered that Nola had been in the house, and that she had been the one to lead her to Petra. It was after Nola had removed her 'ratta' locks that the woman had been shaken from her awe. Hopey had at once realized that Nola's disguise meant trouble, and she panicked and called Val.

What amazed Nola, though, was how the woman had acted after the call. The supposed simpleton had come back into the room with the ointment and acted like nothing had occurred, when all along she'd just sealed Nola's fate. But, then again, why should Nola have been surprised at the woman's acting skills when she worked for the best teacher of all? She could have kicked herself for being so careless. She should have known that Eric McKenzie would not have kept any weak links within the chain around his life!

He was good! That much Nola accepted now. He had built a fence around his life that could compare only to the thickest, strongest links of steel. He'd scaled off those who were disloyal, and had driven so much fear into those who remained around him that there was not one single kink in the link, not even in the halfwitted ones.

They locked Nola in the bedroom with Petra. She hadn't made it easy for them. She'd tried to run—past the smoking woman down the stairs, through the white dining room into the kitchen, but the smoking woman's quick wiry limbs had caught up with her, and she'd grabbed Nola around the waist and pulled her to the ground before she could get to the white phone. Nola had screamed then, trying to claw the woman's eyes, but by then Hopey had lumbered down the stairs and helped to hold her hands above her head while the smoking woman slapped a cigarette-stink palm over her mouth.

Hopey had not looked Nola in the eye. Every time Nola had tried to catch her gaze with a pleading look, the woman had looked away. When the tears began to fall from Nola's eyes, and her chest heaved with sobs, Hopey had used the back of her baby lotion hands to wipe her cheeks, but she still had not looked her in the eye.

"Please ..." Nola had sobbed when they pulled her off the floor and began to lead her back up the stairs, "Please! Him goin' to kill her! You know that! Please don't let him do what him do to Barry! Take her away from here! Hide her, please!"

"Shut your mouth!" the smoking woman had hissed into Nola's ear and hauled her by the elbow up the stairs. "Stupid child! Don't I did tell you not to come back? I never warn you? Now you get what you deserve, you damn fool! Shut up before the rest of them outside hear you, and then when them done with you, you will be beggin' for them to kill you too!"

And they flung her beneath the beautiful blue sky.

Petra did not stir. Even as Nola screamed and kicked at the door, she remained in her trance. Eventually, exhausted, Nola fell to the floor. She'd messed up. Dear God, she'd messed up again and put Petra in even more danger. Even if she found a way out of the house now, she could not take Petra with her in the trance that Aggie's potion had put her in.

She buried her face in her hands and sobbed. So this was it? This was the purpose Aggie had spoken of—to screw up over and over again! She could have stayed and done that in Redding! She should have known not to fall for the nonsensical rabble of an old witch. If it weren't for the memory of that stupid speech, she would not have put on this disguise! She wouldn't have found Petra and put her life at more risk!

So much for finding Eric's weakness. There was none.

The door opened and the smoking woman walked in with pieces of clothing hung over her arm. She stared at Petra's purple-painted face in the bed.

"Hopey say you give her someting to drink? Some sort of stinkin' tea that make her sleep. Is what?"

So the oaf had actually smelled the herbs and pretended ignorance! Nola looked up at the ceiling.

The woman sighed and locked the door, dropping the key into her pocket.

"Look, we take care of the girl. Him beat her, and we fix her. I just want know if what you give her is medicine or poison?"

Nola gasped at the thought of giving Petra poison, and the woman nodded, satisfied with the answer on Nola's shocked face.

"You stupid just like her! Both of you cut off the same fool cloth! Tell me, if you know that someting goin' hurt you, why the hell you keep doin' it? She know him don't want to hear 'bout no baby! She know him don't want hear that she want to go home, so why she keep sayin' it?"

"She's sick!" Nola screeched. "You damn idiot! She's sick and she need her medicine!"

The woman gave Nola a curious look, then her expression cleared. "I should'a know! From all that damn bawlin' she used to put down! Then what she come here for? Why she push herself up into tings she can't manage, like a damn fool idiot?"

Nola scowled, but didn't answer. Who was this flimsy little excuse of a woman to speak so derogatively about Petra when she didn't even know the truth?—Didn't even know that Petra had left home to save her baby from being put into a home. Didn't know that she'd left to prevent Eric from digging his destructive claws deeper into everyone's life. Who the hell was she to speak when she didn't even know that it was Nola who'd brought the curse of Eric McKenzie on to Petra, and that Petra had sacrificed herself to save them all?

"Anyway, you can't stay in them dirty clothes in Eric's yard." The woman gave a scornful nod at Nola's rags and held up the clothing. "Put on these so him don't blow a worse fuse when him see you."

"Take them clothes and stuff them where the sun don't shine!" Nola shouted.

The woman hhmphed and threw the clothes roughly at her.

"Look, is you sneak into the man house and give him woman poison, so you deal with the consequences." She put her arms on her hips. "Hold on, is how you find the house? Is follow you follow me?"

Nola looked at the ceiling again and the woman gave a grating laugh.

"You have guts, that much I will say. And you even get past Bunty and Sasquatch and them boys!" She laughed again. "You have guts for true. Eric goin' fix them business when him find out —'bout them is watchman!" She looked hard at Nola. "Nuh you is the schooler who was in the supermarket talkin' 'bout Merlene?"

Nola's eyes flashed to the woman's face.

The woman shook her head. "Merlene," she spoke the name quietly. "How is she, and Dahlia?" she asked.

Nola swallowed. "You ... you knew them?"

The woman gave a dry laugh. "You askin' me if I know Dahlia and Merlene?" She was about to laugh again, but something in Nola's face stopped her. "Of course I know them. Nuh she send you to me? And who is this child?" She jutted her chin at Petra's sleeping form. "Another spy she send? What she think, that she can get more?"

Nola shook her head. "More?"

"Aw, come now, nuh bother with the pretense. I think it too late for pretendin' now! Why she send such a child, two children to deal with such tings?" Her chin jutted at Nola this time. "Merlene shoulda know better than that! What she thought, that she could trick Eric by usin' little pickney?"

"Merlene and Dahlia dead!" Nola couldn't help herself.

The woman blinked. "What you just say?"

"Them dead, burn up in a fire that my papa set."

The woman collapsed onto the ground and stared at Nola.

"Petra don't know them. I come to Kingston because my family neva want me, and I end up livin' in the same house with Petra. I come to the supermarket to look for Dahlia's

293

papa, and Eric see me and take me home one day, and that's when him see Petra and …" Nola took a breath that merged into a sob. "I come to take her home because is me why she in this trouble."

The woman was not looking at her anymore. It didn't seem like she was even listening. Her hands were on her knees, and when Nola looked closely she noticed that they were shaking.

"Dahlia's father? You was lookin' for Dahlia's father at the supermarket?" she eventually whispered.

Nola nodded, and the woman sighed.

"Him dead too. All of them gone, now."

"What?" Nola gulped in shock.

"Heart attack—three weeks or so after them leave. Doctor say him heart was weak from all the drugs and ting. But I know that him heart did just break. Him never, ever forgive himself for what him did do to them. Him go to him grave prayin' for forgiveness."

"You was there?"

"Him was my brother! Is me help them to leave that night." She paused before continuing. "Me get the money out the safe and take them to the bus stop. I thought him would never forgive me. Him was my brother. I had to tell him that is me help them to leave! That's why Merlene never tell me where she was going, 'cause she know I would'a tell him where they were when him start to beg me. I thought him would never forgive me, but you know what him say to me? Him say, Val, them deserve to be happy, and I was makin' them unhappy, so them had to go."

Nola wiped her wet cheeks and nodded emphatically. "They were happy! She … Merlene started a restaurant in Redding, and them did love each other so much! Took care of each other so much!" Nola shook her head. "All I wanted was to be part of them. That's why I came to the supermarket. I was lookin' for her papa. I just wanted to see one part of them that was still alive."

"And your father? Him was really the one who set the fire?"

"Him never want me to go there to them because of all the things people were sayin' 'bout them. The restaurant had a bar, and the people say it was a evil place, but it wasn't! Merlene and Dahlia treat me like I was one of them. Is the happiest I ever was in my whole life! But my papa find out I was goin' there, and him set fire to the restaurant, and it spread to the house. I went there ... " Nola looked at the woman with tears in her eyes. "I went there to get them out! They could'a come out in time! They could'a lived!" Nola touched the smile singed into her face. "Them never want to live no more. Not with everybody hatin' them like that."

Val was crying. She tried to hide it, slapping her eyes roughly with the back of her hand, but the tears clumped her lashes and pinked her eyelids.

"That was Merlene!" she said after a while. "Proud! And Dahlia grow just like her. I never forget that last night when Merlene say to me, 'Val, I neva goin' make any man ... anybody ... make me have to take my child from her home again!'"

They were both quiet then, each weighed down with the pain of their memories. Nola stared at Val through dazed eyes. All this time she'd been searching for a piece of Dahlia, and there it had been before her all along, trapped in its little cage. Nola searched the woman's pinched face for similarities to Dahlia's. She could find none. She was probably lying. It was probably just another trick to get her to talk. Suddenly Nola remembered something.

"But when I called Merlene's name in the supermarket, you said that him would kill me, like you was talkin' about Dahlia's papa!"

The woman took a shredded piece of toilet paper from her pocket and noisily blew her nose.

"Eric!" she said. "I was talkin' 'bout Eric. I thought Merlene sent you for money. I thought she wanted more money, and I got frightened because I thought she was goin' to make you lead Eric right back to her. You see, is Eric money I give her outta the safe that night."

Nola gasped and the woman sighed again.

"Why you think I'm here, workin' for Eric? Because I like the benefits?" She gave a dry laugh. "Teddy, my brother, Dahlia's father, him get into the gamblin' and the drugs. Years and years we talk to him, tryin' to get him to stop, but... ." Another sigh. "Bottom line was, him get himself into big, big debts, and the more debts him get into, the more him take the drugs and lick up Merlene. Well, who you think come to the rescue, bail him out of all him debts?"

Nola gave her a shocked look. No! Impossible! It couldn't be that he'd wedged himself into their lives too!

Val nodded. "Yup ... that's right—Eric! Eric did own a little liquor shop beside the supermarket, where the bettin' shop is now, and it was doin' very well. Anyway, Eric hear what was happenin' to Teddy and him tell Teddy dat him will pay off all him debts, but Teddy have to pay him back interest each month. Well, what you think my brother do? Take the deal from Eric, pay off all him debts, and start rack up more!" She blew her nose again, leaving flecks of white shredded tissue on her nose. "Teddy was always the spoil one. Granny make him think that anyting him want, him must get, no matter how it affect other people. Spoil! Just like that one!" She jutted her chin at Petra, then thought for a while, her eyes distant again.

"Well," she shook her head as if shaking the memory out. "Eric warn Teddy. Warn him over and over again, and Teddy start to put down the money to pay him back. Well, that night when Teddy beat on Merlene and Dahlia, me take the money out of the safe and give it all to her. Well, after she gone, and Eric find out that Teddy never have no money to pay him, Eric beat him on top of the knife stab! I thought him was goin' to kill him! Well, because I know that Merlene was gone, I tell Eric that is she take it and run away."

She gave Nola's shocked face a defensive look. "I had to!" she exclaimed. "I had to save my brother's life! Eric look all over for Merlene. For a long time him try to find her, but, thank God, she disappear clean, clean! No trace of her or Dahlia anywhere! So, Eric say that Teddy have to pay him back with the supermarket—and me." She nodded and gave a bitter smile. "Yes, me! You see, at first I was so thrilled with the man that Eric was—strong and in charge—different from the other peaw-peaw men that was bouncin' round the place. Yes, believe it! Someting 'bout the way him handle tings make you feel like him would always take care of you." She gave a bitter laugh and shrugged her shoulders.

"Well, with Eric it always get to the point where not even when you do what him say, it can't please him. Him interest just fade away, and nothin' you do can change that. Me? Him tell me that I have to work till I pay off all my brother's debt, and because I knew that it was me who really take the money, I stayed."

So Nola had been right. The smoking woman was one of Eric's bounties in his pirating escapades. She couldn't believe how far his tentacles had reached—even to Merlene and Dahlia!

"But Petra ..." Nola exclaimed, jamming her finger into the bed, "She didn't know what she was getting into! She thought Eric was nice, and when him threaten to put her baby in a home, that's when she come here, to get him away from her baby and everybody." Nola's voice thinned into a pleading whine. "You have to get her back to her baby, Val. Petra is sick, and her baby … her baby not normal. She's like Hopey, the helper, not normal. She need her mama, Val!"

But Nola stopped when she realized that Val was laughing again. "What you just say?"

"Petra need to go back to her baby!" Nola frowned.

"No, no … " she choked again, "the part 'bout the helper?"

"Petra's baby is like the helper, not normal … "

"HELPER!" the woman screeched, "Hopey's not the helper! Hopey is Eric's mother!"

And then it was Nola's time to choke! Val slapped her back to help her catch her breath. When she'd caught it, Val wiped her own tears of laughter from her face.

"That doll that she take everywhere? That's Eric." Val nodded reassuringly at Nola's disbelieving stare. "Rape." She said, and sighed, all of a sudden serious again. "Hopey lived with her granny on a little lane downtown, and one day Granny leave her to go to the tax office. Well, some boys in the lane go into the house and rape Hopey while she was there alone. Nobody know who it was, cause Hopey lock it out her mind and wouldn't talk 'bout it. Well, them eventually find out that she was pregnant, and she have the baby, but she couldn't manage to take care of it. She was young, just turned 14. She used to love that baby, but she would forget to feed it, and bathe it. When the baby cry, she just hush it. Not even Granny she would allow to take the baby from her, so them give her the doll and tell her that was the baby. Of course she knew it wasn't the baby, but that's how Hopey protect herself —lock tings out her mind and just move on."

Hopey, the giant simpleton who cowered at the mention of Eric's name, was HIS MOTHER!

Nola cleared her throat. "I … I … I thought his mother was a nurse, in Mobay."

Val shrugged and wiped her eyes. "Nurse – teacher – lawyer – Eric's mother been all those tings."

She'd found Eric's weakness! Hopey, with her feeble-mind and hanging face, was the thing he was ashamed of!

No wonder he'd despised poor Kendra. He'd hated her so much that he'd taken her own mama away from her, then he'd beaten her mama to near death for wanting to go back! Was he punishing Petra, for having had the audacity to bring another like his mama into the world? No wonder he'd been so insistent about sending Kendra to that home.

Nola shivered. Is that what her own papa had felt—that the more he ignored her, dismissed her with his eyes, was the more the black would fade from her skin? She remembered the glaze in those grey eyes, the frenzy of the licks on her skin.

She had to hold her head between her legs and take deep, gulping breaths. She heard the woman shout for Hopey, but the voice sounded far away, even though she was still there beside her, just like Delroy's voice that night in the rain.

Delroy! Nola's lungs closed, just as Delroy picked her up and carried her out of the freezing rain.

CHAPTER 47

DEAR GOD SHE'D fainted again! She looked frantically around. She was in a bed, but not in Petra's room. This one was not as nicely decorated, but it smelled much better—no stale breath and unbathed skin. A fresh, clean smell, like baby lotion.

Hopey's room! They'd moved her to Hopey's room. Had Eric come home and demanded they get her stinkin' ass out of Petra's room? Her hands flew to her face to feel for bruises. She wouldn't have put it past him to pound her while she'd been unconscious. No, no pain, no swelling.

The room was plain, but comfortable—cream walls, pale yellow curtains at the windows. A faded green bedspread with several holes in it had been thrown over her legs. There was an old dressing table beside the bed, on its surface a collection of grooming items. Her heart leapt as her eyes rested on the old steam bent rocker, just like Granny Pat's, sitting gracefully in the corner of the room. Its smooth wooden handles arched down delicately to become the curved legs of the chair, then rose again to intertwine like a ribbon within the circle of the arms.

Nola slapped the tears off her cheeks and ran to the door, pressing her ear against it. She heard voices, a man's drone followed by a woman's high-pitched laugh. Not Val's laugh. Val's laugh had been deeper, with that smoky rasp to it. She tried to peep through the keyhole, but the key had been left in on the outside and blocked her view. She listened till the voices faded and a door clicked shut.

So, already, Eric had found someone to replace Petra! No-good, dutty dog that he was! He didn't even care that Petra lay just a few feet away, in desperate need of a doctor.

A sound at the door sent her flying back against the wall. The key was being turned! She pressed herself back as the door opened and Hopey's head poked through. Nola moved quickly. Before the woman could focus on her standing behind the wall, she rammed her shoulder into the door, and as Hopey's pained hmmph rang through the room, she ran.

Hopey stumbled backwards, holding her head in agony as Nola raced down the staircase! She jumped them two at a time, frantically pulling the detective's paper from her bra. But as she raced into the kitchen, she ran straight into someone, and it was her turn to hmmph as she was pulled roughly to the ground. A hand capped over her mouth, stifling the scream that was about to rip from her lips. Cigarette smoke!

She didn't even bother to fight when Val straddled her and hissed into her ear, "Stupid pickney! You want to get us all killed?" The woman squinted a warning as she cocked her head towards the doorway.

Eric's voice was echoing from the top of the stairs! "... damn noise so late at night time! Get in your bed and stop haunt the place like duppy!"

Then Hopey's voice, "Trip and lick head on door. Opi get ice."

They hadn't told him! She looked questioningly above the hand on her mouth into Val's eyes.

The flash of answering anger told her that she was right. They hadn't told Eric. That's why they'd hidden her in Hopey's room.

Hopey stumbled into the kitchen, holding her head with one hand and the doll in the other. Nola's heart cracked when she saw the vivid red mark on the woman's temple. Hopey stopped only for a second at the doorway, blinking down at Nola and Val on the floor before lumbering past and removing an ice tray from the freezer.

Val removed her hand from Nola's mouth and sat back against the cupboard. "Stupid pickney!" she grumbled again.

Nola got up slowly and went to where Hopey was snapping cubes of ice into a white towel. She watched as the woman emptied the tray then placed the towel on the gash.

"Sorry, Hopey," Nola whispered, "I thought you was goin' to make Eric kill me."

Finally, Hopey looked at Nola. Her eye glistened with unshed tears, the rim red and swollen. Slowly, she leaned forward and placed her great head on Nola's shoulder.

"Nola angry at Opi," she whispered, "but Opi nuh hurt Nola. Opi nuh hurt Peta. Opi nuh hurt nobody."

Nola squeezed the spongy shoulders. "I know, Hopey. I just get frighten, that's all. I not angry no more. Now I know you wouldn't hurt us."

Hopey sighed. "Opi want help Peta, but Opi nuh want no more beatin'!"

Nola pushed the woman's shoulders upwards so that she could look into the eye. "You don't have to do anyting, Hopey. I goin' call somebody who will take care of everyting! You not goin' to get no more beatin'!"

There was a scoff from the floor and Nola turned to stare down at Val's scowling face.

"Phone call? Who you plannin' to call, m'dear? God?"

302

Nola waved the paper with the numbers scrawled across it. "No, Val. This person goin' get us outta here! Him not 'fraid of people like Eric McKenzie. I . . . I can't explain, but I saw it in him eyes. Him is the right match for Eric!"

But Val just shook her head sadly. "Let me tell you someting, pickney, it's not one or two years me know Eric McKenzie, and me can tell you someting—ain't nobody born yet who can come in here, and get that gal upstairs outta here! Only way that gal can leave is when Eric good and ready for her to leave!"

Nola bent and waved the paper in Val's face. "Val, someting inside me tell me to take this number with me today, and that mean that this is the person born to get Petra out of here! Trust me!" She dropped to her knees in front of the woman. "Eric isn't God, Val, and somebody have to stop all the wickedness him doin'. We have to try, Val. Please."

Hopey tapped Nola's shoulder. "Phone on wall. Opi tell lie. Phone on wall. Call man to help Peta."

Val pulled her hands out of Nola's and jumped up from the floor. "Well, me gone! If you want to do some craziness like that and risk your life, that is your business, but me gone before Eric think that is me set this up! Hopey, go to your room, don't make Eric batter you no more cause of this stupid chile!"

Hopey turned to refill the ice tray at the sink and place it back in the freezer, then she picked up the doll and cocked her eye at Nola. "Nola take Peta to her baba! Baba sad with no mama."

Nola nodded. "Yes, Hopey, I goin' take Petra to her baby. You go to your room, and when the man come to help, you pretend like you never see me before, okay?" Then she turned to Val. "You too, you go home and pretend you never see me before."

Val frowned and jammed her hands on her hips. "You tellin' me to go home? I'm not the stupid one here, m'dear. Me gone!" But she didn't move. She stood there looking at Nola as if she was about to say something else, but turned and flashed a hand at Hopey. "GO Hopey! You don't hear to go to your room? You want another bust ass from Eric?"

Hopey left slowly, the doll perched on her shoulder like a giant, balding spider.

"So, you goin' call or what?" Val's voice was quiet with daring. She jutted her chin at the phone as she walked to sit in the chair.

"I don't want you to stay." Nola replied. "I don't want nobody else to get hurt cause of me."

Val's laugh melded into a rusty cough. She stared at Nola with her head cocked to the side, her eyes watery from the coughing. "How old you are?" she asked.

"Seventeen ... almost."

Val nodded thoughtfully. "My brother ... 'memba I told you that him dead from a heart attack? What I never tell you is that him get the heart attack after Eric continue to give him more and more drugs."

Nola gasped.

"Mmm Hmm," Val nodded. "Eric think I don't know that is him was supplyin' Teddy. But I know. I always say, Val, how you can see this man every day, work with him every day ... knowing that is him cause your brother family to mash up, and is him cause your brother to dead? Well, you know why? Cause I was 'fraid! 'Fraid to lose my life, 'fraid to end up with nothin' like Teddy—no family, no money— just 'fraid! But I know now that this life is not anyting to try and save. All I want to do is put my hands round Eric McKenzie's neck and choke him! Choke him, till every last breath stop in him chest! But now, I see you. I see how you risk your life for that girl

304

up there ... " Her eyes focused on Nola's singed smile. "... how you go into that fire to save my sister and my niece, and I realize something. I realize that sometimes you have to give up a lot to get back a lot. I did that one time you know, when I took that money. I did it once. Well, time to do it again."

And there it was! Nola had looked for it earlier and not seen it, but there it was—the resemblance to Dahlia Daley. It pulsed for just a second across Val's face, like a flash of lightning across a night sky. There it was – that fighting spirit. That blaze of glory.

"So," Val pointed at the phone, "Miss I-Can-Stop-Eric ... make your phone call."

Nola nodded. She lifted the white receiver and dialed the numbers scrawled so flamboyantly across the paper. The ring on the other end sounded so much louder in her throbbing head—one ring, two rings, three rings, four rings, then ...

"Run your mouth!" The voice was thick with sleep.

Nola looked at Val, realizing that she had not thought about what to say, but Val just raised her eyebrows as if to say, Well?

"H ... Hello?" Nola swallowed. "This is Nola Chambers ... the girl from Palm View ... the one you were askin' questions 'bout Barry, by the Rasta shop."

There was no response, but Nola could hear deep breaths passing over the phone.

"H ... Hello?" She said again.

"Yeh! Nola! What you needin' at this time of night, Nola from Palm View? You have some news for me?"

"Not 'bout Barry. Someting else. I ... I want to tell you ... 'bout a kidnappin'. A girl! Petra Ramsey. She live on Palm View, too, but someone take her away, and him beat her up bad! She need a doctor and him not lettin' her go!"

305

"A kidnappin', eh? You sure is not the girl gone on her own free will. How you know sey she get kidnap, Nola from Palm View?"

Was there sarcasm in the tone? "Why you don't come and see for yourself?" She hissed into the phone. "You're a police! You're supposed to save people! Look, this is the same man who kill Barry! Just come and see for yourself! I callin' from ... "

She looked at Val who mouthed the address. "Twelve ... Blair ... Way!" she repeated. "Come now and get us out, or you goin' have innocent blood on your hands!" She'd heard those words once, in a scratchy old black and white movie that Sister Norma had shown one Saturday afternoon at church.

There was silence on the other end of the phone, then a heavy breath and the voice finally said, "Repeat that address?"

Thank God! Him was comin'! Nola's voice shook with relief as she repeated the address. "Down from the bus stop by that hardware store. Steele's! Steele's Hardware!" She added. "Come now! And bring help, him have gunman on every corner!" Then she hung up.

Val stared at her for a long time before standing up. "Well," she sighed, "Might as well get comfortable! Some mint tea?"

Nola realized then that she had not eaten since she'd stuffed one of Imo's gizzadas down her throat that morning. Her stomach felt hollow and gassy, but, truth was, she couldn't think of anything else but the look on Aunt May's face when she brought Petra home and announced to everyone that Eric McKenzie was out of their lives for good!

They must be worrying about her now. She almost sobbed at the thought. What a thing to be able to say! Someone was worried about Nola Chambers!

Val made tea for herself, then sat back in the chair and slurped from the white mug, staring at Nola with that same blank expression. "You have guts, that much I will say. You don't know what it's like to give up, do you?"

Val blew into the mug. "One day when I was a little girl, I was walkin' to catch water by the pipe, and when I look into the bushes, I saw some red flowers. Pretty and so bright. I went to get a closer look and saw that it wasn't flowers! It was cherries! There was a little cherry tree in the bushes, laden with cherries – the sweetest cherries I ever eat in my life! Every day I would go to that tree and eat cherries till my belly hurt! Then, when Granny died, me and Teddy had to go and live with our father, and we move far away from that cherry tree. Well, after that, every time I walk somewhere, I look in the bushes for someting red, and every time I see red flowers, I get excited thinkin' that it's another secret cherry tree. But, never again... from then on, every red flower was just a red flower. And after a while, I just stopped lookin' for cherries."

Nola was silent, waiting for Val to explain the point of her story, but the woman said nothing else, just sipped her tea and stared into space.

CHAPTER 48

THE KNOCK WAS muffled, coming from down the passage, but it still shook Nola in her slippers. He'd come! Even with the moat and the watchmen, he'd made it. She gave Val a look that said, "See?," but the woman's face remained blank. After a second or two, Val sighed and went to open the door.

When Nola heard the muffled voices she was unable to contain herself any longer, and ran and beckoned agitatedly towards the light flooding in from the garage. Val's back was turned to her, but she could make out the top of the detective's head, bowed forward as if asking a question.

"Hurry!" Nola hissed, and Val obediently turned and came back towards the kitchen.

As she passed Nola, she whispered, "Red flowers."

Nola frowned slightly, but the confusion was soon lost to relief when she realized that the detective had entered the house followed by another head. Good! Him bring help, just like she told him to! She rushed ahead of them to the doorway leading into the dining room, her heart racing with the euphoria of her success.

As Winston walked into the kitchen, Nola jammed a finger towards the dining room. "Upstairs! Quick! Petra up in the far room, make me show you!" she almost shouted, now suddenly freed from the fear of Eric overhearing her.

But Winston stopped in the kitchen and just stood there, looking from Nola to Val with a smirk on his face. Those eyes that had pierced her on the sidewalk were now pink and mushy with residual sleep, as if he hadn't even had the courtesy to awaken himself properly for the job.

"Well, well, well," he said with a chuckle that sounded like he was saying the letter 'K' over and over again, "Keh, keh, keh! Wonders never cease."

Val crossed her arms over her chest and stared back at him.

"So, you goin' tell me how she get in here?" He addressed Val.

"How you mean, 'how she get in here'? Eric McKenzie kidnap her! Him won't let her go and she need a doctor!" Nola cried, shaking her head in frustration.

But Winston continued looking at Val, just keh, keh, keh-ing.

Finally, Val sighed and said, "All of you think you're so bad! Well, she get past every one of you, and them idiot dogs too!"

Nola swallowed. Something was wrong! Something was very, very wrong! She felt the acid heat of dread creep into her head, burning her nostrils with its familiar bitter smell—Winston and Val were speaking in a conversational tone—not the tone of strangers.

She took a step backwards and finally, Winston turned to look at her. All at once, it hit her—red flowers, not cherries! Of course, of course, of course! No weak link! There was no weak link in the fence around Eric McKenzie's life! Eric would not have been that sloppy, to have allowed just anyone to handle the questioning of Barry's murder. That's why the detective's eyes had held that look on the sidewalk. It hadn't been a look, it had been a warning, to keep her mouth shut!

309

That's why he'd given her this piece of paper with his number. Because he'd known that of all the people there, she would have been the first one to break. And so she had.

She turned to look at Val's tired, blank face. Nola wanted to say to her, there were some people who never even found red flowers.

Suddenly there was a movement behind Winston, and Nola remembered the other head that had walked in behind him. The person had been so quiet that she'd almost forgotten about him, but now he looked out from around the dim passage. When Nola spotted the rat tail, it was all she could do not to laugh.

"Shit! I just figure it out!" Winston suddenly snapped his fingers then tapped his forehead. "You is the beggar woman from the plaza!" He turned to Necka and shook his head in wonder. "Keh, keh, keh! She good, you nuh! Damn good! Sneak up right behind me and Eric when we was talkin'!"

If Nola's hadn't felt so weak with distress, she would have felt a tinge of pride at the awe in the man's voice. Instead, her hands flew up to her open mouth. This was the policeman! This was the policeman Eric had been talking to in the plaza! The one he'd sent to handle the questioning of Barry's murder, the one in his back pocket!

Necka gave a little giggle and pulled at his beard as he studied Nola's garb. She could only stare wide-eyed back at him.

"Eric know?" Winston asked, turning back to Val.

Val shook her head, but her face remained expressionless.

"So when you was plannin' to tell him?" Necka piped up.

Val cocked an eyebrow at him. "Why bother tell him when all of you are so on top of tings, with all your watchmen out there?"

"Look here, woman, don't fresh yourself with me before I box all your teeth down your throat!" Necka screeched. "How them must know that a old witch like this comin' to try and break into Eric house?"

Val shrugged. "Well, that ole witch could'a have a gun hide up under all them rags, and waltz right in here and blast off Eric head! I don't think Eric would'a like that, what you think?"

It was true, Nola thought, she could easily have come in there that evening and killed Eric. What would have stopped her, when she'd already tried it with her own papa? Suddenly, she felt the familiar gurgle rising up from within her chest.

"ERIC!!" She shouted into the dining room. "Eric, Nola Chambers get in your house and you never even know!" She had to hold her belly as it cramped from the force of the laughter.

"ERIC!" She guffawed again, "You dutty dog! You think you're so smart, but look who is in your house! Me! Clumsy! The clumsy gal get in your house and you never even know! I could'a kill you, Eric ... I could'a kill you if I wanted! I could'a walk up behind you at the plaza and kill you, and nothin' you could do 'bout it!"

She smelled the stench of fish before she spotted Necka beside her, before she realized that his hands were reaching for her throat. At first, she thought he was trying to shut her up, but when the pressure of his hands increased, she realized that he was actually attempting to strangle her. She tried to grab the braided beard, but her hands only flailed helplessly through the air. She heard ugly, gutteral sounds filling the room and realized that the noises were coming from her own throat. The pressure in her head built as she gasped for air and tried to pry the fingers away. She felt as if the blood itself was flooding her eyes, blurring her vision so that the kitchen became a haze, the details retreating farther and farther away as her legs buckled beneath her.

But, mercifully, the pressure ceased and she fell to the ground. Her belly convulsed, wracking her with dry retches. Thankfully, each gasp brought a gulp of air into her chest, and eventually she was able to pull greedily at the air.

She didn't know how long she lay there, for the rush of blood through her head did not subside, even as her lungs ballooned once again. She felt like she had that evening when Mama's peppery fingers had seared her eyes, blind to knowing whether Papa was in the kitchen. Now she wondered if Eric had come down, or if Necka was standing over her, waiting to strike again.

When the noise in her head subsided she realized there was shouting and sobbing around her, and a strange gurgling sound. Nola slowly raised her head and saw that Necka had remained standing above her, but now he wore a strange expression. His eyes bulged grotesquely, and his lips opened and closed nonsensically. It was from those lips that the gurgling sound was coming. Nola squinted to focus on the gasping man.

There was a huge arm around his neck, and behind his reddened face stared Hopey's wide, panicked eye.

Nola pulled herself up by gripping the counter. It was all too confusing. Where had Hopey come from? Where the hell was Eric?

How come Winston hadn't tried to save Necka from Hopey's grip?

She spun around to check behind her, and nearly collapsed once again from shock.

Winston was lying face down on the ground, and Val stood over him with a rolling pin in one hand, while the other she extended pleadingly towards Hopey.

"Hopey, let him go! If you kill him, we goin' be in worse trouble! Let him go NOW! Him can't breathe!"

Val was the one who'd been shouting.

But Hopey just sobbed and tightened the pull of her arm. Necka's eyeballs rolled upwards, leaving the sockets as white and vacant as coconut jelly.

"Hopey! Him can't hurt us no more! You save me, Hopey, you can let him go now!" Nola forced herself to stand, praying that her legs would not collapse. "See, Hopey? I'm okay."

Nola saw the eye blink with relief, then Necka crumpled to the floor. The man squirmed for an instant before becoming deathly still.

"Baba no like Necka!" Hopey sobbed.

The rolling pin clattered to the ground as Val rushed over and pressed two fingers against Necka's neck. She stood up and gave a sigh.

"Unconscious," she murmured.

"Where Eric?" Nola asked. "How him never come down with all the noise?"

Hopey blinked at her, then Val, then she dug into her pocket and removed a bunch of keys. Nola immediately recognized the leather 'E', the key ring that had dangled from Eric's fingers as he'd sauntered around Palm View.

"Opi pick lock, go in room when Eric sleep, take keys, lock door. Eric nuh come out to beat Opi and Val and Nola."

Nola laughed despite her aching throat. This woman was continuing to surprise her more and more by the hour.

But Val scoffed and jutted an angry chin at Nola. "What now, eh?" She pointed at the two men lying on the kitchen floor. "You happy now, Miss Trust Me? This is the great plan to get outta here? And what 'bout Hopey now that you get her involved? When you gone 'bout your merry way, what goin' happen to Hopey?"

Nola looked at the keys in Hopey's hand, her heart sinking rapidly at the pride that beamed from the sagging face.

"Look," Val threw up her hands with resignation. "You have to get that girl outta here before these two wake up. Hopey, give me them car keys. You two go and lift Petra down while I think up someting for them boys outside."

At the mention of Petra's name, Hopey and Nola spurred into action. However, as they turned to hurry through the dining room, Nola suddenly pointed at the men on the floor.

"What 'bout them? What if them get up and let out Eric?"

Val thought for a minute, then rushed to a drawer beside the fridge and removed a handful of white dishtowels. She threw some at Nola.

"Tie up Necka's hand and foot, and make sure it's tight!" she instructed.

Nola held her breath as she obediently bent over Necka's stench. Val hauled Winston's hands behind his back, a towel gripped between her teeth. Nola froze at the image the woman made—squatted over Winston like that. She looked just like Dahlia, squatted over Devon that day with the lizard!

A groan from Necka quickly stunned Nola back to her duty. She watched in horror as the man tried to lift his head, but to her relief he just coughed a few times before dropping back to the tile. Thankfully, his slim body was pliable in its semi-concious state, and she was able to quickly secure his wrists and ankles with the cloths before he moved again.

As she stood up and surveyed her work, she suddenly had an urge to do something. She rushed to the drainboard and removed a sharp knife, then returned to Necka's bound body.

Val stopped in the midst of tying Winston's ankles and gave her a stunned look. "What you think you doin'? Stupid pickney, you gone mad or what?"

But Nola ignored her and held the knife against Necka's fluttering eyelids. She bent over his ear and whispered, "This is for Ab!" then she pulled the rancid braid from beneath his

314

chin and hacked across the hairs. As she held the slimy tail up
in the air, she could hear Hopey giggling by the doorway.

Nola shrugged her shoulders at Val. "You know what them
say, Val—'what go 'round'... "

Val just shook her head, mumbling to herself as she resumed
her task. Nola wrapped the braid in a napkin and stuffed it
into the waist of her rags.

With both men bound like chickens ready for roasting,
they headed for the staircase. As they neared the living room,
Nola was suddenly aware of a dull pounding. It got louder
and louder as they climbed the staircase, and by the time
they reached the landing, the unmistakable bellow of Eric
McKenzie raked their ears.

He was destroying the room. Things were crashing against
the door, punctuated by threats of what he was going to do
with them when he got out. Hopey winced, and Val patted her
reassuringly on the shoulder, but with each crash against the
door, Val's words sunk deeper and deeper into Nola's head.

What had she done? After they took Petra home, and Eric's
door was re-opened, then what? She and Val would surely end
up like Barry, and Palm View would be worse than before!
Eric would go right back there for Petra and Kendra, and
there would be no moat to stop him.

Dare she pray? Dare she pray again, after all her prayers had
fallen on deaf ears all these years? She didn't know if she could
deal with the disappointment again, of hoping that Grampy's
Sweet Jesus would, for once, listen to her.

She watched Eric's door vibrate on its hinges, and panic
staunched her heart. She stood stiff with hopelessness,
listening to the threats, and suddenly realized that there was
another sound coming from behind the door. Sobbing. The
woman! The one who'd been giggling earlier had been locked
in with Eric.

Oh God! Another innocent life pulled into her rusty world!

Nola prayed as Hopey grabbed her hand and pulled her into Petra's room. One miracle, Lord, just one! Just get Eric McKenzie outta our lives!

Petra was still in the deep haze. Hopey lay the doll gently on the girl's chest before lifting her easily from the bed. Her head and limbs flopped backwards in Hopey's arms, and as Nola spotted her bare legs, she gasped.

All along she'd thought that Petra's wounds had been confined to her face, that he'd hit her only in her face, but when she saw the blackened splotches all over Petra's legs and arms, she realized that she'd been wrong. So, so wrong.

Nola flashed an angry look at Val and realized that the woman had been quietly watching her. However, when Nola's eyes met hers, she looked away, bending to pick up the clothes that she'd flung at Nola earlier that evening. She pulled the pants over Petra's bruised legs.

"Him kick her down the stairs." Val spoke with her back to Nola. "She was tryin' to leave. Him say, 'You want to leave? Make me help you then,' and him just kick her down the stairs." Val sighed, then moved up to lift the shirt over Petra's head. "Like I say, she stupid. She knew him wasn't goin' to let her go like that, but instead of waitin' till him good and tired of her, she get impatient." Val stared down at Petra's lolling, broken face. "All I can tell you is that she lucky, the last one who try to leave still missin'."

When she'd finished dressing Petra, Val nodded at Hopey who turned obediently towards the door. Petra's limbs dangled lifelessly with the movement. Val slapped Nola on the shoulder.

"You sure the someting you give her never kill her?"

Nola shook her head. "That someting save my life."

Val hmmphed and followed Hopey to the door, placing one hand over Petra's bushy head to prevent it from knocking against the jamb. She spoke under her breath. "Take time, Hopey, that's not Baba. This one have feelings."

"Wait!" Nola shouted as Val reached for the door handle. "Listen."

They all stood silently by the door, eyes raised towards the sky as they listened.

"Opi nuh hear nothin'."

But just as Nola was about to say, 'Exactly!' the bedroom door flew open and they faced Eric's red-raged face.

CHAPTER 49

EVERYONE EXCEPT VAL took a startled step backward. Poor Val. Since she was the one whom Eric first saw at the door, she was the one who received the first blow.

What was it about those moments that made them seem to happen in slow motion? Nola watched Val's face burst like a ripe pomegranate, its red seeds fanning slowly through the air as Val flailed rag doll arms. She staggered backwards for an eternity before collapsing onto the bed.

"Fool!" Eric rasped at her comatose body. "You don't know that when you lock up somebody you don't leave them with a phone?"

Hopey whimpered, and Eric's eyes immediately flashed to her, narrowing when he spotted Petra in her arms.

"Where you think you goin', buffoon? Put her down before I knock she and you down the stairs this time!"

His voice was hoarse from all the bellowing. He was in a pair of red shorts, made from some kind of silky fabric, and he stood in them with his legs apart, like a mad dog. Under his white tee shirt, the twin saucers of his chest rose and fell with the heavy breaths of his rage. His eyes did an even deeper squint when they saw that Hopey made no move to obey him.

He took a step further into the room, and that was when his eyes rested on Nola.

Even with the breath tight in her chest, Nola felt a rush of satisfaction when she saw Eric's steps falter with shock. It lasted for just a split second, that quick, stunned shift of his eyes, but it gave Nola the power to return her panicked breaths to their normal passage through her lungs.

"Well, well!" Eric gave the sound that posed as a laugh.

"Yeah, Eric, CLUMSY!! Clumsy in your house!" Nola did not know where her voice came from, but it rang crisp through the thick room, surprising even herself with its strength. "What you think of Clumsy now, Eric? Recognize me?" She flashed the tail of her rag skirt. "I could'a come right up behind you at the plaza and sink someting sharp in your back! Or while you was sleepin' tonight, fix you up nice, nice, like how you fix up Barry!"

Eric's lip lifted slightly. "You see now, Clumsy, that's the difference between you and me—you should'a kill me!" He wagged a lecturing finger. "One lesson for you to learn—never should'a kill somebody. When you should'a kill somebody, then sure as Mighty God is in the sky, that person goin' come back and take pleasure in killin' you!"

"Mighty God?!" Saliva slushed from Nola's lips. "What you know 'bout God, you dutty, nasty dog? You is the devil himself, and you talkin' 'bout God?"

The sneer melted from Eric's face. He took a step towards her and she involuntarily stepped backward, but there was nowhere to go. She felt the bedroom wall press unyieldingly against her back just as he reached out and grabbed her chin.

She heard Hopey cry, "Nuh beat Nola!" but Eric ignored his mama's plea and squeezed her cheeks till that familiar tinny taste flooded her mouth. The soft flesh of her cheeks split against her own teeth as Eric's fingers pressed mercilessly. She felt her lips pop outwards like a guppy fish, but she forced herself to stare unflinchingly at the man's squinting face.

He chuckled. "Then Clumsy," he said, "Who you think know more 'bout God than the devil? Don't him used to sit right there with God in heaven?"

"Nuh beat Nola!" Hopey's voice was louder now from behind them.

"You know something?" Eric continued unfazed, "Gals like you and Petra have the same problem—you don't know your place! You think that you is someting great, someting that man can't live without, but unnu is nothin' but worries. The only thing for man to do is eliminate the whole lot of you! Eliminate you so you can stop bring problems to big man like me!"

"You don't even want her!" Nola muttered through her distorted lips. "You don't want her. Look how you mash her up. Why you didn't just send her back home?!"

Eric stared into her eyes. "Because," he finally whispered, "She's mine!"

Nola's heart shimmied with anger. "You think you can just buy people? You think you can just buy them and do whatever you want with them? Is that what you do to Barry? Buy him and use him, and when you done with him you just eliminate him?"

"Barry ..." he spoke the name thoughtfully, as if trying to remember someone from the past. "Barry? Nuh him did thief my money? Thief my money, and when Necka ask him 'bout it, him tell Necka that him goin' to the police 'bout the car ring. The same car ring that was feedin' him and clothin' him? Clumsy, you see how people ungrateful? Imagine, I come to Palm View, give you all the ideas to improve your business, improve your life, and what unnu do? —Turn round and bite the hand that feed you!" He sniffed in mock sadness. "Barry never have such a good life as the one me give him, and just like you, him step over him bounds, lost his place." He gave a cavalier shrug. "Well, Clumsy, him left me no choice but to find the right place for him!"

"But what make you have to torture him like that? Why you never just kill him? Him never deserve to dead like that!" Nola shrieked.

The shouting roused Val. She gave an agonized moan beside them.

"Not me kill him," Eric crooned. "I don't do manual labour, Clumsy. You know I have my people to deal with them things for me. You see, to my people, dealing with a thief like Barry is a treat, like when you fling a bone to a dog." Soft chuckle.

"Coward!" Nola hissed. "You can't even do your own dirty work!"

Eric leaned closer and brushed his lips against her pulsing ones. "No," he whispered sensually, his hot breath caressing her face, "I just save the special ones for myself."

Then he shoved her face so hard that her head cracked against the wall. He gave a little smirk at her involuntary cry, then sauntered from the room.

Nola's hands flew to her throbbing face. She turned to look at Hopey.

She still stood there, holding Petra in her arms and blinking her single eye in fear.

Val's painful snort suddenly reminded Nola of the other woman's distress. She quickly rushed to the bed and stifled a sob at the face before her. Dahlia! Dahlia's lip nose ... Val's nose and mouth were swollen and twisted, globs of blood blocking the nostrils like slimy swabs of cotton. Nola grabbed up a section of the sheet and pressed it against the bleeding face, lifting the woman's head upright onto the pillow to free her breath.

The blood was clogging the nose, and Val made another painful snort. Nola instructed her to blow her nose, but Val would not comply. She just sat and stared ahead, snorting something into the bundle of sheets over her face. Nola leaned closer to try to decipher the words, but it was not until Hopey released a wail that she spun around and saw what Val had been staring at.

Pedro! ... leaning as easy as cheese against the doorjamb. The expression in his eyes was hidden beneath their shelf, but Nola did not need to see them to understand his motive, for in one hand he held a black gun.

He stood silently, as if having been waiting for their attention, and when Nola finally turned to face him, he casually lifted the gun, pointing at first to Hopey, then at the door.

Hopey looked at Nola, her eye wide with despair as she gripped Petra tightly. Mustering the most reassuring smile she could on her shaking lips, Nola nodded, telling the woman to go. Save yourself and Petra, her eyes said. Run!

Hopey lumbered to the door, but as she passed Pedro, he tapped her shoulder with the gun, then pointed it at Val and said, "Put down that one, then come back for this one."

So he wanted to kill her alone. Nola did not know if she should feel disappointed that she wasn't one of the 'special' ones that Eric had chosen to kill himself, or happy that she didn't have to spend her final moments with the creature she despised so. There was some relief, however, in knowing that maybe the others had been spared.

Hopey came back for Val, her eye shifting fearfully from Nola to Pedro. When she padded the sheet around Val's seeping face and murmured, "Nuh cry, nuh cry," Nola knew that she was speaking to her. At the door, with Val in her arms, Hopey turned to give Nola a last look, and once again, with all her might, Nola smiled. Is this how Merlene and Dahlia had felt when they'd seen her out of their house that night?—this longing to continue with life, yet this knowing that you didn't have the choice but to accept the end?

There and then, looking into Hopey's weeping eye, Nola realized something – She did not want to die!!

She did not want to die! She did not want to say goodbye to Kendra, or Aunt May, or Nathan, or Mrs. Lyndsay. She did not want to leave Ab or Mams, or even this deformed eye staring at her from the doorway.

Pedro gave Hopey a rough shove and slammed the door. Then he sauntered to the bed and dropped the gun on the bare mattress. "You think you smart. You think you smart, and you think you nice. You think I never notice how you used to cut your eyes at me at the Rasta shop?"

She hadn't even been aware that he'd noticed her, much less acknowledged the dislike on her face.

As he removed his shirt, her breath stopped within her chest. He didn't want to get blood on his shirt when he shot her!

"Eric did want to finish you right here, you know? Him come outside to get him irons to done you right in here. Him did want just pop you so," he used two fingers to imitate a gun barrel at her forehead. "But I say, Nah, man! That girl have to bring down to size first. She can't disrespec' big man so, and get to dead without learnin' her lesson! Me tell Eric, gimme a chance to teach her a lesson, then you can deal with her when me done."

Nola gasped. How stupid she was! How stupid not to have remembered Barry's horrific torture. Of course Eric was going to kill her! Of course she was one of the 'special' ones! But she had to have her lesson first—a lesson that involved Pedro taking off his pants.

Nola recoiled as he circled the bed to approach her, his crotch bulging like a scandal bag wrapped around a large Haden mango. He grabbed the knot of cloth at the top of her shoulder. Her legs stumbled forward as the cloth scraped roughly against her skin. She thought she heard herself whimper, but she could not be sure, for her mind was racing with disbelief. Not this! Her hands flew up to cover the black bra that was exposed as the cloth fell at her feet. She felt the release of the little bulge in her waist as Aggie's package and Necka's beard fell into the midst of cloth.

Pedro grabbed the straps from her shoulders and hauled them down to her belly. His fingers scraped away her skin as he grabbed the waist of her panties in the downward haul.

She moved one hand from her breast to cover the shadow between her thighs, closing her eyes, unable to look into the eyes beneath that shelf. She didn't want it to be her last memory.

She shivered, but decided she would not fight. The quicker it was over, the quicker she could get into that field with Grampy and Ellie.

"Open your eyes, gal, and look on big man!" His breath stank. It smelled of rancid sleep. "Open your eyes before I open them for you!" He hissed again.

Pedro stared down at her body, and when she shivered and her small breasts shook, he covered them with his hands.

Nola swallowed the bile that swarmed her throat.

"Why you shakin' gal, like you 'fraid? Nuh bother with the pretense, like you innocent. Barry tell us how him used to work you good, how you love your rudeness, so stop gwaan like you nice." His voice sounded so strange, now—fast and thick, like it had grown plump in the narrow space in his throat.

Her shivering stopped as the meaning of his words hit her. A rush of anger stiffened her back—no wonder Barry hadn't been able to look her in the eye that last night!

324

"Him was so boasty, that one," Pedro continued, "Him wasn't so boasty when him was beggin' for him life though!" (Chuckle) "That's why I make them chop out him tongue first, teach him not to boast round big man! By the time them done with him, him was mewing like a puss!"

Nola swallowed hard again, he was goading her. He wanted her to fight, to give him a reason to punch her till she begged for her life.

Suddenly he released her breasts and shoved her towards the bed. "Turn round and lay down!"

She gave him a confused look despite herself.

"Lie down on your belly—I don't want see that ugly grin on your face while I doin' me business."

A hundred thoughts ran through her mind. Her eyes flew to the gun on the bed and he gave a chilling laugh.

"Don't bother with it, gal! By the time you reach it, me done sail a bullet straight through that grin on your face!" He pointed to the mattress. "Lie down!"

He shoved her hard, and she fell flat onto her belly across the bed. She closed her eyes and waited. She thought she would hear the loud explosion before the nothingness came, but there was no sound. Pedro was neither shooting her, nor touching her. She turned to look behind her and saw that he was still standing above her, still in the red briefs, but the mango had shrunk. He was staring, his mouth pulled into a tight, disgusted scowl.

"What's that all over your back?"

Nola sat up quickly, turning her scarred back away from his scowl and covering her breasts with her hands. It was funny how she'd forgotten about the chords of raised flesh that had been her greatest shame in Redding.

"What's that on your back?!" He demanded again.

Nola crossed her legs, feeling even more naked now than when he'd first torn off her rags and panties.

"My papa ... "

"Your papa what? You father beat you!" he sneered down at her, answering his own question and shaking his head in disgust. "You nasty, man! You is damaged all round, eh? Scar pon your face, scar pon your back!" He sucked his teeth. "Nah, man. Pedro Ellis have too much nice gal around to go nasty up himself with a mullet like you!" He picked up the rags from the ground and flung them at her. "Put on your tings."

Nola swallowed. "What?"

"Cover your nasty self!"

And with that, he bent to pull on his own pants.

So many years! So many years of that very same look on Papa's face, and she'd felt so humiliated. And now—now she was free?! That very same disgust that had once caused her to be whipped till her skin split open, was now releasing her from a final humiliation before her death? Those scars that she'd painstakingly hidden from the world were saving her from a horrible torture! Wonder of wonders, Papa had saved her!

She scrambled off the bed and hurried to haul on her underwear and gather the cloth around her body. Her hands shook with a mixture of relief and disbelief, and they fumbled so much with the cloth that she gave up trying to tie it and just rolled it tightly around her waist. As she stuffed Aggie's package and Necka's beard into the twist, she checked anxiously to make sure Pedro had not changed his mind and was about to push her onto the bed again.

But he was fully dressed, pushing the gun into his waist.

As Nola watched as he pulled his shirt down to cover the weapon, she froze. It was as if a ray of light had broken through the painted clouds in the ceiling and was illuminating the man in the centre of the room. Val's muffled words from behind the padding of sheets were coming back to her, and

326

Nola realized that it wasn't that she hadn't heard what the woman had said, it was that she hadn't understood!

Peter! That was what Val had mumbled over and over. Peter! Of course! Nola had known him as Pedro, so the muffled name had made no sense then, but now, with Pedro's statement—'Pedro Ellis have too much nice gal around'—it all became very, very clear. Pedro Ellis—Peter Ellis!

"Peter! Peter Ellis!" she sputtered, pointing excitedly at him.

He spun around, pointing his double-barreled fingers at her face. "Pedro! Me name is Pedro! Is that bitch, Val, eh? Is she tell you that me name Peter? That bitch won't call me by me right name! Watch me and her out there!" He turned to scowl at the closed door.

"Yes, but, isn't Peter your real name?"

"What the hell that have to do with you, gal? "

"Peter Ellis—June 23rd—17 Pine Crest." Nola almost choked on the words.

That day in the parking lot, when she'd snuck up behind Eric and Winston, it was Pedro they'd been speaking about!

Pedro froze for an instant. Before she could speak again, he was in front of her, gripping her cheeks in the same spot that Eric had grabbed earlier. Her jaw sang with the awakening bruise, but she was too worked up to pay it attention.

The man leaned close to her puckered face. "Where you get that address from?" His voice was so cold that it made her numb to the bitterness of his breath.

"From Eric, the day I sneak up behind him at the supermarket. Him was tellin' it to Winston, the police downstairs," she mumbled.

Pedro shook his head and spoke in the same threatening tone. "No police was downstairs, just Necka and the brother for the gal who you lock up in the room with Eric. Speak the truth, gal, before I cut that smile cross to the other side of your face! Where ... you ... get ... that ... address ... from?"

Nola pointed agitatedly at the door. "Winston is a police! Is me call him here cause him was the one Eric send to question us 'bout Barry. I thought him could help me get Petra outta here! Eric was tellin' him that the others round you is cool, that them know where them bread butter."

Pedro stepped back, and there it was—that shifting, sideways look! That flash of fear.

Nola got the answer she'd been searching for. Eric and Pedro had been afraid of each other! They'd sat together at Ab's, conversing and laughing like the best of friends, when all along they'd been deathly afraid of each other. It had just been a matter of time, who would have turned on whom first.

Pedro backed away, and Nola immediately felt a fresh surge of power flow through her. She could see his mind reeling, his eyes shifting like a ping pong ball.

"Imagine, all that time, not eatin' or drinkin' or smokin' from anybody else, and this whole time is your friend who was settin' you up! What him was plannin' to do, Peter?—kill you there?"

Nola continued, her voice gaining strength from the shock on his face, "Pedro, now you owe me! Now you have to save us—me and Val and Petra and Hopey! Get us outta here before Eric kill us like him was plannin' to kill you!"

In a flash, he grabbed her shredded cheeks even harder than before. "Who you think you talkin' to, gal? Pedro don't owe nobody nothin'! You hear me? Nothin'! Me dust off men three times bigger than me own self. Me not 'fraid of nobody! If I want blow off your head right now, nothin' can stop me, you hear me, gal?"

He shoved her head away and she stumbled to the floor. He looked down at her for a while, scorn spitting from his eyes once again, then turned and walked to the door.

"Get up," he commanded over his shoulder. "Some people have some explainin' to do!"

And he kicked the door open.

CHAPTER 50

As she walked from the room, Nola's eyes locked immediately with Eric's. He was sitting in the reclining chair, and he turned to watch her with amusement as she walked out in front of Pedro.

He was dressed now, in a pair of cream pants and a shirt so lightly peach that it could have been mistaken for pink.

Leaning casually against the staircase was Winston, and on the floor a few feet away from Eric's chair was Necka. No one else was in sight. Neither the woman from Eric's bedroom, Hopey, Val or Petra. She searched the floor for traces of blood, but, to her relief, there were none. She noted that Hopey's bedroom door was shut, and she prayed that they were in there—alive.

Eric's eyes eventually slid off of her and fell onto Pedro. "So, yout," he said with a conspiratory laugh, "You done with her, now? Me can deal with my business now?"

"Where Petra?" she asked in the most nonchalant voice she could muster.

Winston sucked his teeth and raised himself from the staircase. "But what do this gal, eh? Shut your mouth before you lose every teeth in it!"

The unfrozen side of Nola's lip lifted into an involuntary snarl, and a shiver rocked her spine.

"Winston ..." she said, "Winston, Winston, Winston! Where's your sister, Policeman Winston?"

Silence filled the room, and an unmistakable look of warning flashed between Eric and Winston. Winston was the first to gather himself, sucking his teeth again and pointing 'gun-barrel' fingers at her forehead, just as Pedro had done earlier.

"A wha' do this gal, though Eric? You don't see she disrespectin' big man and beggin' to dead!" He turned the two fingers on to Pedro, cocking his head to the side. "Oy, Bredren, you is a man or a mouse? You never teach the gal any manners in the room deh? She come out just as feisty and full of chat like she did go in!"

Pedro did not answer. Instead he walked slowly up to Eric's chair and stood silently behind it.

Winston touched the bulge in the waist of his pants and jutted his chin at Eric. "You want a real man deal with this gal for you, Eric, or you goin' deal with tings right now?"

"Easy, Star. Don't tell me when to do my business! I want to deal with she and the one name Petra at the same time." Eric looked up at Nola from his reclining throne, his eyes holding a gleam of promise. "I want this one to see when her friend dead, then I will deal with her after!"

Petra was still alive!

"Nah, man!" Pedro's voice came with its cold chill from behind Eric's chair. "Me interested in meetin' this man's sister, too." He leaned forward and rested his elbows casually on the back of the chair, looking down onto Eric's shiny head.

On hearing the man's voice above him, Eric quickly made to get up, but as he tried to stand, Pedro pushed his shoulders back into the chair.

Necka gave a gasp and jumped up from the floor. In one fluid movement, the switchblade was out of his pocket and flicked open towards Pedro. It was the same one that had hacked Ab's locks.

"What you think you doin', Bredren, puttin' your hand on my boss like that? Who you think you disrespectin' so?" Necka crackled, taking a step towards Eric's chair. But before his other foot took the next step, he froze.

Nola spun to see what had shocked him, and her gasp was simultaneous with Winston's hand flying once again to the gun in his waist.

Pedro's gun was at Eric's head, pointed downwards from the top of the chair like a thick, black arrow!

"Don't bother with it, my yout," Pedro cautioned, nodding at Winston's hand. "If you don't want see your boss' brains all over this chair, I would throw that ting over here right now!"

Nola did not see what look passed between Winston and Eric, for she was too busy staring at the gun over Eric's head, but whatever the look said, it made Winston remove a silver pistol from his waist and kick it across the floor. It skated towards her, and without thinking, she put her foot out and caught it. Her instep tingled on the cold metal.

"You too, little yout!" Pedro nodded at Necka. "Fling that ratchet over here! And make sure that blade don't land nowhere near me, or this trigger goin' definitely pull tonight!"

Necka obediently threw the knife, but it sailed over Nola's head and landed with a clatter by the bedroom door.

"What this all 'bout, Boss man? Is what goin' on why you stressin' out so?" Eric's voice sounded tight from his throne. His pretty peach shirt had developed two large wet circles beneath the armpits.

"Is the little gal sweet you so why you actin' like this, man? You actin' like you never get pum-pum yet! And it's not even

332

good pum-pum!" He gave a dismissive wave at the vicinity of Nola's crotch. "You don't see how she mash up, man? Me can get you some nice, quality pum-pum, man! This one can fling away on the roadside, Boss."

Nola moved before she could stop herself. She walked right up to the chair and leaned forward, staring into Eric's eyes. They squinted, as she knew they would, and his lip lifted with disgust.

"Wha'ppen Eric? Don't like my clothes? Don't like these rags?" She imitated his sneer. "Well, is cause of these rags, not my pum-pum," she cringed inwardly as she repeated his crude words, "why I'm standin' here, and you're sittin' in that chair with a gun on top of your head!"

He didn't get it. He still looked scornfully smug as he stared back at her.

"June 23rd—17 Pine Crest," she whispered.

And the squint gave way to a blink.

"What? How the gal know 'bout that move?" Necka squawked from behind her.

"From them!" Nola pointed at Eric and Winston. "I sneak up behind them at the supermarket, and I hear them talkin' 'bout it! Them was settin' up to kill Pedro!"

Eric shot a look at Winston. The policeman remained silent. Then Eric laughed. "You see wha'appen when you don't know 'bout tings and you just chat shit?" Eric shook his head in mock sadness. "Pedro, don't tell me that you believe this little country gal? Of course I was tellin' Winston 'bout the move, him is the man goin' keep the heat low. Him is the man in control of all the police, Star, goin' set it up so no heat don't fall on us, you check me?"

Pedro's head jerked slightly at Eric's mention of the word 'police'. "So ..." he eventually said, "let me get this straight. The heat was comin' too close to you, so you told me that me and Necka was supposed to go to the house on June 23 rd, and steal the Benz. Then me was supposed to shot Necka in the car to make them think is him who was behind the whole car ting, take the heat off of you." (Gasp from Necka) "And now, what you sayin' this bredren was goin' do?" He jutted his chin at Winston. "Take the heat off of me? So tell me someting, my yout, what the rass you think me was goin' do when me spot this bredren, who me don't know, come up on the scene? Hail him up? Introduce myself? You think me stupid, Star?"

Winston hmmphed and crossed his arms across his chest, but he still said nothing.

"Boss," It was Necka's turn to shake his head disbelievingly at Eric, "After all me do for you, is so you was goin' to fix me up, Star?"

Eric looked at Necka as if trying to force him into silence with his gaze, the stiff smile still on his lips.

"Tell him nuh, Eric. Or you don't 'memba?" Pedro nudged his head. "You don't 'memba tellin' me that the youth Necka gettin' too greedy, and him so damn stink you don't want him round you no more?"

"After all me do for you, Boss?" Necka repeated, rubbing his barren chin sadly.

Eric sucked his teeth but did not lose his smirk. His words directed at Necka were made to sound casual, humorous, even. "After all me do for you, you goin' believe this shit?"

Necka sniffed and threw confused looks from Eric, to Winston, to Pedro. Then he scratched his head.

Pedro nudged Eric's head with the gun, causing the man to jerk ungracefully. "Anyway, Star," he said, "Just so me can continue to clear the air without any misunderstandin', beg you just pass your irons up here, and don't try nothin' stupid, or you goin' leave your head behind right here pon this chair!"

Winston bristled. "Is what do this bwoy, though? Is what him a chat 'bout, leave head pon chair? You think is little bwoy business we dealin' with, yout? Me is BIG police!" He slapped his chest. "When me done with you, you won't even know where you is, not even your teeth them goin' be able to find when me done with you!"

Eric laughed that dry, humourless laugh, but he gave Winston a warning glance before obediently reaching into the section of the chair between the cushion and the side and removing a gun similar to the one resting atop his head.

He looked at it. Nola saw his eyes move from the gun to Winston, as if relaying some silent message, and then he said,

"All because of a little country pum-pum."

And then he fired.

The sound rattled Nola's teeth. She saw Winston fall flat on to his face.

The landing shook with the weight of his body and the reverberating echo of the gunshot. Nola stared in horror at the face pressed into the floor, as if trying to sniff something on the tile. The arms were by the sides, one foot bent as if ready to run to catch up with its departed soul.

Her knees went weak, and she closed her eyes to erase the image she'd just seen. Petra! Her eyes flew open again and flew to Hopey's bedroom door. It remained shut. They must have thought it was she whom Eric had shot, and were too afraid to come out.

"Rass! Rass!" Necka was screaming, pressing back against Eric's bedroom door. "Why you just shot him so, Eric?"

Eric chuckled, then lifted the smoking weapon and handed it to Pedro. "See, Star?" he said. "Now you don't have nothin' to worry 'bout! You think me would' a do that if him was any business interest to me?"

Pedro calmly took the gun from Eric's hand and shoved it into the waist of his own pants.

Nola could not believe it. Not even a raised eyebrow did Pedro give at Winston's prostrate body.

He nodded at her. "Bring that one over here!" he commanded.

It was then that Nola remembered the gun at her feet. She jumped back sharply, as if the thing had suddenly bitten her, and as she stared down at the silver barrel, she realized something. What about them—Petra and Val and Hopey? Couldn't Eric or Pedro shoot them just as easily as Winston had been shot?

She picked it up, her hand shaking as she gripped the handle. It felt rubbery within the sweat of her palm, and heavier than she imagined it would. The barrel tipped forward even as she used her other hand to support it. She turned the barrel towards Pedro.

"Seein' that … " She shook her head, attempting to shake some volume into her squeaky voice. "Seein' that I don't really care if Eric's brains end up on the chair back, I think I'm goin' to keep this ting with me till I get outta this place—leave you two alone to sort out your worries."

Pedro turned his head slightly to the side, but made no other move. Eric chuckled again, resting his chin on his hand as if watching a movie plot unfold.

"Necka! where Petra?"

Necka's eyes flew first to Eric, then to Nola, then to the pool beneath Winston's body.

"Tell the gal where them is so me can deal with what me need to deal with, Star!" Pedro demanded.

Necka pressed his palms up against his shorn chin as if trying to push his jaw closed, then jabbed a finger towards the stairs.

"In the car trunk. She in the car trunk, and the other two tie up on the back seat."

336

Nola's heart plummeted. They'd locked weak Petra in the car trunk! By now she could have suffocated!

She took a step backwards, ready to turn and race down the stairs, but she froze when she heard another satisfied chuckle from Eric.

"Tell me someting, Clumsy," he cocked his head to the side, leaving Pedro's gun to point vacantly ahead for a quick second. "When you was tellin' Pedro all what you tell him, when you was usin' your nasty country crotch to fill up him head with shit, you never think to remind him that this is my yard, and nobody can leave here till me tell my people that them can leave. Listen me good," he wagged his finger at the gun above his head, "you see that shot that them just hear, them think that is you me just deal with, Clumsy. Them think that is you lyin' dead on my floor! Them just waitin' for me to tell them when to come and clean up your shit! So answer me this, Clumsy, exactly how the hell you plannin' to get outta here?"

Suddenly, Necka pulled himself up from the door and said, "Me will take you." And as Eric squinted, he shrugged and muttered, "Nuh me is the messenger? Nuh me is the one who always do the dirty work?"

Eric sniffed. He squinted at Necka for a quick, disbelieving second, then he said, "Remember that you have family, bwoy. Family that can get hurt bad."

Necka stopped and stared at his boss sitting on his throne. "Family, Boss?" he repeated, then shook his head. "And what would'a happen to my family on June 23rd? What them woulda have after me was dead and gone?"

He jutted his chin at Nola, then at the stairs, indicating that he was ready to go.

"Wait!" Nola shouted.

She did not know if it was the silent defeat in Necka's tone, but she suddenly realized that she could not leave just like that. Eric had damaged too many lives. She walked up to the chair with the gun shaking in her hands, and as his neck craned to look mockingly up at her, she stared into those eyes that had haunted her dreams for so long. It was all she could do not to shiver at the coldness in them.

"You better run, Clumsy. Run far," he whispered in a melodious tone.

Nola felt her spine straighten, as if someone had come from behind and pressed a firm, steadying hand against her back. She laughed. "You don't get it, eh Eric? You just don't get it!" She leaned forward and imitated his whispering tone, "Me name is Nola Chambers, not Clumsy, and yes, me come from the country, and yes, me mash up because my papa used to beat me, but me is the one walkin' outta this house now, Eric, while you can't! You see, Eric, when you put someone on the outside of your house, them can watch tings when you don't even know them lookin' through your window. Me was watchin' you Eric. Watchin' you!" She gave a nonchalant little shrug. "Now you have to explain everyting to my friend Pedro here!"

He hit her before she could move. His arm shot out before she even realized that he'd moved, and it was only the pain in her face that told her she'd been struck. The gun flew out of her hand and clattered across the floor, and Eric then tried to grab her neck. He tried to put his hands around it to choke her, but Pedro had already gripped his shiny hair and hauled him back into the seat.

"Siddung! I don't done with you yet!" Pedro shouted, pulling so roughly that Eric's eyebrows were hauled upwards.

Nola held her face as blood pooled in her mouth. Her lips were split and her nose vibrated with pain, but she laughed again, making the blood bubble through her fingers as she registered Pedro's gun pasted against Eric's temple.

338

She was free! They were free! All of them—the ones from this house and the ones from Palm View Road—finally, free of Eric McKenzie!

The smirk had fallen from Eric's lips, and this time, when he squinted, Nola swore that his eyelids shook.

"I'll take that last lick, Eric!" she gurgled, "I'll take it from you, cause a lick is nothin' to me! But just 'memba one ting—next time you come round to Palm View, make sure that you check in with me first before you go anywhere else on that street!"

She felt her heart soar as his eyes dulled. He remembered! It was the line he'd first used on her when he'd dropped her home on that fateful day. Nola gave a triumphant grin with her swelling mouth, then she turned and stepped over Winston, her feet slipping a little in the pool around him, and followed Necka down the stairs.

CHAPTER 51

IT WAS NOT the same three men from the street who greeted them in the garage. Maybe it was the darkness, or the nature of events that had just taken place, but these two looked even more cruel than the first three from the street.

One of them seemed quite fat, but as he turned to face them, Nola realized that it was hard muscle that padded his stocky frame. The other one was slim and well-dressed, like Eric, but had a scar that marred his face. The raised ridge of flesh ran from behind his left ear right up to the corner of his mouth.

"Him never dust it?" He asked Necka.

Nola's heart beat wildly. She was afraid to look at the men lest they saw the sudden rush of fear that ruddied her face. The surge of strength that had stiffened her spine in front of Eric moments ago was suddenly sucked out of her. Now her body wobbled like jello. Her knees actually buckled with relief when she heard Necka say, "Nah! Him fire one shot when she try step out of line little while, but him say him don't want no blood in him house. Him say I must take her round to Palisadoes and finish them off round there."

The big one chuckled. "Them fish and shark out there must be glad the day when Eric born!"

Necka giggled back. "Unnu can gwaan to unnu bed. Eric say him just goin' finish talk some business with Pedro and the one name Winston. Him say unnu can leave now." He grabbed Nola's arm and shoved her roughly towards the black Honda. "Me will take care of tings. This one nah give no more trouble! You see what Eric do to her face? Him fix her business good and proper!"

The well-dressed one grabbed her braids and pulled her neck so far back that Nola felt as if it would crack right off into his hands. He stared down at her battered face.

"Gal, that will teach you not to use big man name when you a thief into people yard!" he hissed.

"Easy, Hitler." Necka warned, "Eric say me musn't kill her till she watch her friend dead first." But he left her in Hitler's hands and walked around to the driver's door.

After several seconds of staring down at her face, the man roughly shoved her head away, sending her stumbling against the car. Nola could only feel a surge of joy as Necka opened the car door and the light beamed on.

Val and Hopey were huddled together in the back seat. She scrambled into the passenger seat beside Necka.

Their faces were bloody. Val's nose had been bandaged roughly with a piece of the sheet from Petra's bed, and Hopey's good eye now swelled to match the sealed lid of the other. Nola swallowed a sob.

"Necka!" she whispered. "Necka, get Petra out the trunk before she stifle to death!"

"Shut the car door, gal, before I change my mind and shot you right here!" he hissed back.

"You don't have no gun, Necka, and Pedro take your knife. Get Petra out the trunk now!"

He turned to face her, "Look here, gal, stop talkin' 'bout tings you don't know 'bout! If me take her out now, then them two out there goin' know that someting not right, and trust me, after them been waitin' so long to see somebody dead tonight, them will deal with tings right here! So shut the rass door!"

The big one opened the gate so that Necka could reverse through, giving a little salute as the car passed. Nola looked behind at Val and Hopey. Their heads rocked unsteadily as the car headed towards the moat. Two men, also different from the ones from the afternoon, appeared from the shadows and placed the grate on the gutter, then after the car had driven over they lifted it back off and disappeared into the night. Duppies. That's what they looked like. Duppies, nodding respectfully at the black Honda as their shadowy forms crept over the wall.

They drove down road after road, turning corners and driving through red stoplights and past sleeping street figures and hungry dogs till Nola felt the panic crescendo through her chest once again. Had she fallen for another trick? Was Necka really going to kill them? After all, she had cut off his beard, and Hopey had strangled him to within an inch of his life. And Petra was surely going to die in that trunk! Then, as she was about to grab the steering wheel from the fishy hands and swerve the car into the sidewalk, Necka pulled over and said, "Go get the gal!"

Nola did not hesitate. In a flash she was at the back of the car. The hot stench of sweat and bile hit her like a physical force. She reached into the dark space and could only sob when she felt the breath lifting the chest. It was slow and laboured, but Petra was breathing! Nola lifted, unfolding the brittle arms and legs from the cramped space.

It was too much, the relief of finding Petra alive and finally holding her in her arms, and before she could catch herself, Nola collapsed onto the damp sidewalk with the girl clutched against her chest.

Petra's eyes remained closed, still caked beneath their thick mucous, but her tongue flickered slightly over her lips when she felt the cool rush of air on her face.

"Peta okay?"

It was Hopey! Necka had freed her! She stood before Nola with her swollen eye and shattered lips, her doll clutched to her chest.

Nola nodded as Hopey lowered herself to the sidewalk and gently touched Petra's face. Another shuffle told them that someone else had joined them.

This time it was Val, stumbling towards them and also collapsing onto the sidewalk, lying back on the dirty concrete with her bony legs splayed wide. She lay there, staring up at the purple sky without saying a word.

Not one head turned to look at the car as it drove off.

It was not until Petra moaned that Nola looked around to see where they were. That was when she saw the sign.

RAPLEY CHURCH OF GOD
COME PRAY FOR YOUR NEEDS –
MONEY, HEALTH, SALVATION
GOD ANSWERS PRAYERS!

Sitting on that sidewalk with Petra in her arms, she began to laugh "Red cherries!" Nola gurgled at Val. "Red cherries, Val. We got some of them red cherries tonight!"

Val's distorted lips spread into a smile, and soon she was laughing too. "You know the only ting that went wrong tonight?" she chortled.

"What's that, Val?" Nola gulped, wiping her eyes with the back of her hand.

"I left my rass cigarettes!"

And they laughed all over again, while the night dew washed over their broken faces.

CHAPTER 52

THE NEWSPAPER REPORTS said that the fire that razed the house of businessman Eric McKenzie seemed to have been caused by a cigarette which had fallen from the hands of the owner, when he fell asleep on the upper floor of his home. It also stated that two other bodies were found within the burnt shell. Details were given about the attempts of other residents of Blair Way to quell the flames after the dispatched fire truck had collapsed into a ditch at the top of the road and broken its two front axels. All in all, five of the closest houses were burnt to the ground.

Nola stared at Aunt May's mouth as it moved over the words of the newspaper, willing herself to accept that Eric was finally, permanently, gone. She stared at Val and saw that the bony snake of the woman's throat worked up and down. She didn't believe. Eric never smoked. He was just too vain to risk the sour smell on his breath.

It was Pedro who'd done it. They knew. He'd burned it with Eric and Winston inside, and the poor screaming woman from the bedroom.

Aunt May finished reading the article and flung the paper into the garbage bin, slapping her hands together as if dusting off dirt.

She'd lost so much weight. Her hips and arms sagged with the loss of substance, like a balloon that was slowly deflating. The weeks of Petra's absence had been hard on her, and when Nola went missing she fell apart. Nathan said that she'd cried all night, and in between the tears, she'd knelt in the corner of the kitchen and prayed.

It was Val who told Hopey about Eric's death, beneath the ackee trees while the sun was setting. The woman gave no reaction. No tears. No sob. No sigh. No glee. Nothing. She just stared back at Val, blinking that fleshy lid and rocking her doll.

Later reports stated that autopsies of the charred remains revealed that Eric McKenzie, Eloise Bernard, a hairdresser from Portmore, and Winston Holness, a policeman from the Area One Police Division, had actually died from gunshot wounds.

Four other bodies had been found dumped over a wall at the top of Blair Way, the road on which the fire had occurred. The report identified them as Desmond Cower (alias Booley D.), Polack St. James (alias Hitler), Richard Gibson (alias Smiley) and Preston Miles (alias Powda). They were also reported to have suffered from gunshots, all administered from behind. The report stated that investigations were being conducted into the gruesome murders, and had already led to the apprehension of several other residents of Blair Way, many of whom were wanted for various crimes.

Nothing was mentioned of Pedro or Necka.

One and a half weeks after the fire, Val returned to the supermarket and resumed her job as manager, but it was not until she went to the tax office to file for the proper housing benefits for the employees that she discovered that the supermarket ownership was still listed under her name. Eric had not changed the name of ownership after her brother died. All those years, as Eric dilly-dallied around the taxman, he'd been forging Val's signature, no doubt to protect himself if his tax tricks eventually caught up with him.

Val's hands were still shaking when she brought the papers to show Nola and Aunt May. Smart, conniving wretch! Aunt May had said when she'd seen them.

Smart, DEAD wretch, Nola had said, and they'd all tried not to laugh because of the morbidity of the joke.

It meant arranging a long payment schedule for all the taxes that Eric had reneged on over the years, but it didn't matter. The supermarket was Val's. No more handing over the profits at the end of each week and receiving a pittance of a salary in return. No more answering to the barks of a dog like Eric McKenzie.

Petra's healing on the outside was quick. She spent only one week on the ward of the public hospital. Two ribs and her left index finger had been cracked in her tumble down the stairs, and her right leg had to be fitted back into the hip socket. The doctor marveled at how fast Petra's lesions purged their puss and meshed into scabs. Nola marveled along with the nurses and doctors, making absolutely no allusion to the thermos of bitter tea that she brought to the hospital each day.

But, the deep emotional scars that had been re-opened by Eric's brutal treatment and subsequent abandonment, combined with Petra's guilt at having left her baby, created a wound that needed more than Aggie's potion could heal.

Petra had locked herself away. No tea, none of Aggie's scriptures, none of her weekly sessions with her doctor, could get her out. Even as her skin glowed, once again, with health, Petra's eyes reflected the glazed state of a numbed soul. Even after Kendra became familiar, once again, with her face, and began smiling and chatting with ease around her, Petra only touched the child hesitantly. It was as if she was afraid to

346

become attached, as if she didn't trust herself to stay. Even within Aunt May's hugs that had always brought delighted giggles, Petra stiffened and turned her head away.

He'd taken Petra away, Nola thought angrily. He'd cracked her open and removed her soul, and they'd only retrieved the empty shell to repair. She knew only too well about an empty shell. Her own mama had lived in one.

It would take time, Aunt May told them, and Nathan nodded solemnly as he touched Aunt May's shoulder in reassurance.

Hopey did not leave Petra's side. When Petra was eventually discharged from the hospital and Hopey transferred her watch to the bedroom, she would play with Kendra in there, bouncing the child on her lap and laughing raucously at her antics. Many times she would look hopefully at Petra and say, "Peetty baba, Peta. Peta baba so peetty!"

When it was obvious that Hopey had no intention of leaving Petra's side to go to live with Val, they put her to sleep in Nola's room while another cot was placed in Olive's room for Nola.

As to Nola, the first thing she did on returning to Palm View was to go to Ab's shop and tack Necka's beard over the doorway. The thing looked even more flimsy hanging over the door. Like a stinkin' wad of tangled old thread, Mattie said.

That morning after she'd returned with Petra, when she'd walked to the shop with her swollen face, Ab had looked at her as if he'd seen the devil himself. He'd been up all night, Mams said, waiting for word on her whereabouts. His face had darkened with rage when he spotted her face, and when she held up the little beard, he just turned and walked away.

Mams said she'd had to tell him, about the locks and the disguise when Nola did not come home that night. He had not known who to call, or where to tell anyone that she might have gone, and he'd cussed out poor Mams for her carelessness.

"Him was a fret, Nola," Mams said, "Fret like it was him own head that did lost!"

But he left the beard up, and many times Nola found him looking up at the wingy tail, a look of perplexity on his wide face.

Two months after bringing Petra home, Nola went back to school. She'd decided that she would the moment Eric had announced in the kitchen that she 'smoked weed all day'. She'd resolved she would, when she'd seen how distraught they'd all been at her disappearance that night. And she'd determined she would, when she'd seen the despondency in Petra. She would give Aunt May no more reason to sit over her Milo and pray into the steam, or to set her jaw so that it rippled beneath the strain, like Mama's.

Truth was, even with Petra's dark moods, the house crackled with the electricity of renewed beginnings—Hopey and her delight in Kendra, Val and her ideas for Nathan to package and sell his magical fertilizer, Hopey plucking long white hairs from Mrs. Lyndsay's chin beneath the ackee trees in the evenings, Ab and Mams's shop and the rest of Palm View and Preston Roads running once again without the shackles of Eric and his cronies—new beginnings.

Nola worked hard at school since she had missed out on so much. Many evenings found her sitting in the living room with Aunt May till the house was filled with the breaths of everyone else's sleep. They hashed over math and science problems. Nathan woke periodically to bring them hot mugs of tea or Milo. Mrs. Lyndsay tried one night to bring them hot drinks, too, but after mixing two cups of a white, chalky liquid, using flour instead of cocoa, she was asked to help them by checking in on Kendra and Petra.

* * *

In two and a half years, at nearly the age of nineteen, Nola graduated from high school and went straight into what she'd felt had been her calling from the very first time she'd sat over that math book with Dahlia Daley. She registered to study teaching. She then went on to specialize in 'special needs' education at the Mico Teachers' College. It was, Nathan who said, "a gift", one he could have seen clearly from the time she'd spent with Kendra, teaching her how to eat and speak. Nola did not tell him that her desire to help those with challenges was the farthest thing from a gift. Rather, that it arose from a pain. A pain so severe that it sought to be numbed by fixing others. Those who were weak, and different, and exiled—those were the ones Nola craved to help. Those were the ones she wanted to hold against her chest and show them that they were special.

With Aunt May's help, and everyone else cheering on from the sidelines, Nola graduated with honours. Her first move was to look for somewhere to open her own school, one where Kendra and children like her could be taught in a comfortable environment.

It had not been easy for Kendra at school. They had all watched with aching hearts as day after day Kendra came home cranky, sometimes with welts on her arms for the spankings she'd gotten for not cooperating with the rules of the school. They all knew that Kendra always needed extra coaxing when it came to following rules and regulations. The teachers just never had the time or patience to deal with such needs, even though half the school was made up of students like Kendra, some with even more severe disabilities. Aunt May had stormed into the school many times after Kendra had come home withdrawn and sad, demanding to know the reasons for the welts on the child's arms, but it never made a difference.

Eventually, the school told Aunt May to take Kendra home and deal with the child herself, since she was so dissatisfied with their attempts. And, so she did until she and Nola opened the Dah-Lilly School for the Challenged.

At first, it was only one room, rented at the side of a Chinese restaurant where the smell of food had everyone's mouth running like leaking pipes all day.

The wailing on the first day of school was nerve racking, even though the total number of students in attendance was five. The crying was so bad that Hopey had to be taken outside by Nathan and hushed like one of the children when she held her head and sympathetically joined in the sobbing.

Petra drew up the registration forms and wrote down the names and addresses of the students, their allergies and medical histories, and fee payment schedules.

Nathan planted five hibiscus plants (in clay pots so that when they moved to a larger property, the plants could be moved with them) in honour of the first five students, to commemorate the great day, while Hopey prepared chicken soup on a hot plate outside, the commencement of the lunch programme to be offered each day.

One of the students, Deborah, sat quietly in a corner, and when Aunt May approached her and asked if she wanted to use the brand new crayons, she told her that she just wanted to go back to her fucking yard. When Nola saw Aunt May's eyebrow strings haul the two brows up to her hairline, an involuntary snort of laughter escaped her lips, and when Aunt May turned a startled glance in her direction, Nola could not control the giggles. Before she knew it, Aunt May had joined her with chuckles of her own. Soon, they were both laughing so hard that they could not stand, and they stumbled around the classroom, slapping the walls and their knees in mirth.

It was not till they stopped to catch their breath that they realized that the crying had stopped and the children were staring at them with wide eyes and open mouths.

And so began the first day of the Dah-Lilly School for the Challenged.

As to Palm View Road, unfortunately Eric McKenzie had only been the first of a long line of his type to venture onto the street. Things were changing in Kingston, and the pulse of the change was occurring right around Palm View and Preston Roads. Once again, faces began to appear at Ab's shop that brought the grip of familiar fear to Nola's heart. The faces were like giant mirrors, positioned on Palm View, but reflecting the cruelty and harshness of life in areas miles and miles away, areas that were growing concentrically nearer to Palm View. Many wore scars slashed into their faces and chests, and those who had none on their outer body carried them on the inside.

Times were hard, jobs were scarce, and those businesses which sought employees skimmed the thin surface of society for the more educated. Rising food costs and living expenses were viewed as sabotage from the government to keep the 'Black man down', and the anger and resentment for the upper crust of society diffused into the streets like a poisonous gas. It was as if Barry had formed a secret church, and his doctrine was suddenly spreading like the flu.

The eyes that filtered on to Palm View were numbed to the softer elements of humanity, and they spread their diseased ways of thinking among the boys who already lived there. The government had taken their living away, and they had to take it back—from whomever they could get it.

Nola saw the change in those she knew, saw the way Panhead's walk altered, with the head now cocked to the side as if daring the world to defy the authority of his shadow.

351

They, too, now stepped into the streets in front of speeding cars, as if life had become a game of 'dare'. They, too, leaned on walls and smoked their joints, speaking of 'shipments' and 'payments' and 'irons' and 'shottas' as if they were discussing the weather. Nola recognized the expressions. She'd seen them all on the day she'd snuck past Eric's street. Hungry and greedy at the same time.

Palm View was changing before their very eyes, like a beautiful ripe mango left to rot. They'd wrestled Palm View out of the hands of Eric McKenzie, and now a larger army had come to claim it. The homeowners who'd once stood in their gardens, watering their plants and catching up with neighbours now remained behind tightly shut doors. The fresh coats of paint that had whitewashed their walls and curbs every Christmas were replaced with flyers advertising dances in the surrounding areas. Litter lay in the gutters along the street, and after heavy rainfalls it galloped with the run-off and piled high at the entrance of the narrow tunnel that led to the main gully. With the gully entrance blocked and the run-off having nowhere to go, the rainwater backed up and flooded the streets, sometimes even entering the lower floors of the homes.

Close to Christmas, the bakery closed its doors and moved to a plaza near Red Hills, commemorating its grand opening with Mattie's four-pounder Christmas puddings. They were a hit and the large orders required that the bakery employ Hopey for one whole month, to help wrap the puddings in their festive burlap and red ribbons.

By early January, Ab and Mams had come down to Aunt May's to announce that they'd been approved to open a vegetarian stall in the food court of a Constant Spring plaza. They were going to rent a house nearer to that area until they could afford to build their own. Everyone knocked their stout bottles together and wished Mams and Ab good luck.

It was, therefore, within the natural flow of things that Aunt May decided to sell the house. Everyone would have to find somewhere else to live.

The announcement brought much wailing and tearing at chests in the kitchen that night, but the sadness was short-lived, for the next morning Nathan marched into the kitchen and announced that he could not bear to carry his secret burden any longer, especially when faced with the threat of losing his one true love all over again. He got down on his soil-chapped knee and asked Aunt May if she would be his most honourable wife. When Aunt May's cheeks turned red and vibrated with her blushing acceptance, it was decided there and then that Mrs. Lyndsay could not return to Connecticut since the cold winters would most certainly aggravate her arthritis and send her straight to the grave. Then Hopey hid herself within Nathan's gungu bushes and blinked unwaveringly from between the leaves when they tried to coax her out, refusing to budge until they promised 'never, ever, ever' to separate her from Kendra. All, but Olive who had signed up for a one year job as a waitress on a cruise ship, decided that they were not to be parted, and the task at hand changed from looking for separate new homes, to finding one large enough for them all in a 'nicer' but affordable neighbourhood.

* * *

It had been Dahlia and Merlene's house. That was the only thought that passed through Nola's mind as she stood on the patchy front lawn and stared at the stripping, mildewed walls. This had been Dahlia and Merlene's home, the one that Dahlia had spoken so lovingly of; the one where she'd made those special memories and dreams. It was as beautiful as she had described it.

Nola did not see the collapsing eave that hung like a broken fingernail over the front door, nor the wooden window box whose skeletal remains screamed of a termite infestation. While the others stood around her and commented on the amount of work the house would need, her heart only soared. Aunt May was quiet, too, watching Nola intently as Nathan rattled on about the crab grass he would use to create a luscious lawn. Aunt May knew that Nola only saw Dahlia and Merlene's beaming faces, looking out from that rotting window box and beckoning for her to come inside.

She had come home! Imagine that. She had traveled a full circle—from the pink house, to the street shack, to Palm View, right to this home in Havendale, St. Andrew. Imagine that! The once lonely, shunned Nola Chambers now stood in front of Dahlia's Kingston home, surrounded by a family—not a family bound by blood, but solely by the happenstance of Fate. Here they stood, within the gaps of the broken barriers which should have kept them apart, but, instead, had formed their own fence of strong links. Their bundle of sticks.

CHAPTER 53

THE SALE OF Palm View was surprisingly quick. It was bought by a woman with a huge silver knob pierced through her right nostril. She never even looked upstairs when she emerged from her sparkling white BMW and met with Aunt May in the living room, exclaiming only at Palm View's easy access to downtown Kingston—Bam, bam, bam and you can take Mountain View straight to the airport!

She apparently made frequent trips to Panama to supply her 'roving boutique' business. Aunt May, thinking the woman would negotiate the price right down to nothing, named a ridiculously high figure for the house, the woman lit a cigarette thoughtfully and then offered cash up front. Aunt May blinked for a good few seconds before handing her an ashtray.

However, even with the sale of Palm View, the tenants in Dahlia's old home in Havendale had to be given notice, and what was supposed to have been a three-month wait to gain possession of the property turned out to be a five-month wait. The tenants—a man, his common-law wife and her brother—had been paying 'cash only' rent to Eric, which Necka had collected each month, and which Val had continued to collect when she'd discovered her ownership of the house. Val had not wished to live there, the memories too painful to face, so when she'd heard of their plight for a home, she'd offered to sell it to Aunt May.

The tenants were outraged, insisting that Eric had promised them first option to purchase if the house went up for sale. When Val explained that Eric had acted without her approval, the tenants embarked upon a campaign to make the move as disagreeable as possible.

Once in possession of the house, they cleaned, they painted, they hammered, they planted and, together, they made their new house a home. It took five weeks, and at the end of it all, Hopey cooked a pot on mannish water with the genitals of a ram goat; curried goat and rice; and a huge cornmeal pudding—and they had a wedding.

Everyone came—Ab, Mams, Val, Miss Myrtle, Peaches, Mattie, Ruthie, Miss Dillon. They all 'oohed' and 'aahed' at how beautiful the bride looked in her pale yellow dress and crisp curler-lined hairdo. Nathan beamed in his grey church suit and shiny black shoes, and when it was time for him to say his vows, he wept openly. Poor Hopey howled.

Nola and Petra stood beside the blushing bride, Petra taking the flowers when it was time for the bride to place her dimpled hands into Nathan's calloused ones, and Nola patting the sweat from the resurrected 'dusky-brown' mask.

Afterwards, they danced to Ernie Smith and Pluto Shervington songs, and when Pluto's song "I Man Born Yah" played, they all sang raucously—'I man born yah, I nah leave yah, fi go a Canada, no way Sah, pot a boil yah, belly full yah, sweet Jamaica!'

The party lasted till way past midnight. If a flushed Aunt May had not said "Oh how I laugh" one hundred times, then she hadn't said it at all. Eventually, Nola had to steal away to the coolness of the front yard to rest her throbbing feet.

356

When she heard a shuffle behind her she thought it was Nathan coming to fuss about her treading on his newly-planted lawn, but it was only Ab, grinning from ear to ear as he handed her a stout.

"Nice time, Princess, nice time."

Nola nodded as she gratefully sipped the cold drink. It really had been a nice time. Even Petra had danced with Kendra, holding the child's hand and spinning in circles to Bony M's "Brown Girl in the Ring."

Nola sighed as she stared at the fresh wood that had replaced the hanging eave over the front door. "Why you think love dies, Ab? First it come on so strong, then it just dead soh?"

Ab shook the locks that had grown back into stubby rolls. They reminded Nola of little bronzed sausages. "True love don't die, Princess!" he exclaimed. "The kind of love dat die is not real love."

Nola took another sip of stout and smiled as a burst of laughter came from the house.

"Alright," Ab said, tugging at the collar of her dress, "When you buy this dress, you did love it, right?"

Nola nodded, frowning quizzically at his serious face.

"And when you put it on this afternoon, you did still love it, right?"

Her frown deepened, but she nodded again.

"Well, when you tek it off tonight, you goin' still love it, but you mind not goin' be on it, cause you done wear it and it serve it purpose for today. Next time you want to dress up nice, you might put on this same dress, but I guarantee you someting, Princess, 15 years from now, you not goin' love dat dress. You mightn't even have dat dress in your closet, might be you think it gone out of style."

Nola laughed. "So that is love? In your mind one minute, out the next!"

357

"Nah man, Princess!" Ab gave her an exasperated look. "Dat is not the real ting, man! Just listen to me nuh! Suppose I tek a knife right now and cut you there?" He pointed at her wrist.

Nola held up her stout bottle. "Then I would have to lick you cross your head with this bottle here!"

Ab chuckled. "You would bleed! And it would hurt you for a long time, nuh true? And then you would get a scar, and every time you look on dat scar you 'memba how Ab cut you."

"What you sayin' Ab? That real love is like a cut, that hurt you bad?"

"It can hurt, yes, but what you really must think 'bout, Princess, is the cut—that it go deep. Dat cut is forever. You can't choose who cut you, but when dat person cut you, it affec' you for the rest of your life! Dat is love, Princess, true love, what Rasta call agape! Can't stop dat love, Princess." Ab cocked his head meaningfully at the house where another burst of laughter erupted. "But when it come, it cut your heart deep, and dat scar stay there forever. Agape, Princess … never die!"

Nola laughed and slapped his shoulder playfully. "You're a good one to talk, Ab—you who have a new empress for every month of the year!"

Ab tugged at her collar again. "Maybe I just still dressin' up, Princess, still waitin' for dat cut."

Nola stared at the eave once again, suddenly serious. "Boy Ab, I been cut plenty times, and it don't feel much like love to me."

Ab did not answer. They both sat quietly beneath the night sky, sipping their stouts and listening to the cheers that wafted from the house, while the dew descended and glistened on his bronzed locks and her dark skin.

CHAPTER 54

FINALLY, LIFE WAS good. Nola woke each morning with that excitement in the pit of her belly, the same feeling she'd had when she'd first been to Dahlia and Merlene's home. Had Fate tired of playing its cruel pranks on her? This was the time when she should have quaked in her shoes, waiting with bated breath for Fate to sweep through her life and turn it upside down once again, but she became too busy to wait.

The Dah-Lilly School took so much of her time that she barely had time to eat. She worked with each child, individually, throughout the day, assessing their progress and set-backs and designing lesson plans for each challenge. Aunt May helped in conducting the lessons, while Nola took turns with each child outside in the yard beneath a jimbilin tree. She found that the children were calmer and more responsive outside, where the leaves whispered above their heads and birds cawed punctuation marks at the ends of their sentences. She couldn't bring herself to teach at a desk like the teachers had done with such distracted interest at Redding Secondary. Instead, she spread a cloth on the grass, and taught just as she'd done with Dahlia under the mango tree. And soon, there were results.

Louisa continued with her periodic calls to the new house in Havendale, relating stories that held little interest for Nola. Mr. Spence had developed colon cancer and was dying in a New York hospital where his daughter had taken him to get 'top, top care'; Pastor Peppers and Sister Norma had been discovered in the church office, stark naked and in a compromising position on top of Pastor's desk; Lydia had cursed Mrs. Spence in the churchyard one morning, telling her she was a fat, interfering buttu before running off at the age of 14 to live with a taxi driver named "Mr. Hype"; all seemed very distant from Nola's life. With the trauma of losing first Mr. Spence, then Lydia, Mrs. Spence had taken to her bed, and Louisa was put in full charge of Razzle Dazzle.

Each time Nola hung up the phone from Louisa's excited chatter, she was left with a strange numbness in her chest. The calls brought no laughter when there was humour, no tears when there was sadness, no surprise when there was shock, no joy when there was pleasure. So, when Louisa called late one night to announce that she would be getting married the following month, Nola could only mumble a distracted 'congratulations'. She did not ask to whom her sister was getting married, nor she did ask where the wedding was going to be, or how happy Mama and Papa were. She just said "congratulations" and hung up the phone.

After that Louisa stopped calling.

Petra remained withdrawn. It broke Nola's heart when Kendra sobbed because Petra told her to leave the room so she could lie alone in the sour darkness of her unbathed skin. They all tried to fill Kendra's life with distractions during those times—visits to the zoo to see the emaciated lion and dazed snakes curled in their cages, long walks along the Havendale sidewalks to identify all the flowers and trees that they passed in the gardens, lessons in cooking Hopey's popular soups and stews.

"Bad wind," Kendra came to refer to her mother's episodes. "Bad wind blowin' on Mammy," she would say, and they knew that Petra had just locked her door. They knew that they would just have to wait the two or so days until Petra would once again emerge from the darkness and pat Kendra apologetically on the head.

Petra droned through life like a worker bee whose only goal was to make the honey for the queen, claiming none for itself. Even the achievements that made Kendra into the bright, self-sufficient person that Petra never thought she would be, brought nothing more from Petra than distracted smiles.

In the end, Nola realized that she'd saved Petra from Eric McKenzie, but she'd been unable to save her from herself. In Petra, Eric had glimpsed the incomplete painting, and he'd taken his paintbrush and splattered his dark, hideous strokes across it.

Nola tried many times to talk to the girl, to let her know the secrets that had ripped her away from her own family in Redding and brought her to Kingston; to let her know that just as she had survived, so could Petra. But Petra did not want to hear.

Then, the dreams began. Dreams about Petra, sitting in a drum of bubbles; the bubbles flowed over the rim, covering the girl's mouth and leaving only her wide, frightened eyes to stare at Nola. Nola tried to slap the bubbles away so that Petra could breathe, but just as she got to the drum, Petra sank beneath the bubbles.

The dream haunted Nola for several nights, but each morning when she woke to seek Petra, she found with relief that the girl was going through one of her 'good spells', playing 'Go Fish' with Kendra and smiling with those muted smiles.

Nola dismissed the dream, at the time not knowing that her dreams were not to be dismissed.

Petra did it in the early morning, while the new sun was perched on the horizon—the time of the dew angels. Nola often wondered afterwards if she'd told Petra about the dew angels if she would have still done it. Would she have gone outside instead, and sat on the wet grass and allowed the wash to take the darkness away? Would she have felt the sun's new light tickle her skin despite the 'bad winds' within her head?

Hopey had found her. She smelled the acid melting the body and followed the smell into the kitchen. She found Petra lying on the floor in the choppy ocean of her own vomit.

She'd drunk the half bottle of drain cleaner that had been left beneath the sink after Nathan had cleared the drain the week before.

It must have been a horrible, painful death, yet Petra had uttered not a sound, had not called for anyone to come to her aid as her body had contorted with pain. When Nola heard Hopey bellow, and ran to see the sight for herself, she could hear nothing but Petra's words echoing through the kitchen, bouncing from one wall to the other— 'I too bad for this world ... don't belong in it'. Nola had understood as she'd stared at the face on the floor, frozen in the pain that had digested the lips right off the face—only someone who thought of herself as rotten, could have done such a terrible deed to herself.

They did not allow Aunt May or Kendra to see the body, and Aunt May did not fight as Nathan led her into the living room. She went quietly with him, and even when Hopey tore off her clothes and ran wailing down the street, Aunt May did not budge from the chair.

The neighbours brought Hopey back, and Mrs. Lyndsay wrapped her in sheets from the laundry room. By then Val and Ab had come, and they spoke to Hopey in soothing tones until she stopped wailing, hiccupping up at the police when they asked her if Petra had said anything when she found her. The police didn't understand that Petra had already been dead when Hopey had found her, that she'd planned it that way so that they could not save her again.

They had to keep the casket closed at the funeral. They buried her at Dovecot Funeral Park, yards away from where her mother and father had been buried. The inscription on her tiny, aluminium tombstone read:

PETRA
BELOVED MOTHER, NIECE, FRIEND.
AT PEACE AT LAST.

They stood for a long time at her graveside. Long after the shellshocked faces of their friends had stumbled away. They were left there alone, Petra's family and adopted family—Aunt May, Kendra, Nathan, Mrs. Lyndsay, Nola, Hopey, Val, Ab and Mams. The air did the same thing it did when Dahlia and Merlene had died. It warbled loosely around them, flapping the folds that had once held the now absent life.

It was Kendra who surprised Nola. She'd not shed one tear since the moment they told her that her mother had gone to heaven and that she would never see her again. The child stood by the grave in the brand new white dress that Val had bought for her, holding Mrs. Lyndsay's hand and moving her lips silently as if in conversation. When Nola went to stand beside her, to give her hand a supportive squeeze, Kendra leaned against her and whispered, "Listen ... Nola. Listen, Miss Linsy!"

"What, Kendra? Listen to what?" Nola bent to the child while Mrs. Lyndsay cocked her ear curiously.

"Mammy talkin'," the child answered, staring up at the trees, "Mama say that, bad wind stop blowin' now."

Nola stared down in awe at the heavy, wise, childish face. What was it about people like Kendra and Dahlia and Hopey that saw so deeply into the truth of life when others just merely skimmed the surface?

After the funeral, while everyone else rested from the grief that had left them weak, Nola sat in the kitchen and stared at the spot where Petra had chosen to silence her winds. This was where it had happened for Dahlia, too; where she'd stabbed her papa and earned her lip-nose. In this same kitchen, another life had been cleaned and scrubbed and disinfected from the ground as if it had been a spill of milk. The floor had been left shining with the brilliance that vinegar gave to tile.

Aunt May walked into the kitchen, stopping when she saw Nola, her eyes blinking dazedly through the green frames, as if trying to remember who Nola was. She said nothing, just continued over to the stove and poured water from the thermos.

It was strange to see her without Nathan behind her. He'd not left her side since they'd found Petra. He'd been such a good choice for Aunt May, despite what people whispered about the gardener with the educated teacher. He'd tended to her every need, and he'd comforted her, and everyone else. They wouldn't have been able to plan the funeral if it hadn't been for Nathan's and Mam's and Ab's calm control of all the painful details. He must have fallen asleep, for he would not have made Aunt May come to make her own Milo if he'd been awake.

Nola watched as Aunt May's cheeks shook as she stirred. They were so vulnerable with their freckles and without their mask. That's probably why she'd worn it at Redding Secondary—to hide her humanness. To hide her vulnerability.

"Aunt May," Nola whispered, "I've been wanting to ask you something for a long time. Remember that time when I was friends with Barry, and started smoking weed and everything? How come you never stopped me? How come you just let me drop out of school and do what I wanted to do, even though it was mashing up my life?"

Aunt May stopped stirring, but she did not look up. She stared at the garbage bin in the corner of the kitchen, her chin quivering slightly. Eventually she removed the spoon from the mug and placed it on the saucer, lifting the mug so that the steam snaked over her face. Her freckles sparkled with moisture.

"I couldn't stop you," she said. "You wouldn't have listened. You know how broken you were when I picked you up from that roadside?" Suddenly her voice broke and the flesh of her neck rose and fell as she swallowed hard. "You were there trying to walk to that taxi by yourself, and you didn't even know where you were going." Crisp curls shook as she opened her palms towards Nola. "You just put your life in my hands without asking one question, with all those scars and burns all over you." She took a deep breath. "I knew it would take plenty time for you to heal, Nola, not just overnight, so ..." she shrugged, "I knew that the breakdown had to come. When you met up with that Barry fellow—all that weed smoking and drinking and other such delights?—I knew that was all your pain, all your anger, all your sadness coming out. I couldn't force you to do anything that you didn't want to do. I would only have driven you away. You were too busy looking for somebody to hate for me to put myself in your way."

She sighed heavily. "I knew you would come around. I knew you would find yourself after all the anger was spent. Remember, Nola, I was at that school from the time you were just learning to talk and other such delights. I knew you well,

Nola Chambers, and I knew all that bad behaviour wasn't you. It hurt me to see you like that, but I knew it was just a matter of time before you found yourself."

She gripped a curl that had fallen onto her forehead and pushed it back up into its indented line. "For many years after that fire, I blamed myself, you know. I only wanted to help you, when I gave you and Dahlia that assignment. I saw you in that classroom, around the town, always alone except for when you sat with Dahlia at lunchtime, and I saw how unhappy you were till you were with that girl. But you wouldn't allow that friendship to go any further, because of the way everyone else looked at her."

Nola opened her mouth to protest, but Aunt May held up a hand.

"You got to know them when I gave you that assignment, when you saw for yourself that everything you'd heard was all a lie. You got to know them and I saw the change in you— overnight! I knew it was a good thing, Nola. It was a risk, but a good thing for you and Delroy. Dahlia Daley loved life, and I wanted both of you to learn about some of that love." She shrugged her shoulders and looked down at the kitchen floor. "Maybe because of Petra..." Her voice cracked again, and once again, she swallowed hard. "Maybe because of Petra I could recognize the unhappiness in you. I just wanted to give you joy, a little joy, so you could just know the feeling of being a child, of being carefree."

"But they made the choice to die, Aunt May! Just like Petra. To die instead of fighting."

Aunt May nodded. "But that's the thing, Nola. I once told you that I saw something special in all of you because of the struggle. It wasn't the struggle I meant. It was how you fought it. Some people just get tired of fighting, Nola. Some people just can't manage it any longer."

"What about Petra, Aunty? She wasn't fighting. She gave up a long time ago."

Aunt May's chin quivered again as she stared at the garbage bin. Eventually, she shook her head slowly. "You know why I had to leave Kingston and go to Redding, Nola? Because I had to give Petra a chance to bond with her father, to learn how to manage on her own and stop leaning on me. She was like my own daughter—my brother's child, but like my own daughter. The things that she saw when she was a baby were things that no normal person could forget. You see, Petra's mother wasn't the type of woman who was ready to be a mother. Pretty like money and other such delights, Tricia was! Made people stop dead in their tracks when she walked past, and she used her looks to get what she wanted. But Petra wasn't one of those things she wanted—'a mistake' is what she used to say that child was, from the first time they put that tiny baby on her chest in hospital. But my brother ..." Aunt May gave a little laugh, "My brother was a good man, and he married that woman same way, knowing that she didn't want him or the baby, thinking that in time she would come around. But she never did." Aunt May distractedly picked up the spoon and began stirring again.

"Tricia had so many men on the side that people used to leave buns on my brother's doorstep to make fun of him. Till one day, it stopped. You see, one of the men she had was very jealous, a carpenter from Spanish Town, 'hurry-come-up boy' who thought he'd made it, thought everything he wanted he should get, even if it belonged to someone else. One night he came to my brother's house and told Tricia that she had to leave her husband and come live with him right then and there. But Tricia was spoiled, she loved that good life that my brother was giving her too much to leave ... nice house, nice clothes. Tricia liked eating her cake and having it too. The carpenter

367

just couldn't guarantee everything my brother was giving her, so she told him to leave, to get out of her house. Petra was only five, but I swear to you, up to the night before she died, every time I looked into that child's eyes, I saw everything that she saw that night ... when that man took out that knife and stabbed Tricia in her neck."

Nola's hand flew to her mouth.

"We took Petra to doctors all her life to try to put those terrible things out of her head—psychiatrists, counselors, even a doctor in Florida. That is the one who put her on the medication. You saw it— sometimes it helped, sometimes the memories were just too bad for anything to help. To tell you the truth, Nola, I loved Petra more than I loved myself, and I knew that child was getting tired of fighting ... I saw it in her eyes."

The tears rolled freely down Nola's face as the mystery of Petra unraveled before her. Aunt May reached across the table and gripped her hand.

"She's at peace now, Nola, that's what I know in my heart."

"Is that ..." Nola gulped, "Is that what stopped her from getting close to Kendra?"

She squeezed Nola's hand. "I don't think she knew how, Nola. I don't think Petra knew how to love something that she made, whether that child had been born perfect or not. In Petra's eyes, nothing she did was ever good enough." Aunt May blinked at Nola as if her own thoughts had suddenly shocked her. "I ... I ... think that Petra almost willed that baby to be born like that."

And yet, it was Petra who'd given Nola the reason to step off her own destructive path. Through Petra's lost way, Nola had found her own path.

Petra, dear Petra, you never lived in vain. You saved me! You were one of my angels!

She felt Aunt May give her hand a final squeeze before she went over to the sink to rinse out her cup.

"Aunt May," Nola whispered as the woman turned to leave the kitchen. "Aunt May, thank you for taking me with you."

"Thank you for coming with me, child."

Come, Thou Holy Spirit, Come

O most blessed light divine,
Shine within these hearts of thine,
And our inmost being fill;
Where thou art not, man hath naught,
Nothing good in deed or thought,
Nothing free from taint of ill.

Heal our wounds; our strength renew;
On our dryness pour thy dew;
Wash the stains of guilt away;
Bend the stubborn heart and will;
Melt the frozen, warm the chill;
Guide the steps that go astray.

On the faithful, who adore
And confess thee, evermore
In thy sevenfold gifts descend:
Give them virtue's sure reward,
Give them thy salvation, Lord,
Give them joys that never end.

Hymn 156
Church of St Margaret's Hymnal

Unknown author, Twelfth century, translated from Latin to English by Edward Cassell

* * *

CHAPTER 55

T HEY SAY THAT when you leave somewhere as a child, then return as an adult, the place always seems much smaller than you remember. That was not so with Calabash Street. The street had so widened that Nola descended from the bus and stood for several seconds, wondering if she had come off in the right village. For one thing, the road was beautifully asphalted, the pot holes replaced by the smooth gleam of tar. Even the bus stop beamed with a spanking new roof, this one asking the question in bright red letters, WHAT WOULD JESUS DO?

The stop had been relocated further up the street from the school gate, in front of a pale yellow building which had the words REDDING POST OFFICE beaming proudly above its double front doors.

It was as if the little town had spilled from its boundaries and was creeping down the fattened road. Even the undeveloped land which had once sat on both sides of the road leading to the highway, the area where Nola had sat and waited with Aggie, was now covered with an array of new buildings. Redding had certainly flourished with her out of it.

She looked around at the faces that walked up and down the sparkling street. She recognized so many of them, but they did not give her a second glance as she descended from the bus. She was supposed to have been dead, so they would not have known to look at her and recognize the similarities to Nola Chambers.

She was grateful for the anonymity. Her heart raced and her legs trembled too much to have to deal with the stares and questions of the villagers.

Could she really do this? Could she really walk into this village, go up that hill, and walk into that house again? She took a deep breath and clutched her bag to her chest. She had no choice. Mama was calling.

She walked up the new sidewalk, past the post office and into the busy street, holding her head down slightly so as not to make eye contact with anyone.

There were more cars, too. Not as many bicycles as before, but a lot more cars. The school looked the same. The windows still with their dark gashes of missing louvres. The yard was still dusty and barren, except for the faithful lignum vitae tree that stood in the middle like an old friend. The only difference Nola could see was that a chain-linked fence now circled the perimeter, already showing gaping holes for shortcuts into the school yard.

She stopped by the gates and stared at the lignum vitae tree, an involuntary smile lifting her lips. School had finished for the day, but a few students lingered beneath its shade, laughing loudly at a magazine that one of them held in their lap. She remembered laughing under that tree at some nonsense that Dahlia had said. Laughing at the world that had laughed at them.

She walked a few more yards, taking in the sights as if walking through a foreign country. Her eyes widened as she came to the Razzle Dazzle window. Gone was the glass cage that had showcased the headless mannequin in her various finery. In its place was a whole other building! Even Razzle Dazzle had grown!

The extension had a higher ceiling, extending from the old structure like a large, ill-fitting appendage. It was a household section, Nola could see, its windows boasting shelves of crockery, multicolored clothes hampers and bath towels stacked like rainbows across the shelves. RAZZLE DAZZLE HOUSEWARE, the gold letters on the window said, and beneath those, smaller cursive letters read, WELCOME HOME.

So Louisa had been speaking the truth. During one quick call, before that last call about her wedding, she'd gushed to Nola about how pleased Mrs. Spence had been with her innovative ideas for Razzle Dazzle, how fast the store was growing beneath her position as manager.

Nola quaked as she stared at the old entrance doors, sealed now with a chain and padlock so that the patrons entered through the gold-lettered doors. She hadn't realized how much she'd hated walking through those doors. She'd always felt so out of place amongst those sweet-smelling lotions and pretty clothes. Not Louisa. She'd found her true calling.

Nola hurried away, dazed by her racing heart and throbbing head. By the time she got to the spot where Aggie's stall used to be, she was almost hyperventilating. Calm down, Nola. You come this far! Don't faint and make them see.

Three vehicles were parked against the sidewalk where the shack used to be, all bearing license plates with the 'P' before the numbers, indicating that they were licensed for public transportation—Taxis.

The area on the sidewalk where she'd once slept, where Aggie had lisped her life-saving scriptures, now bore a concrete building painted in orange and green with white fretwork over the windows. School children laughed raucously by the doorway, some holding the typical cardboard 'box lunch'.

COUNTRY HUT offered a variety of pizzas as well as regular cooked lunches.

The left side of the building, the section of the grass where Aggie had boiled her soups and herbs, had been covered with gravel and now held four round plastic tables each with its set of chairs. Four school girls huddled over a game of jacks at one table whilst at another, three boys fought for forkfuls of food from one greasy box. Beside them, a man slept with his head on the table.

The area was filthy, strewn with empty food and juice boxes. As Nola watched, one of the boys tiptoed over to the sleeping man and dropped a forkful of rice and peas onto his hat. Immediately, flies swarmed his head while the boys guffawed loudly. The man did not budge.

Nola felt the hairs on her neck rise, as if an electric charge had surged through her. She had to hold herself back from going over to the boys and emptying the rest of the contents of the box over their own heads.

So even though the town had changed, the people had not—the joke was still on the helpless.

Nola turned away, memories jolting her like a physical blow. She felt her eyes welling over, and she had to blink vigorously as she looked ahead for the two roads that had been the crossroads of her life—the one that had led her uphill to her beatings, and the other to joy at that pink house.

Her eyes snagged on just one thing—the tree tops which had once been stripped barren by the fire were green again, lush and full. Like the rest of the village, they'd flourished.

She decided to take a taxi up Macca Hill. Her legs felt too weak to make the walk she'd made almost every day for the first 15 years of her life.

"How much to go ... ?" She stopped, a gasp swallowing her words.

374

The man had turned around at the sound of her voice, bringing his face into full view. Jasper! Clars the plumber's eldest son! She held her breath, waiting for the recognition and disgust to strike the man's face. He'd left school a couple years before her, joining his father on his jobs in order to learn the plumbing trade. Surely this was not his taxi? She'd heard Clars boast many times in the churchyard that his son was a natural, and was going to make an even better plumber than himself.

"Unjith" he said, using his tongue to expertly flip the cane in his mouth.

"What?"

"Unjith! Un-jith!" he repeated, and flipped the cane again.

Nola cocked an eyebrow. "One hundred dollars to go up Macca Hill!"

Jasper stopped chewing, his cheek bulging with cane trash as he cocked his head. "Roath bad!" he said. Then he spat the trash on to the pile by his feet. "Better you walk, then baby! That road too bad for my vehicle! Pot hole won't mash up your foot, but it will knock my car tyre clean off, and me sure you not goin' buy my car tyre back!"

Macca Hill still had its pot holes.

"Okay," Nola nodded, eager to get off the street. "Chambers' house," she said, and climbed into the back seat.

"Chambers," he repeated as he started the engine, "Come to see Miss Sadie, eh? I hear she soon dead."

As Nola's heart jolted, he spun the taxi into the road and screeched towards Macca Hill.

They passed Shamoney Leach, her hands gripping her back as she trudged up the hill, pregnant.

They passed Pastor Pepper's house. Louisa said he'd moved from Redding shortly after the scandal with Sister Norma. She wondered if anyone lived there now, but as she spotted the

375

garden, she realized that someone certainly did. The garden was pristinely manicured, the beds of lantana and hibiscus so straight that they seemed to have been lined off with the aid of a ruler. It was a beautiful garden. The Haden mango tree still stood magnificently in the centre, now surrounded by an impressive bed of giant-leaved Spathophilum.

There was Miss Cicely's house, beside its field of cabbage and lettuce. And the churchyard had about ten or so young children chasing each other around some broken church benches.

"So, which parts you come from?"

Nola pretended not to hear over the noisy radio.

The hillside was green and lush with its undulating fields of cabbages, lettuce, scallions, watermelon vines, and, of course, the tall spokes of yam vines that Grampy used to call 'the watchmen of Macca Hill'. The wild guinea grass and the prickly privet that had given Macca Hill its name still dominated the steeper and stonier areas, and along the shady roadside, ferns clutched the bank like a fluffy layer of cotton.

Nola had forgotten how beautiful the hillside was. That was the thing about the smudged sketches—they smudged the good along with the bad. She'd not remembered the awesome wonder of Macca Hill, with its the varying shades of green, punctuated every now and again by the vibrant reds of sweet peppers and tomatoes, or the bright yellow bonnets of the scotchie peppers.

The car slowed for another crevice by Mass Tackie's house. Nola did not know if it was her imagination, but the house actually seemed lower down the hill than when she'd left. However, the area which had once been bald and smooth now held several patches of green where hardy grass had fought its way up from the soil. Nola's heart sank with sadness when she realized the significance of the growing grass—the soil was no longer being swept.

Her house looked so small there off the side of the road. It seemed to have shrunk, like a coolie plum seed left in the sun. The dying thumberga vine was completely gone now, but the wall still held the imprint of the roots as they'd peeled off the paint and stained the concrete with their sap. The house resembled some sort of skeletal remains, like the lizard bones she used to find by the river within the rotting roseapple leaves.

She paid Jasper the hundred dollars through the window, and as he took the money, she felt his sticky fingers linger on hers.

"What you doin' later tonight, sweet ting? Me woulda like show you a ting or two 'bout Reddin'." He winked, his lips puckering suggestively.

Suddenly, an uncontrollable rage welled into her chest and she bit her lip hard. She knew herself well enough now to know that anxiety and rage always made her reckless, so she knew that poor Jasper was going to pay the price. She leaned through the car window and put a seductive smile on her lips, staring into the pleased eyes.

"Jasper ..." she whispered, and his tongue flicked eagerly over his lips. "Jasper, 'memba when you came to this house with your papa to connect up the tank, and Nola was shellin' cocoa pods on the kitchen step, and when you thought nobody was lookin', you chew up some of them seeds and spit them right in Nola's face?"

The shock on the man's face was so rewarding that Nola could have stopped right there. But, she didn't.

"Well, Jasper," she leaned so close to him that she could smell the cane juice on his lips, and when she saw the sudden recognition hit his face, she said, "You can't show me nothin' 'bout Redding that I don't know, Jasper!"

And she spat straight into the man's paling face.

When the car screeched down the hillside, it left a cloud of red dust circling in the air, and a hundred dollar bill floating to the ground. Nola put her hand to her mouth in realization of the lewd act she had just committed, and discovered that she was shaking violently. The humiliation that day when Jasper had spat at her had been unbearable. She'd run all the way to the river and dunked her head under the icy water till her lungs had threatened to burst open, but the pain in her chest had done little to ease the burning shame.

Now she stood at her gate, not believing that she had done something so vile. It was just as she'd thought—Redding brought out the worst in her, made her lose control and become just like that trapped animal once again.

"No need to fight, no more," she mouthed into her hand, "them can't hurt you no more, Nola. You have your own school, your own family, now. Them can't hurt you no more!"

CHAPTER 56

ONLY ONE HALF of the gate was there, leaning open on its broken hinge. The mongrel must have died, for if it had been alive the gate would have been closed to prevent it racing out to chew up people's goats and chickens.

Nola picked up her bag and walked through the gateway, her legs shaking violently as she stepped onto the walkway. The last time she'd seen this walkway it had carried Ellie's blood away in a rusty stream.

There was the coolie plum tree with its circles still etched into the trunk, and the spot where Elllie had looked into Nola's eyes and taken her last forgiving breath; and there was the pen, like another skeleton, its rotten roof sagging defeatedly inward, its sides gaping open where planks of wood had fallen out, no doubt the result of the large termite nest that sat on the upper corner like a big red sore.

Nola's hand involuntarily flew up to her face, to the spot that now tingled on her lip as if the memories were resurrecting the sore. Even after all these years, her lip still smiled slightly in that spot, the nerves forever frozen by Dahlia's spark.

There was the kitchen window and Mama's face was not at it. Under the window, the spot where Nola had stooped so many times, was a clutter of Mama's large pots. There was a sheet of newspaper on the kitchen step, covered in the bald seeds and split skins of guineps. A few flies pitched lazily on the seeds, but were not frenzied since the seeds had been sucked clean of their silky pulp.

Nola stepped over the paper and knocked on the kitchen door.

No answer, but she could hear the faint sound of something being pushed across a floor. She turned the knob and the door creaked open as if objecting to her entry.

She was in Mama's kitchen! Gone was the smell of onions. Nothing except the precisely clean scent of Savlon. It seemed to permeate the entire house. Gone were the jars and the pots and the chopping boards. The only things visible on the counter were a round plastic tray covered with vials of tablets, and, beside that, a black thermos.

The room seemed so tiny. Could this little place have really produced so many jars of chutneys and jams? Mama had always wanted to extend her work space. It had been her dream.

"Hellooo … !" Nola put down her bag and called towards Mama and Papa's closed bedroom door.

Footsteps immediately tapped towards the door and there was another creak as it was partially opened. A woman peered out, her face glowing with a film of sweat. It was not a face that was familiar to Nola, and returning Nola's confused look, the face blinked questioningly back.

"Yes?" the woman said, raising her eyebrows impatiently.

"I … I … sorry … I lookin' for Louisa, or … or Sadie Chambers."

The woman frowned and cocked her head towards the interior of the room. "Miss Sadie in here, Hon, but I'm tidying her right now. Who are you? Cause it's not everybody Miss Sadie want to see."

380

Her voice was rounded, in the way that Olive would have called 'stocious'. The manner in which the 'uptown' Kingstonians spoke.

"Tell her ... Nola. Tell her Nola come."

The woman's frown gave way to a widening of the eyes. She walked slowly from behind the door and approached Nola, touching her cheek in amazement.

From the doorway she'd seemed to be in her early thirties, but up close Nola could see creases beneath the film of sweat, panning out from her eyes and mouth, and grey streaks within the tight bun of her hair. She was probably in her late fifties, like Aunt May.

"So Sades wasn't speaking foolishness after all," the woman whispered, "You really are alive! She told me what happened, you know, how you got outta here before those scavengers ripped you apart, but I didn't believe her, thought it was just the pain talking. Everybody round here says that your bones long gone with the witch. You know something, Hon?" she whispered conspiratorially, her eyes still moving disbelievingly over Nola's face, "now that you're older, you look just like your poppa!"

Then she turned and went back into Mama's room. "Come quick. She's been asking for you."

But, Nola could not move. She just stood there, staring at the empty doorway until the woman's face appeared again with its original frown.

"Come!" she said, and when Nola still did not move, she walked up to her and gripped her shoulders. "Look here, Hon," she said, her voice coaxing and gentle now, "She doesn't have much longer, and now that I see you, I realize what she's been waiting for. You need to take a deep breath and get yourself together and come see your mama. I know it's not easy. I've been through it with my own poppa, but you have to help her find some peace, Honey. She's in a lot of pain."

"I just … don't know … what to say," Nola stammered.

The woman cocked her head to the side and gave Nola's shoulders a slight shake. "Don't know what to say?! You don't have to say anything! That's your mama in there! She just want to see you, Hon, to know that you came back to her, that's all."

Nola swallowed the lump in her throat. Lady, you don't understand. It's not the villagers why I had to leave home, It's my own mama and papa who didn't want me! How could she explain to this woman, this stranger, that the shame of her existence had been too great for this same mama who was now asking for her? How could she understand, with her gentle, sympathetic, unknowing eyes, that the last time Nola had tried to get close to her mama, her mama had stuck her in the eye with pepper on her fingers, and for days after that Nola's eyes had watered, not just from the pepper, but from the unbearable pain in her chest? But she swallowed her words and nodded at the woman.

The woman gave a satisfied nod and gently pushed her towards the bedroom door.

"Go on. I'm going to pick some mint from the yard to make tea." Then she pointed again at the door before stepping over Nola's bag and going outside.

Nola looked towards the dim living room. The clock had stopped ticking. Its dusty face stared silently back at her, its hands frozen beneath the hazy glass. She sighed and moved towards Mama's door, pushed it open and stepped in.

There were curtains hanging over the windows now, yellow curtains which were drawn shut. They gave the room a yellow glow, as if everything had become covered in gold. It was the same bed, the one over which she'd bent to touch Papa's cheek. Mama was lying in the middle, now, not on the left side where she'd always slept, but in the middle, tucked tightly within crisp white sheets. There was a pink wash basin

382

and a pile of folded wash cloths on one bedside table, and on the other, a bottle of rosewater, the bottle of Savlon and a few tablet vials similar to the ones in the kitchen.

"Mama ..." Nola said, but her voice only came out as a whisper. Mama did not hear her. She moved closer to the little body, and it was only when she got to the foot of the bed that she saw that her mama's eyes were open.

They were staring at her.

Nola took a deep breath. The eyes seemed so big, so overpowering in the skeletal face. The skin was pasted back against the sheets, and the bags and folds that had once covered Mama's eyes now lay like pouches at the sides of her face. Despite the shockingly gaunt look of Mama's face, it was the eyes that shocked Nola the most. They shone. They shone as if thay did not belong on that fading face.

Never in all her years of being on this earth, had Nola thought she looked anything like Mama or Papa or Louisa, or Grampy. Never had she seen anything of herself in her family. She had only seen a resemblance in that tiny picture beneath her bed, to that sad, dark face that had stared back at her like an omen. But now, after all these years, she looked at Mama's fading face and she saw what she saw in the mirror after she'd removed Grampy's towel, when she'd looked at herself for the first time through her own eyes, and not the eyes of the Redding folk—I have Mama's eyes!

"Hello, Mama." she whispered.

Imagine that? Eight years of not seeing or speaking to the woman who gave birth to her, and she greeted her like she would anyone else on the street—Hello Mama!

But Mama just kept staring. Nola wondered if she was really awake, or under the effects of some medication that had put her into a wide-eyed daze. She looked anxiously to the door for some sign of the strange woman, but she could hear nothing in the kitchen. She guessed she would just have to wait until Mama woke up. She pulled the plastic chair closer to the bed and sat uncomfortably beside the wide eyes. It was then that she recognized the other smell in the room—the slightly stinking odour of something rotting—Dear God! Mama!

Before she could stop herself, she reached out and touched Mama's cheek. The skin felt like dry ash, ready to disintegrate if she squeezed too hard.

Then, suddenly, Mama turned her face into Nola's palm. Nola felt the wetness before she saw the tears, falling like drops of dew down Mama's face and onto her hand.

"Don't cry, Mama. I ... I ... come. I come back," Nola choked.

Something was moving beneath the sheets, slowly, from side to side. It was Mama's hand. It stopped for a while, then moved again, this time up and down, with a little more urgency to it.

"What you need, Mama? More medicine? Let me get the lady. I don't know what to give you."

But Mama shook her head and pumped her hand more vigorously. Nola watched helplessly, looking from the pumping sheet to the empty doorway. Then it hit her—Mama wanted her hand free! She hurriedly pulled at the sheet that had been tucked tightly beneath the mattress, and immediately Mama's hand wafted up like another piece of ash from the bed.

The knuckles seemed to exist all by themselves, the frail bones of the fingers, overpowered by the large knots, as they rose up to touch Nola's face. The hand was as cold as the river, shaking in the effort to touch Nola's mouth. It whisked its ice over the spot that had frozen into its smile, then rose to the cheek that had been branded into a smooth, slippery patch. Then it fell back to the bed, and Mama's eyes opened even wider to stare up from her pool of tears.

384

"Little ... Bird," she whispered. "Little Bird."

Nola felt her face crumple like a piece of paper. She could not stop the sobs that racked her chest. That had been Grampy's name for her, the name that told her she was his special little one.

"You are ... You are a little bird." There was a touch of wonder in the soft voice. "You spread your wings ... you fly ... even in the storm. You soared."

Nola stared in shock through the thick tears. The wings! The bird! It was her that Mama had been staring at in the dream! In her pain, in the rotting of her body, Mama had imagined her as a great bird, covering the earth in the black shadow of her wings. Or was that what Mama had thought of her all along?—as a dark shadow that would not go away?

"Have ... something," Mama was whispering again, "Have something ... for you. Look in the ... wardrobe ... in the ..." she closed her eyes tightly and took several deep breaths, the skeleton of her ribs printing the sheets. "Look under the basket ... with my sewing things ... the flour bag." Her hand lifted then fell back onto the bed in a failed attempt to point.

Nola knew the wardrobe. It had always stood in the corner of the room, like an old security guard with its scratched doors and scuffed legs. It had been carved lovingly by Granny Pat's pappy for his only daughter, many years before she met and married Fin Thomas. It was not one of the large double door types that Mams had in her room, or that was common in most Redding homes, but a smaller one, with a single door on one side, and a stack of drawers on the other. Grampy used to tell Nola that the wardrobe was a special one, because within its meagre space, it held a very large lesson. Grampy said that Granny Pat's pappy had made the wardrobe with one single cupboard because that was all he could afford to fill with dresses for his daughter. He told Granny Pat that whenever she opened her wardrobe and saw it filled, she would always be satisfied with what she had, but if he'd made the wardrobe larger, with double doors, she would have opened it and seen the empty spaces, and her heart would have yearned for more.

Nola had never been able to tell Grampy when he spoke of that wardrobe with such love, that she hated it. She abhorred it. She could never let him know how much she despised that single door with its delicately carved handle. Behind that door with its special lesson, were Papa's belts.

Now she walked up to the despised piece of furniture and pulled the handle. She was greeted by the overpowering scent of mothballs. Mama had always kept her church dresses there, and she'd always hung gauze sachets of mothballs around the hangers to keep insects away. She'd kept Papa's good jacket in there too, and his belts. Now there was no sign of the jackets or belts, just the dresses that had hung from the wiry hangers of Mama's shoulders.

The basket was at the bottom, brimming with the coloured threads and button boxes that Mama had used to darn Grampy's and Papa's pants. Nola lifted the basket, and there, as Mama had said, was the flour bag.

There was a time when that bag would not have been just lying around at the bottom of the wardrobe. There was a time when the recipes that the bag held were hidden and guarded like a precious family fortune. They were the recipes developed by Granny Pat's mammy, when she'd used overripe fruits left over from her day of selling to make jams and chutneys for her family and friends. Those age-crisped, fruit-stained sheets of paper were passed on to Granny Pat, who'd passed them on to her eldest daughter Irene, from beneath whose mattress Grampy had retrieved them when the woman had died of a ruptured appendix. Grampy had given them to Mama, who'd come to know them so well that she had not needed to read the painstakingly formed letters when she made her chutneys.

Nola also knew those recipes by heart. She used to whisper them out as a child, even though Mama didn't need them, whisper them with the conspiratory reverence of being part of a special secret—a special family secret. It used to give her so much comfort, to know she was part of that legacy that even the beatings could not take away.

Mama's eyes were closed when Nola returned with the bag. Her breathing was not as laboured, but the outline of her ribs was still apparent with every intake of breath. It hit Nola then that Mama already wore the body and odour of death, even though life still pulsed through her. But then, maybe that's how it had always been with Mama—a flimsy shell of flesh over a dazed spirit. That was why her eyes had shocked Nola so. They looked more alive facing death than they had facing life.

"Mama ... " Nola whispered, touching her cheek again. "Mama, I have it."

Mama made a sound, a little murmur, then opened her eyes again. "Tomorrow ... give you ... tomorrow. Lettie ... call Lettie."

"What? No, Mama," Nola looked at the empty doorway. So the woman's name was Lettie. "I ... leavin' early in the mornin', Mama. I won't be here tomorrow. You want me to give the bag to Louisa for you?"

Mama shook her head as a frown marred her forehead. "No!"

Nola blinked at the forcefulness of her voice.

"Tomorrow! Tomorrow ... I give you! Lettie ... call Lettie ..." Then she closed her eyes again, biting her lip and grimacing so that the pouches of her face shook.

Nola ran to the door. "Lettie!" she called into the kitchen, and immediately a chair scraped across the floor.

The woman appeared with a plastic jug in her hand. She did not come inside immediately, but stopped and stared at Nola so hard that Nola had to look away uncomfortably.

Nola pointed at the bed. "Mama callin' you. I think she feelin' pain."

The woman nodded and walked over to the bed. "Ready to take the medicine now, Sades?" she crooned soflty. "We going to take that medicine and brush up those teeth, and then we going to get a nice sleep, right Sades? A nice, nice sleep."

Mama moaned and the woman turned to face Nola. "I made a sandwich and a thermos of mint tea for you, Hon. Just cheese, but I know you must be hungry. Eat." She nodded towards the bed. "She going to sleep little now. Go eat. I soon come."

Nola looked hesitantly at Mama. She was moving her head from side to side, the moisture of tears making her face glisten. She made an approach towards the bed, but the woman's voice stopped her.

"Go eat!" She commanded. Then she sighed when she saw the shivering of Nola's lips. Her voice was gentler the next time she spoke. "We used to this, me and Sades. We know how to get them cells to start behavin', so just leave us to it. She soon get to sleep and the pain will go away. You go eat, so when she wakes up you can talk some more."

Nola nodded and slowly left the room. She heard the bedroom door click firmly behind her as she stood in the kitchen. The sandwich was on the counter under a meshed food cover, but just the thought of putting it to her lips made her belly lurch. It remembered that it wasn't supposed to eat in this house.

She walked down the passage to Louisa's and Grampy's room. The door was open, and Nola realized with shock that it was totally empty. The only item was a dented curtain rod, leaning against the wall in the right corner. The bed was gone,

388

the chest of drawers was gone, even the curtains were gone. Nola held her chest and sniffed the air greedily. Grampy's smell was gone!

"Hello Grampy, " she whispered at the walls.

Nothing.

She walked to her old room. Empty too. Barren, like Louisa's. The walls had been painted red. Even the window sills had been painted, with smudges lining the panes. The colour that kept the evil spirits out.

Nola almost laughed out loud. They'd painted the room red to keep her evil spirit out and here she was, standing right in the middle of the room.

"Him don't live here no more, you know."

Nola spun around, startled by the voice behind her.

Louisa! Louisa was standing behind her. A much plumper Louisa, but still so pretty, even with her heavy bosom and the face of a woman.

"Louisa," Nola said, smiling at her sister.

Louisa stared back at her. "Nola . . . You heal up so good! You face is so . . . pretty."

Nola shook her head. "Louisa, please, I heal up because of the things Aggie gave me. She saved my life."

Louisa nodded. "Is like she was waitin' just for you all those years. After you left, she just disappear into thin air—like a duppy."

Nola laughed. "Trust me, she wasn't no duppy."

Louisa laughed too. "That's what Delroy say . . ." Then, as Nola's head jerked up, Louisa stopped speaking.

"How is he? How is Delroy?"

Louisa walked across the room to the window, the one which Dahlia and Delroy had pelted with stones on her birthday. The one through which Louisa had stuffed the red cloth.

Nola stared at the image her sister made against the barren red walls. Louisa had been right. She did look just like a real working lady —in her linen skirt and high heels. Just like the ones Mrs. Spence used to wear.

"Things change a lot round here, Nola. Things change a lot." She sighed. "Papa don't live here anymore."

"His belts gone from the cupboard." It was the only thing her brain could muster to say.

Louisa turned to face her with surprise. "Everything gone," she eventually said.

"So where? Where him live now?"

Louisa shrugged. "All 'bout the place. Him have some friends in Nainsville, sometimes him even sleep in him car. Wherever him feel like. Him say that your duppy won't leave him alone, that you follow him everywhere, and slap him up when him sleepin'." She shrugged again. "Finally, I had to tell him the truth, that you was in Kingston, because him was really goin' off him head, Nola. But him never believe me, say that I just protectin' your spirit, as usual."

Nola didn't realize that her hands had covered her mouth till she tried to speak and her voice was muffled. "So, him don't know 'bout Mama being sick?"

"Of course him know! Him say is she harborin' your spirit, that's why she sick. Him say that she holdin' on to you, that's why you won't leave. Him don't come round here too much, just check with me at the store from time to time."

What was Louisa saying—that after all those years of Mama dedicating her life to Papa, chopping and chopping all day to buy him his new red car, he didn't come around now that she was dying?

She sniffed. "So who look after Mama?"

"Paulette. You remember Paulette, Mass Tackie's daughter? She went to study nursin' in Kingston, and she came back to Redding when Mass Tackie got sick. It was right after him dead that Mama got sick, so Paulette stayed to take care of her. She don't even charge me, Nola ... she say that she and Mama are sisters."

Paulette—Lettie! So that was who the woman was!—Mass Tackie's 'nurse' daughter of whom he'd been so proud. Her heart dropped at the confirmation that Mass Tackie had died, but she knew that he and Grampy were nowhere else if not playing a game of checkers underneath a tree in that field.

Paulette! Grampy had spoken a lot of Paulette, the friend with whom Mama had got into all her escapades as a child. She'd left Redding when Nola had been very young, so Nola had not recognized her, but here she was, taking care of Mama when Papa wouldn't.

Nola looked around the empty room as a thought suddenly hit her. "So where you live now, Louisa?"

Louisa gave a watery smile. "Memba I told you that I got married, we ... ." Her voice faltered over the word 'we', but she looked away and continued, "We bought Pastor's house. That's where I live now. I been beggin' Mama to come and stay there with us, but she won't leave here."

Nola smiled. "So Papa was right. You found your prince."

Louisa laughed. "We take care of each other. Him work with me in the store. We bought that too, you know. We bought Razzle Dazzle! We bought it with the money from his father's business, when Mrs. Spence couldn't handle it no more after the stroke. Him sell his father's business and we used the money to buy it."

Nola's head felt as if it was buzzing with all the news that Louisa was throwing at her. It had been easier to listen in Kingston, when she'd been so distanced from it all. Now each bit of news pelted her like a rockstone—Papa not living there anymore; Louisa owning Razzle Dazzle; Mrs. Spence having a stroke!

Louisa gave a nervous laugh. "How you think I knew you was here? When you're at Razzle Dazzle, you see and hear everything that happen in Redding!"

Nola wanted to say, "Yes, that's how Mrs. Spence knew everybody's business," but she did not.

"It was that Jasper. Him take you up in the taxi, right? Well, him run right into the middle of the street, screamin' that him just see Nola Chambers' duppy, and it spit right in him face! You should'a see what happen, Nola!" Louisa chuckled, her hand covering her mouth delicately. "Some people drop to them knees and start to pray that your duppy don't come and trouble them too!"

Nola hung her head with renewed shame. "I don't know what happened to me, Louisa. Nobody recognized me when I was walking through the street, like they forgot 'bout Nola Chambers, and I was happy 'bout that. Then, when I got up here with Jasper, I just felt so angry that I . . ." She shook her head in frustration, her mouth searching for elusive words.

Louisa touched her shoulder gently. "I know. I was there, 'memba?"

So sweet, Louisa. Still the same sweet soul, trying to make Nola feel better.

Nola smiled gratefully. "So who's the lucky man?" she asked. "Who in this place was lucky enough to marry Louisa Chambers?"

Louisa twisted the thin band of gold on her left finger. "That's what I wanted to tell you, Nola, but you never seem to be interested." Her voice fell to a whisper. "Delroy." She swallowed, and blinked long lashes anxiously at Nola. "Delroy, Nola. Delroy is the person I got married to. I am Mrs. Louisa Reckus."

CHAPTER 57

S O FUNNY, HOW after all those years, Redding still had the knack of putting Nola right back into her place. No matter what Aunt May had preached, about her being an adult now, a teacher, with her own school, her own 'family', Redding had, in just a few hours of her standing on its red soil, put her right back into her place.

Who was she to have loved Delroy Reckus? Who was she to have loved one of Redding's golden boys? Delroy Reckus belonged to Louisa! He belonged to beautiful, perfect Louisa. Of course! The laws of Redding didn't apply to anywhere else but Redding, and no matter what had happened in Kingston, no matter how happy or contented or successful she was there, it had nothing to do with Nola's place in Redding.

Delroy, the one thing in Redding that Nola had yearned for, was married to her sister. Nola had not even realized, until Louisa had made the announcement how much she had yearned to see that face with its adolescent dusting of hair. She had been yearning, so, so badly, for the chance to finally finish the conversation that they'd begun on the hillside, right before the green truck had barreled over her life. She'd tried to quell the yearning, tried to hang that face in the midst of all the other sketches on the fence and tell herself that he was just like the rest of them, but it had been there all along, lurking like a virus in her bloodstream. Those arms that had lifted her out of the rain, and wrapped her in Grampy's towel, were now wrapped around Louisa.

She did not ask if Delroy knew that she had not died in the fire; that she'd been in Kingston the whole time. She just fell into place. She told Louisa how happy she was for them, then she asked if Paulette now lived in Mass Tackie's house.

Louisa only paused for an instant at the change of subject, then she explained that Paulette slept in Mama's room to administer her medication through the night. Then she invited Nola to stay at her house—at hers and Delroy's house, but Nola told her no, that she wanted to be able to sleep in Grampy's old room.

After Louisa left, Nola sat with Paulette in Mama's room, wondering if the house had always been this silent. It seemed that when she'd lived there it had always rung with sounds. During the days, there had been the constant scraping of Mama's knife on the chopping board, or the hiss of pots bubbling their sugary juices over into the fire. During the nights, there had been the tinny beat of Papa's radio, the night creaks of the house, the heavy sleep breaths of everyone, and of course, the ticking of the living room clock.

Now there was just silence, as if the house had stopped living.

She asked Paulette questions, to try to stop the ringing and to fill the empty silence.

She proved to be easy to talk to. She scooped her words from the air with a smile as she spoke of Mass Tackie and his pride in her. She loved her job as a nurse, she explained, because her poppa had always told her that she had a gift for making people feel better. She loved living in Kingston (in

Mona, near the University Hospital where she worked), but she'd taken a year off to tend to Mass Tackie when he'd gotten ill, and that year had now stretched into sixteen months when she'd realized how ill Mama was.

Paulette asked her about her own life in Kingston, and Nola told her about Nathan and Aunt May and their surprising love for one another, of Kendra and Hopey and Ab and Mams. When she told Paulette about the Dah-Lilly school, and the woman raised her brows and scooped the word 'really' from the air, Nola's chest pulsed with pride.

Nola asked if Mass Tackie had suffered before he'd died like Grampy had, and Paulette smiled sadly and said not for long, he'd been tired—eager to go. They laughed quietly about the friendship that he and Grampy had shared, and they both agreed that wherever they were, they were sitting under some tree together playing a game of checkers, goading each other about who was the bigger cheater.

Then the conversation switched to Mama's illness, and Nola asked how come they'd never taken Mama in to Kingston to see the specialty doctors there. Paulette hesitated, then told her that it had been too late when they'd found out how sick Mama was. She told Nola that Mama had known she was sick long before she'd told anyone. She'd felt the lump in her breast, felt it becoming a pulsing mass with a life of its own and she'd let it be.

Mama had done the same thing that Petra had done! They'd both chosen to have their bodies eroded.

"What you think changed her, Paulette?" Nola whispered. "What you think made Mama stop laughing?"

Paulette stared down at Mama's sleeping face, leaning forward to blow a piece of cotton off her forehead. "The same thing that eventually change all of us, Hon ... love."

Mama did not sleep well through the night. She tossed and moaned, and once or twice she called Nola's name, but when

Nola stood over her and murmured, "Yes, Mama … see me here," she looked right through her. Paulette explained that she was not really awake. Only dreaming. That was how it was at night, Paulette said. Always worse at night because of the moon. The same magnetic powers that pulled the waves to and from the shore, also pulled the dreams from the soul. It was so with all her patients, Paulette said.

So they rubbed her legs as she moaned, put cool cloths on her forehead when she became drenched in sweat, and warm cloths on her neck when she shivered.

Nola had no time to cry as she watched Mama's torment, for Paulette kept her busy with her brisk orders—Drip some ice on her lips, Nola. Pull her leg back on the bed and pump it so, let the blood flow through it.

By daybreak Mama fell into a restful sleep, her body flopped across the bed like a broken doll. Paulette slept too, her legs splayed wide in front of her in the plastic chair, her snores scooping up the quiet dawn air.

But Nola could not sleep. She lay in the cot that Louisa had sent up for her, listening for the whisp in Grampy's room. The heavy silence just made her heart heavier. Where you are, Grampy? Why you gone and leave me?

Then suddenly it hit her! Grampy had always spoken to her when she'd been on her way to the dew angels! The dew angels! She hadn't thought of them in so long. She laughed to herself. Imagine her, 23 years old, and still thinking of an old man's stories!

She flung the sheets off her body and ran to the kitchen. She pulled the door open and stepped outside, turning to ensure that the door clicked properly behind her. Then she stopped. It didn't matter! It didn't matter if the door was open or closed! The mongrel was gone. Papa was gone. There were no belts hanging in Granny Pat's wardrobe, no one to bellow her name across the mist and make her knees weak with fear, no sore on her lip to smart beneath the wet dew. She released the door handle and watched as the door swung open, pulling a white swirl of mist inside. It dissolved in the warm kitchen like a bashful ghost.

She giggled in the giddiness of the moment, spreading her arms wide. She jumped off the steps and ran through the mist. Free! I am free! She chuckled again as her arms sliced the mist, sending the silver swirls upwards towards the blue-grey sky. The grass cramped her toes and lifted its scent into her nostrils, and even with Mama's sickness resting so heavily on her soul, she could feel her spirits lift. Her spirit had craved this for so long—the peace of the Redding dawn.

"Ellie!" she said breathlessly as she reached the coolie plum tree. She wrapped her arms around the trunk and pressed her face into the deep creases. "Ellie, I miss you so much."

Where Ellie's hooves had once trampled the ground into barrenness, grass now grew like a thick carpet. It was grass that would have made Nathan stammer with excitement.

Nola was surprised to see that the tree stump was still there. When she left Redding, it had been rotting, softening from the inside out. As she leaned closer, she realized why it still stood. It had been burned. The stump was charred, the top smoothed from flames and subsequent weathering. Then her heart pulsed. This was where they'd burned Ellie! The fire had sealed the trunk as hard as a rock.

Nola sat on the hardened wood and listened. There it was, the light rustle through the leaves. She felt her skin prickle with the excitement of their welcome. I'm back, she whispered, I'm back! She held her head towards the sky, smiling as the dew settled on her. Even though her hair was now in cornrows, she could still feel the moisture creating its silver cap. She felt her body getting lighter and lighter, glowing from the wash, and suddenly, in the midst of the rustling, Nola realized something—She was this stump! She too had been burned, and the insects that had been gnawing her to mush destroyed. She was still alive, and best of all— She had come back! They'd thought she'd been destroyed, but they'd only made her strong. Yes, she was charred, but she'd also been weathered smooth, and tough.

She'd been preserved. Preserved! The word was like a soft answer to her soul. Hadn't she stood over the heat of the stove and stirred the jams till the sugar melted and the fruit juices were preserved, could no longer ferment? How could she not have seen that the fire was necessary? How could she not have seen that you couldn't hate a match for its flame, for that was what it had been created to do? Nola knew then that they had been the flames for her—every one of them—Papa, Mrs. Spence, Clarice—her matches. She could not hate them anymore, for they had been only doing what they had been made to do.

NOLA

T HAT WAS THE day that I stepped into my body. You may think it strange, that I had lived outside of my body for so many years, even when I became happy with my new life in Kingston, even when I overpowered a creature like Eric McKenzie and carried my friend home to her family. Well, this story is proof that I did.

Until that morning with the dew angels, I had always thought of that black vessel of my body, the thing that transported my soul, as my enemy. It was the thing that had caused me too much pain to claim ownership of it. So, like a child caught marking on a wall, then shaking its head in denial that it was the one responsible, I stood aside from my body and shook my head in denial of it. Until that morning, my spirit walked beside my body like a prisoner handcuffed to its enemy.

My name is Nola Chambers, and the story you have just read is my life. People who glance at me as they are passing will notice that there is something strange about my face. The right side of my lip rises into a slight smile, as if I am always smirking at the world. It is not until they look closely that they see the gleam of the skin where the natural lines have been smoothed and tightened by fire. Those are my scars, and it took me a long time to grow into them, to wear them as my badge of honour for having survived my life. My expression is not mocking.

If anything, it is filled with awe and gratefulness because I have been so blessed.

In answer to the many questions of, What happen to your face? I used to mutter, Was in a fire—long story, and then to the persistent ones, I would relate my story as if it had happened to another, a girl named Nola that I once knew. I do not claim deceptiveness in having told my story in the third person. I can only claim to have been so unwhole that I could not speak in my own voice. I can only claim to have felt so much hatred and fear for myself that I had to hide behind the words of some distant soul.

You see, in hanging the smudged sketches of my past on that fence, I had also hung myself. I told my story at a distance from that fence, with the details of myself smudged and distorted just like the others, so the pain would not have been as sharp. I tried to clarify my place in this world through someone else's voice. I did not know that the one person whose acceptance I needed most was my own.

One day as a child, after I had been beaten by my papa and kicked into the rain, I accepted the fact that I was in my skin, and I would always be hated for it. But that was a lie, for I told myself that I accepted the fact that I would be hated by others, what I really meant was, hated by myself! I hated that I was born into the dark, wide-eyed body that was passed on to me by my ancestors. I thought I was the 'shame' of my family— the mistake brought back to taunt them in their hard earned, light-skinned perfection. Deep down, I did not even believe that it was my right to be alive. I had always felt that every day of me being alive was undeserved, for every day of my life meant another day of that beautiful little boy being dead.

400

I had not always been aware of my pain. I carried it deep in the core of me, and it had come in waves, sometimes with a force that knocked me to my knees, sometimes with a dull ache, that, with enough distraction, I could ignore. I had worn my body as I had my sister's hand-me-down dresses, as an ill-fitting garment that had been deemed for someone else, and by default had ended up wrapped around my soul.

When I arrived back in Redding, I thought that I had found understanding of myself and the world in the choices that I had made, and that I was healed because I'd knitted a protective cloak around my wounds. But there is a difference between understanding someone, and loving them, and a healed, contented soul should not need a protective weave. That is why I had shocked myself and spat in Jasper's face. Jasper had brushed against the tender scars beneath my weave, and my actions had been none other that the involuntary retaliation of a wounded animal. My wounds were as raw as the night I had stumbled into that taxi with Aunt May, and even though the souls of my feet had shed the possessive yellowing from the Redding soil, my soul had not. My soul had still been in its chokehold.

My wounds did not truly heal until that morning when I returned there. They did not heal until I'd seen myself in that charred stump. My hatred for my skin, my eyes, my face, my soul, my life, came to an end that morning. No lightning bolt. No clap of thunder. Just the dew and a stump of wood. It came when I realized that there had been no mistake in my creation. My life had been carefully and meticulously planned by God, and I had been preserved.

That morning I realized that all through my ordeals, I had been pampered. I had been passed from soft hand to soft hand while I was being weathered. You see, from the ashes of my fires, I had risen, with friends so dear to me that I could not imagine my life without them —the dear, sweet, loving hands of Grampy, Louisa, the river, Dahlia, Merlene, Delroy, Aggie, Aunt May, Nathan, Mrs. Lyndsay, Kendra, Ab, Mams, Mattie, Hopey, and even Petra—yes, Petra, despite her confused resentment of me, had taught me more about myself than anyone else ever could. She showed me my strength, my loyalty, my bravery, all qualities which would have remained stagnant within me if she had not pulled me from my daze. Petra had been my mirror, the looking glass that had made me straighten my shoulders and brush back the matted tufts of my hair.

They were all angels, every one of them. They were the dampness of the dew on my skin after the harsh burn of the fire, tending my bruised soul and helping me to stand once again on my shaky legs.

Even the anger and hatred in me had served a purpose. I could not have faced Eric and his cronies without it. I could not have brought Petra home without it. The hate had been part of the plan too, as much as the love.

Yes, I had been surrounded by love, all my life, but I could not see it in the midst of the hate within me. It took a stump of wood to make me see it, and that morning it allowed me to take possession of my skin, my eyes, my body. I pulled in those loose, flapping folds, and fitted them perfectly to my soul.

I hated myself right till the day before my mama died.

I returned to Mama's kitchen that morning knowing that Papa would be there. I felt him. The crackling electricity of him roused me from the pen. Just as I'd felt Mama's death from Kingston, I'd felt my Papa's presence from the pen. You see, as much as Papa would have wanted to pretend that I was not a part of him, our shared blood had bound our spirits too. That night I had stood over his sleeping form and breathed in his breath, our spirits had knotted, through my love and his hate.

I stood by the kitchen door and watched his head loll over the steaming mug on the table. The stench of him reached me even from outside the door, the whiskey and the sweat. His hair had become grey, and in the middle of his silver pate the strands had thinned so that his sun-rusted scalp formed a startling contrast.

He must have sensed me there, for he suddenly looked up, and instantly I saw fear flash across his face.

For one second, my steps faltered. It had been such a habit to wait till I'd assessed Papa's mood before entering the kitchen, that my feet involuntarily hesitated.

"Hello, Papa," I said.

Those grey eyes blinked in confusion. I looked into them, searching for the ice I'd remebered so well, but it was not there. It had melted into a watery, whisky-pinked film. The eyes seemed smaller too, no more the grand silver that had once dominated his beautiful face. It was the lines! The lines that had once crinkled so handsomely when he'd smiled, now pleated his face so heavily that his jowls hung low, dragging his eyelids with them.

I stepped closer. The stench burned my nose.

"Hello, Papa," I repeated, more to convince myself of his identity than to get a response.

He blinked again. And then he fell off his chair.

One minute he was blinking up at me, and the next, he was on the ground, the coffee mug shattering into pieces between his legs. I think that he had tried to jump backwards, forgetting that he was seated, and the chair tipped over.

I grabbed a towel from the counter and ran to help him up, to sop where the steaming liquid had darkened his filthy pants, but Papa crawled backwards, away from my outstretched hands.

Just then Paulette appeared at Mama's bedroom door, looking into the kitchen with confused, sleepy eyes. It took a while for her dazed mind to grasp the scene before her. She looked from Papa, huddled against the fridge with a trail of brown coffee leading from the table, to me, standing in front of him with the kitchen towel dangling helplessly from my hands. I saw the clarity overtake the slumber within Paulette's eyes, saw her bottom lip scoop decisively over her top lip, and she gave me a long look, a triumphant glimmer in her eyes.

Then she turned her gaze back to Papa, and said, "What happen, Troy? Not happy to see your daughter?"

And with that she closed the bedroom door and left Papa whimpering on the floor before me.

You might think that I was happy to see my papa like that, crying before me with his hands held protectively over his head. You might think that I was happy about it since that was the same position he'd forced me into so many times. But that was not the case.

I was not happy to see my strong, handsome Papa groveling on the floor. If I had been, then I would have been no better than the rest of them, and I would not have benefited from my journey.

This was not what I had wanted from my papa. I had wanted his love, never his fear. But I knew then that I could not have what had never existed, and I knew that I loved my papa too much to see him so afraid. Remember what I had learned just minutes before in the dew, that I could not hate the match for starting the fire. My papa had done exactly what he'd been supposed to do. What would I have become if my papa had not deemed me different and unworthy of his love? I would have become one of them, looking for a fair-skinned donor to 'wash the black' out of me, the very black that Fin Thomas had fallen in love with. The black that had created my dear, dear Grampy.

So, once more in my life, to make my papa happy, I left my home. I dropped the kitchen towel onto his wet pants and he cried out when it landed softly on his leg. Then I walked out the door.

I saw his car parked outside the gate, the one he'd bought from Mr. Spence with Mama's kitchen money. At first I did not recognize it, for all that was left of the red paint were a few dull red patches within the rust. The rear window was completely gone, a greasy piece of cardboard taking its place, held in by layers of duct tape. Suddenly, while staring at the dilapidated car, I was jolted by a memory—this had been the car parked behind Jasper's on the side of the road! I looked at the license plate and sure enough, there was the 'P'. Papa's beautiful red car had been converted into a taxi!

I walked back up to my stump and sat with my back to the house. I heard the shuffle of his feet as they hurried down the kitchen steps, but I did not look around. I knew that the whimpering man whose urine had expanded the amber pool of coffee across the kitchen floor was just the rot in the stump that had finally been exposed.

When I returned to Mama her eyes were wide with knowing. She watched me silently as Paulette wiped her emaciated limbs with rosewater, her eyes telling me that she had heard Papa's fall, and that she knew that I had seen what he had become.

Even in her illness, she had not changed—never to utter a bad word about my papa. While Paulette took the bottle of Savlon to wash the bed pan at the outside pipe, I fed Mama warm cornmeal porridge. She swallowed slowly, as if even the tiny grains were too large for her throat.

"You went ... to the angels," she finally whispered.

I blinked at her. Of course she must have known about the dew angels! She'd once been Grampy's little girl, listening to his tales as eagerly as I had. I smiled at the sheepish way she'd said the word 'angels', like an older child not wanting to let go of the notion of Santa Claus. I nodded and put another spoon of porridge to her lips, but she shook her head indicating that she wanted no more.

"Lettie and I ... we used to go. We use to watch ... it run off each other's ... face."

I laughed again, partly because of the image of them as girls in the dew, partly because of how strong her voice sounded.

"Grampy was full of story, eh, Mama?"

Mama shook her head. "Not story, Nola, the angels come. Not all the time, but ... when you need them. God's ... helpers." I nodded.

"So beautiful." Mama closed her eyes and swallowed. "I saw you, you know ... on those mornings when you ... came back from them. So beautiful. You had that glow. That's how I knew ... you were going to be ... fine."

I could not speak.

"God was always ... with you. From you were born, I could see ... you had Him right there with you." She looked at me with her wide eyes. "You were born with your eyes open. We had to wash them ... with aloe, cause you came out with them wide open, like you knew everything that was goin' on. I heard them whisperin' that it was the devil. Them think that I never hear ... but I heard them whisperin'. But Grampy took you from them, and him put you on my chest and him say, Sadie, she small like a bird, but she have the wings of a vulture!" Mama laughed softly, her eyes glazed with memory, but I could not laugh back.

My heart was too hungry for her words to even smile. Her eyes focused once again on my face.

"You think I ... let you go."

It was not a question, so I did not answer, and Mama sighed deeply, rippling the sheets. "It was ... the best I knew to do." She lifted her hand from mine and pointed to the wardrobe. "Get it," she said.

406

I did not move right away for I did not want to break the mood of Mama's unusual chatter, but when she closed her eyes and turned her head exhaustedly into the pillow, I went to the wardrobe and retrieved the flour bag.

"Open it," Mama whispered when I put it beside her on the bed.

I pulled the knot of cord and peered inside. The thick wad of papers were folded over once and tied with another piece of cord. I could see some of the letters on the edges of the paper, the blue of the ink now bleached pink with the combination of fruit splatters and age. I took the recipes out of the bag and handed them to Mama, but she brushed them away.

"No, the other thing." She pointed weakly at the bag.

I looked inside again and saw a brown paper bag, also tied tightly with a pale green strip of cloth. I took it out and handed it to Mama, and this time she took it from me and held it against her chest.

"I never let you go. I kept part ... of you with me. The part ... I prayed over. I knew you were doin' good when I held it ... against me and my heart ... sang, and I knew you were havin' it ... bad when I held it and my heart sank. This was how I spoke to you, my child... from all those miles. I never let you go."

Mama handed me the brown bag, and tentatively, I pulled the cloth and opened it. What I saw made me laugh and cry at the same time. I couldn't believe that Mama had saved it all – Grampy's belt, Granny Pat's picture, and Delroy's blade of grass. The things from under my mattress.

"Mama," was all I could say, for my throat burned with emotion.

"I saved you." Her fingers chilled over my hand again. "You couldn't stay. He was too afraid of you, Nola ... and it was gettin' worse when you started ... staring him down; taunting him. When I saw that ... cutlass, I knew it had to stop."

Taunting him? What was Mama talking about? I never tried to taunt Papa when I looked at him. I just wanted to see his eyes. "Mama, I wasn't ..."

"Yes, the fear was goin' from you ... and he saw that. That was enough ... to taunt him."

I touched Grampy's belt, the old leather shedding a fine powder on the bed. I rolled Delroy's dried blade over my fingers. Then I stared down at Granny Pat's face. She stared back from my own face. Funny how I'd never noticed before how sad her eyes were.

"Did she smile a lot, Mama, even with everything that they did to her?" I asked.

Mama looked blankly at me. "I didn't know her so good."

"Didn't know her?" I gave Mama a confused laugh, thinking that exhaustion was now affecting her memory. "Grampy say that she used to rock you and tell you stories! You don't remember Granny Pat, Mama?"

Mama twisted her head to the side and gave me a slight frown. "Nola, that's not Granny Pat ... that's Papa's Aunt Linette ... the one who raised him."

When people speak about their head spinning, it may sound like an exaggeration, but I can tell you that after Mama's words that morning, my head reeled. Her words hit me like someone had taken the flour bag of recipes and pounded me over my head. I remembered when I'd found the picture in Mama's drawer, and when I'd seen my own face staring back at me, I'd assumed it was Granny Pat's picture.

But now Mama was saying that this black face was not Granny Pat's, but Papa's aunt! Papa's family! It was not just from Mama's loins that I'd unearthed a secret, but from Papa's also!

"Why you think he was so 'fraid of you, Nola? Why you think he had to keep you down ... keep you weak? Because he couldn't face that ... power again."

408

So this had been my papa's ghost.

"You had to go. You couldn't stay. That's why... I gave you nothing to stay for. That's why I was happy... when you stayed away from us... away from him!. I had to get you strong. I had to get you not to need us!" Mama took a deep breath and her lips shook. "Those wings that Grampy said you had ... Papa would have torn them off. When the witch told me she had you ... I told her, Please don't make him kill her! If him find her, him goin' kill her ... "

I saw the tears in Mama's eyes, but she was not looking at me. She stared into the distance, and I saw the same glaze that had opened her eyes wide, but blind, during her sleep. I realized then, that my Mama had not forgiven herself. Even though she had sent me away to save me, she had not forgiven herself for what had happened to me. That was why she had called me, why she could not sleep at night, and why she could not die.

I wept. Finally, I let the pain out of my chest. The pain that had been harboured there through my happiness and my sadness. I opened the plug in my heart, and I let the pain flow from me till my body was weak and I could not sit up in the chair.

Mama reached for my head and put it on her rotting chest, the spot I had dreamed of lying on all my life. Finally, I had the answer to my mama's frozen face, why she had stuck me in my eye that afternoon instead of hugging me. It was because from the moment I was born, from the moment she saw my face, she was preparing me to leave. She was giving me nothing to stay for, nothing to pine for when I left.

She gripped my sobbing head and held me so tight that I could hear the light flutter of her heart, like a baby bird's wings, getting ready to fly from its nest.

Mama, with her skeletal face and unsmiling lips, had loved me enough to not love me. She'd saved my life, for if I had remained in Redding, I would have done what Dahlia and Merlene did. I would have done what Petra had done. I would have done what Mama had done.

Those words my Mama spoke to me that morning were the last words she spoke except for the two she uttered in the early hours of the following morning. When I lifted my head from her chest, her eyes were closed and she was breathing deeply, finally in a peaceful sleep.

When Louisa and Delroy came, we could not rouse her. Neither could we rouse her for her midday broth, or her evening supper. She slept as if she had not slept in years, as if she had walked for miles and miles with a laden market basket, and it had finally been hoisted down so she could rest.

I knew what they didn't. That Mama had finally lifted her feet from that rotting scallion field and was heading towards the open gate.

Louisa and Delroy stayed that day, for they knew it was close to the time, and across my mama's bed, my eyes told Delroy 'thank you' for all he'd done for me, and 'thank you' for taking such good care of my sister.

His eyes answered me, "Never break".

In the early hours of morning, while we all sat around her bed, my mama lifted a finger, ever so slightly. I bent over her, pressing my ear against her lips.

"The angels," she whispered.

We did not for one instant question Mama's wish. It was so fitting that she'd spent her dying hours with all who'd known about Grampy's tale, about the miracle of the angels – me, Delroy, Paulette, and even Louisa. We all knew Grampy's tale, and we all knew that that was where Mama wanted to spend her last hours on this earth.

Delroy lifted her feathery limbs from the bed and Paulette wrapped her in blankets while I rushed to get the cot's tiny mattress from Grampy's room. As Louisa opened the kitchen door, we all stopped in awe at what greeted us.

If I had been by myself, I would have thought I was seeing things. I would have blinked my eyes to clear the vision, but as I turned to look at the others, I saw the wonder on their faces too, and I knew that what was before me was real.

The mist swirled outside as if a breeze were blowing through it, but the leaves on the trees stood still. Silvery swirls snaked like fingers into the kitchen and beckoned us out into its folds. We walked within the chilly blanket to the coolie plum tree, and I placed the mattress on the carpet of grass so that Delroy could lay Mama on it. Paulette sat on the ground beside her, putting Mama's hand to her lips, whispering softly against the fragile twigs of her fingers. Then Delroy, then Louisa whispered in her ear, and I saw Mama's eyelids flutter at my sister's words.

When it was my turn, I put my hand on my Mama's chest, the spot that I had wept on, and I told her how much I had felt her prayers in Kingston, how much they had swooped down and lifted me out of trouble. I told my Mama that she had not let me go—that she had saved my life and I told her that I knew how much she loved me.

As my lips brushed against her cold cheek, I felt the wetness of the dew settling on her skin, and when I looked up at her face, I gasped at how beautiful she looked. The chill of the dew had plumped the sagging lines of Mama's face, and she smiled from a face that looked like that of a young, eager girl.

I had never seen my Mama look so beautiful as that morning when she passed from this world, when the dew clung to her skin and gave her her halo. I knew then that the miracle of the dew angels was just that, a miracle. I knew that just as Mama said, they came when you needed them, and as with any other miracle, when you believed.

411

Just as the sun tipped its first ray on to the earth, and the mist became blue with its promise, my mama's spirit left her body. She simply closed her eyes, and went to sleep. The hands that had chopped incessantly, that had worked themselves to the bone, fanned their fingers out against her sides in the rest that they had so craved. My heart soared knowing that Mama was finally where she'd waited so long to be, just like Petra, with the winds finally silenced.

EPILOGUE

THEY SAY THAT Papa did not attend Mama's funeral, but when the new preacher of the Open Bible Church began reciting the Twenty-Third Psalm, I felt the hairs on my neck rise, and the electric pulse tingle through me.

He came. I did not see him, but I knew he was there, watching from somewhere as they put his Sadie into the ground.

He loved Mama. I knew he did, and she knew that he did. There are just some kinds of love that cannot go beyond the boundaries that a person constructs. That was my papa's love for my mama—confined to its boundaries.

Louisa has never told me why Papa had come from her room that night, because I have never told her that I saw him. But I understand, now, that when love is given unnatural boundaries, it can take the wrong path, like a dammed river finding a tiny hole in the wall. The pressure of that one little drip could soon burst that reinforcing wall apart.

I satisfy myself in accepting that God knows best, and that he brought Delroy into my sister's life through me, when she needed him most desperately. Louisa had said—"We take care of each other." They had needed each other, Louisa and Delroy, and their union had been no mistake.

And me? They all stared at me at Mama's funeral. They stared and tapped each other as they had the night I killed Ellie. Some nodded greetings and exclaimed at my survival of the fire, others stayed far away, their eyes doing that familiar shift reserved for guilty or fearful souls. I smiled at them all, not just with the smile that their fire had granted me, but my own. I smiled because I was grateful that they had released me from their stifling boundaries.

I returned to Kingston the day after Mama's funeral and found a love of my own. You see, before my lesson that morning in the dew, I had closed my eyes to so many things around me, and I had blocked love without even realizing it. When I returned to Kingston accepting myself, it allowed me to accept others, and their love. I accepted my agape.

My sister was not able to come to my wedding. She gave birth to a little girl three days before my wedding, nearly a month before her scheduled time, but the baby was strong and healthy. A fighter, Delroy told me proudly on the phone. Her name was Sadie Dahlia Reckus. I could not speak when he said the name and it was not until I heard Delroy's own wet intake of breath that I realized that we were both crying.

I knew that as soon as my niece was able to understand, I would tell her about the dew angels and the promise for her life, and when she asked me where was the proof of something so mysterious, I would tell her, Right here in front of you—me. I am the miracle, not just 'cause I'm alive, but that I WANT to be alive! I would not tell her that in just eight years of my life, I had lost five people who were very dear to me, four of whom chose death over life. I would tell her about Grampy, about his great wisdom that led to the stories that helped me to cope. And when she asks me why I smiled with only one half of my mouth, I would tell her, "Because I know true happiness, and I know true pain."

414

Mine was the second wedding to be held in the house in Havendale, and I knew that Dahlia must have been guffawing in glee when I walked across Nathan's beautiful crab grass in my yellow dress. Yes, I chose to get married in yellow because it was the colour that to me represented the essence of life. I learned that life didn't always go along with our plans. Through my journey, I learned that imperfections are not hindrances. To the contrary, it is our imperfections that make us perfect for each other.

Kendra made the most beautiful and eager flower girl, throwing bougainvillea petals on the lawn as she walked ahead of me in her peach dress. My husband-to-be waited across the lawn for me, with his best man, Nathan, fussing over the collar of his suit. As I met his eyes across the crab grass, my heart soared because of the love I saw in them. I had been blind not to have seen it all along. He said I had cut him deep, from the moment I had walked past his stall with my large ackee-seed eyes. He said he knew that he had cut me too, when I brought that rat-tail of a beard back to him, but had to wait till I'd realized it for myself.

I soon realized—after all, when I had first met him, he had fed me fish, and said I was his beautiful princess.

At last, I had found my own luscious, delicious red cherries.

IT DUN

415

ACKNOWLEDGMENTS

I'D LIKE TO thank my three angels – Briana, Daniel and Claire, for never tiring of my bouncing paragraphs off of them, and for never complaining when my writing cut into a lot of 'mummy duties'. Thank you Chunky, for allowing me the gift of staying home with he children, an opportunity which granted me blessed time with them, and the six years which it took me to write this novel.

My gratitude to Annmarie Vaz, Jackie Lechler and Cynthia Hamilton, for telling me that I was a 'writer'. Your faith in me was a light in many discouraging times.

My dear sister, Charmian – you are my rock. To my brothers, Warren and Gregory, I say thank you for teaching me that laughter and love are more valuable than the material things in life.

Very special thanks to Hazel Campbell, Gail Whiteman Moss-Solomon, Maxine McDonnough and Camille Parchment, for holding my hand to see this project through, and for having the wisdom to cut where I was afraid to.

My heartfelt thanks to my Jamaican people… your humour and pride are the sugar on top of the bitter pill we sometimes have to swallow. You are the essence of this novel.

Lightning Source UK Ltd.
Milton Keynes UK
UKOW02f1052180516

274491UK00001B/1/P